CLUB ZERO-G

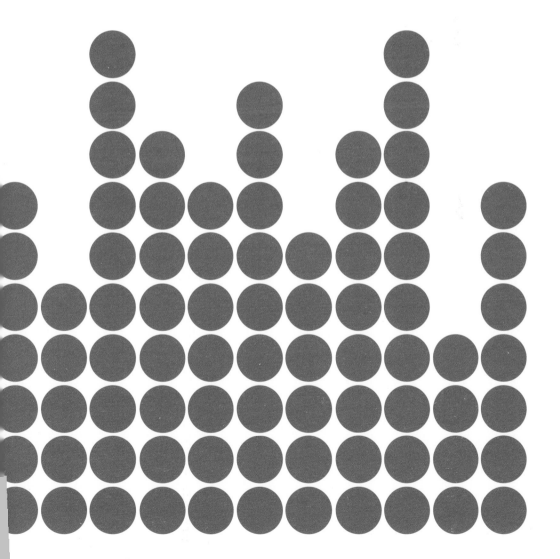

Published by:
The Disinformation Company Ltd.
163 Third Avenue, Suite 108
New York, NY 10003
Tel.: +1.212.691.1605
Fax: +1.212.473.8096
www.disinfo.com

Library of Congress Control Number: 2003113893

ISBN: 0-9729529-3-4

Printed in USA

Distributed in USA and Canada by:
Consortium Book Sales and Distribution
1045 Westgate Drive, Suite 90
St Paul, MN 55114
Toll Free: +1.800.283.3572
Local: +1.651.221.9035
Fax: +1.651.221.0124
www.cbsd.com

Distributed in the United Kingdom and Eire by:
Turnaround Publisher Services Ltd.
Unit 3, Olympia Trading Estate
Coburg Road
London, N22 6TZ
Tel.: +44.(0)20.8829.3000
Fax: +44.(0)20.8881.5088
www.turnaround-uk.com

disinformation
www.disinfo.com

MAD YAK PRESS
www.madyakpress.com

CLUB ZERO-G

STORY
Douglas Rushkoff

ART
Steph Dumais

COLORS
Anne Marie Horne

TYPEFACES
Blambot

EDITOR
Patrick Neighly

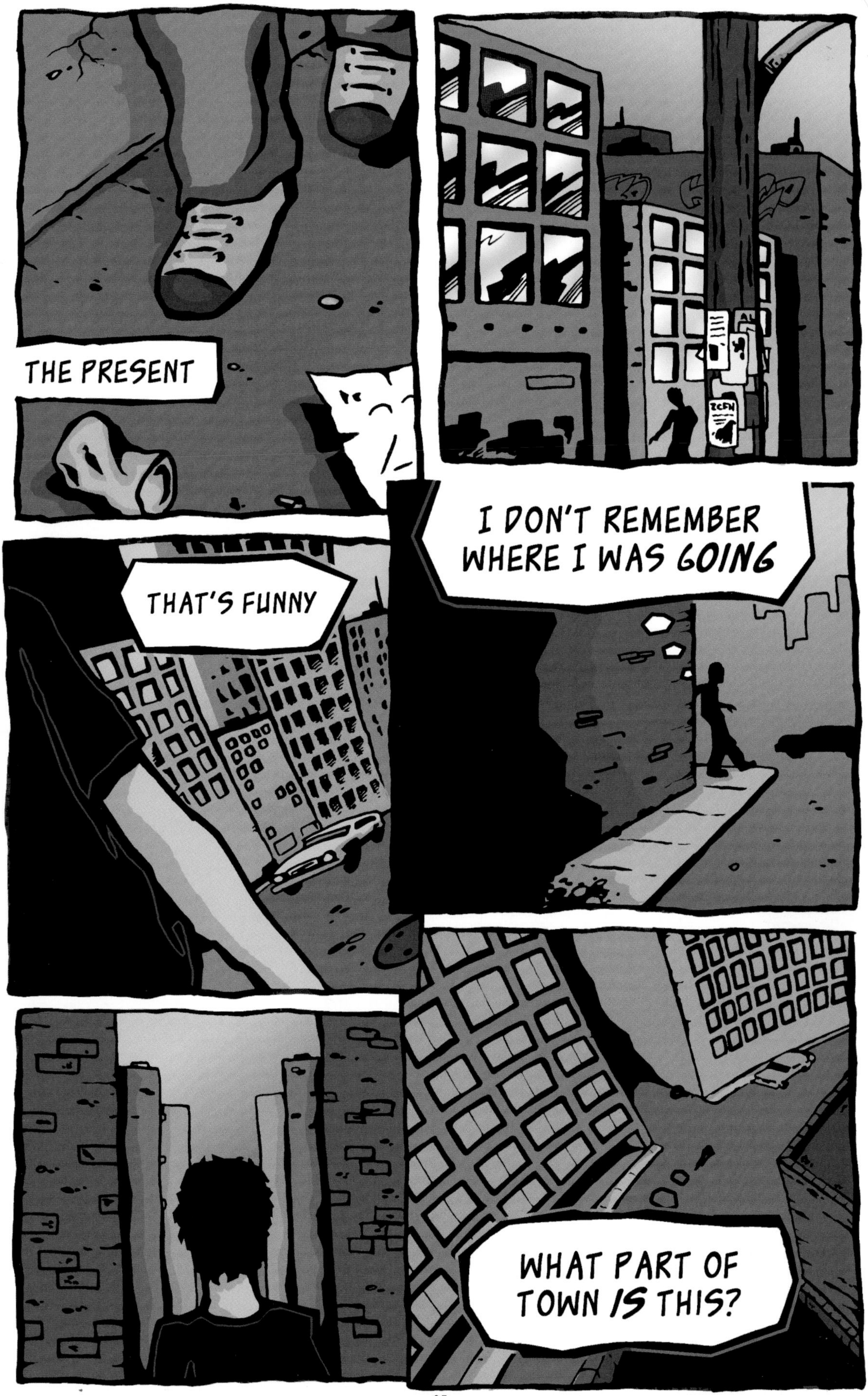
THE PRESENT
THAT'S FUNNY
I DON'T REMEMBER WHERE I WAS GOING
WHAT PART OF TOWN IS THIS?

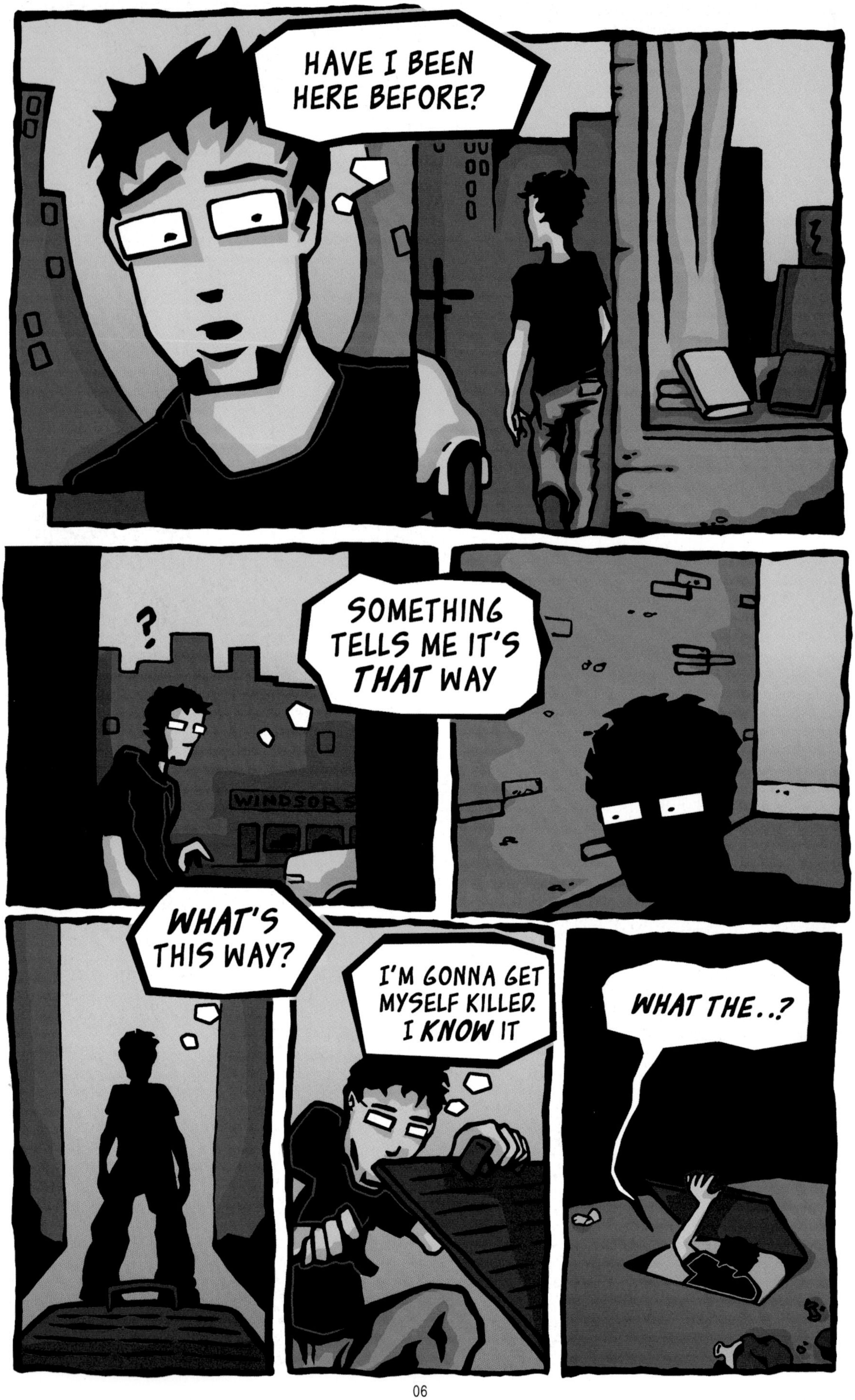
HAVE I BEEN HERE BEFORE?
SOMETHING TELLS ME IT'S *THAT* WAY
WINDSOR S
WHAT'S THIS WAY?
I'M GONNA GET MYSELF KILLED. I *KNOW* IT
WHAT THE..?

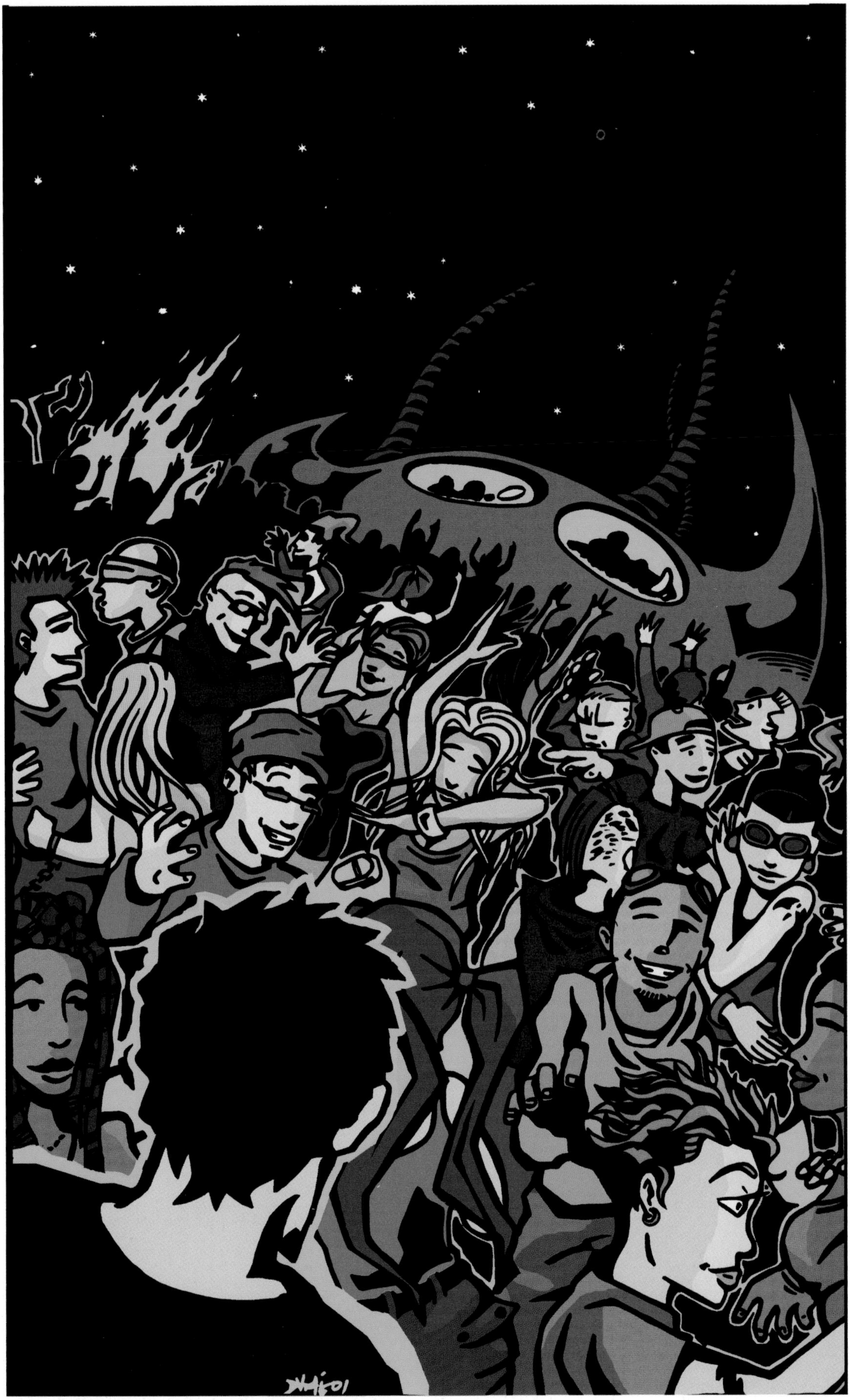

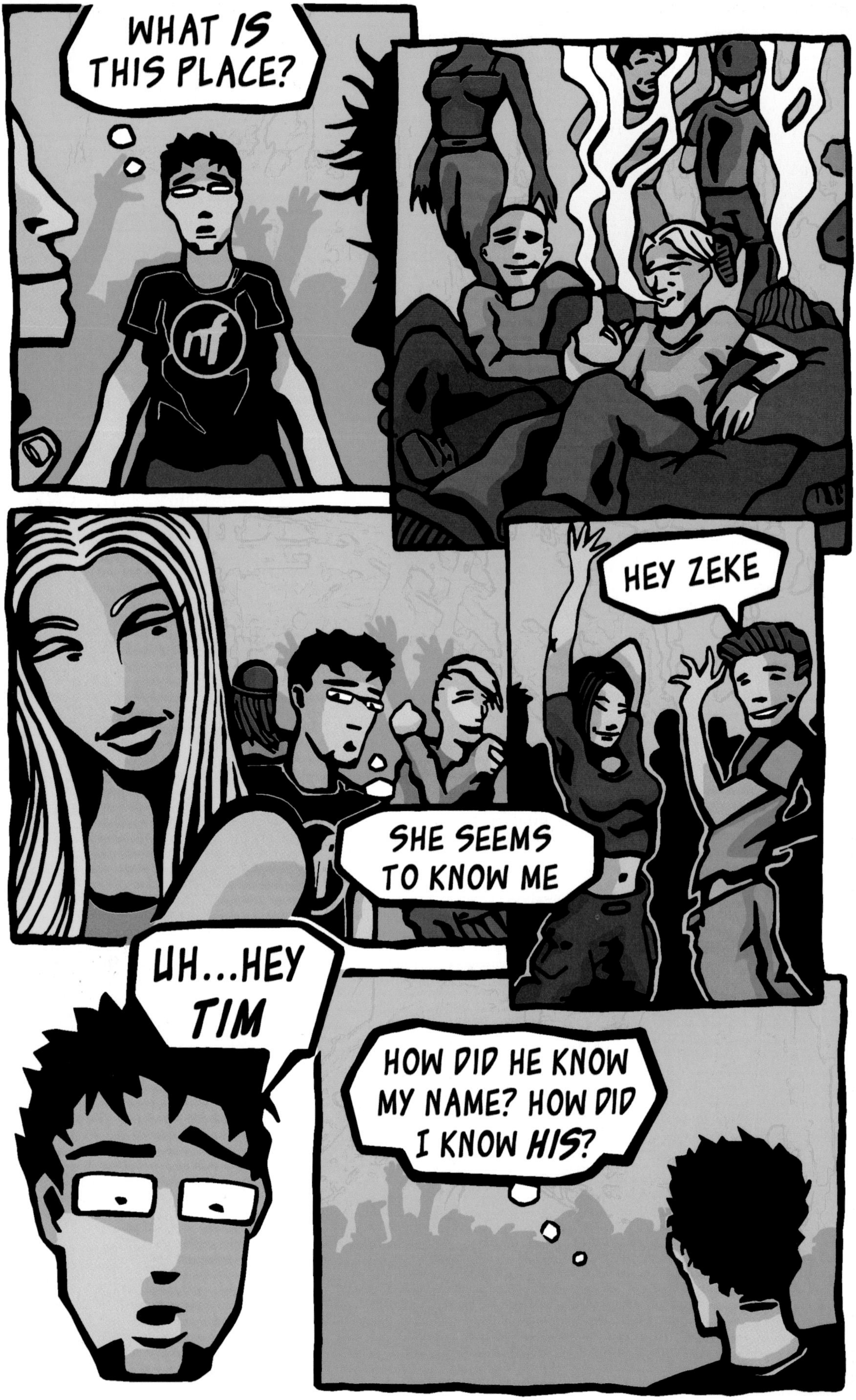
WHAT IS THIS PLACE?
HEY ZEKE
SHE SEEMS TO KNOW ME
UH...HEY TIM
HOW DID HE KNOW MY NAME? HOW DID I KNOW HIS?

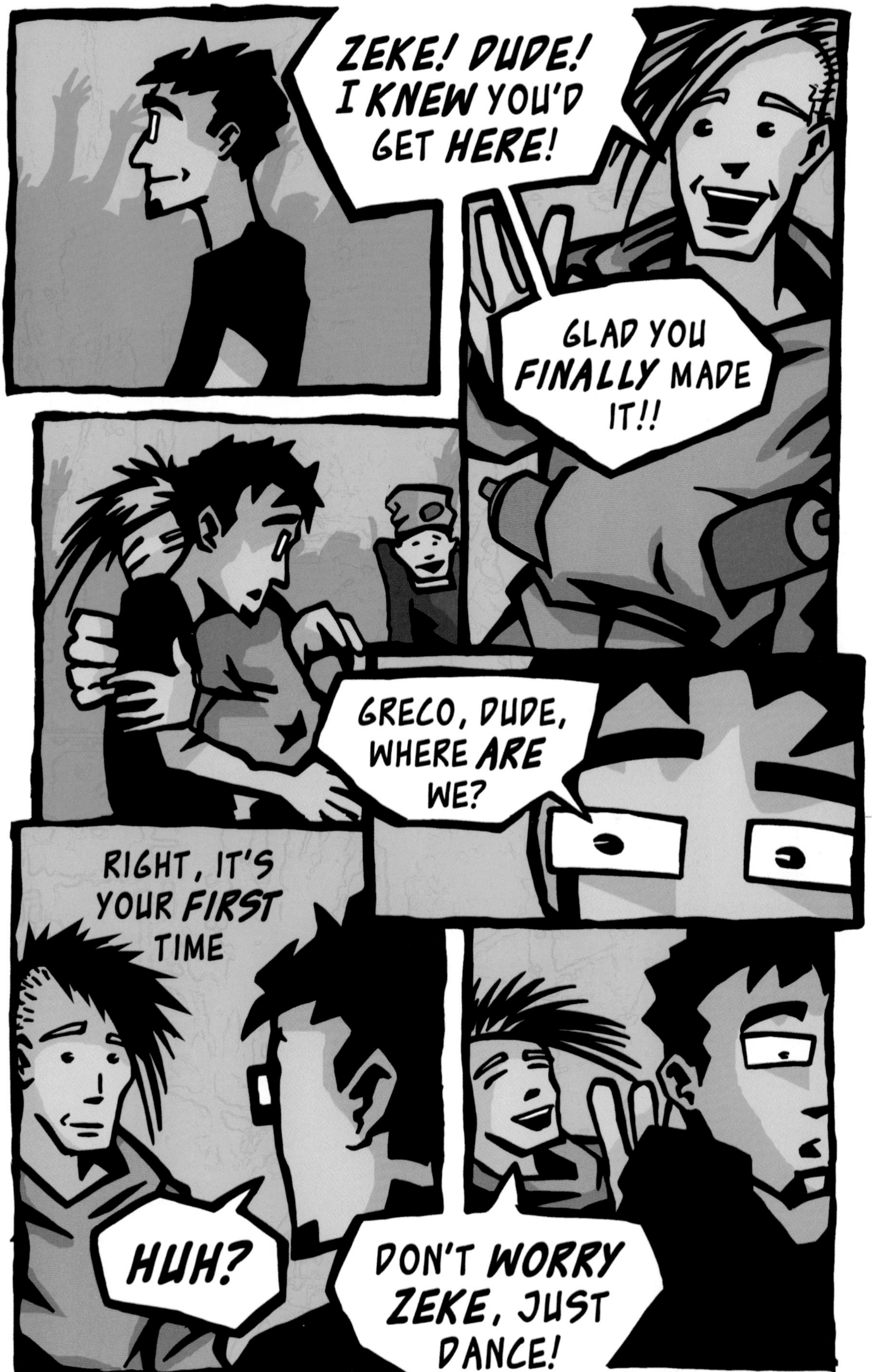
ZEKE! DUDE! I KNEW YOU'D GET HERE!
GLAD YOU FINALLY MADE IT!!
GRECO, DUDE, WHERE ARE WE?
RIGHT, IT'S YOUR FIRST TIME
HUH?
DON'T WORRY ZEKE, JUST DANCE!

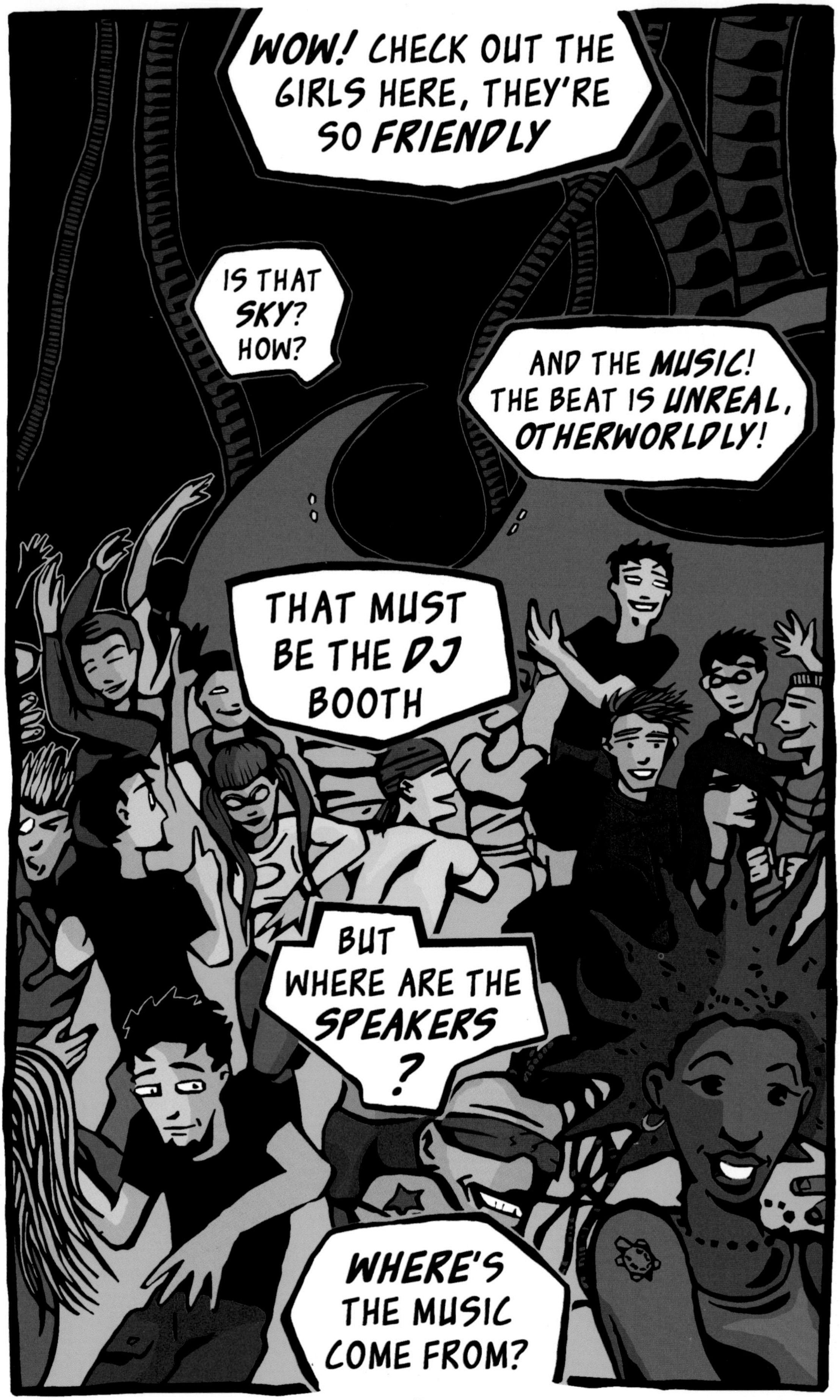
WOW! CHECK OUT THE GIRLS HERE, THEY'RE SO FRIENDLY
IS THAT SKY? HOW?
AND THE MUSIC! THE BEAT IS UNREAL, OTHERWORLDLY!
THAT MUST BE THE DJ BOOTH
BUT WHERE ARE THE SPEAKERS ?
WHERE'S THE MUSIC COME FROM?

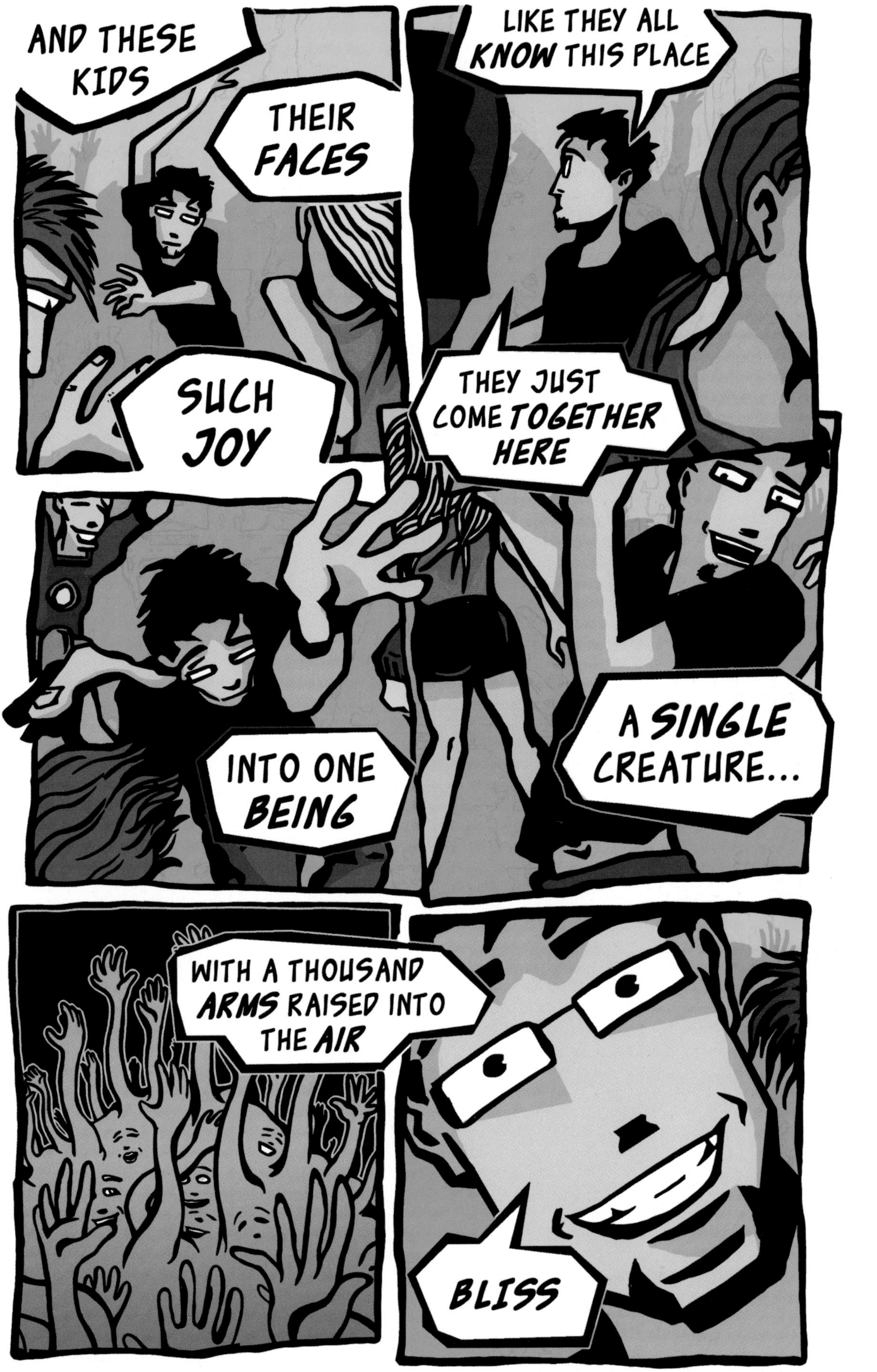
AND THESE KIDS
THEIR FACES
SUCH JOY
LIKE THEY ALL KNOW THIS PLACE
THEY JUST COME TOGETHER HERE
INTO ONE BEING
A SINGLE CREATURE...
WITH A THOUSAND ARMS RAISED INTO THE AIR
BLISS

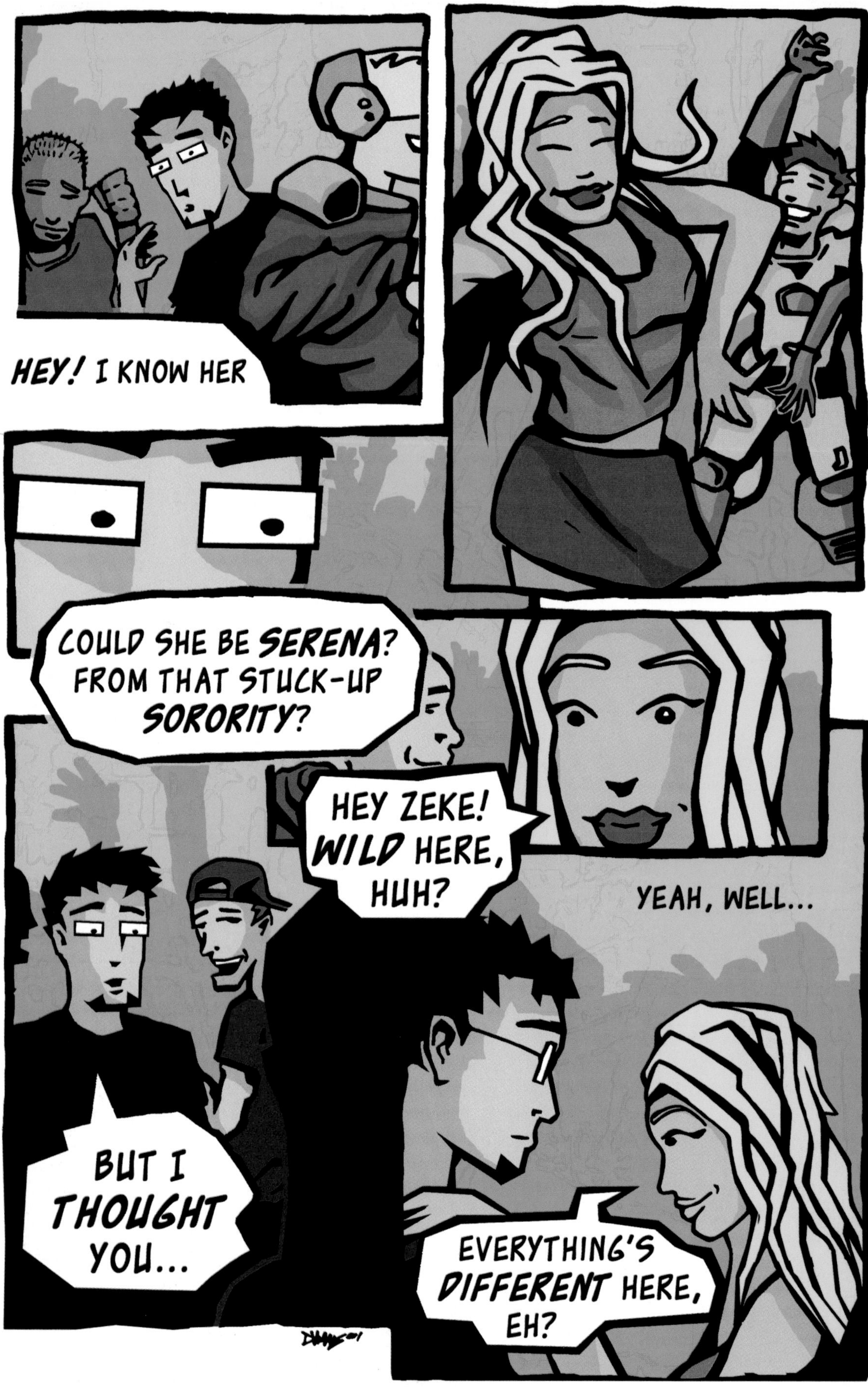
HEY! I KNOW HER
COULD SHE BE SERENA? FROM THAT STUCK-UP SORORITY?
HEY ZEKE! WILD HERE, HUH?
YEAH, WELL...
BUT I THOUGHT YOU...
EVERYTHING'S DIFFERENT HERE, EH?

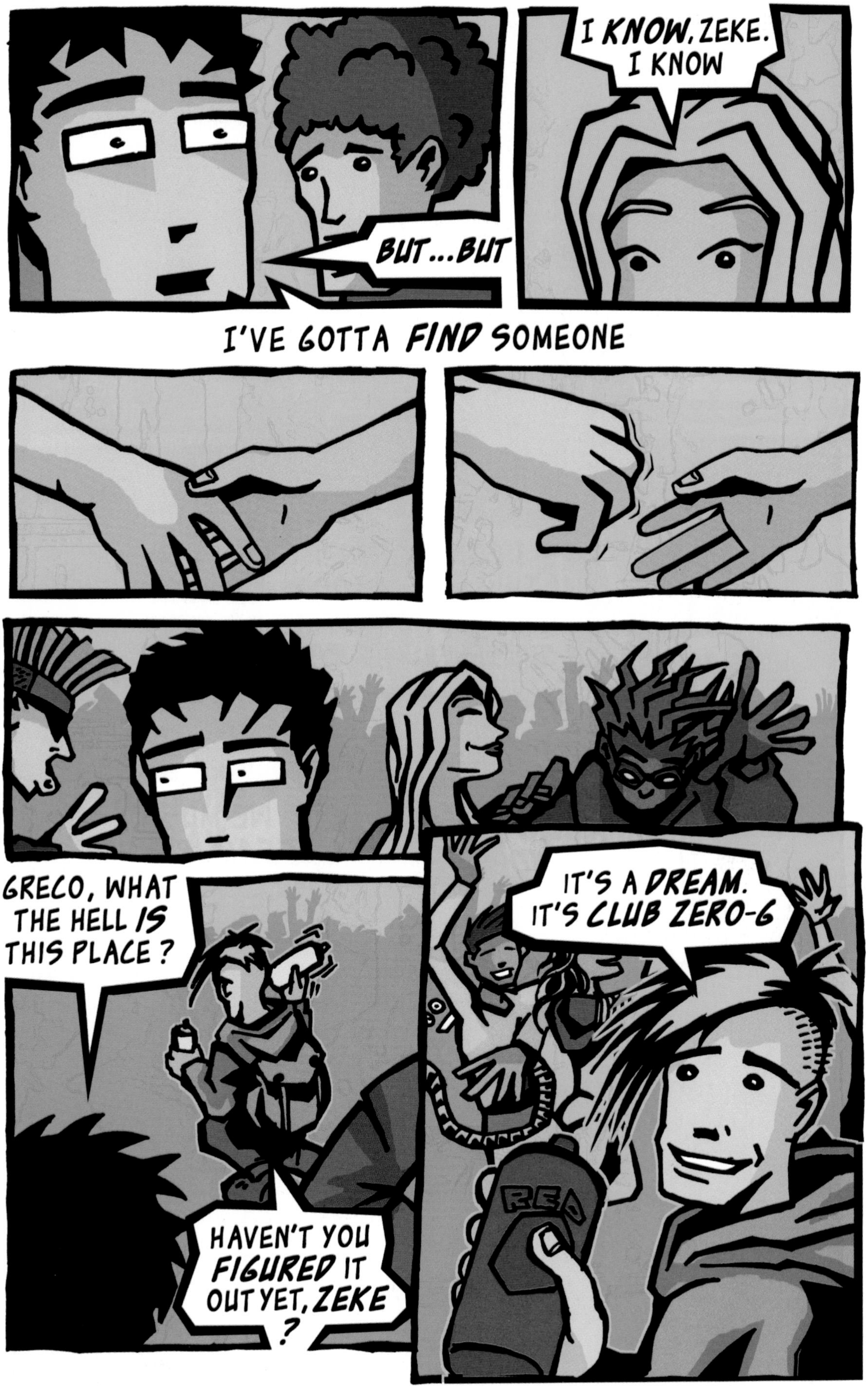
BUT...BUT
I KNOW, ZEKE. I KNOW
I'VE GOTTA FIND SOMEONE
GRECO, WHAT THE HELL IS THIS PLACE ?
IT'S A DREAM. IT'S CLUB ZERO-6
HAVEN'T YOU FIGURED IT OUT YET, ZEKE ?
RED

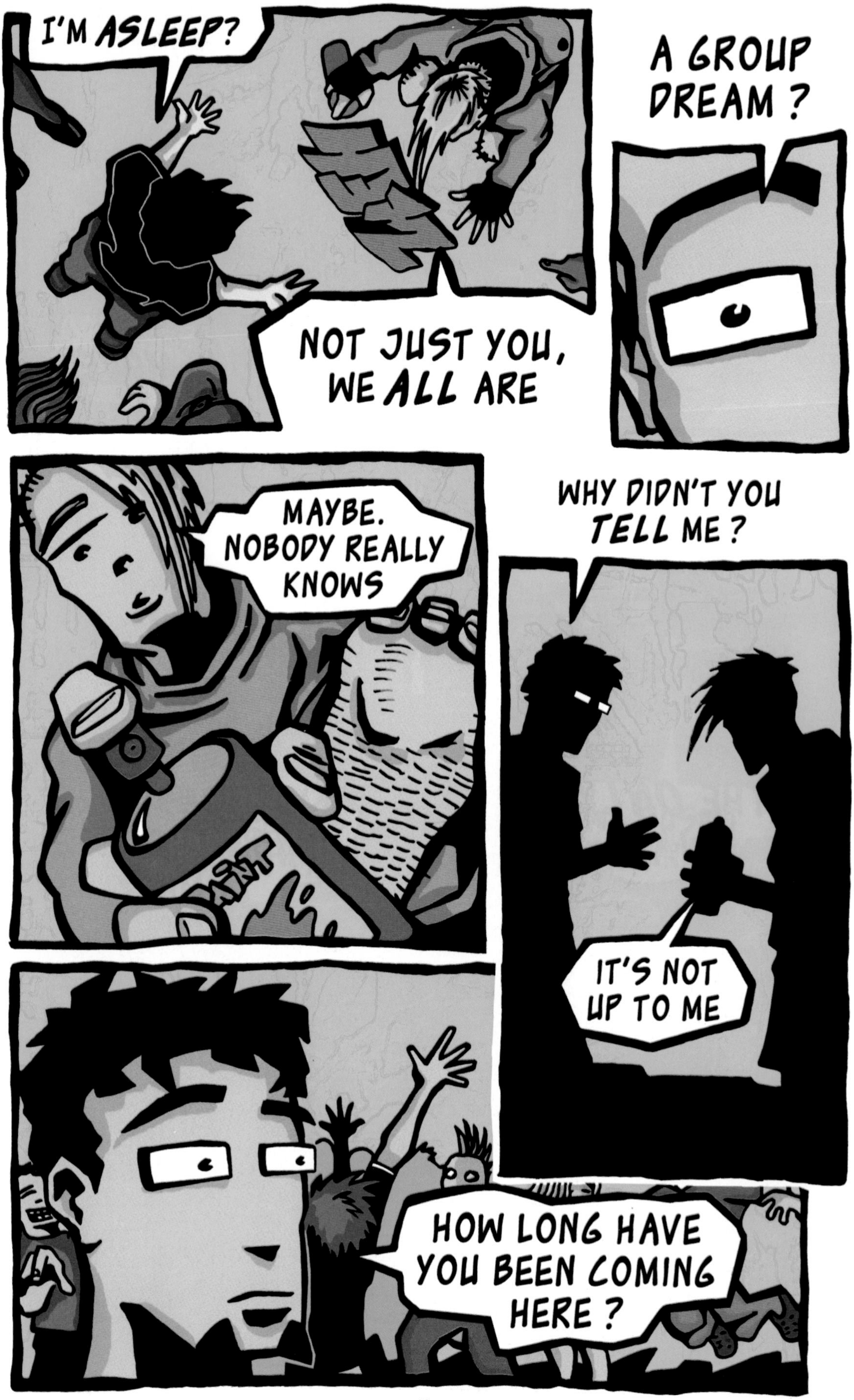
I'M ASLEEP?
NOT JUST YOU, WE ALL ARE
A GROUP DREAM ?
MAYBE. NOBODY REALLY KNOWS
WHY DIDN'T YOU TELL ME ?
IT'S NOT UP TO ME
HOW LONG HAVE YOU BEEN COMING HERE ?

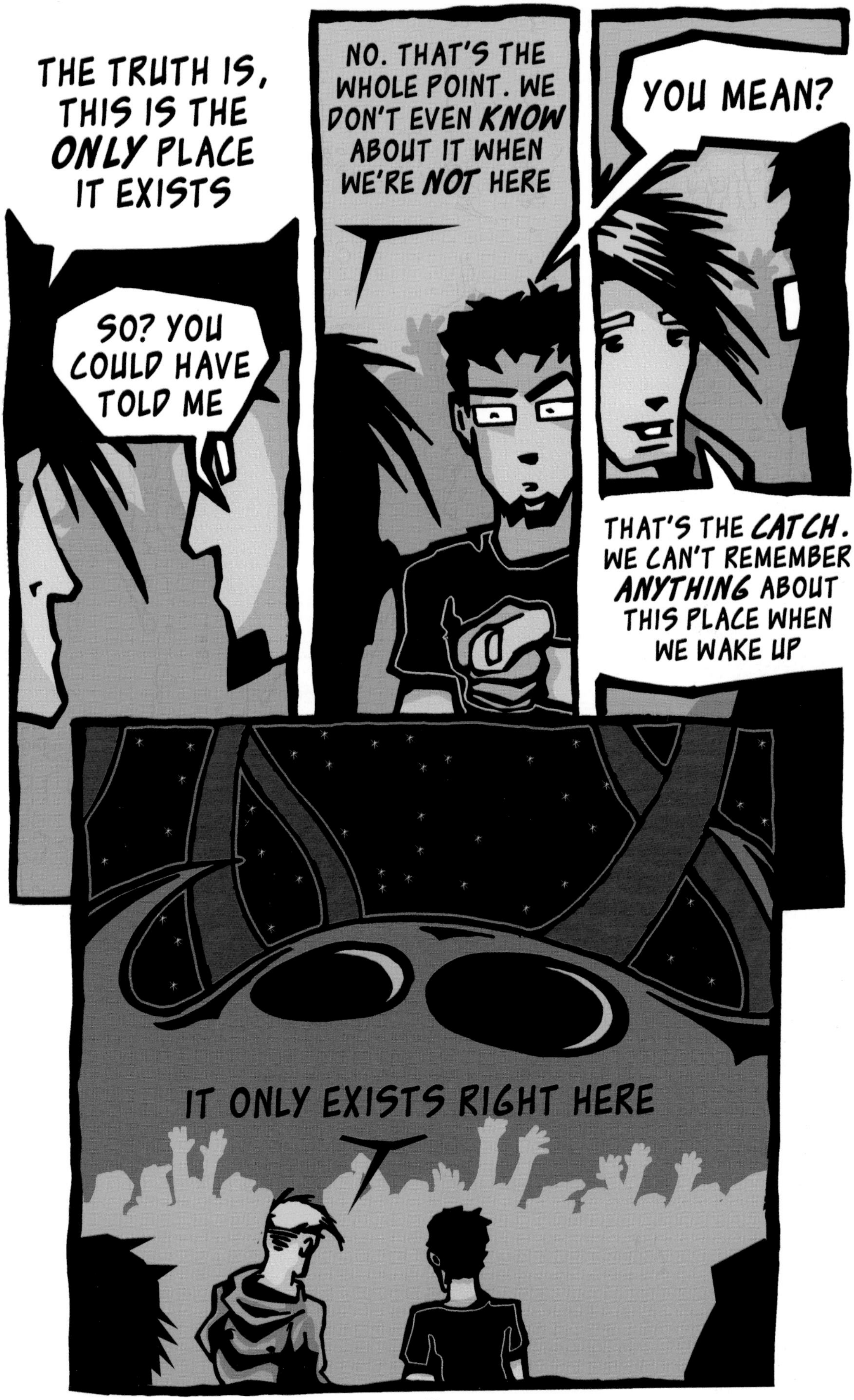
THE TRUTH IS, THIS IS THE ONLY PLACE IT EXISTS
SO? YOU COULD HAVE TOLD ME
NO. THAT'S THE WHOLE POINT. WE DON'T EVEN KNOW ABOUT IT WHEN WE'RE NOT HERE
YOU MEAN?
THAT'S THE CATCH. WE CAN'T REMEMBER ANYTHING ABOUT THIS PLACE WHEN WE WAKE UP
IT ONLY EXISTS RIGHT HERE

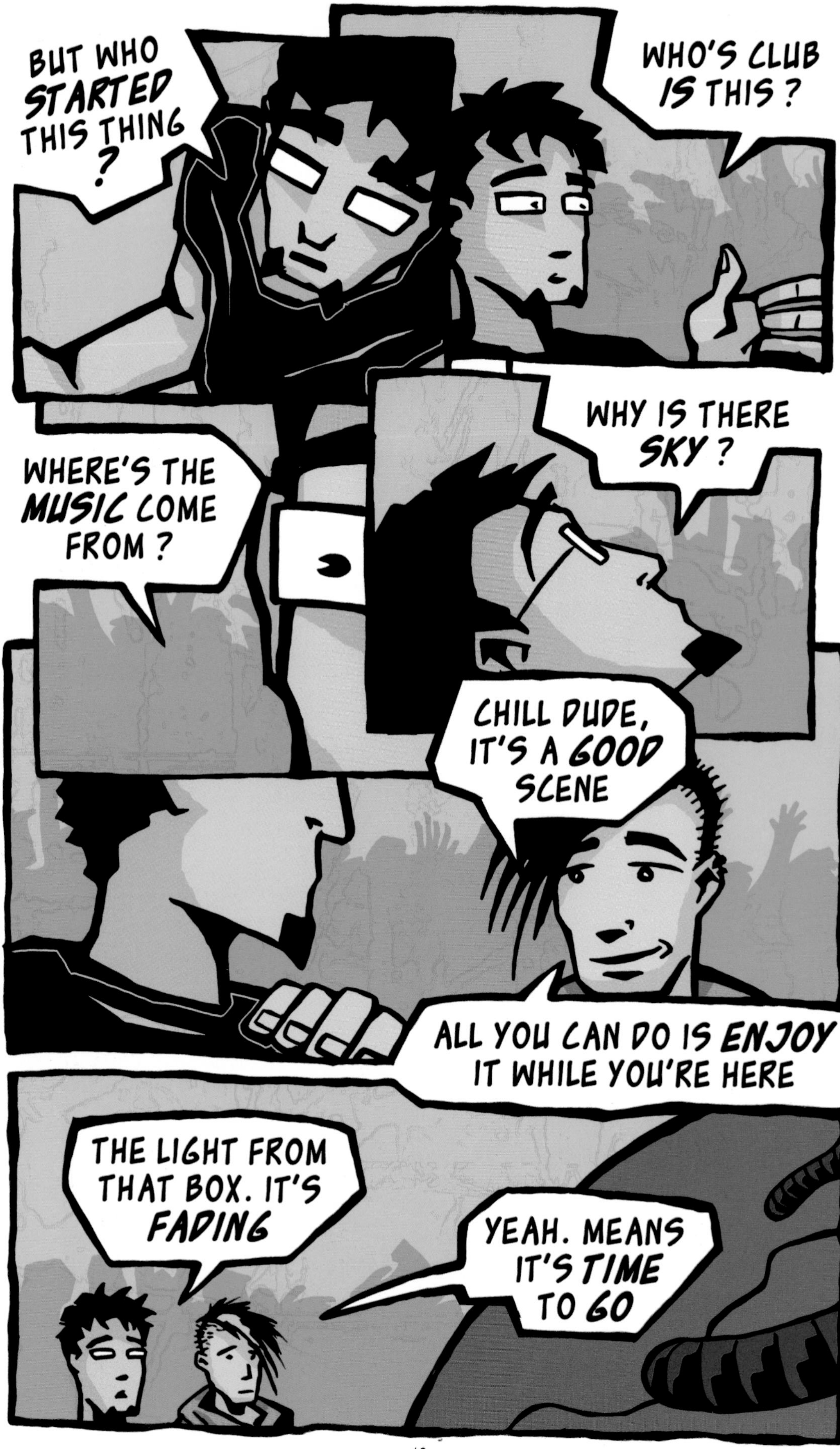
BUT WHO STARTED THIS THING ?
WHO'S CLUB IS THIS ?
WHERE'S THE MUSIC COME FROM ?
WHY IS THERE SKY ?
CHILL DUDE, IT'S A GOOD SCENE
ALL YOU CAN DO IS ENJOY IT WHILE YOU'RE HERE
THE LIGHT FROM THAT BOX. IT'S FADING
YEAH. MEANS IT'S TIME TO GO

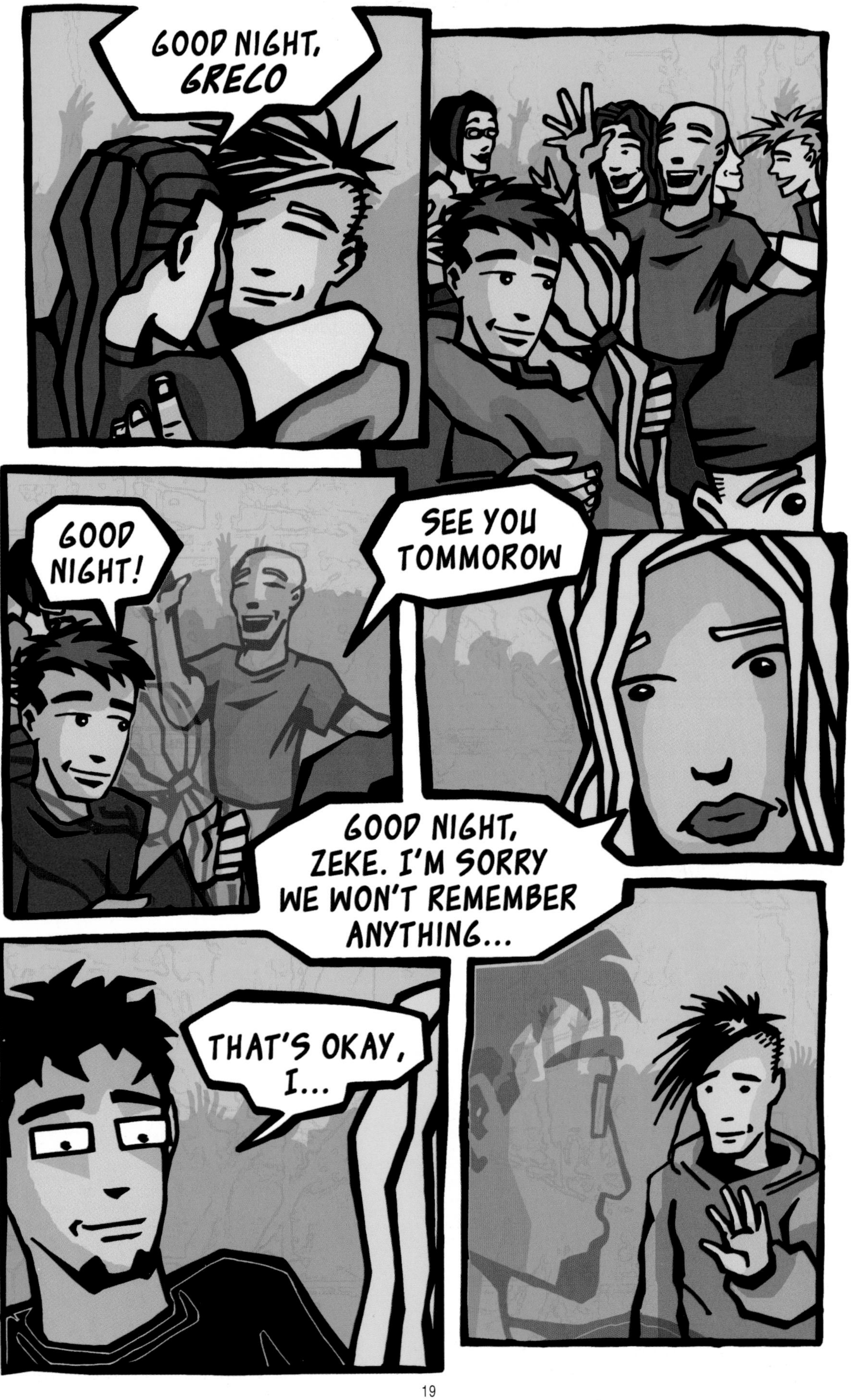
GOOD NIGHT, GRECO
GOOD NIGHT!
SEE YOU TOMMOROW
GOOD NIGHT, ZEKE. I'M SORRY WE WON'T REMEMBER ANYTHING...
THAT'S OKAY, I...

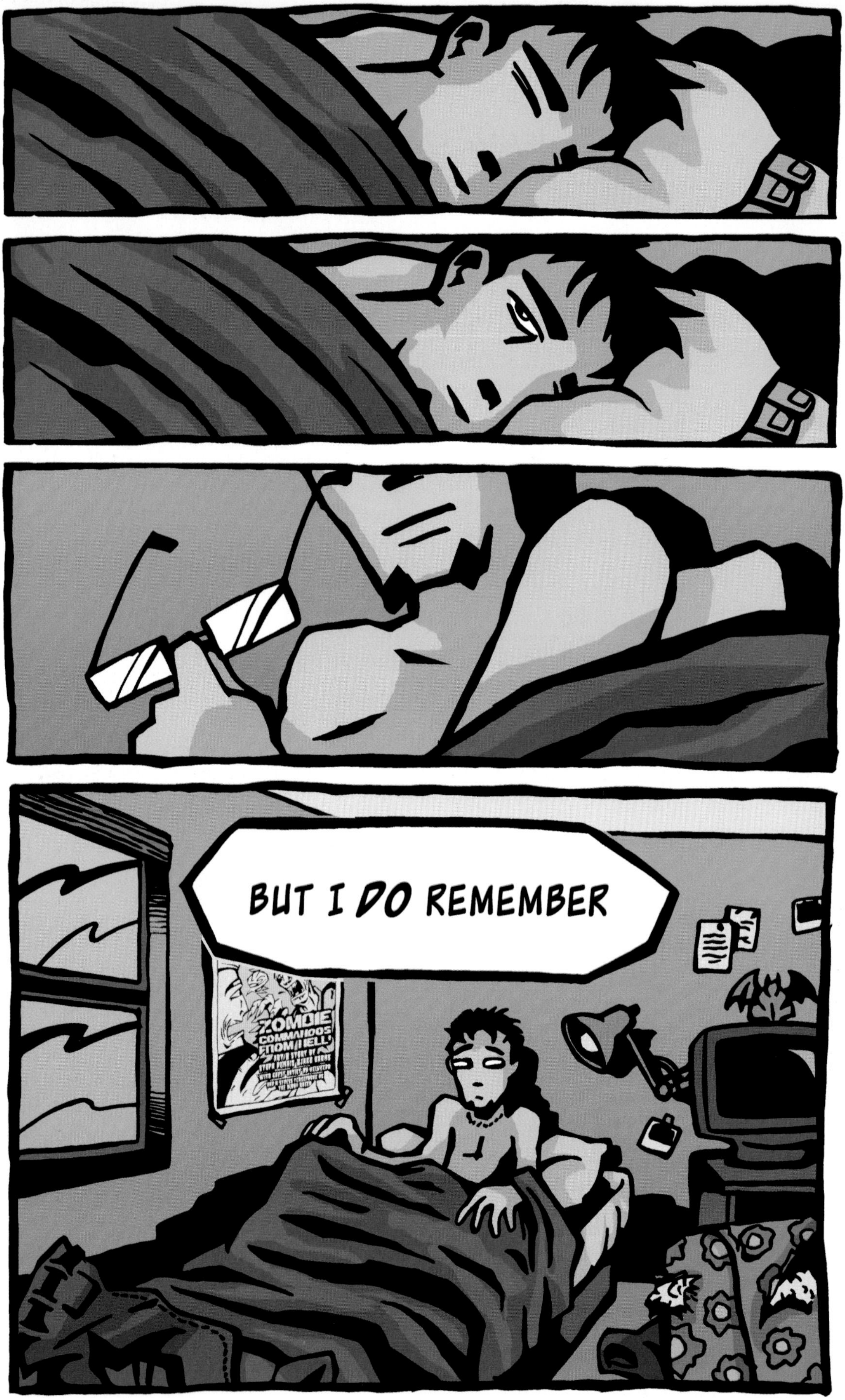
BUT I DO REMEMBER

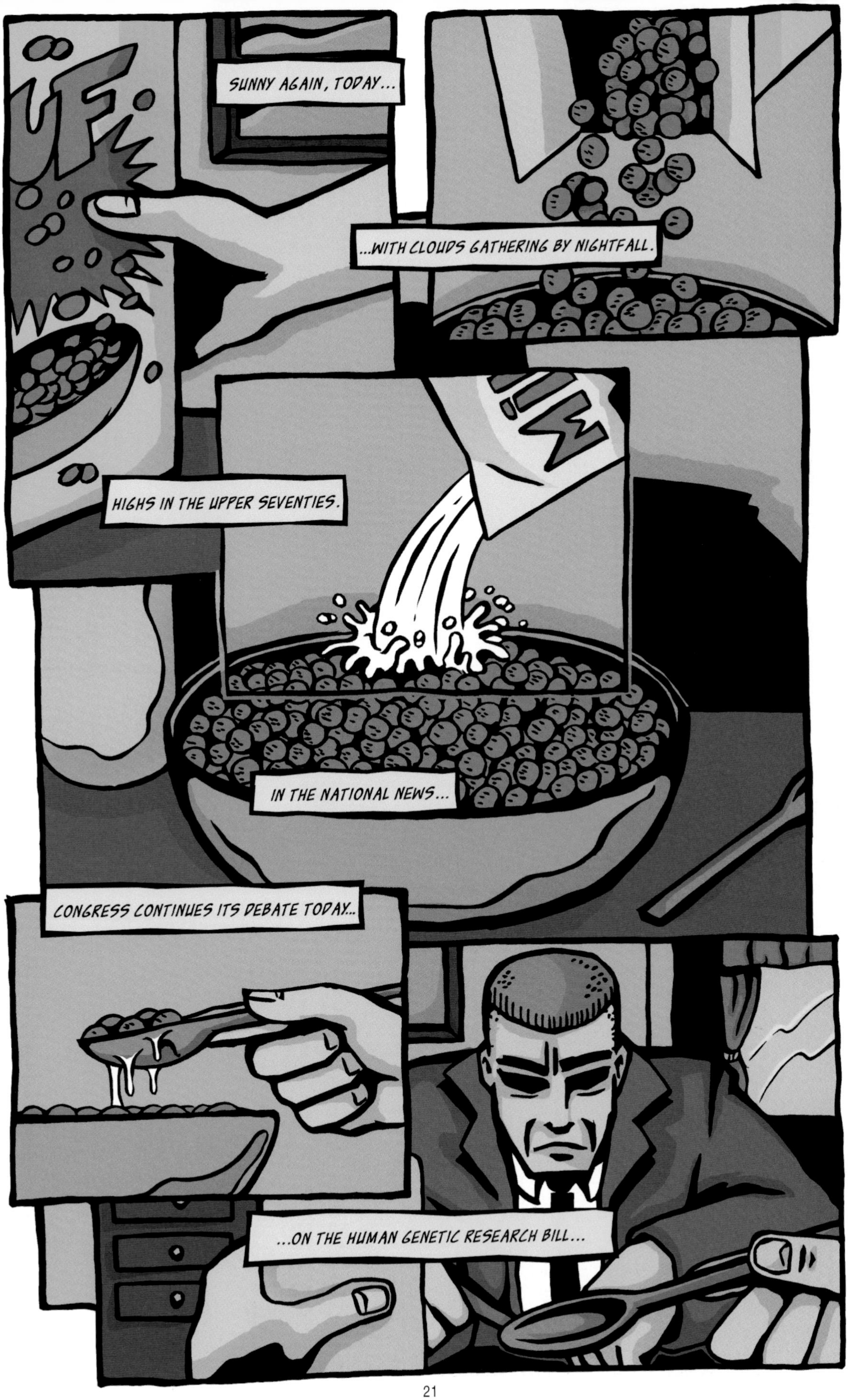
SUNNY AGAIN, TODAY...
...WITH CLOUDS GATHERING BY NIGHTFALL.
HIGHS IN THE UPPER SEVENTIES.
IN THE NATIONAL NEWS...
CONGRESS CONTINUES ITS DEBATE TODAY...
...ON THE HUMAN GENETIC RESEARCH BILL...

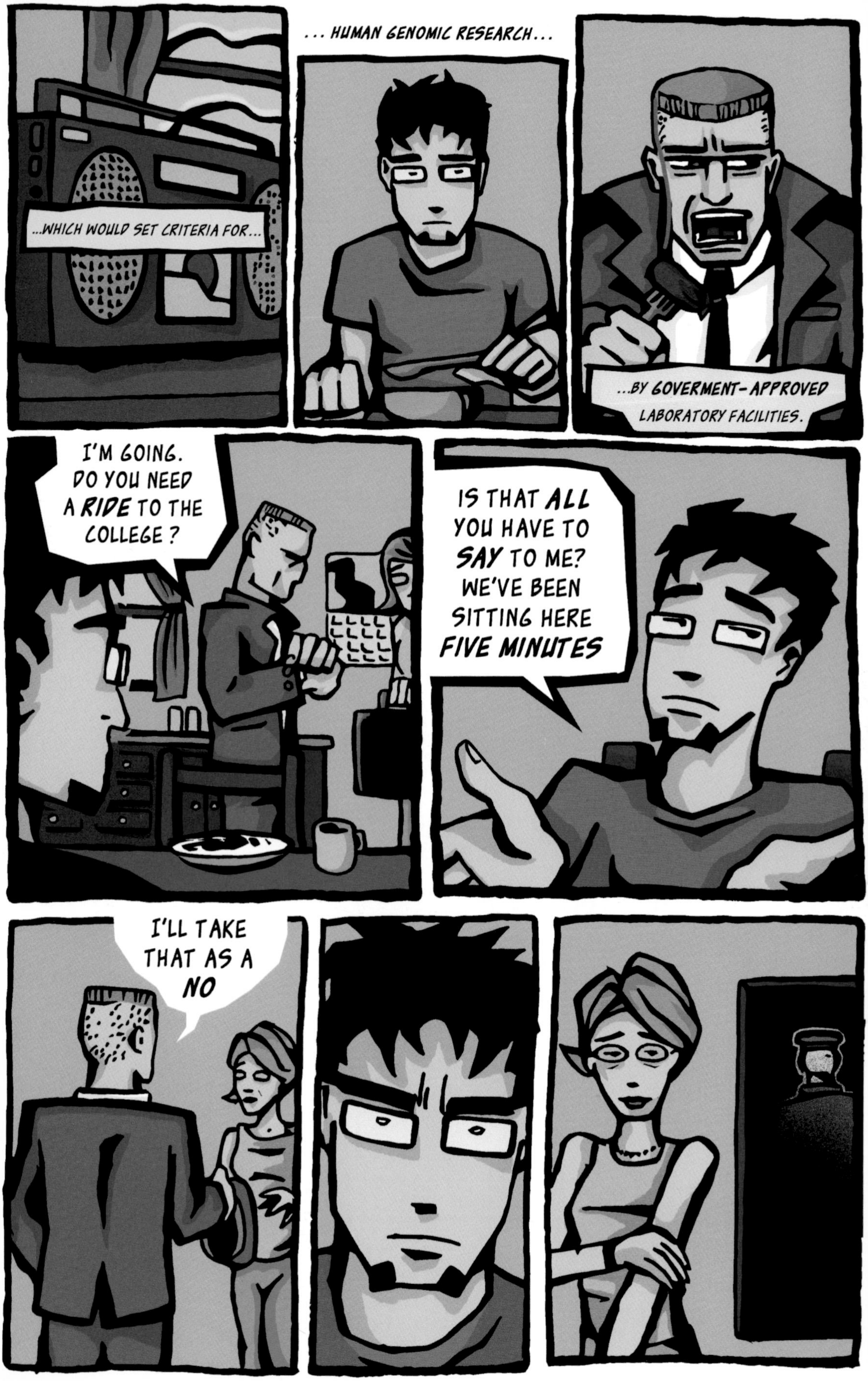
...WHICH WOULD SET CRITERIA FOR...
... HUMAN GENOMIC RESEARCH...
...BY GOVERMENT-APPROVED LABORATORY FACILITIES.
I'M GOING. DO YOU NEED A RIDE TO THE COLLEGE ?
IS THAT ALL YOU HAVE TO SAY TO ME? WE'VE BEEN SITTING HERE FIVE MINUTES
I'LL TAKE THAT AS A NO

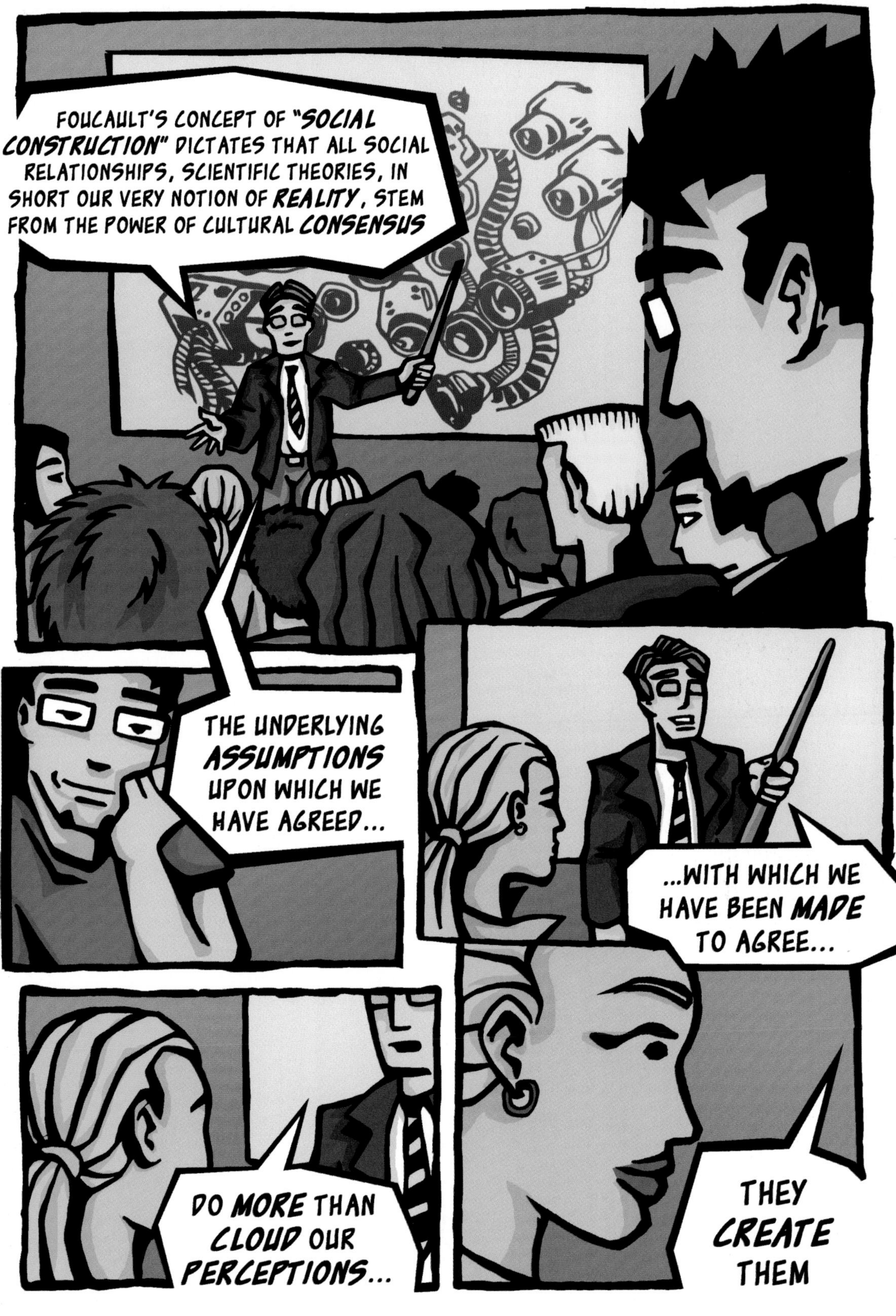
FOUCAULT'S CONCEPT OF "SOCIAL CONSTRUCTION" DICTATES THAT ALL SOCIAL RELATIONSHIPS, SCIENTIFIC THEORIES, IN SHORT OUR VERY NOTION OF REALITY, STEM FROM THE POWER OF CULTURAL CONSENSUS
THE UNDERLYING ASSUMPTIONS UPON WHICH WE HAVE AGREED...
...WITH WHICH WE HAVE BEEN MADE TO AGREE...
DO MORE THAN CLOUD OUR PERCEPTIONS...
THEY CREATE THEM

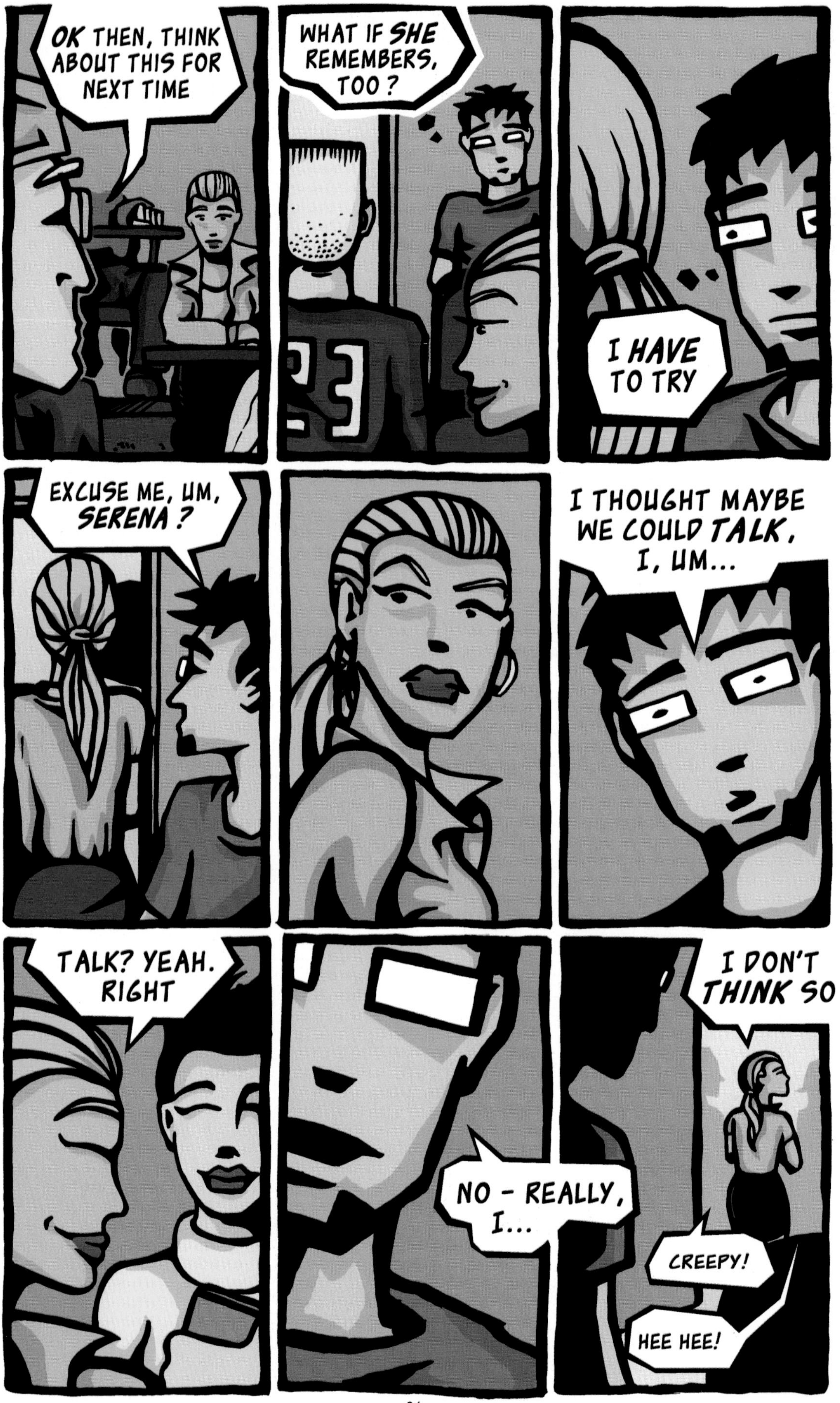
OK THEN, THINK ABOUT THIS FOR NEXT TIME
WHAT IF SHE REMEMBERS, TOO?
I HAVE TO TRY
EXCUSE ME, UM, SERENA?
I THOUGHT MAYBE WE COULD TALK, I, UM...
TALK? YEAH. RIGHT
NO - REALLY, I...
I DON'T THINK SO
CREEPY!
HEE HEE!

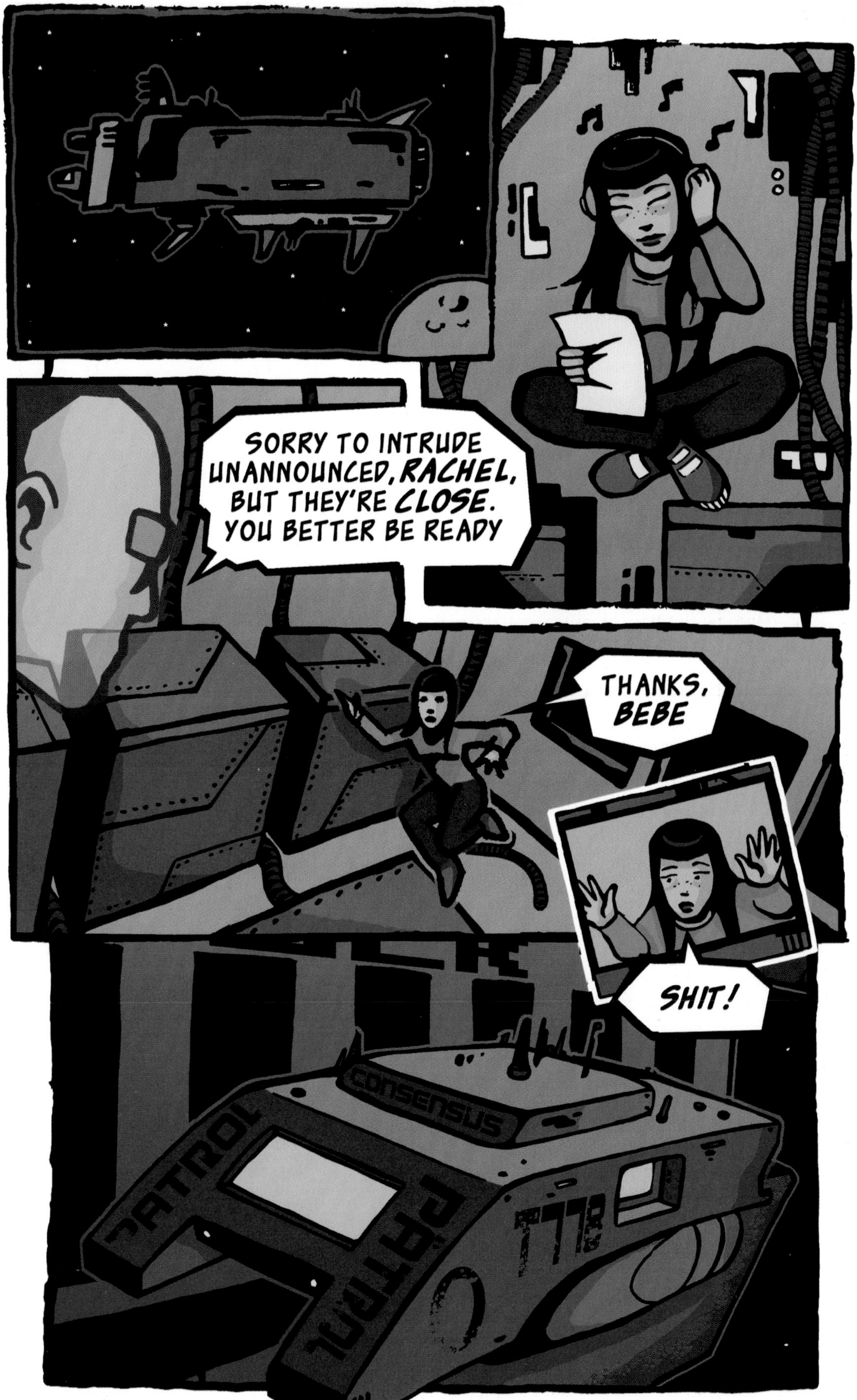
SORRY TO INTRUDE UNANNOUNCED, RACHEL, BUT THEY'RE CLOSE. YOU BETTER BE READY
THANKS, BEBE
SHIT!
CONSENSUS
PATROL
PATROL
T778

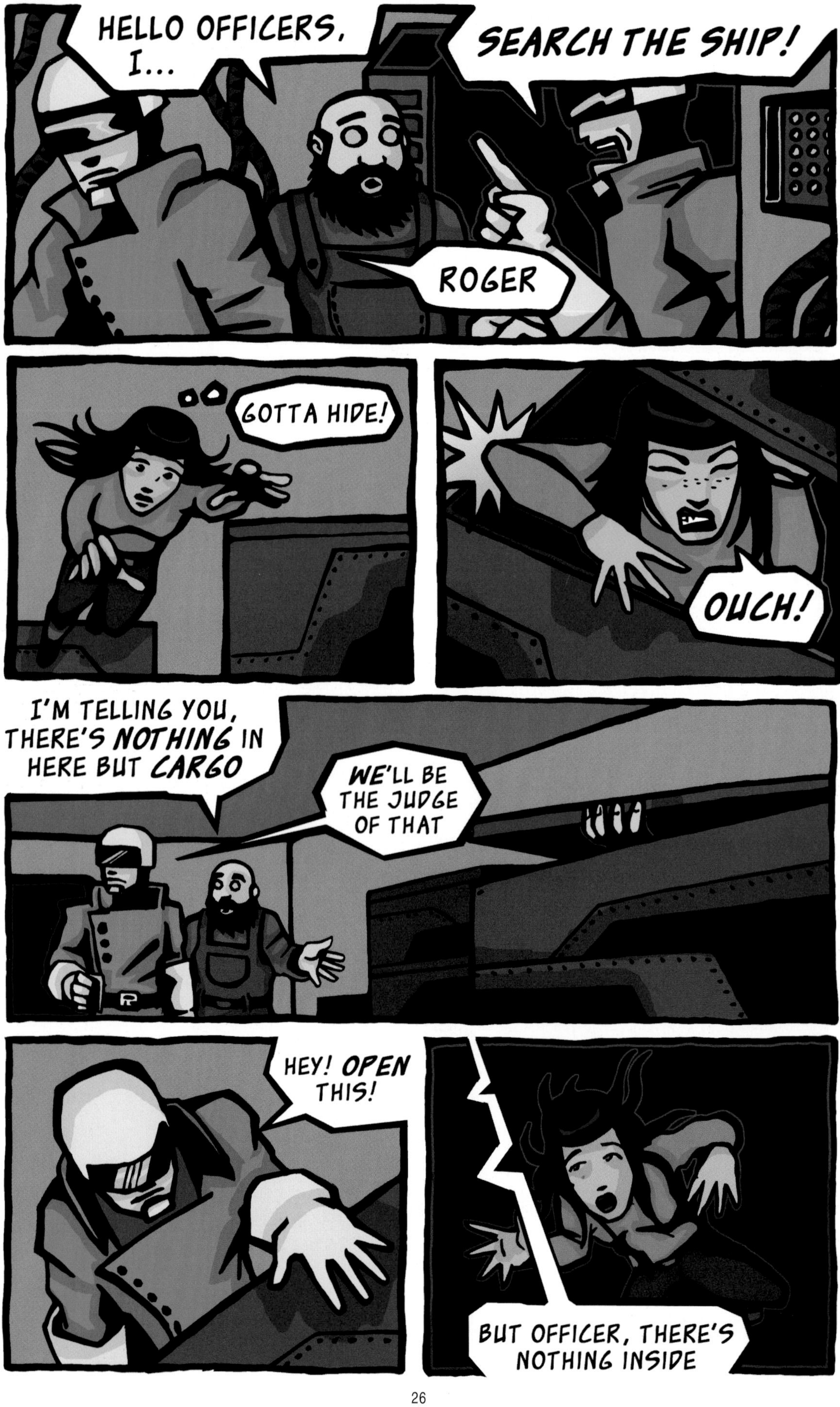
HELLO OFFICERS, I...
SEARCH THE SHIP!
ROGER
GOTTA HIDE!
OUCH!
I'M TELLING YOU, THERE'S NOTHING IN HERE BUT CARGO
WE'LL BE THE JUDGE OF THAT
HEY! OPEN THIS!
BUT OFFICER, THERE'S NOTHING INSIDE

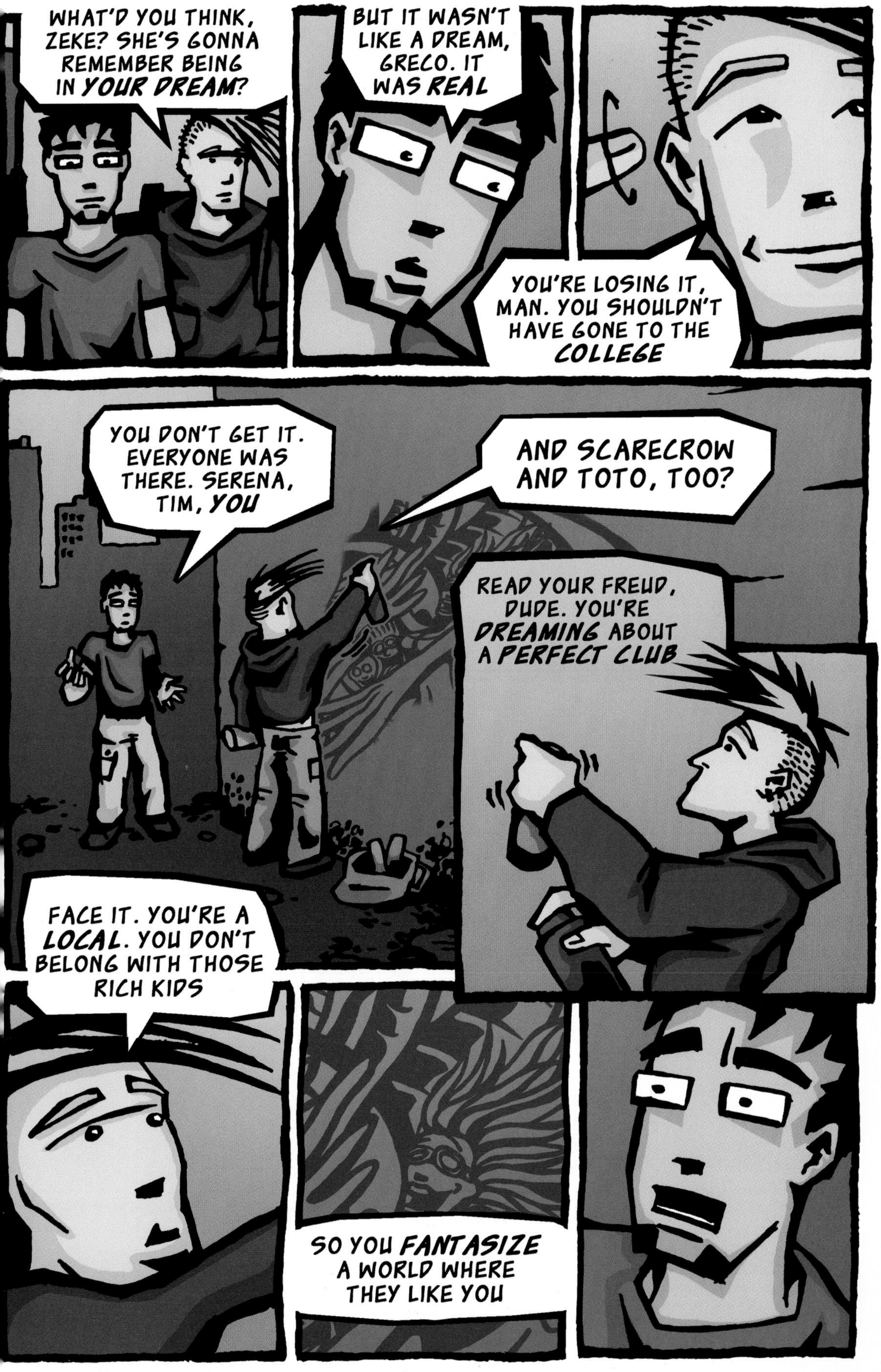
WHAT'D YOU THINK, ZEKE? SHE'S GONNA REMEMBER BEING IN YOUR DREAM?
BUT IT WASN'T LIKE A DREAM, GRECO. IT WAS REAL
YOU'RE LOSING IT, MAN. YOU SHOULDN'T HAVE GONE TO THE COLLEGE
YOU DON'T GET IT. EVERYONE WAS THERE. SERENA, TIM, YOU
AND SCARECROW AND TOTO, TOO?
READ YOUR FREUD, DUDE. YOU'RE DREAMING ABOUT A PERFECT CLUB
FACE IT. YOU'RE A LOCAL. YOU DON'T BELONG WITH THOSE RICH KIDS
SO YOU FANTASIZE A WORLD WHERE THEY LIKE YOU

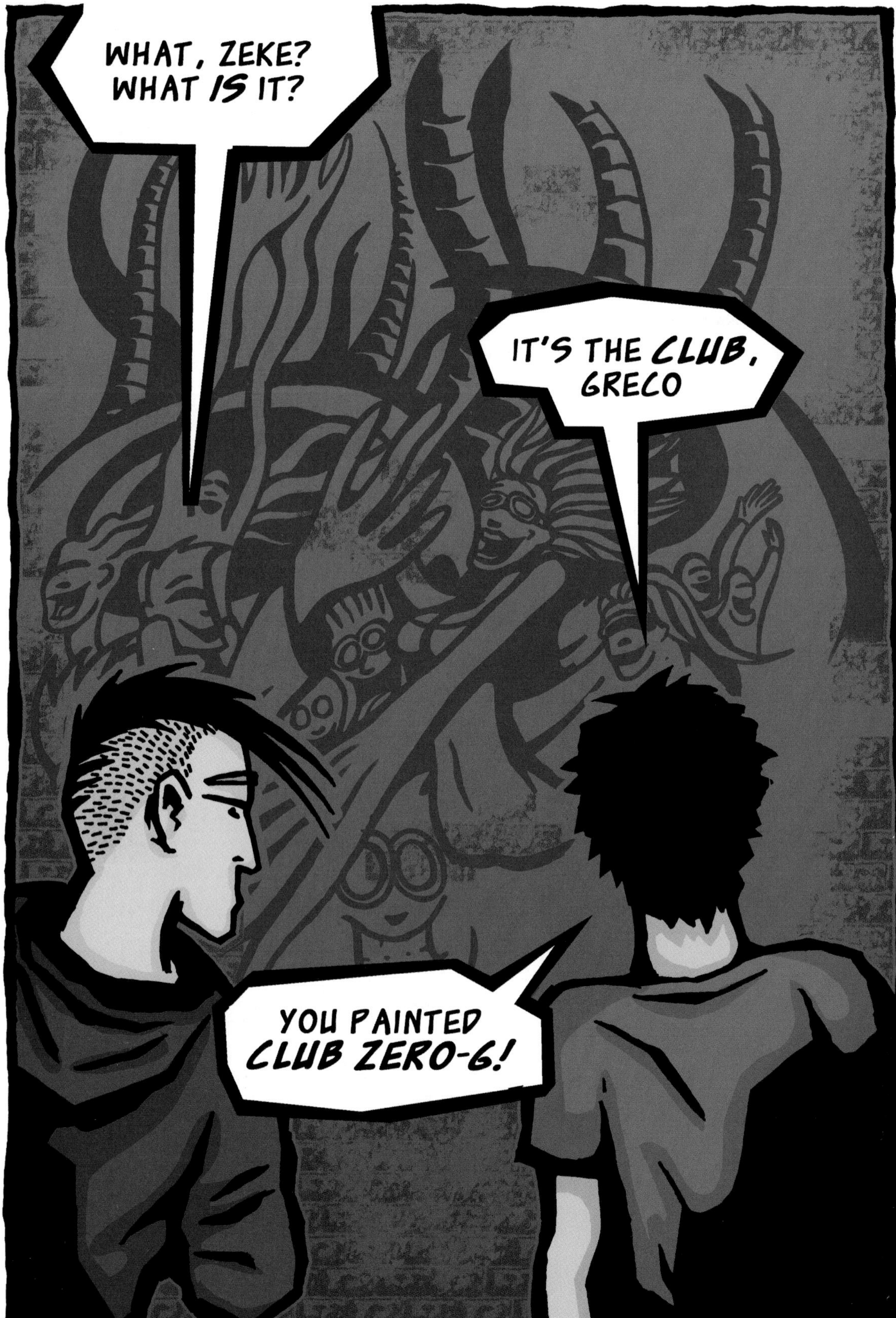
WHAT, ZEKE? WHAT IS IT?
IT'S THE CLUB, GRECO
YOU PAINTED CLUB ZERO-6!

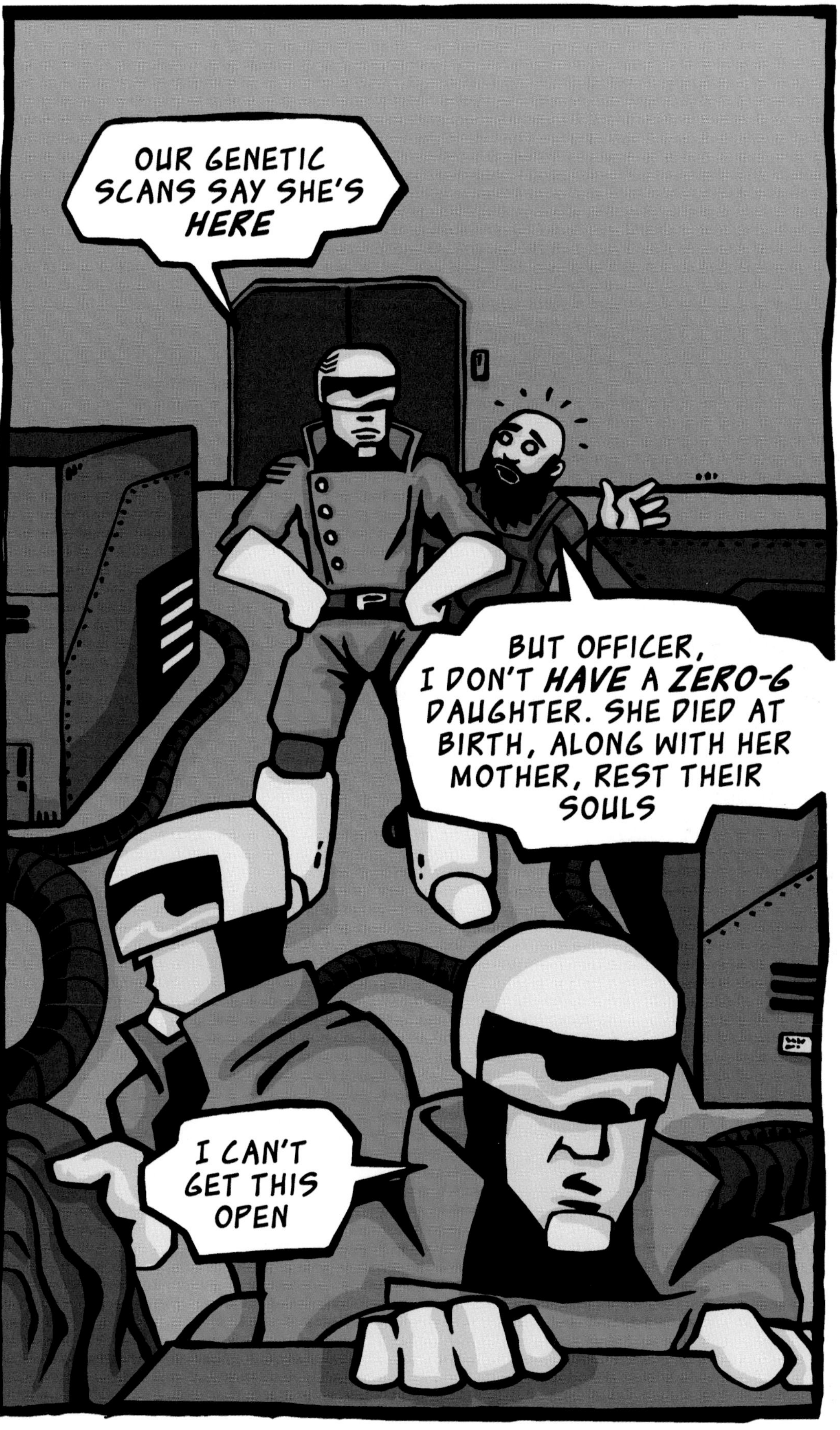
OUR GENETIC SCANS SAY SHE'S *HERE*
BUT OFFICER, I DON'T *HAVE* A *ZERO-6* DAUGHTER. SHE DIED AT BIRTH, ALONG WITH HER MOTHER, REST THEIR SOULS
I CAN'T GET THIS OPEN

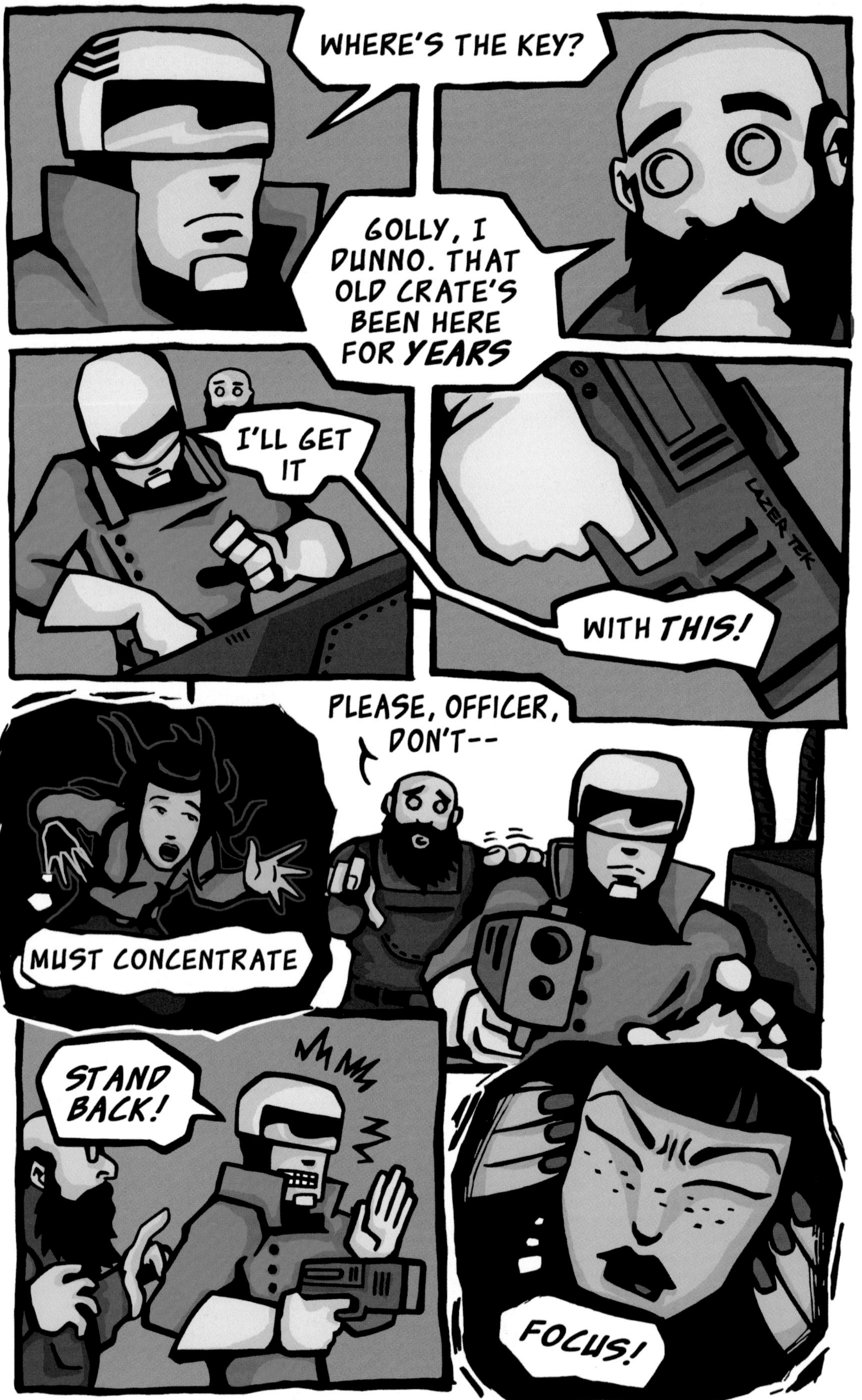
WHERE'S THE KEY?
GOLLY, I DUNNO. THAT OLD CRATE'S BEEN HERE FOR YEARS
I'LL GET IT
WITH THIS!
LAZER TEK
MUST CONCENTRATE
PLEASE, OFFICER, DON'T--
STAND BACK!
FOCUS!

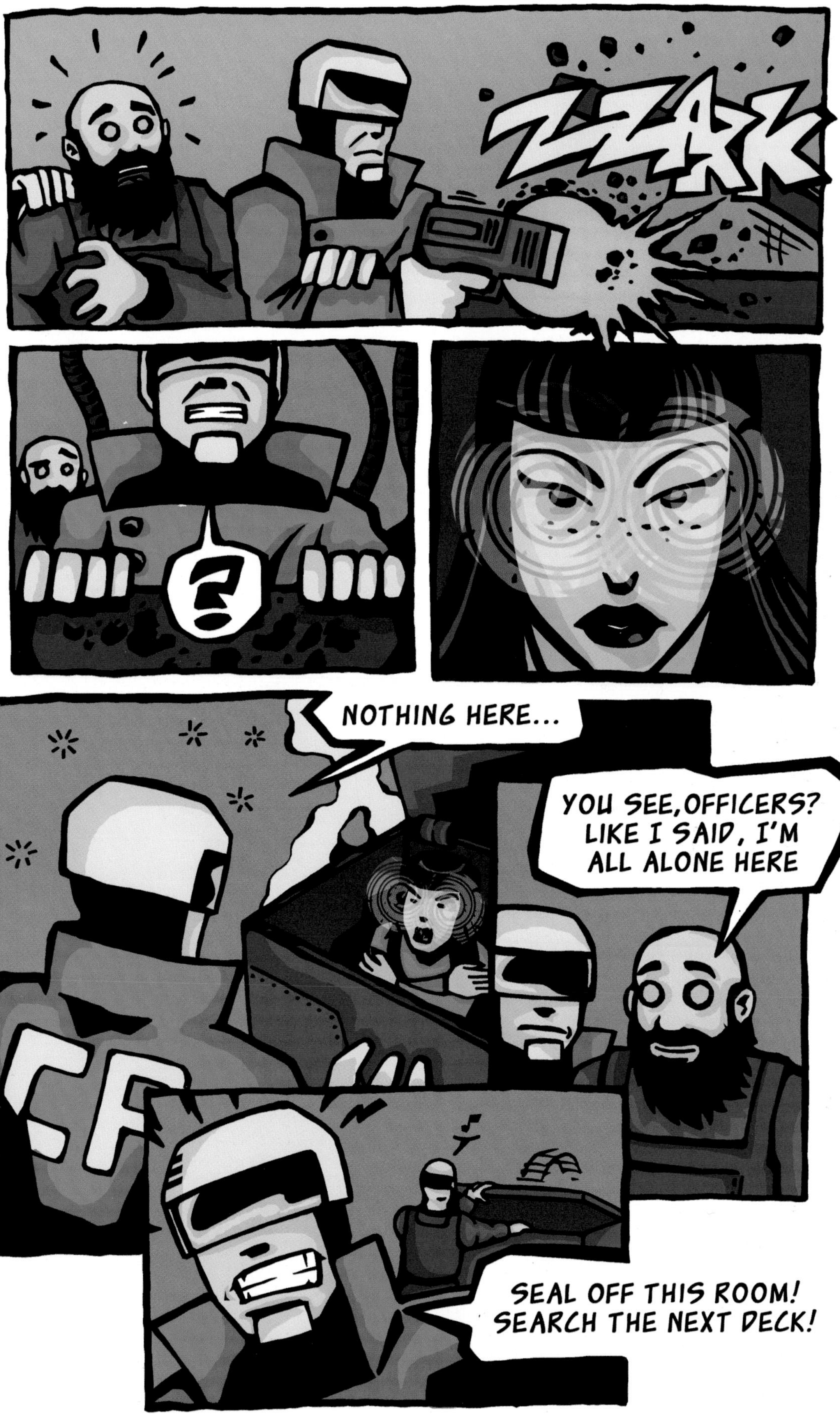
ZZAK
?
NOTHING HERE...
YOU SEE, OFFICERS? LIKE I SAID, I'M ALL ALONE HERE
CF
SEAL OFF THIS ROOM! SEARCH THE NEXT DECK!

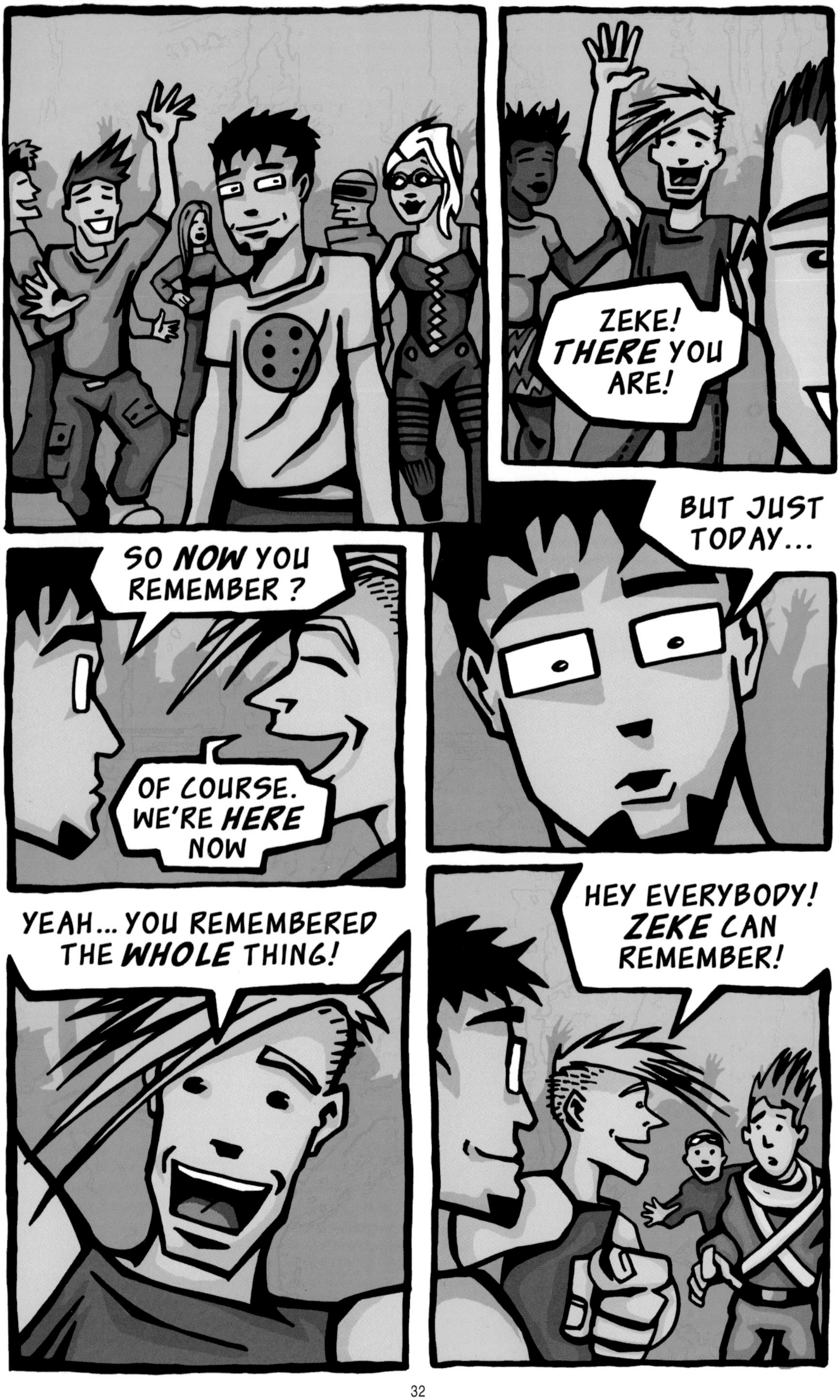
ZEKE! THERE YOU ARE!
SO NOW YOU REMEMBER?
OF COURSE. WE'RE HERE NOW
BUT JUST TODAY...
YEAH... YOU REMEMBERED THE WHOLE THING!
HEY EVERYBODY! ZEKE CAN REMEMBER!

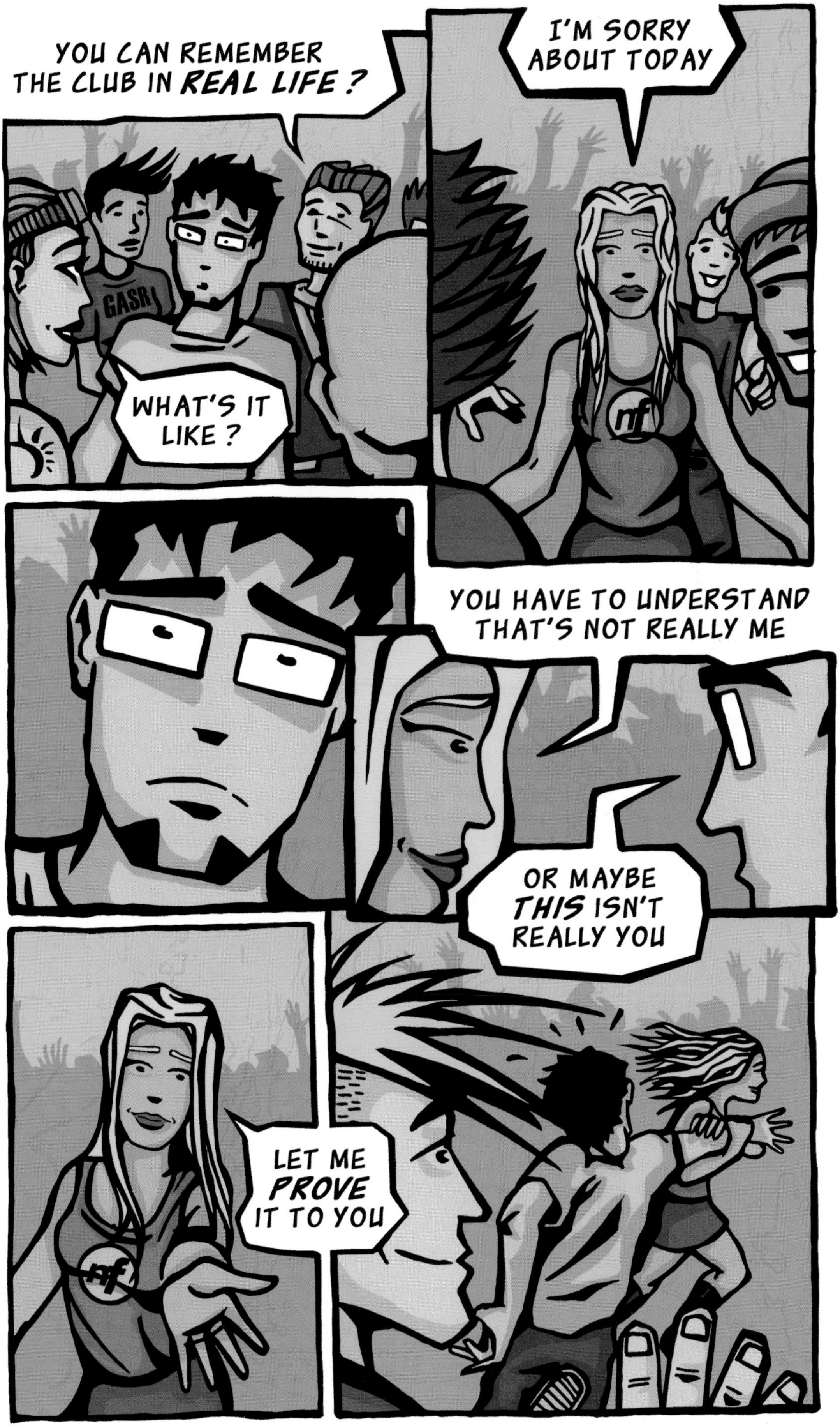
YOU CAN REMEMBER THE CLUB IN REAL LIFE?
WHAT'S IT LIKE?
I'M SORRY ABOUT TODAY
YOU HAVE TO UNDERSTAND THAT'S NOT REALLY ME
OR MAYBE THIS ISN'T REALLY YOU
LET ME PROVE IT TO YOU
GASR

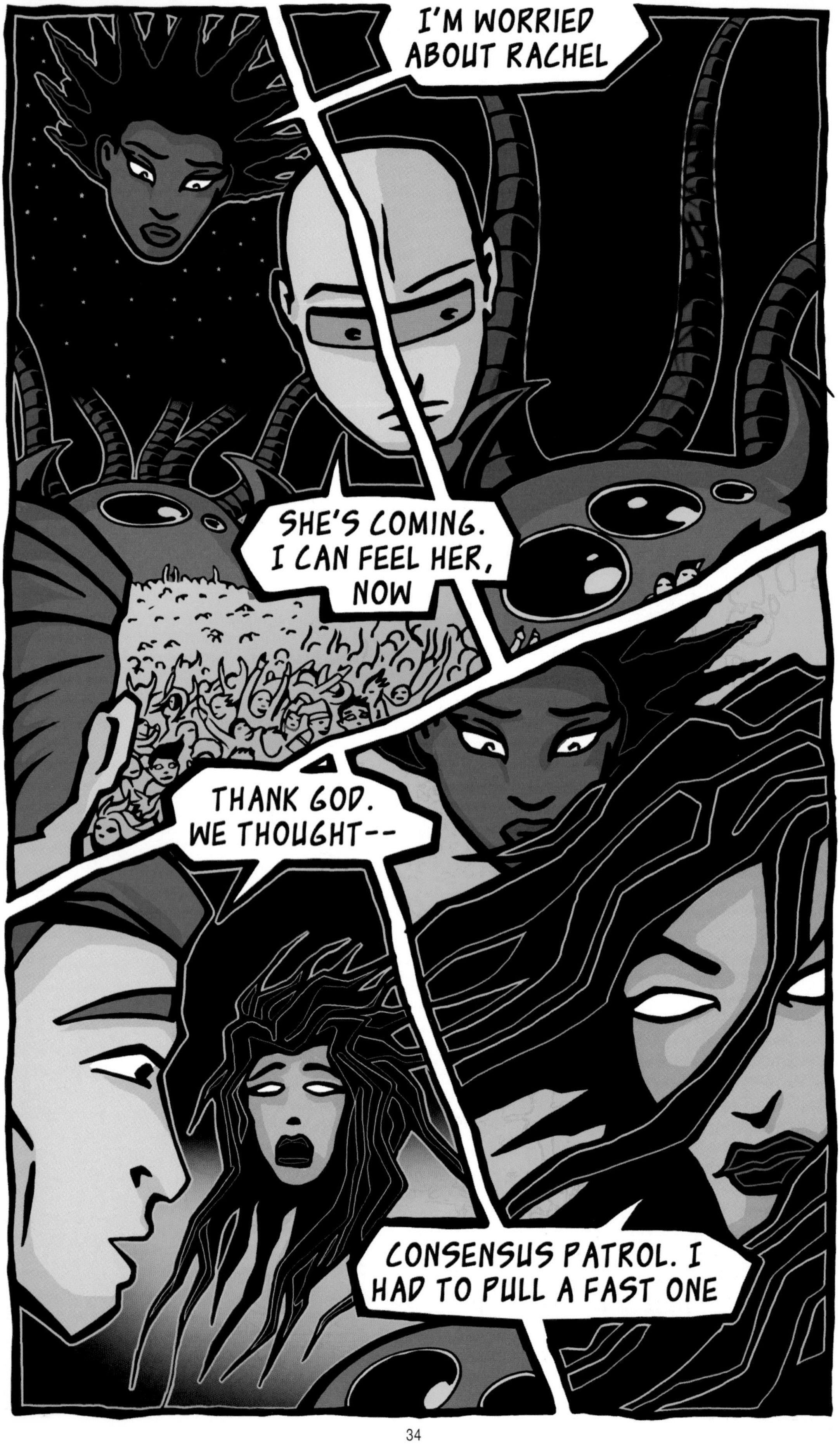
I'M WORRIED ABOUT RACHEL
SHE'S COMING. I CAN FEEL HER, NOW
THANK GOD. WE THOUGHT--
CONSENSUS PATROL. I HAD TO PULL A FAST ONE

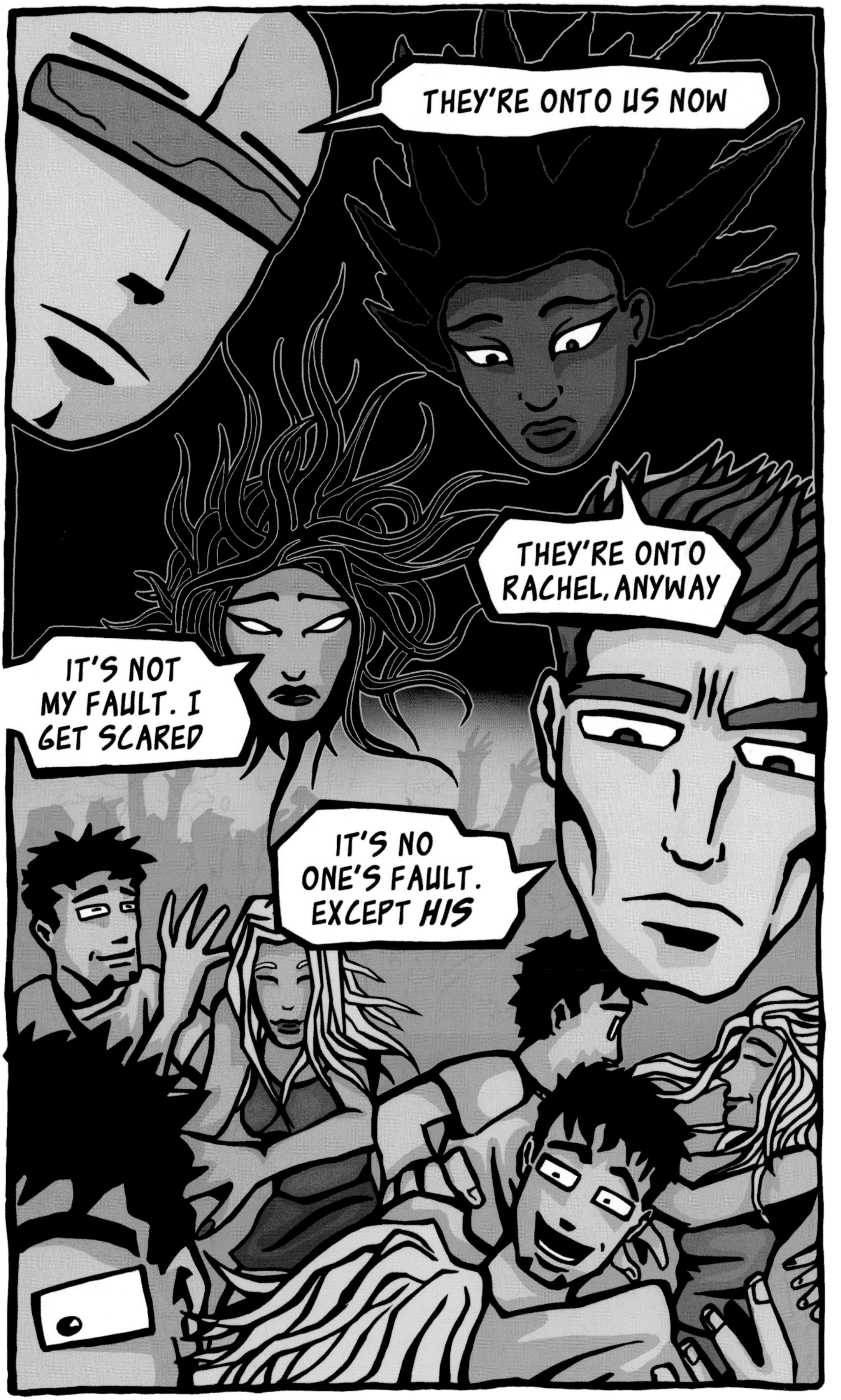
THEY'RE ONTO US NOW
THEY'RE ONTO RACHEL, ANYWAY
IT'S NOT MY FAULT. I GET SCARED
IT'S NO ONE'S FAULT. EXCEPT *HIS*

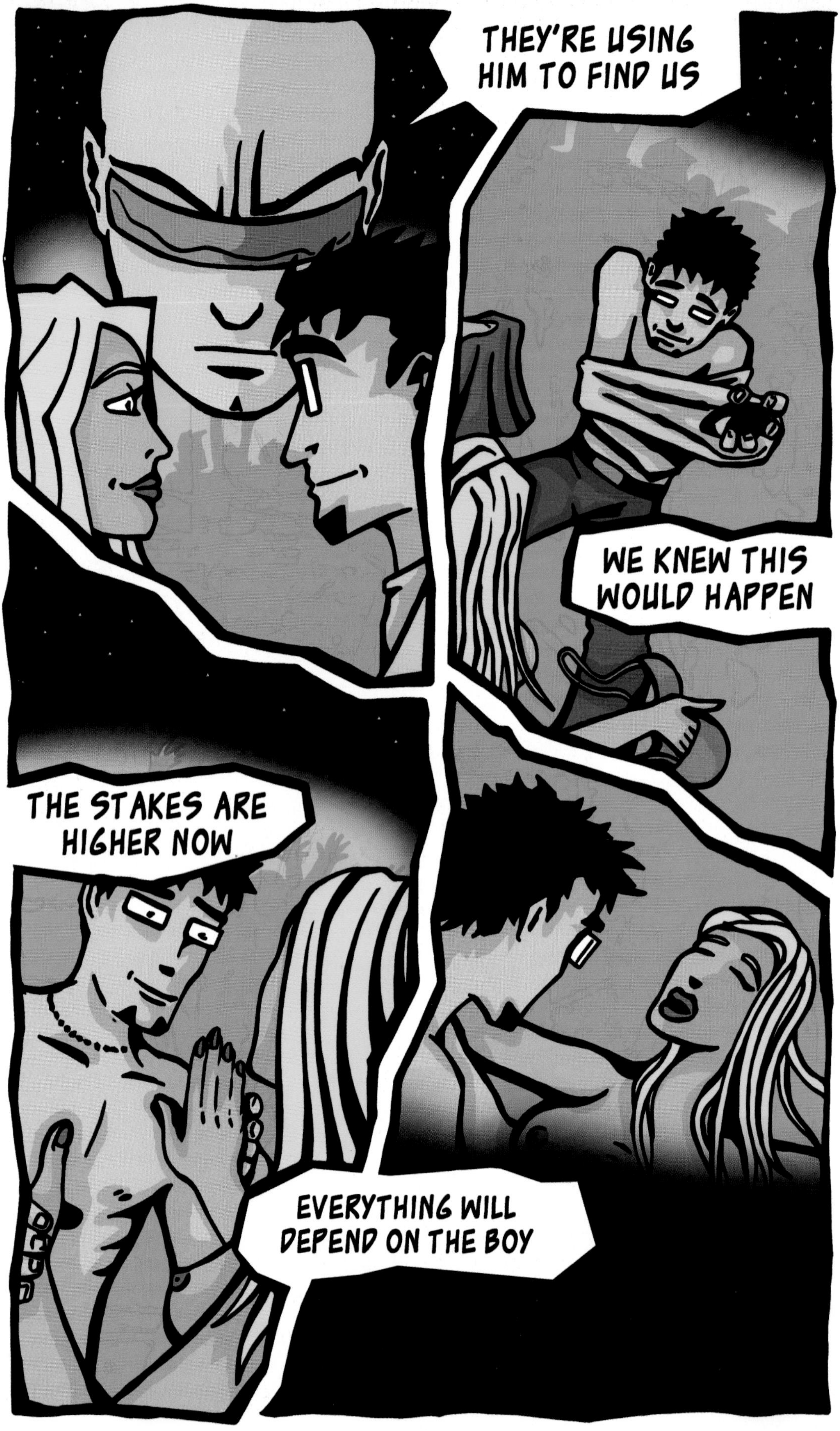
THEY'RE USING HIM TO FIND US
WE KNEW THIS WOULD HAPPEN
THE STAKES ARE HIGHER NOW
EVERYTHING WILL DEPEND ON THE BOY

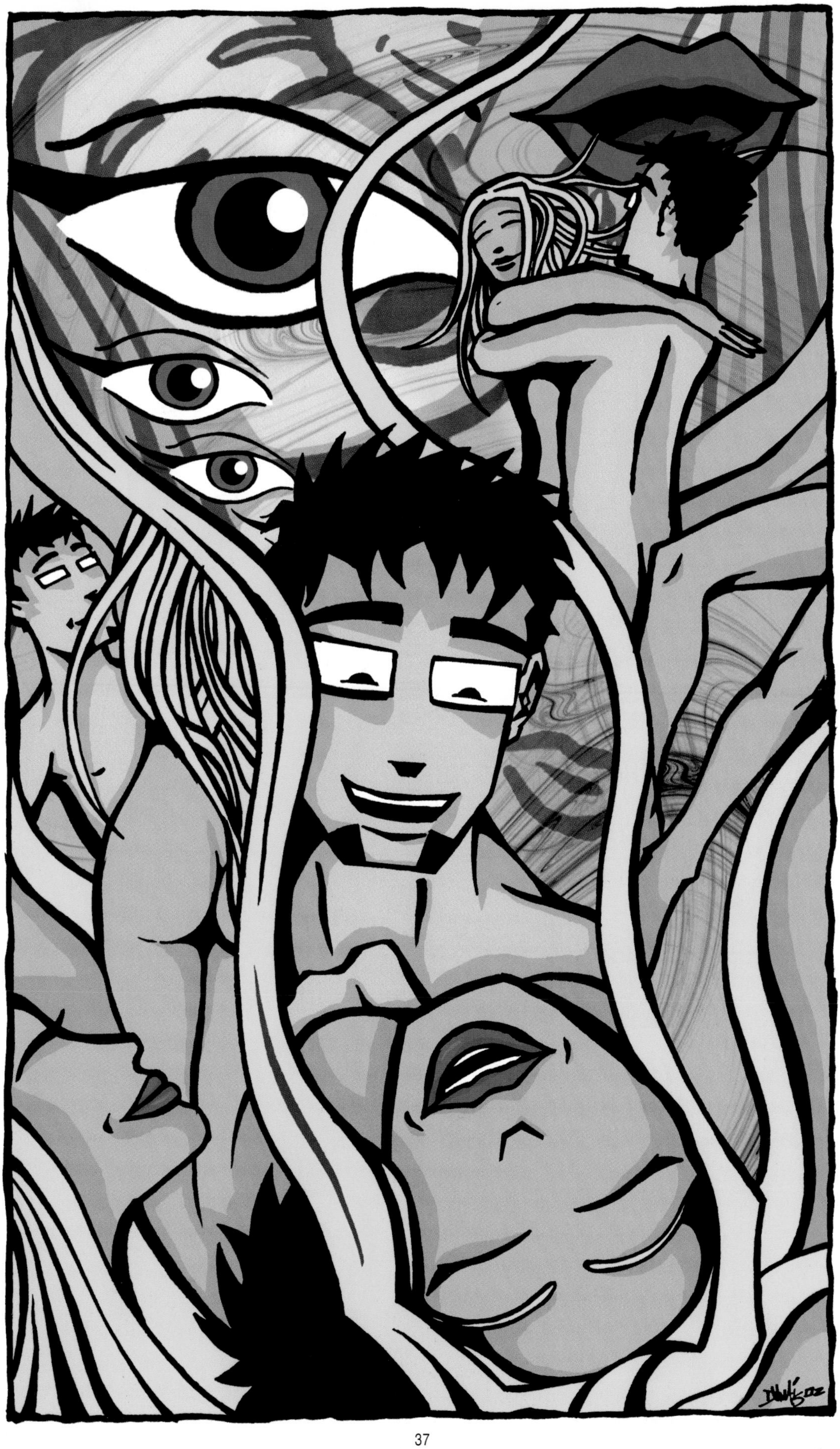

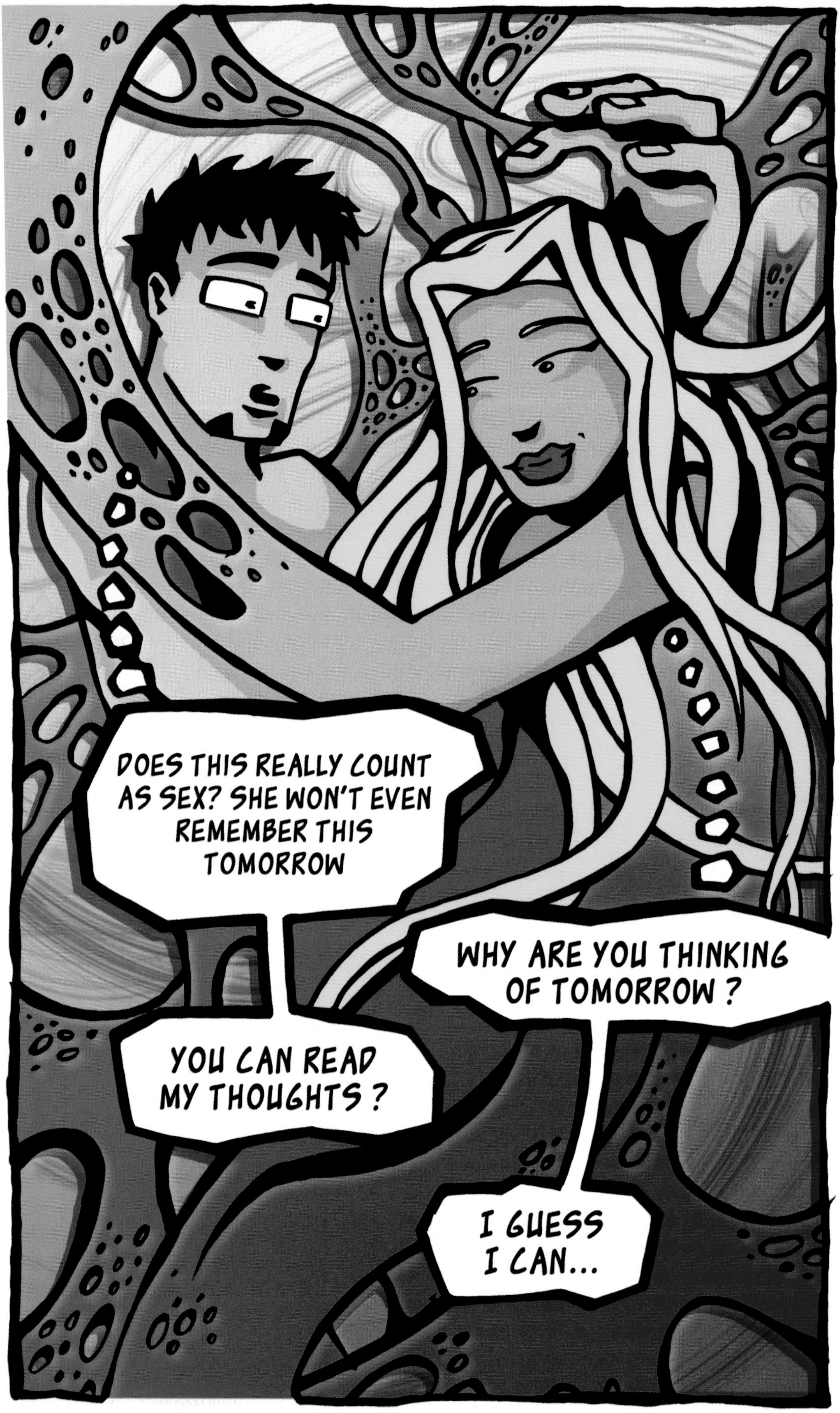
DOES THIS REALLY COUNT AS SEX? SHE WON'T EVEN REMEMBER THIS TOMORROW
WHY ARE YOU THINKING OF TOMORROW ?
YOU CAN READ MY THOUGHTS ?
I GUESS I CAN...

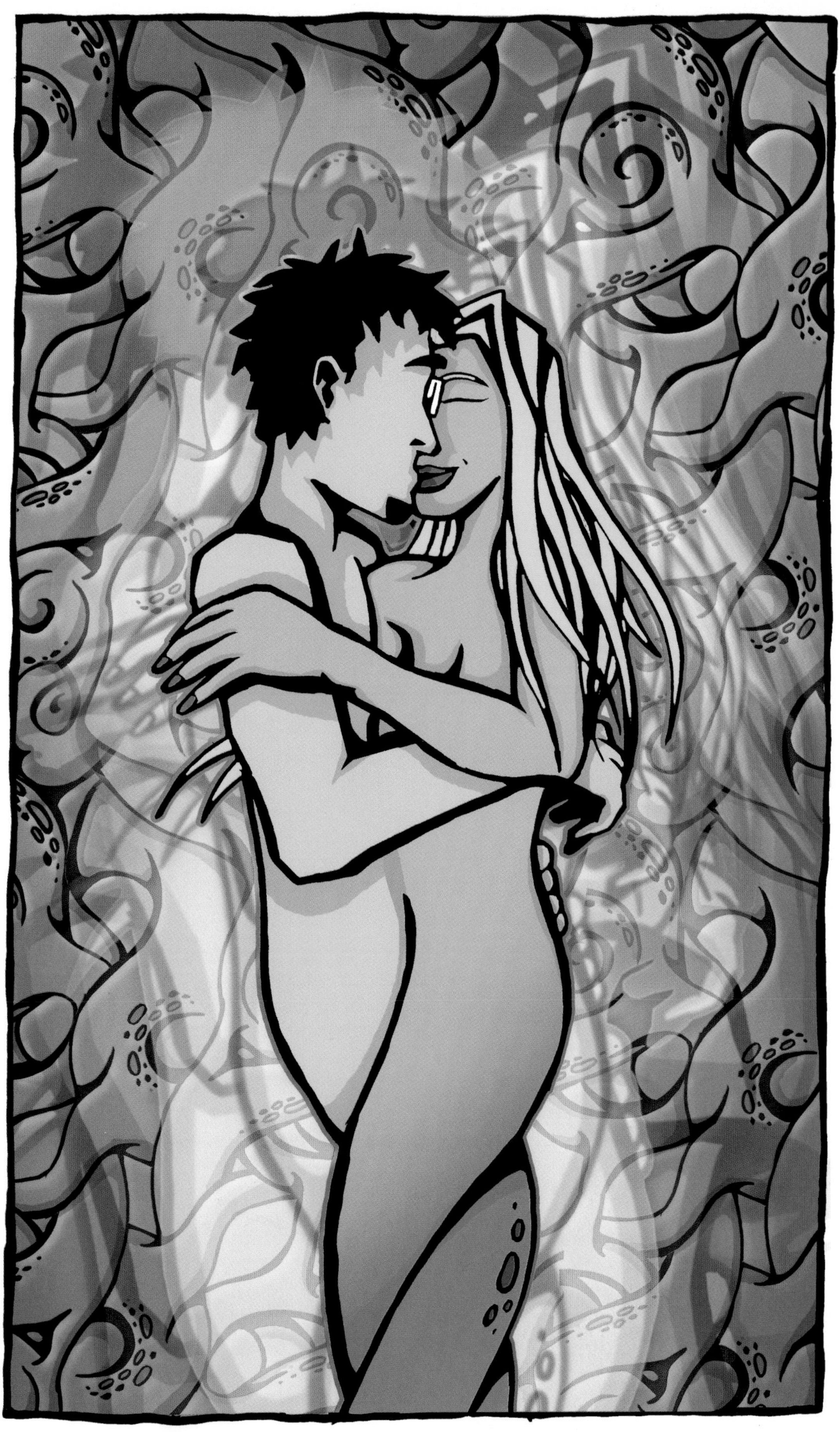

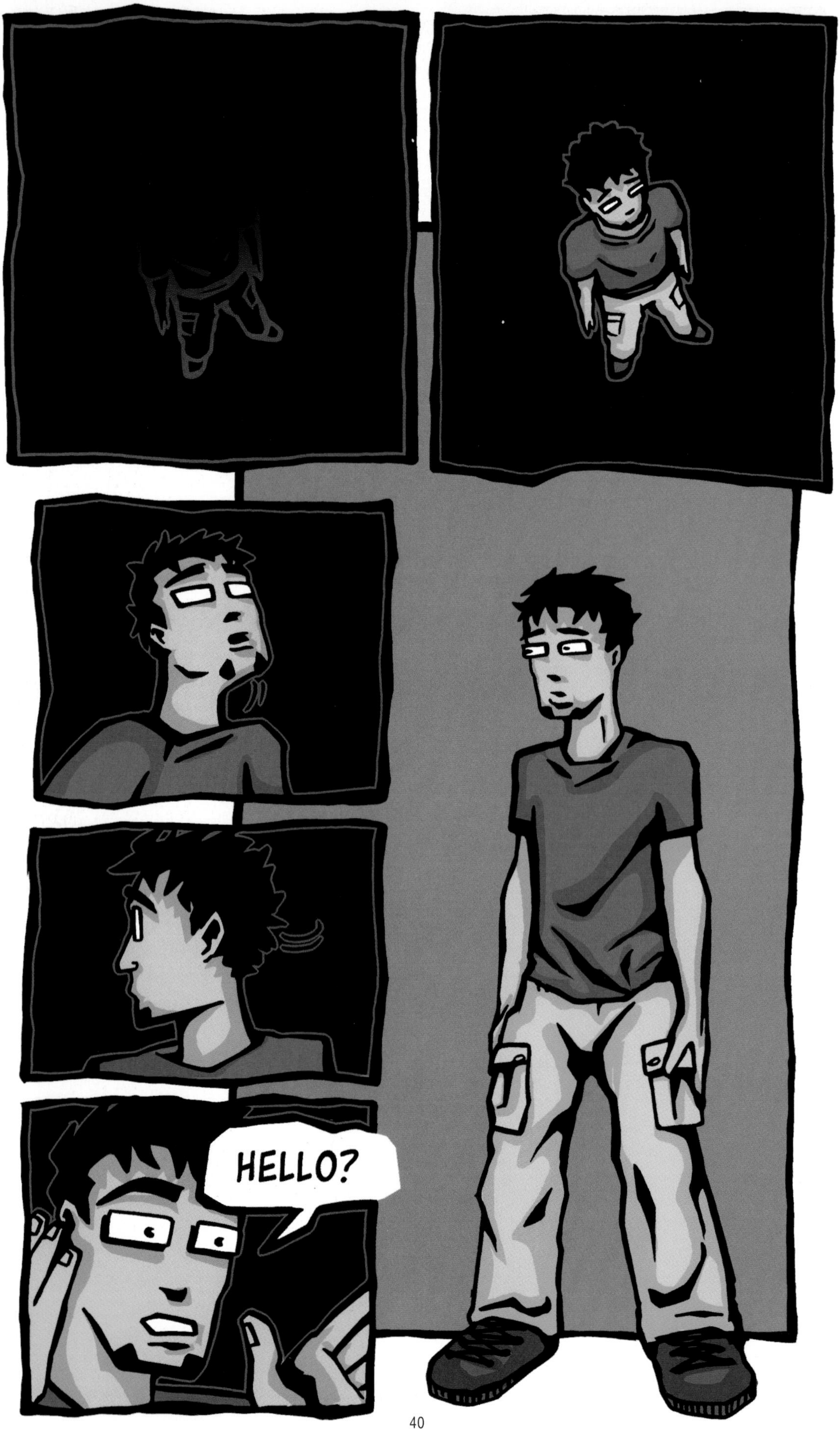
HELLO?

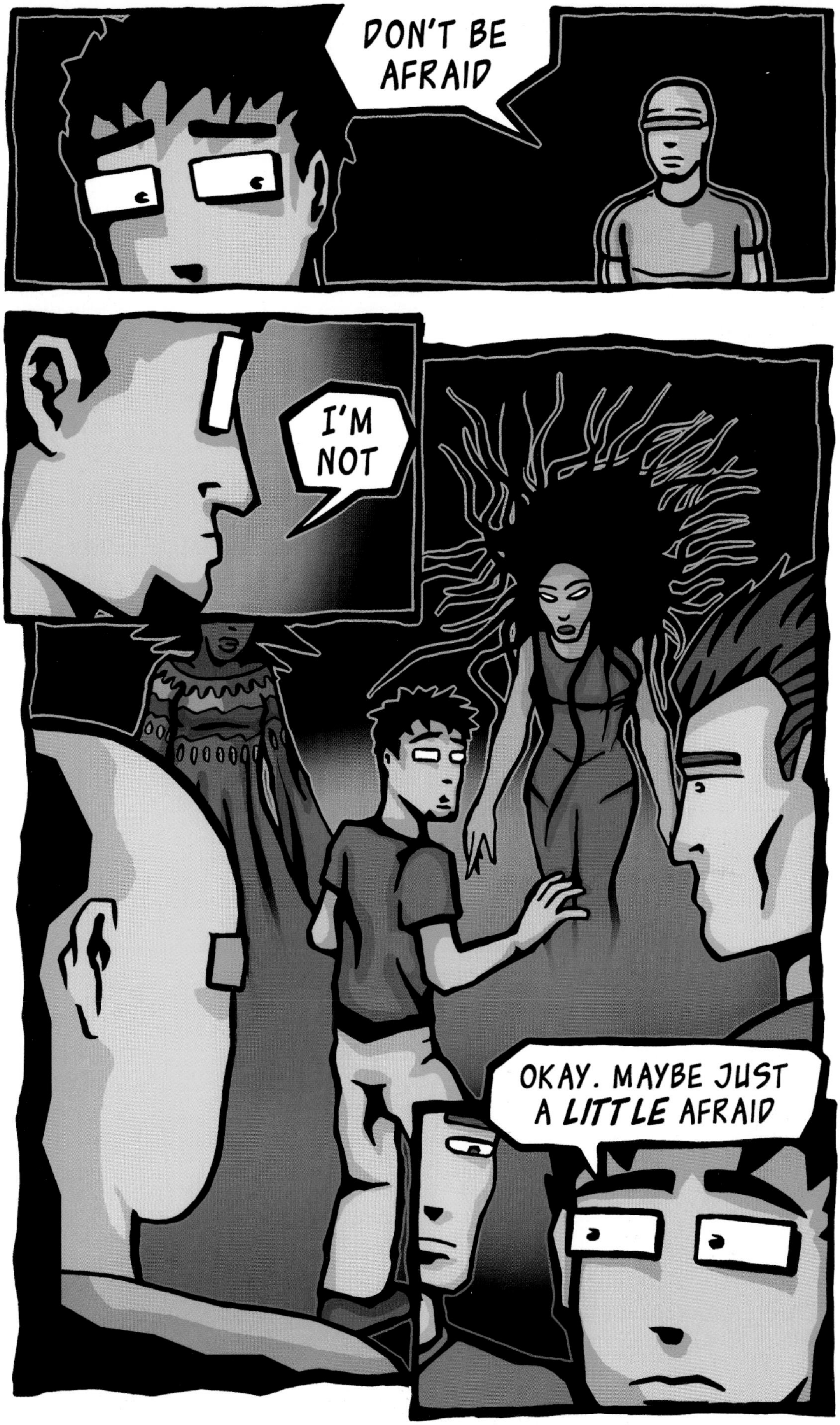
DON'T BE AFRAID
I'M NOT
OKAY. MAYBE JUST A *LITTLE* AFRAID

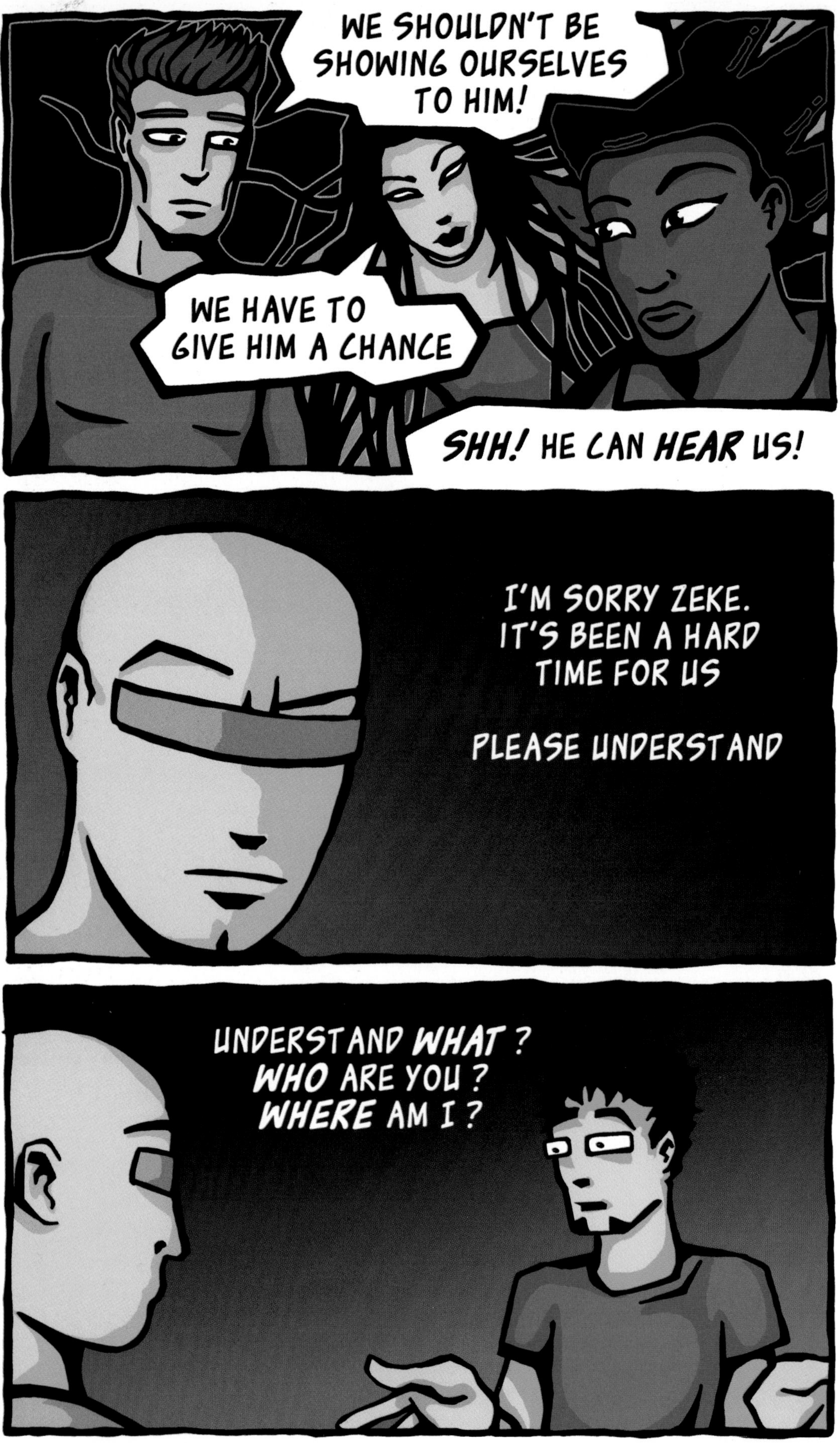
WE SHOULDN'T BE SHOWING OURSELVES TO HIM!
WE HAVE TO GIVE HIM A CHANCE
SHH! HE CAN HEAR US!
I'M SORRY ZEKE. IT'S BEEN A HARD TIME FOR US
PLEASE UNDERSTAND
UNDERSTAND WHAT ? WHO ARE YOU ? WHERE AM I ?

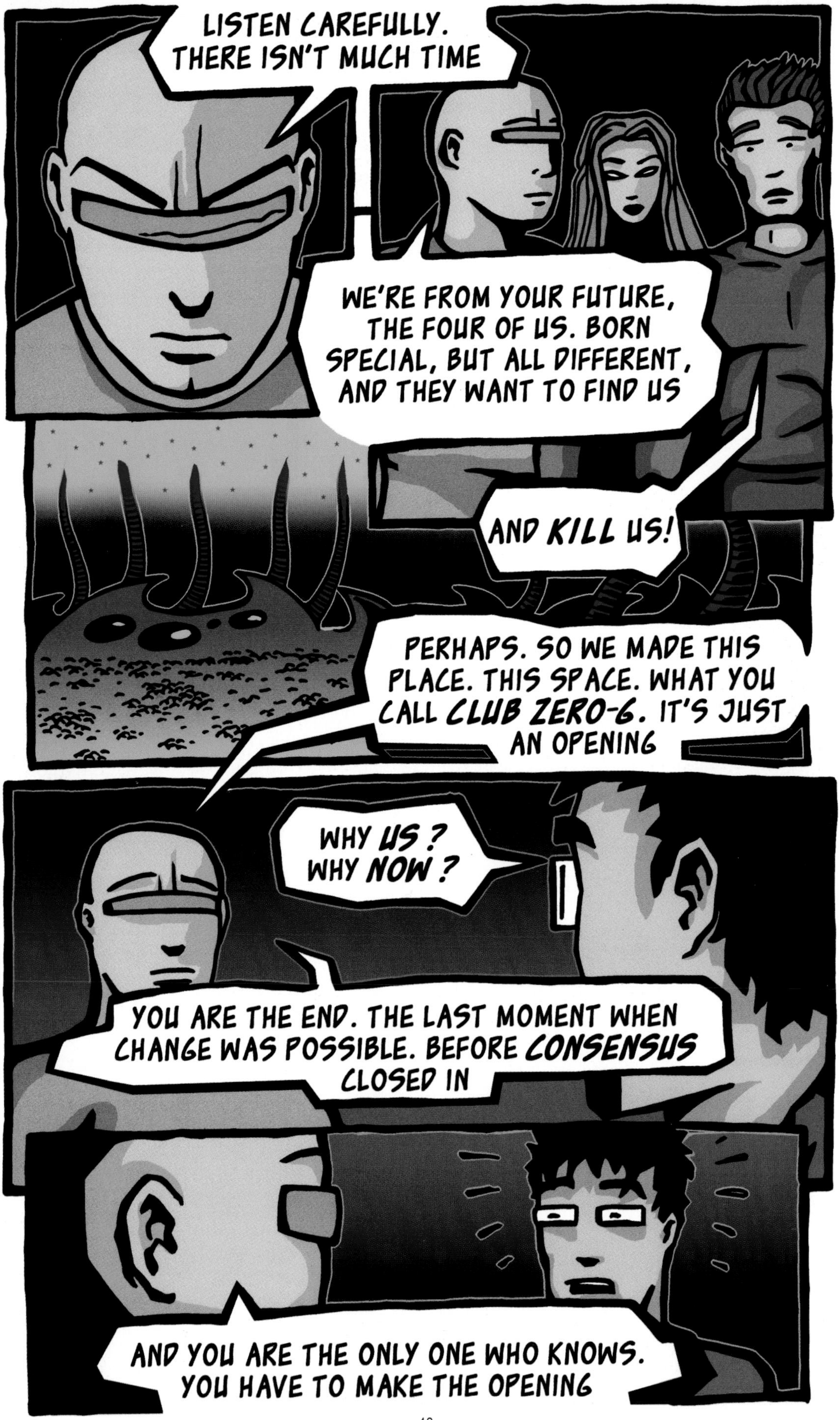
LISTEN CAREFULLY. THERE ISN'T MUCH TIME
WE'RE FROM YOUR FUTURE, THE FOUR OF US. BORN SPECIAL, BUT ALL DIFFERENT, AND THEY WANT TO FIND US
AND KILL US!
PERHAPS. SO WE MADE THIS PLACE. THIS SPACE. WHAT YOU CALL CLUB ZERO-6. IT'S JUST AN OPENING
WHY US? WHY NOW?
YOU ARE THE END. THE LAST MOMENT WHEN CHANGE WAS POSSIBLE. BEFORE CONSENSUS CLOSED IN
AND YOU ARE THE ONLY ONE WHO KNOWS. YOU HAVE TO MAKE THE OPENING

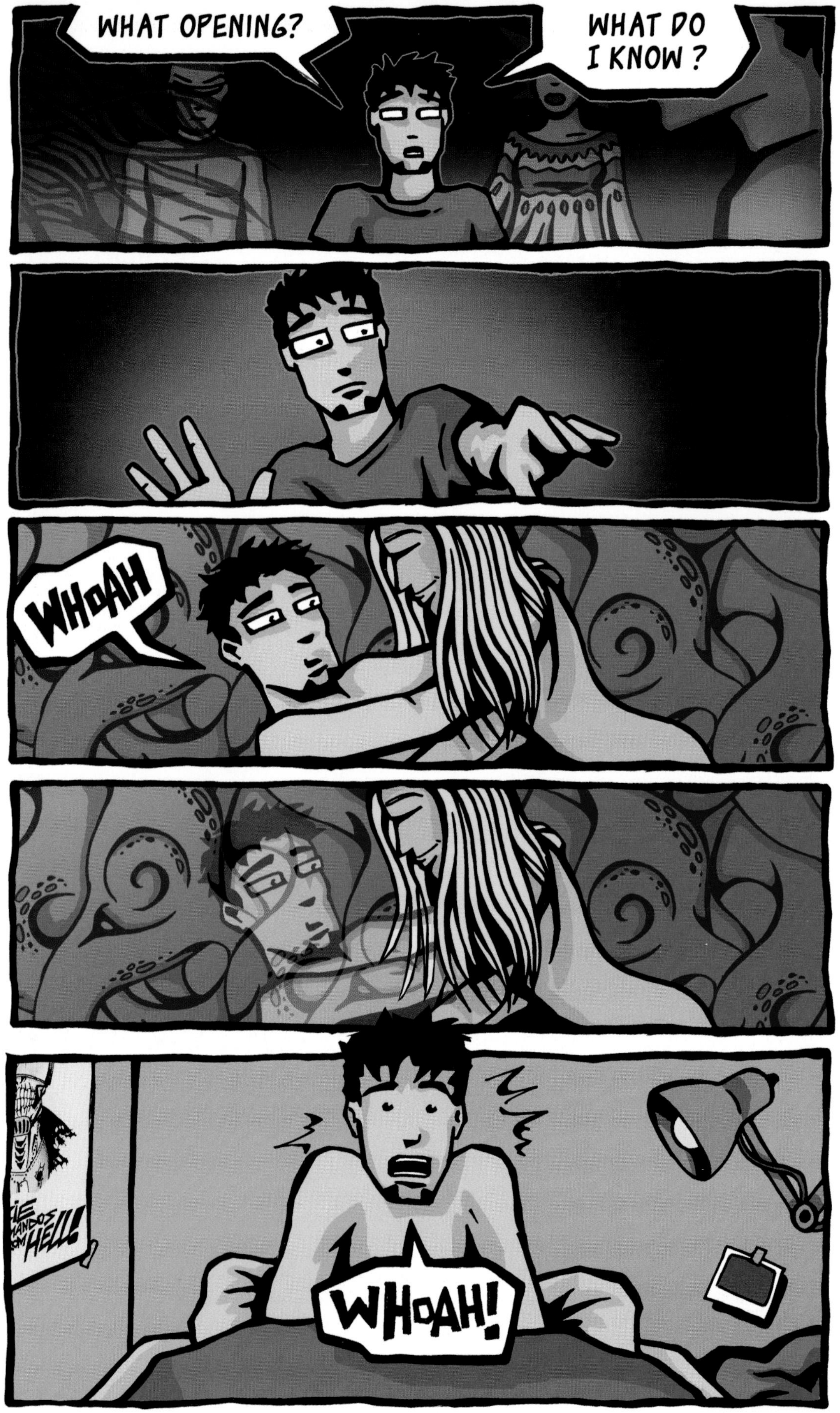
WHAT OPENING?
WHAT DO I KNOW?
WHOAH
WHOAH!

DOCUMENT CASE FILE 0099782-A

Rachel

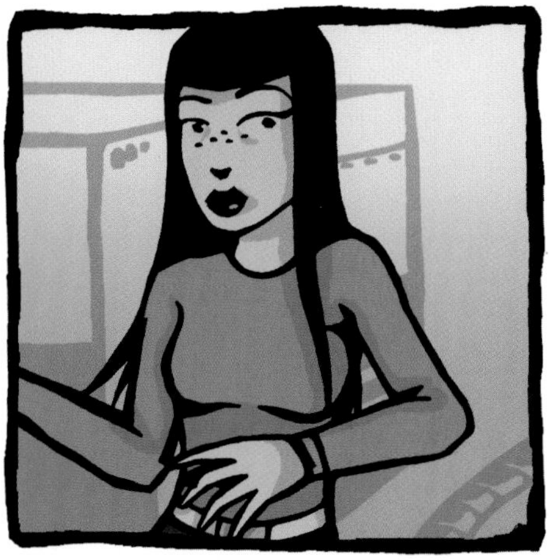

Location: Her father's freighter, on return from Neptune mines.
Cause of mutation: Two months gestation in Zero-G
Disability: Photosensitivity, contact sensitivity; bruises if touched.
Notes: Freighter searched, 9/11. No sign of her. Must have disembarked previous.

Demeter

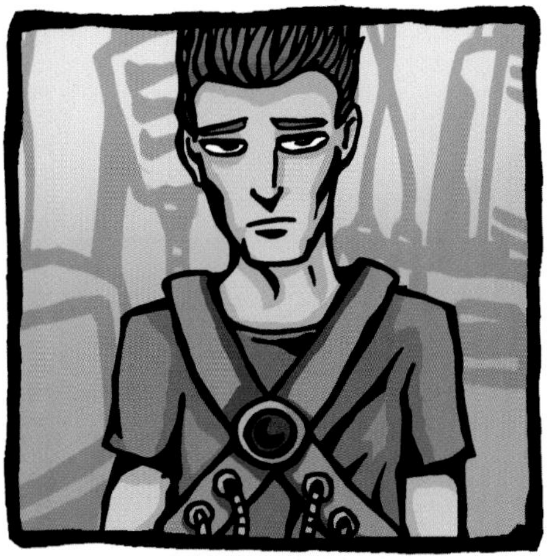

Location: Mars dome.
Cause of mutation: Unknown.
Disability: Electrocardial. Requires shock resuscitation.
Notes: Possibly of aristocratic or government origin. Paper trail on his whereabouts destroyed at high level.

Ikara

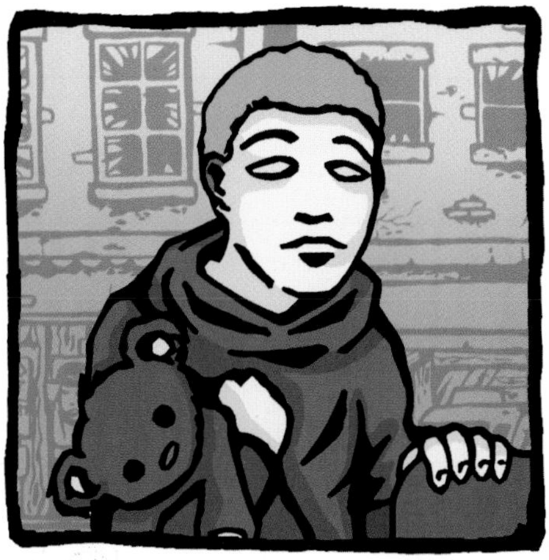

Location: Earth Slums - Urban Sub-Sahara
Cause of mutation: Father worked Station 43B; pre-sterilization procedure incomplete.
Disability: Blind. Albino?
Notes: Most likely protected by escaped workers collective or Sahara Resistance Movement.

Bebe

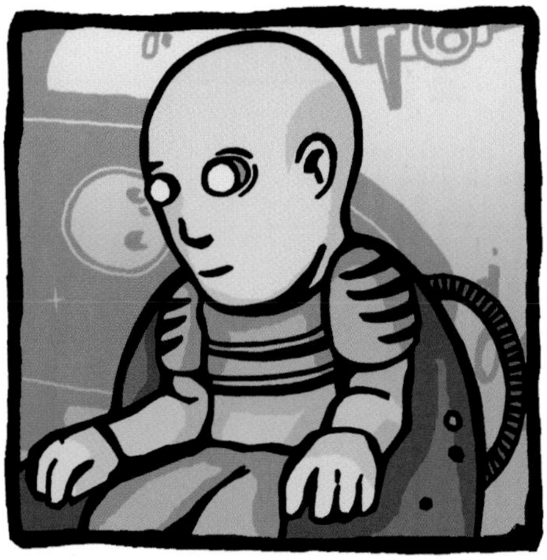

Location: Unknown.
Cause of Mutation: Radical colonist parents - killed in second raid on Io.
Disability: Unknown.
Notes: Parallax of Bebe's signal indicates possibility of presence in or relay through deep space.

DOCUMENT CASE FILE 0099782-B

Rachel

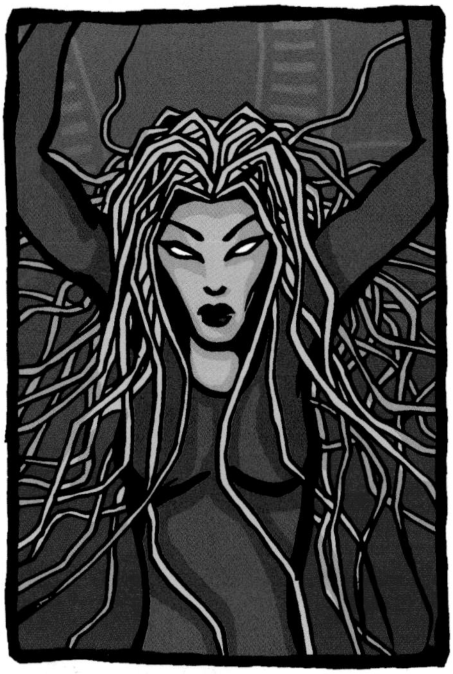

Ability: Persuasion, hypnosis, mind control.

Demeter

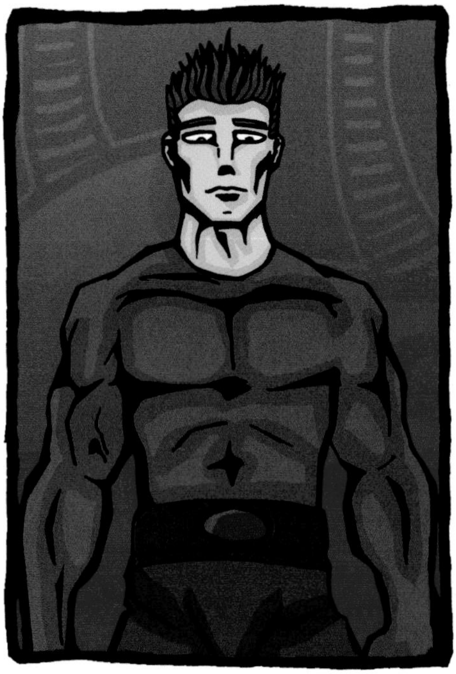

Ability: Electrostatic manipulation. Three fatalities reported.

Ikara

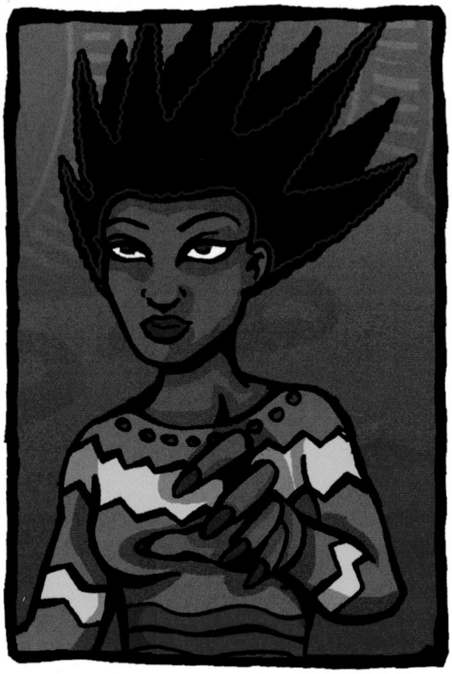

Ability: Remote viewing. Telekinesis?

Bebe

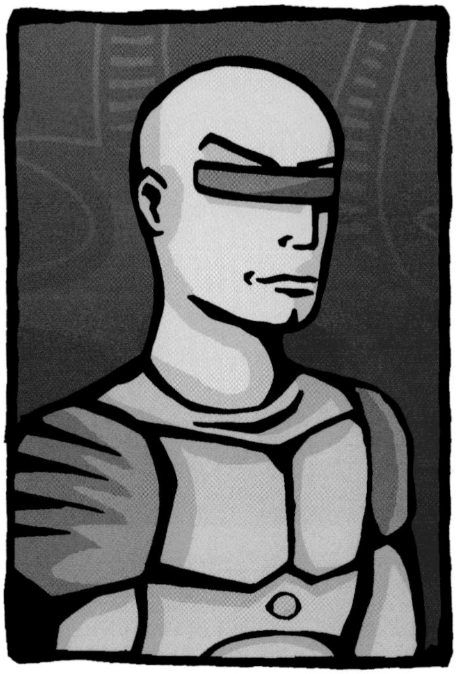

Ability: Still unknown. Appears he is essential component to the psychic field created by the other three. Space-Time key?

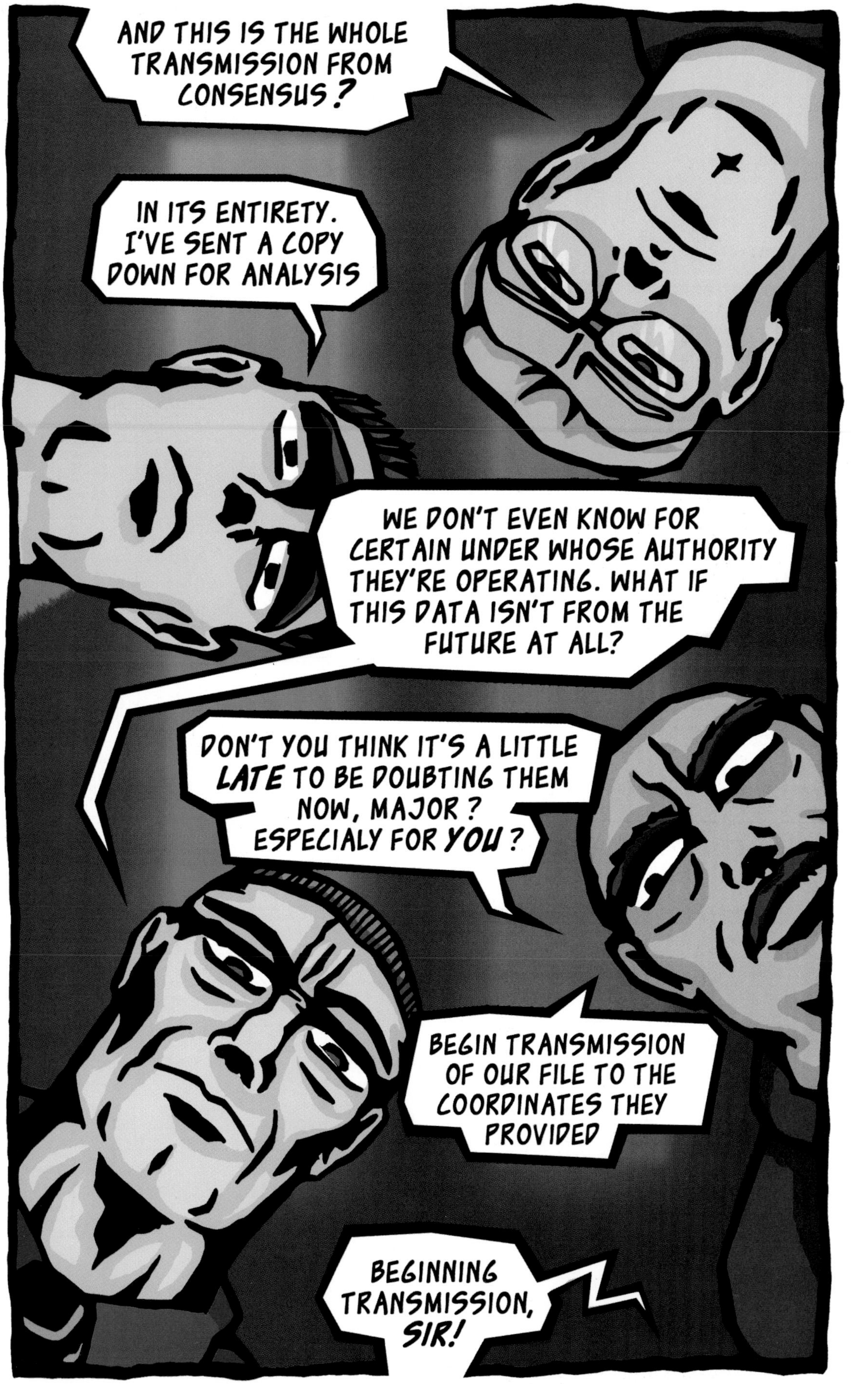
AND THIS IS THE WHOLE TRANSMISSION FROM CONSENSUS?
IN ITS ENTIRETY. I'VE SENT A COPY DOWN FOR ANALYSIS
WE DON'T EVEN KNOW FOR CERTAIN UNDER WHOSE AUTHORITY THEY'RE OPERATING. WHAT IF THIS DATA ISN'T FROM THE FUTURE AT ALL?
DON'T YOU THINK IT'S A LITTLE LATE TO BE DOUBTING THEM NOW, MAJOR? ESPECIALY FOR YOU?
BEGIN TRANSMISSION OF OUR FILE TO THE COORDINATES THEY PROVIDED
BEGINNING TRANSMISSION, SIR!

DOCUMENT CASE FILE 0099782-B

Zeke Gibson

Location:
Base 234, California

Age: 19

Parentage:
Major Gibson's "son"
genetic sample 32B

First Penetration of Zero-G Psychic Field:
10/12/2004

Special Abilities:
None yet detected.

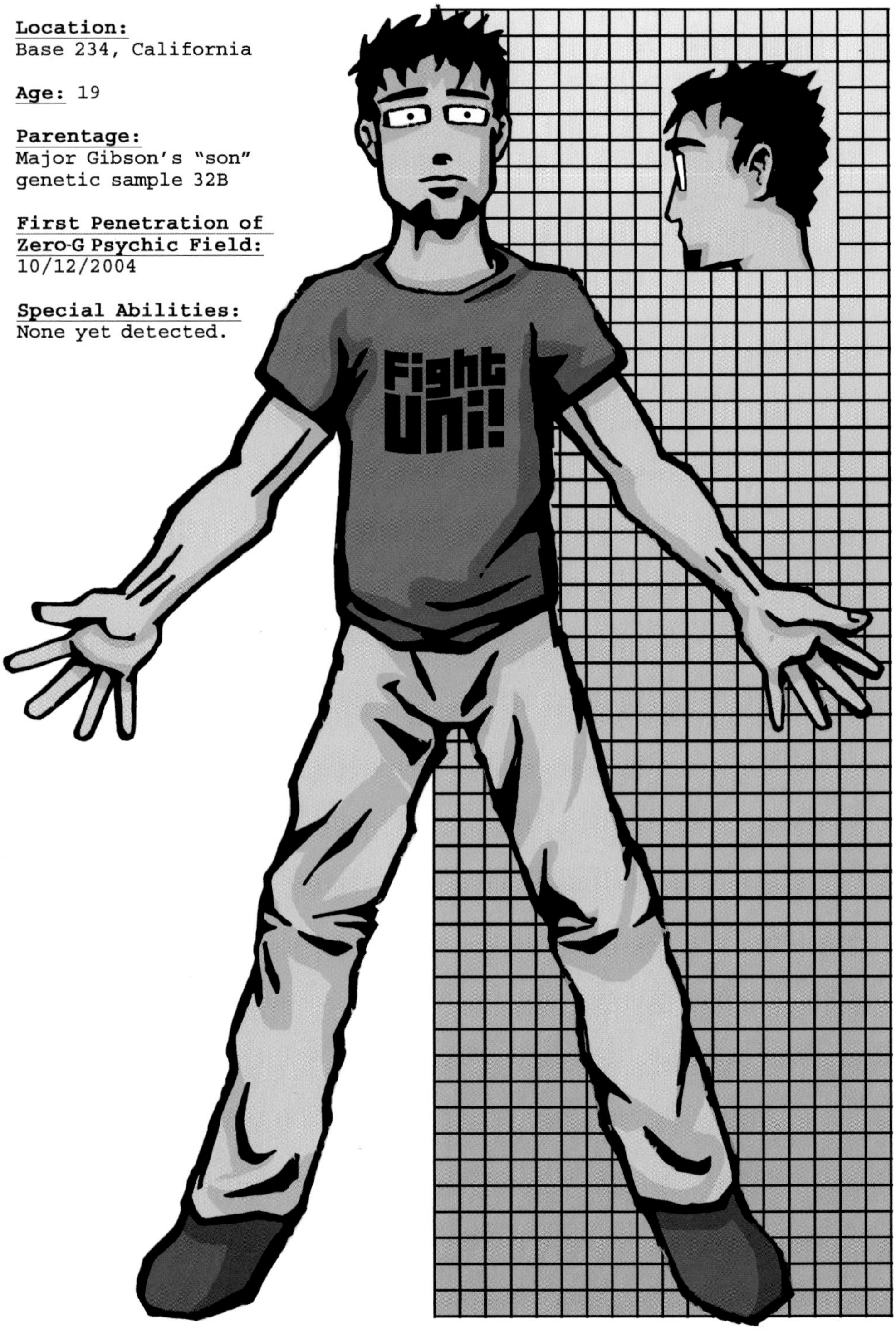
Fight Uni!

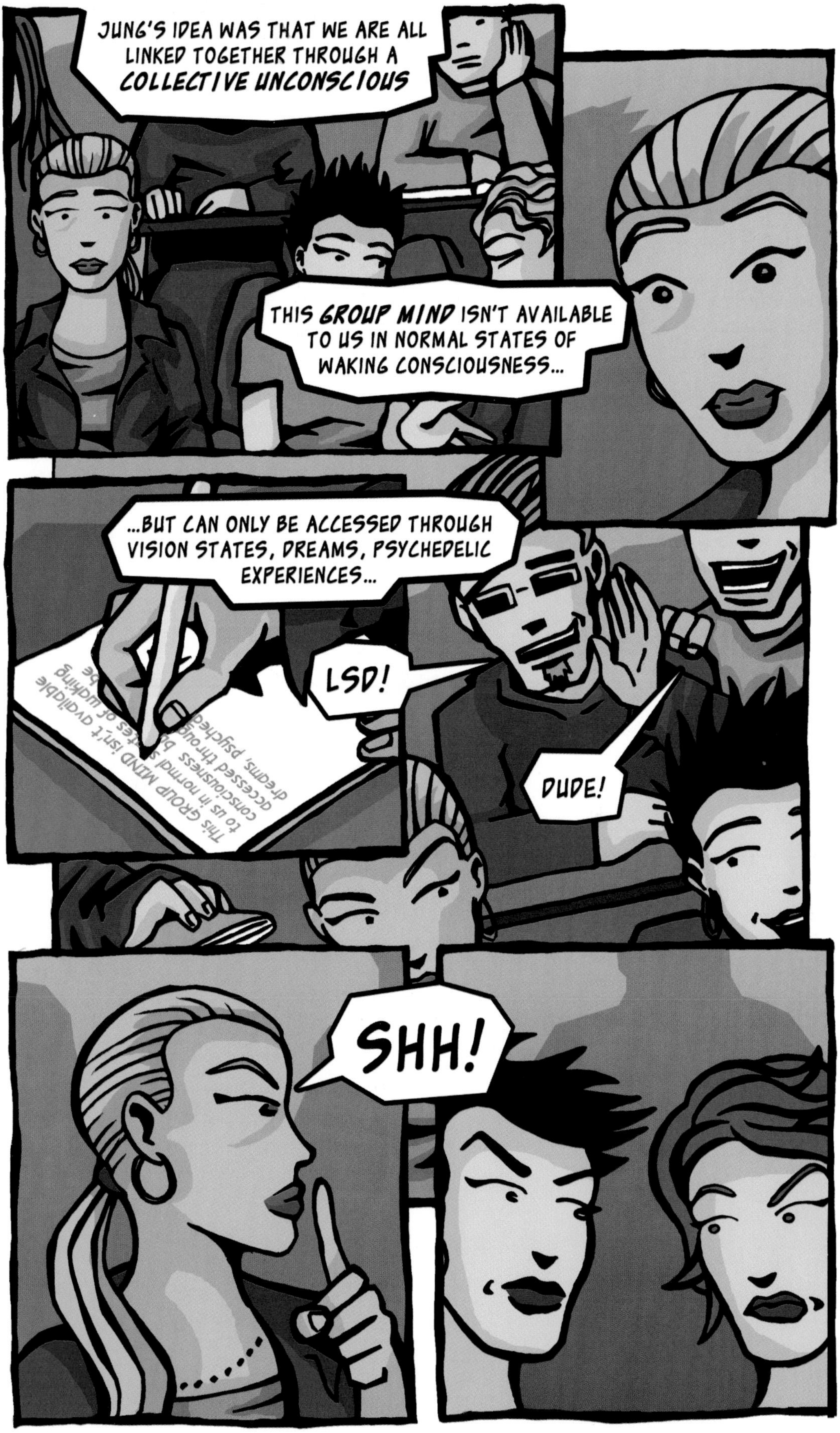
JUNG'S IDEA WAS THAT WE ARE ALL LINKED TOGETHER THROUGH A COLLECTIVE UNCONSCIOUS
THIS GROUP MIND ISN'T AVAILABLE TO US IN NORMAL STATES OF WAKING CONSCIOUSNESS...
...BUT CAN ONLY BE ACCESSED THROUGH VISION STATES, DREAMS, PSYCHEDELIC EXPERIENCES...
LSD!
DUDE!
SHH!

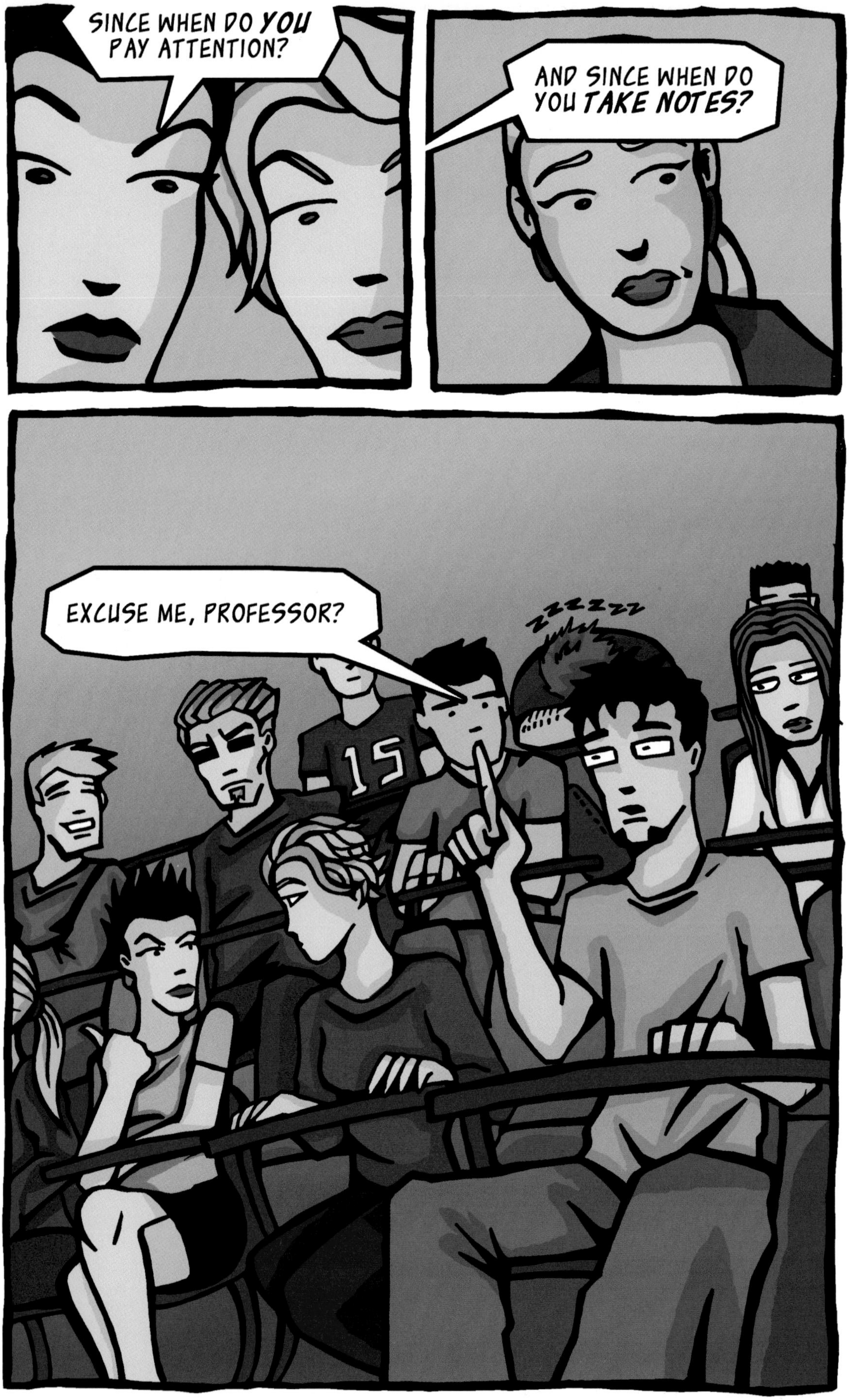
SINCE WHEN DO YOU PAY ATTENTION?
AND SINCE WHEN DO YOU TAKE NOTES?
EXCUSE ME, PROFESSOR?
ZZZZZZZ
15

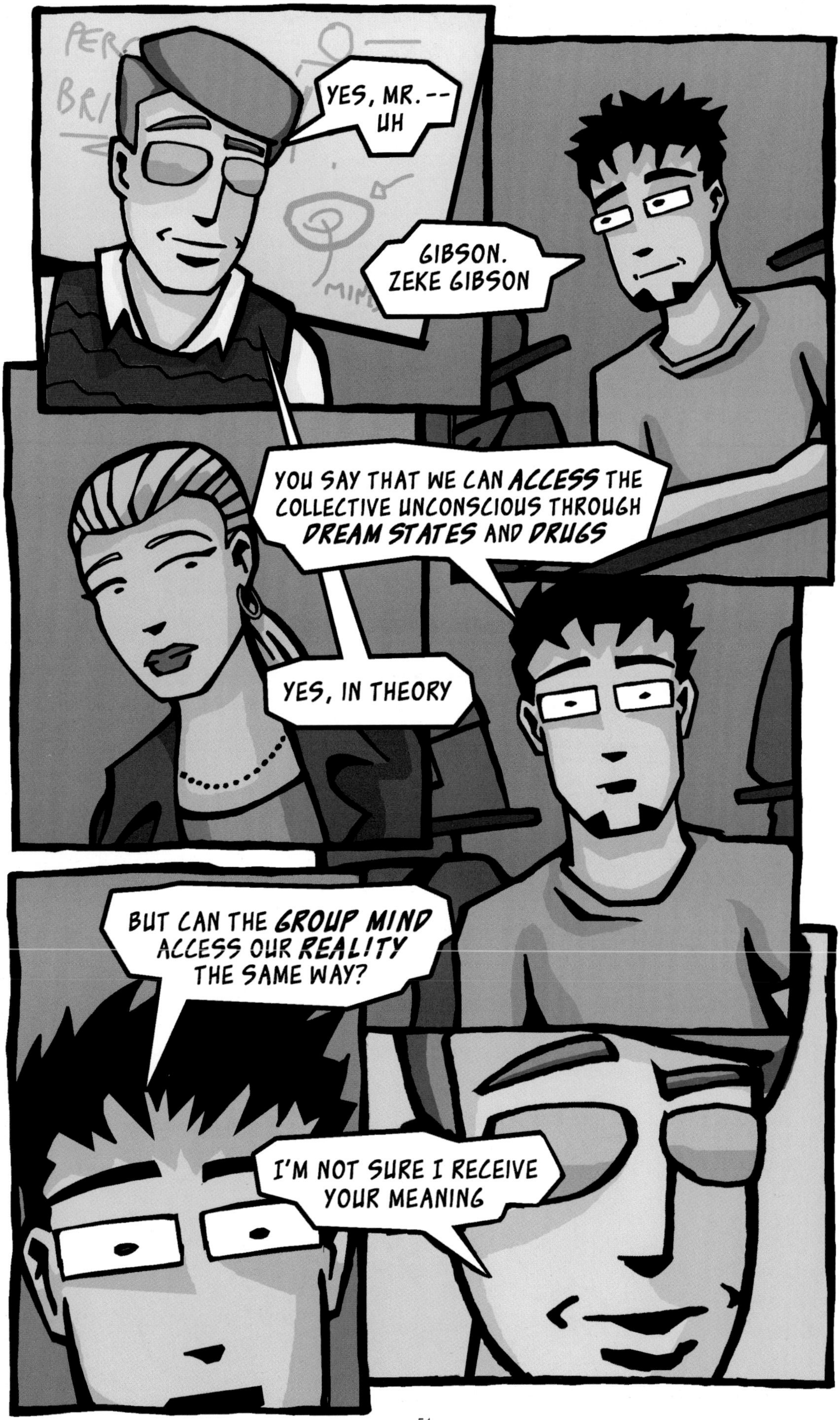
YES, MR.-- UH
GIBSON. ZEKE GIBSON
YOU SAY THAT WE CAN ACCESS THE COLLECTIVE UNCONSCIOUS THROUGH DREAM STATES AND DRUGS
YES, IN THEORY
BUT CAN THE GROUP MIND ACCESS OUR REALITY THE SAME WAY?
I'M NOT SURE I RECEIVE YOUR MEANING

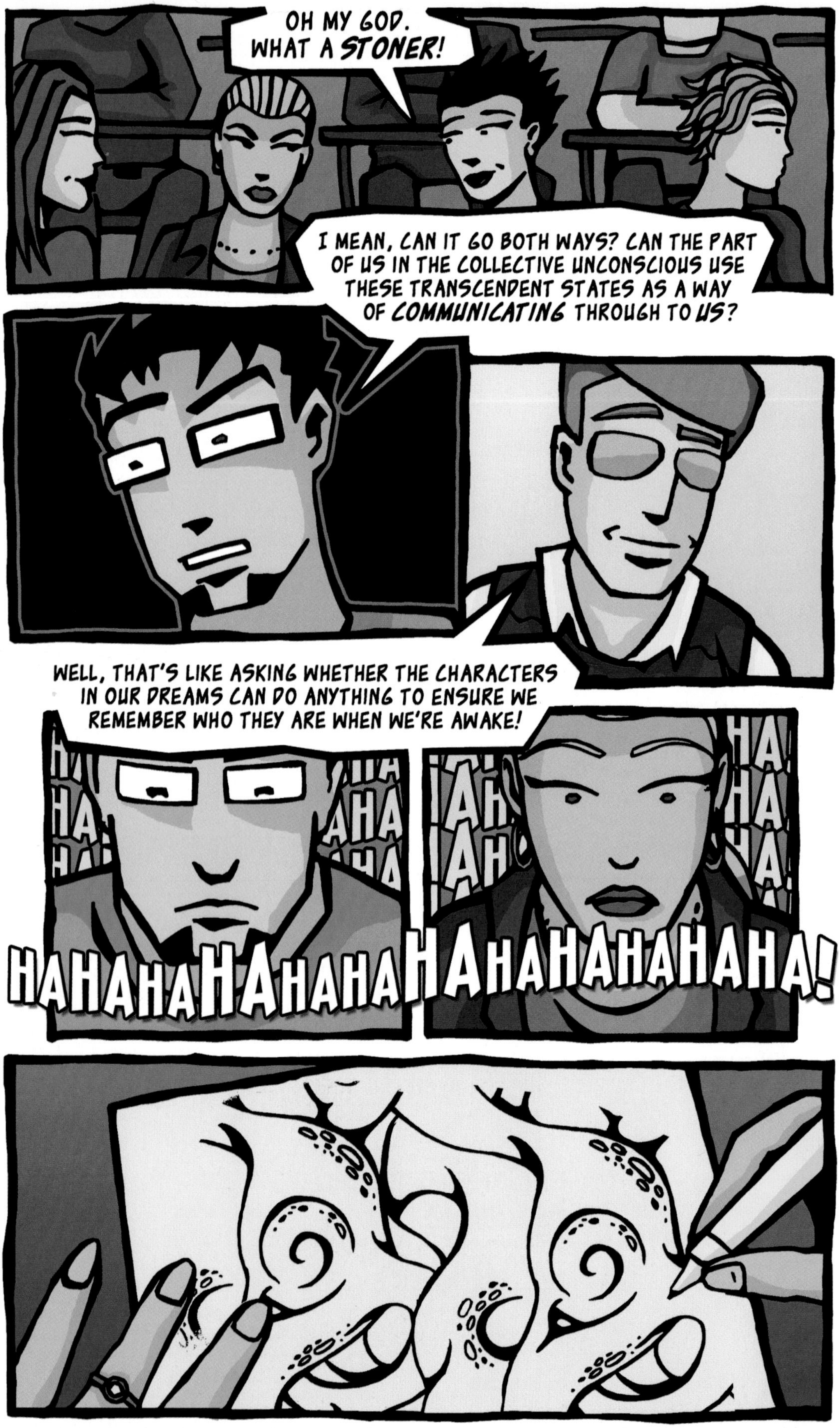
OH MY GOD. WHAT A STONER!
I MEAN, CAN IT GO BOTH WAYS? CAN THE PART OF US IN THE COLLECTIVE UNCONSCIOUS USE THESE TRANSCENDENT STATES AS A WAY OF COMMUNICATING THROUGH TO US?
WELL, THAT'S LIKE ASKING WHETHER THE CHARACTERS IN OUR DREAMS CAN DO ANYTHING TO ENSURE WE REMEMBER WHO THEY ARE WHEN WE'RE AWAKE!
HAHAHAHAHAHAHAHAHAHAHAHAHAHA!

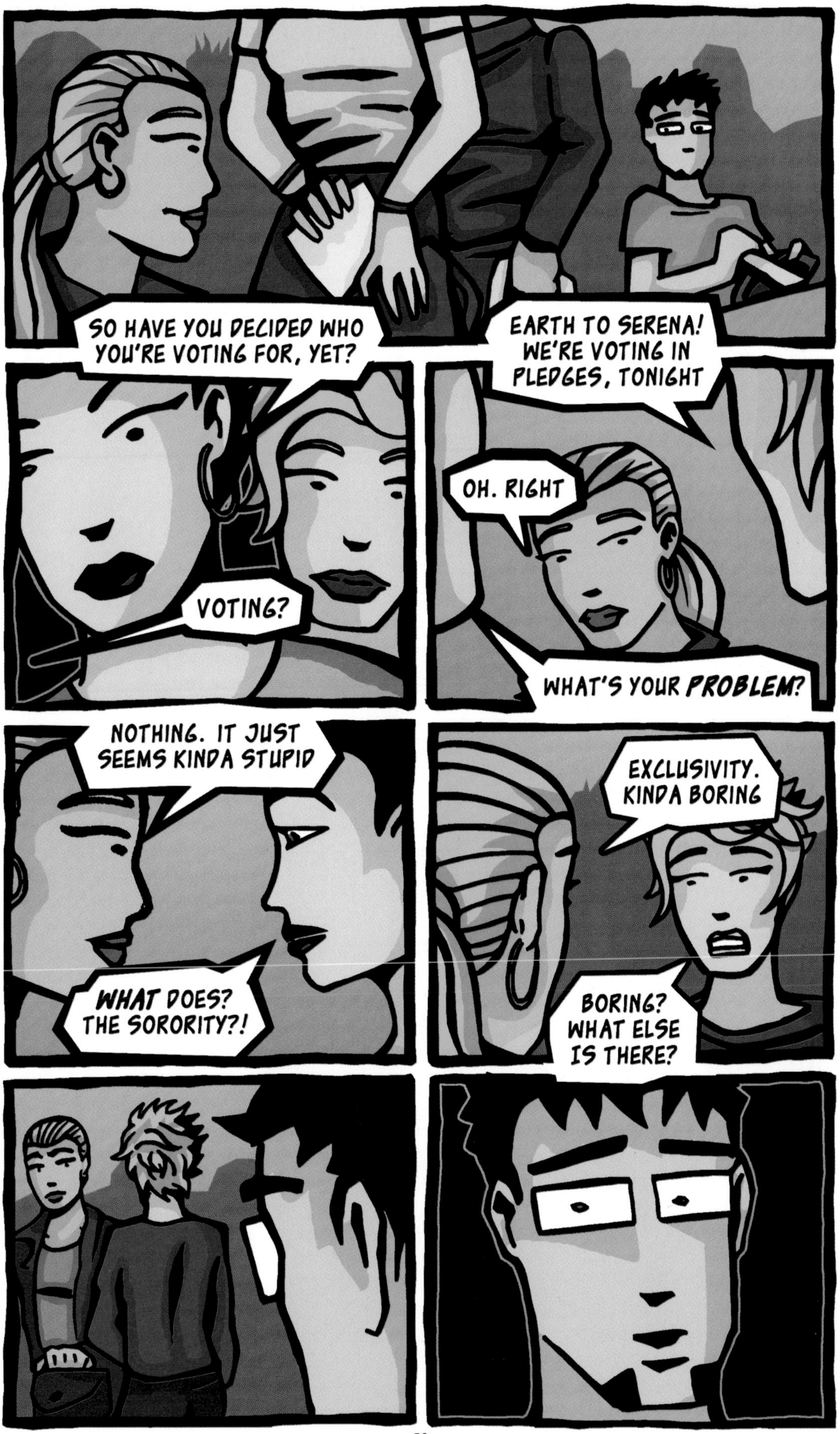
SO HAVE YOU DECIDED WHO YOU'RE VOTING FOR, YET?
VOTING?
EARTH TO SERENA! WE'RE VOTING IN PLEDGES, TONIGHT
OH. RIGHT
WHAT'S YOUR PROBLEM?
NOTHING. IT JUST SEEMS KINDA STUPID
WHAT DOES? THE SORORITY?!
EXCLUSIVITY. KINDA BORING
BORING? WHAT ELSE IS THERE?

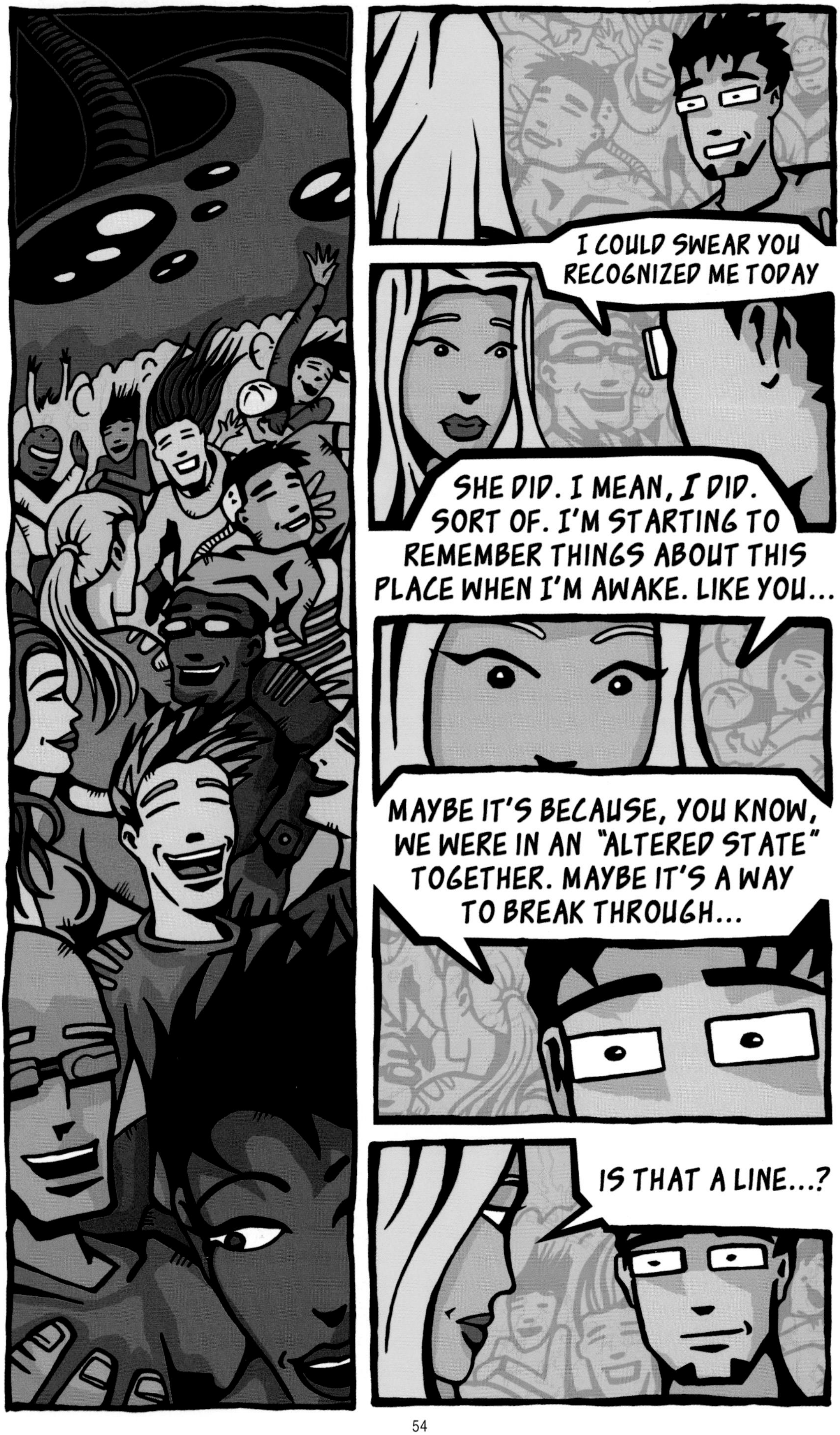
I COULD SWEAR YOU RECOGNIZED ME TODAY
SHE DID. I MEAN, *I* DID. SORT OF. I'M STARTING TO REMEMBER THINGS ABOUT THIS PLACE WHEN I'M AWAKE. LIKE YOU...
MAYBE IT'S BECAUSE, YOU KNOW, WE WERE IN AN "ALTERED STATE" TOGETHER. MAYBE IT'S A WAY TO BREAK THROUGH...
IS THAT A LINE...?

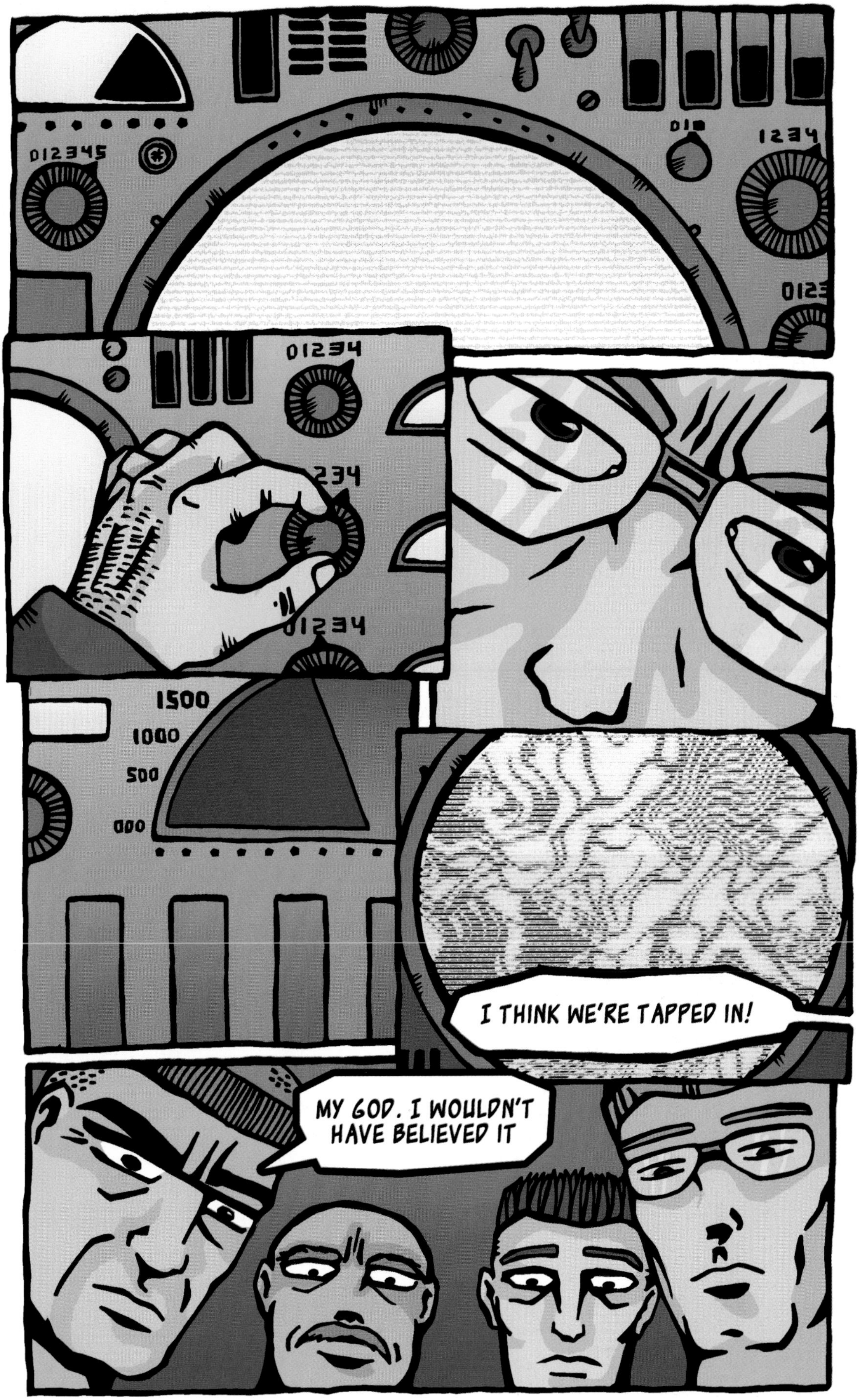

I THINK WE'RE TAPPED IN!
MY GOD. I WOULDN'T HAVE BELIEVED IT

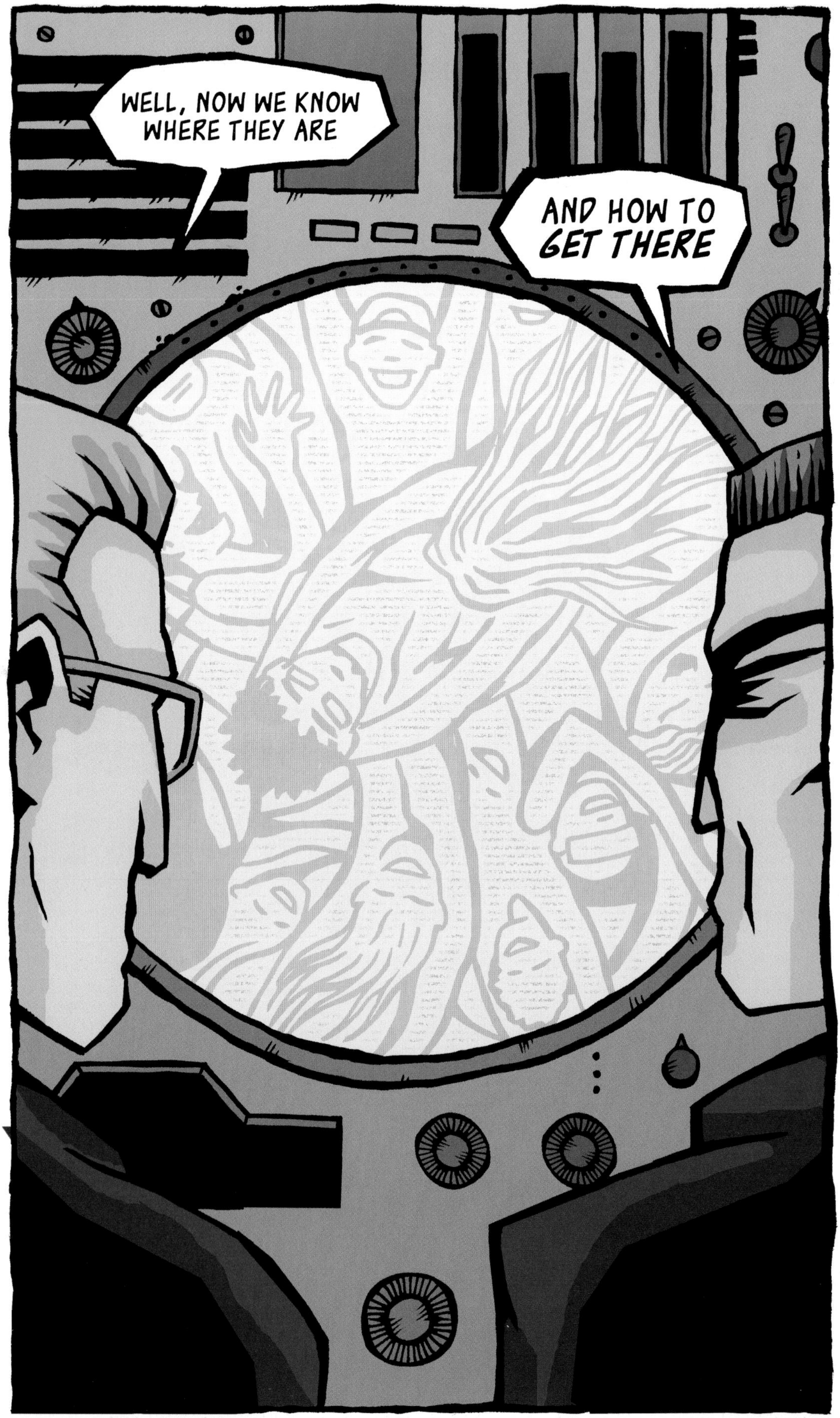
WELL, NOW WE KNOW WHERE THEY ARE
AND HOW TO GET THERE

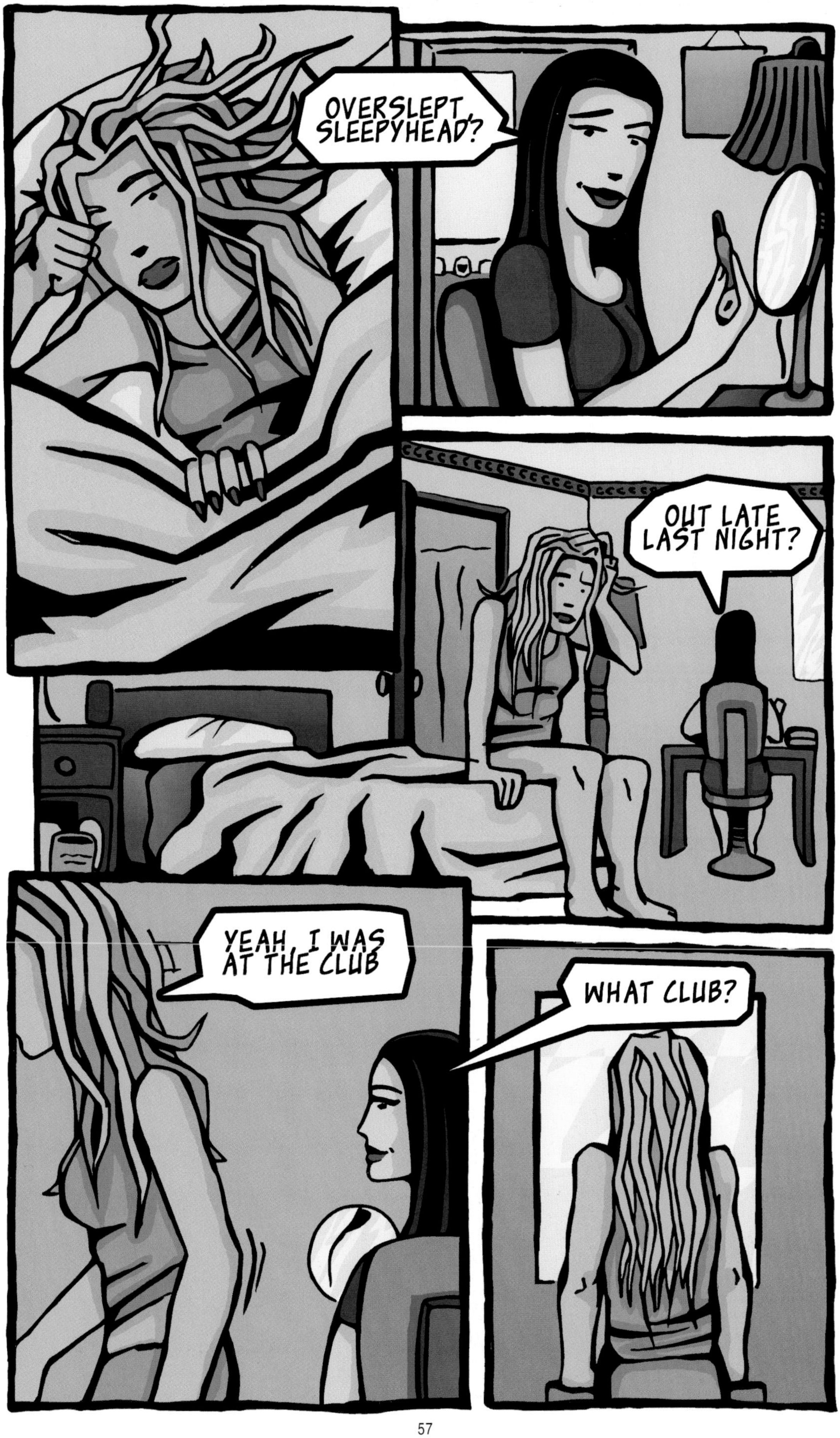
OVERSLEPT SLEEPYHEAD?
OUT LATE LAST NIGHT?
YEAH, I WAS AT THE CLUB
WHAT CLUB?

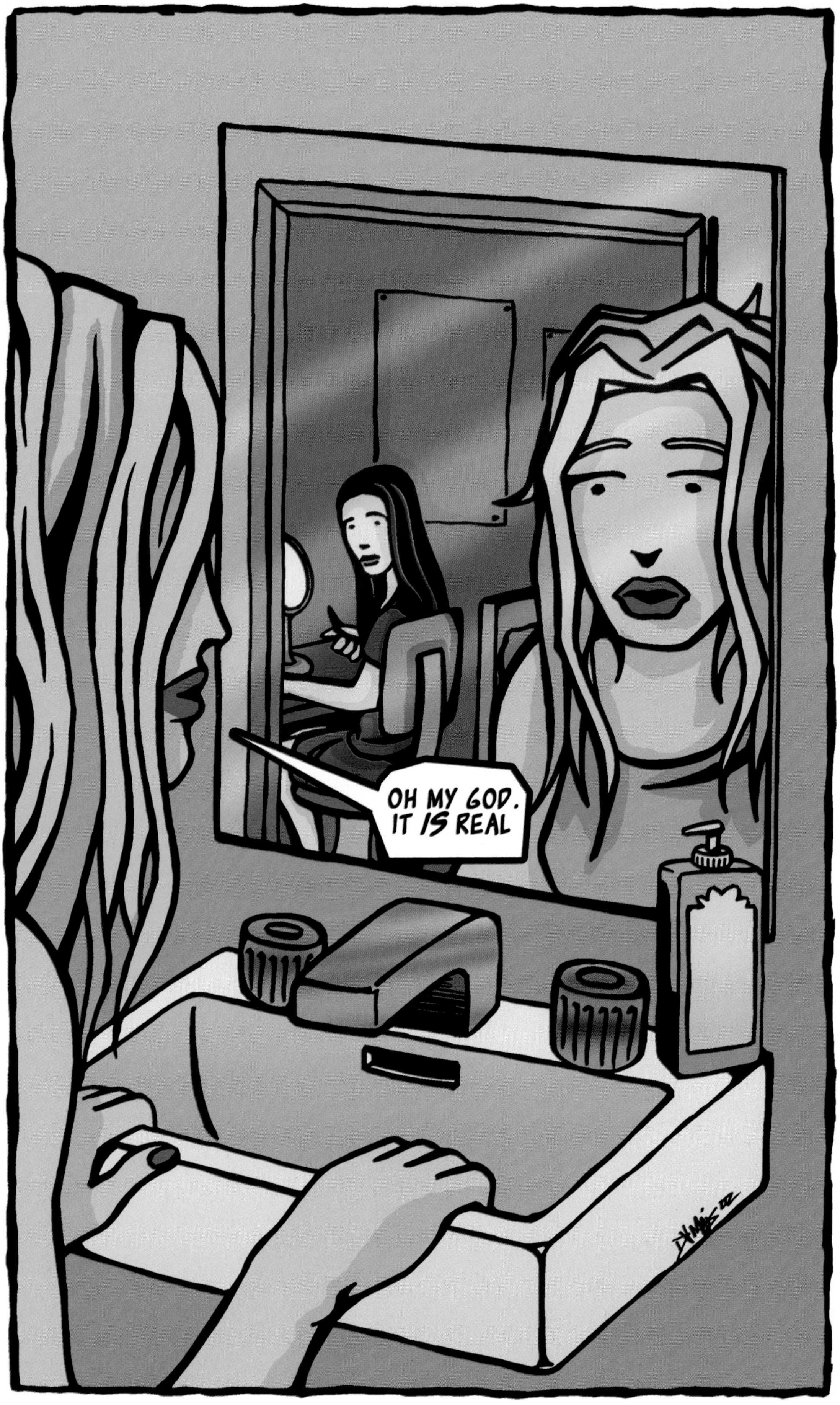
OH MY GOD. IT IS REAL

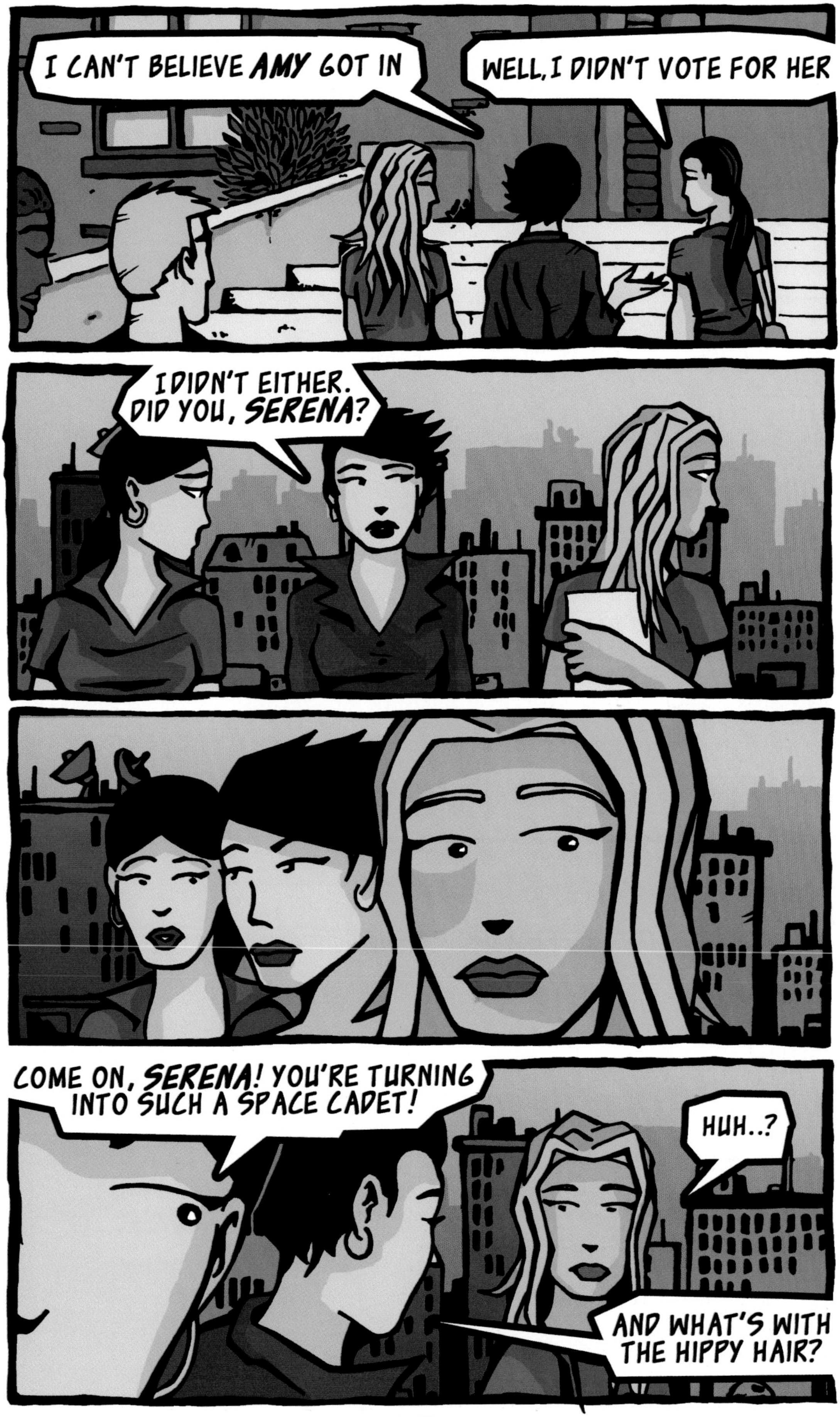
I CAN'T BELIEVE AMY GOT IN
WELL, I DIDN'T VOTE FOR HER
I DIDN'T EITHER. DID YOU, SERENA?
COME ON, SERENA! YOU'RE TURNING INTO SUCH A SPACE CADET!
HUH..?
AND WHAT'S WITH THE HIPPY HAIR?

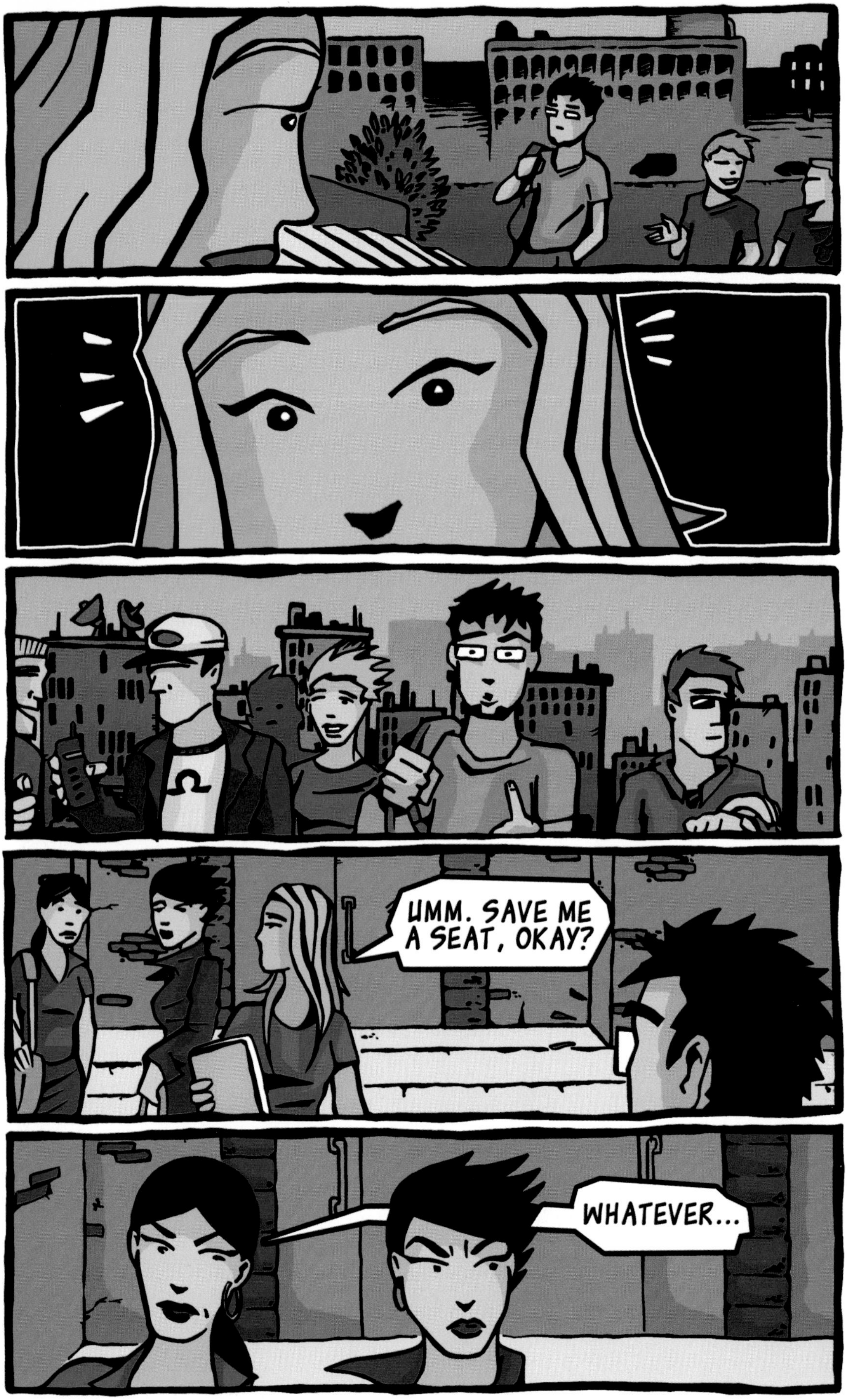
UMM. SAVE ME A SEAT, OKAY?
WHATEVER...

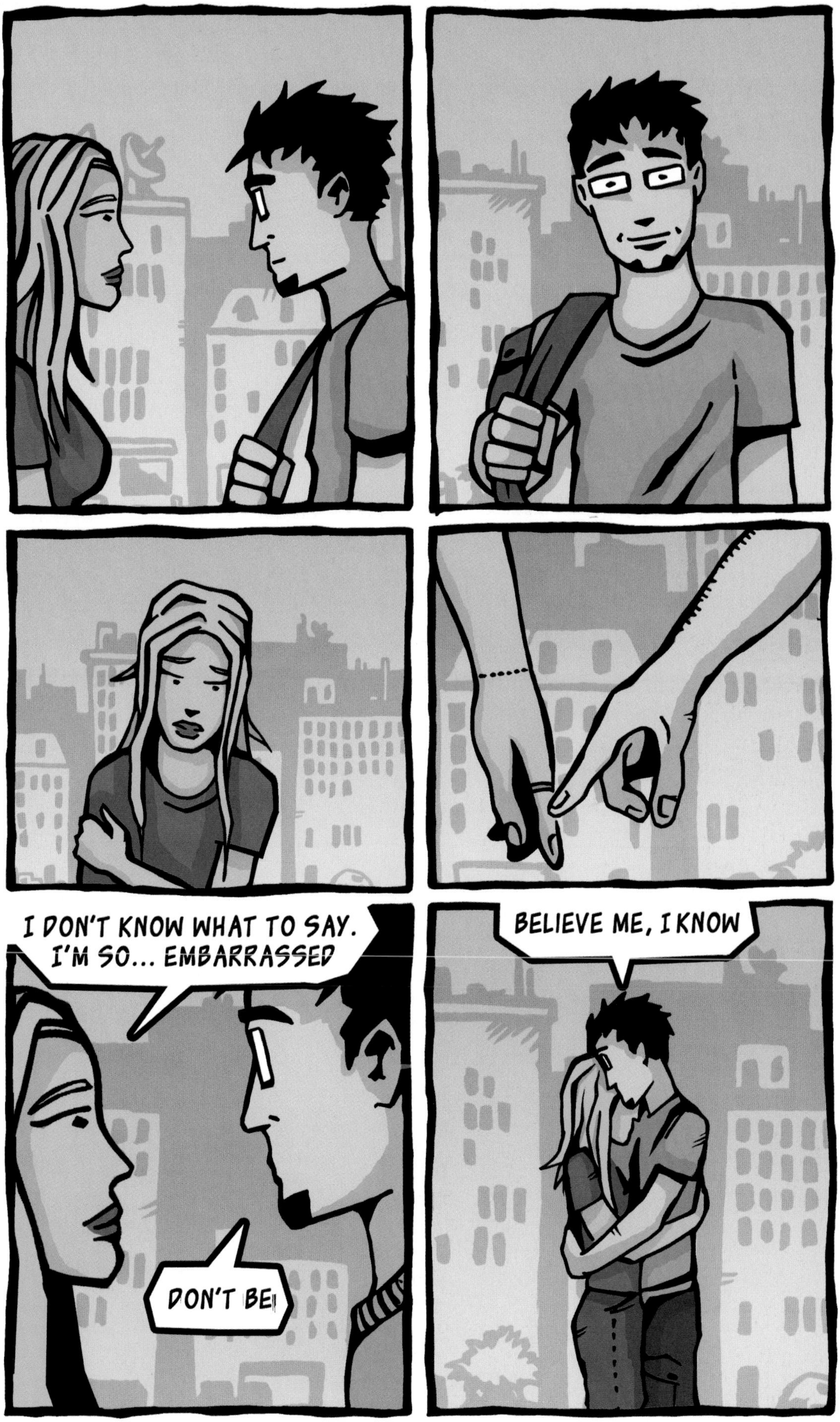
I DON'T KNOW WHAT TO SAY. I'M SO... EMBARRASSED
DON'T BE
BELIEVE ME, I KNOW

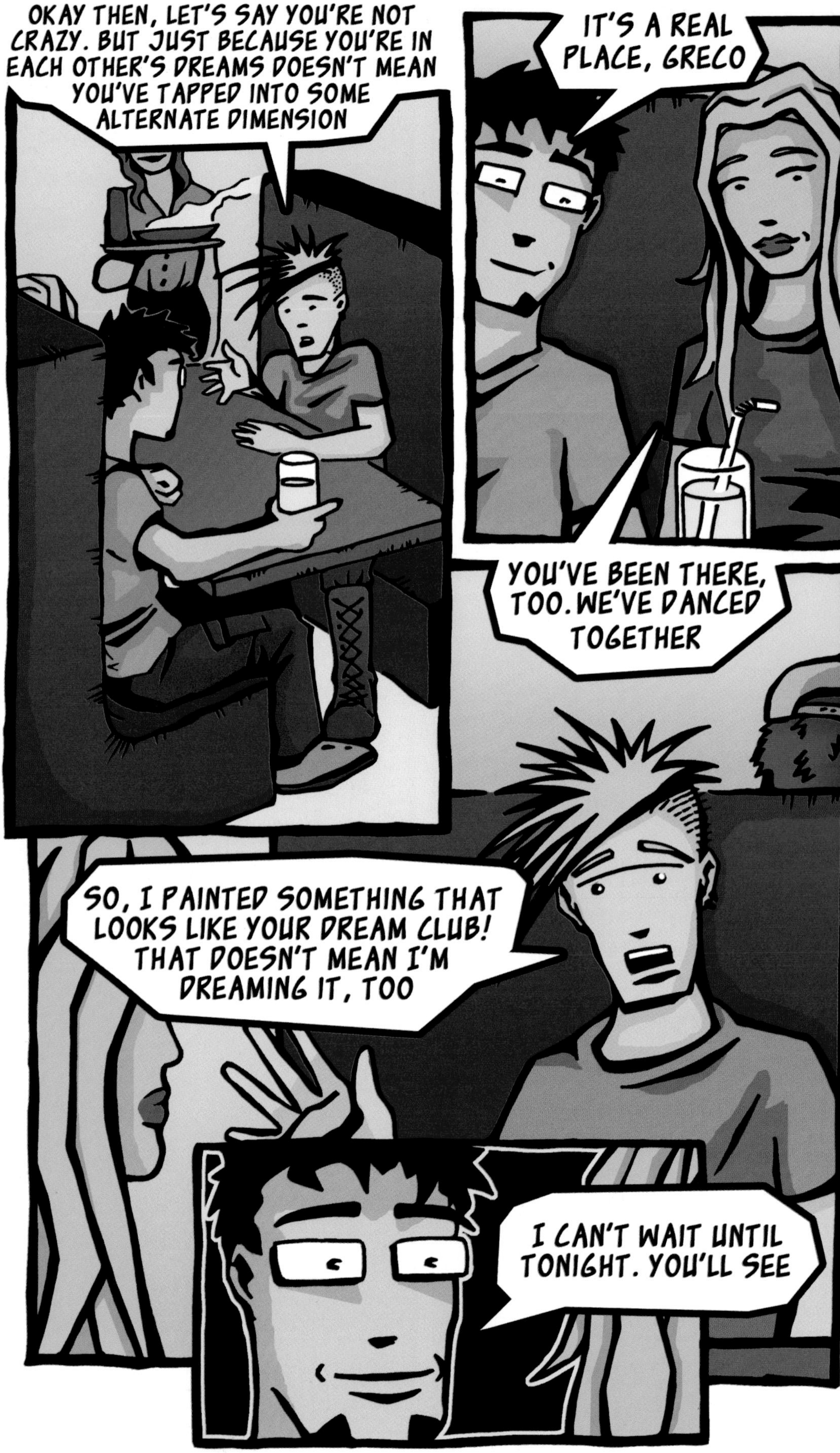
OKAY THEN, LET'S SAY YOU'RE NOT CRAZY. BUT JUST BECAUSE YOU'RE IN EACH OTHER'S DREAMS DOESN'T MEAN YOU'VE TAPPED INTO SOME ALTERNATE DIMENSION
IT'S A REAL PLACE, GRECO
YOU'VE BEEN THERE, TOO. WE'VE DANCED TOGETHER
SO, I PAINTED SOMETHING THAT LOOKS LIKE YOUR DREAM CLUB! THAT DOESN'T MEAN I'M DREAMING IT, TOO
I CAN'T WAIT UNTIL TONIGHT. YOU'LL SEE

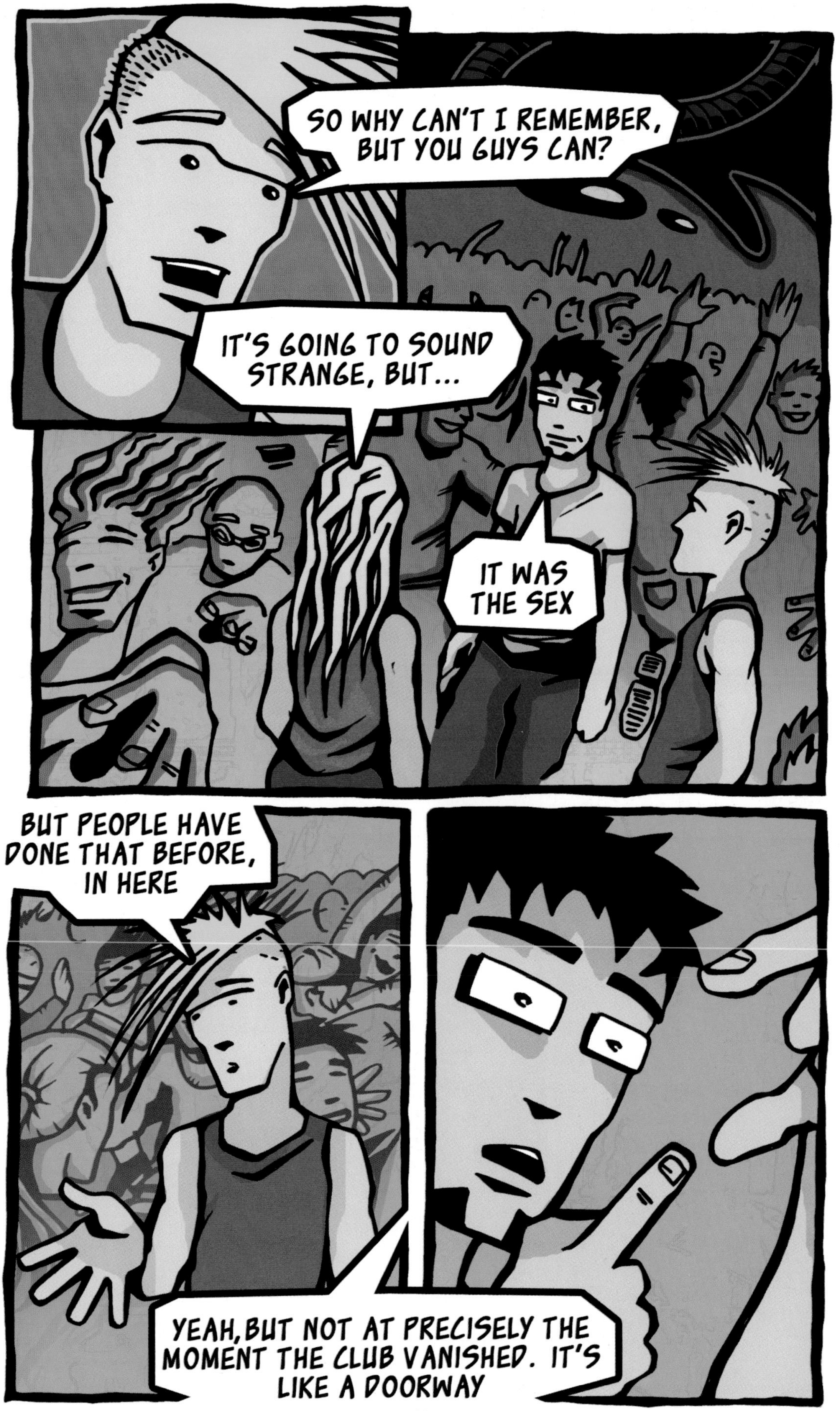

SO WHY CAN'T I REMEMBER, BUT YOU GUYS CAN?
IT'S GOING TO SOUND STRANGE, BUT...
IT WAS THE SEX
BUT PEOPLE HAVE DONE THAT BEFORE, IN HERE
YEAH, BUT NOT AT PRECISELY THE MOMENT THE CLUB VANISHED. IT'S LIKE A DOORWAY

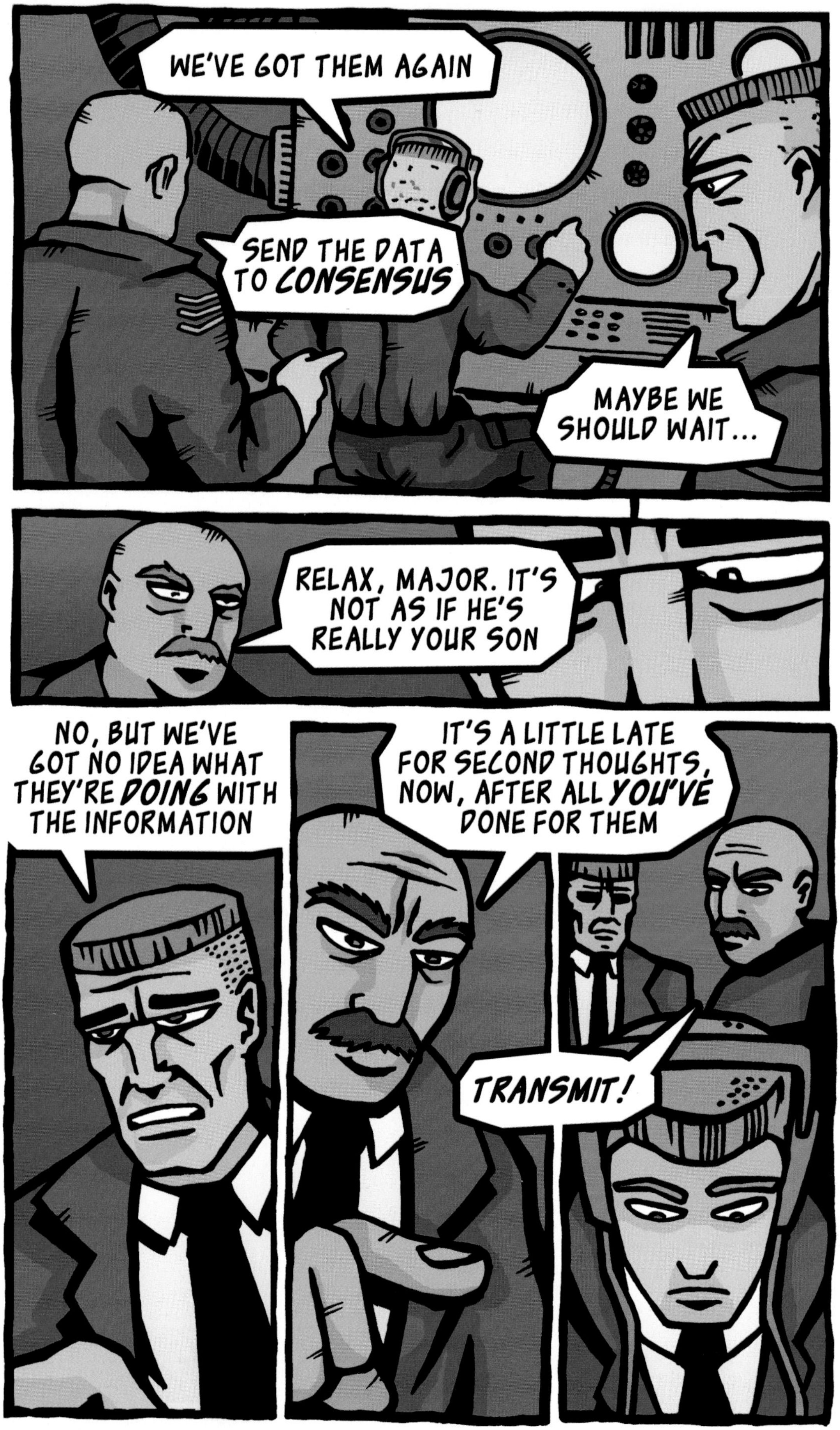
WE'VE GOT THEM AGAIN
SEND THE DATA TO *CONSENSUS*
MAYBE WE SHOULD WAIT...
RELAX, MAJOR. IT'S NOT AS IF HE'S REALLY YOUR SON
NO, BUT WE'VE GOT NO IDEA WHAT THEY'RE *DOING* WITH THE INFORMATION
IT'S A LITTLE LATE FOR SECOND THOUGHTS, NOW, AFTER ALL *YOU'VE* DONE FOR THEM
TRANSMIT!

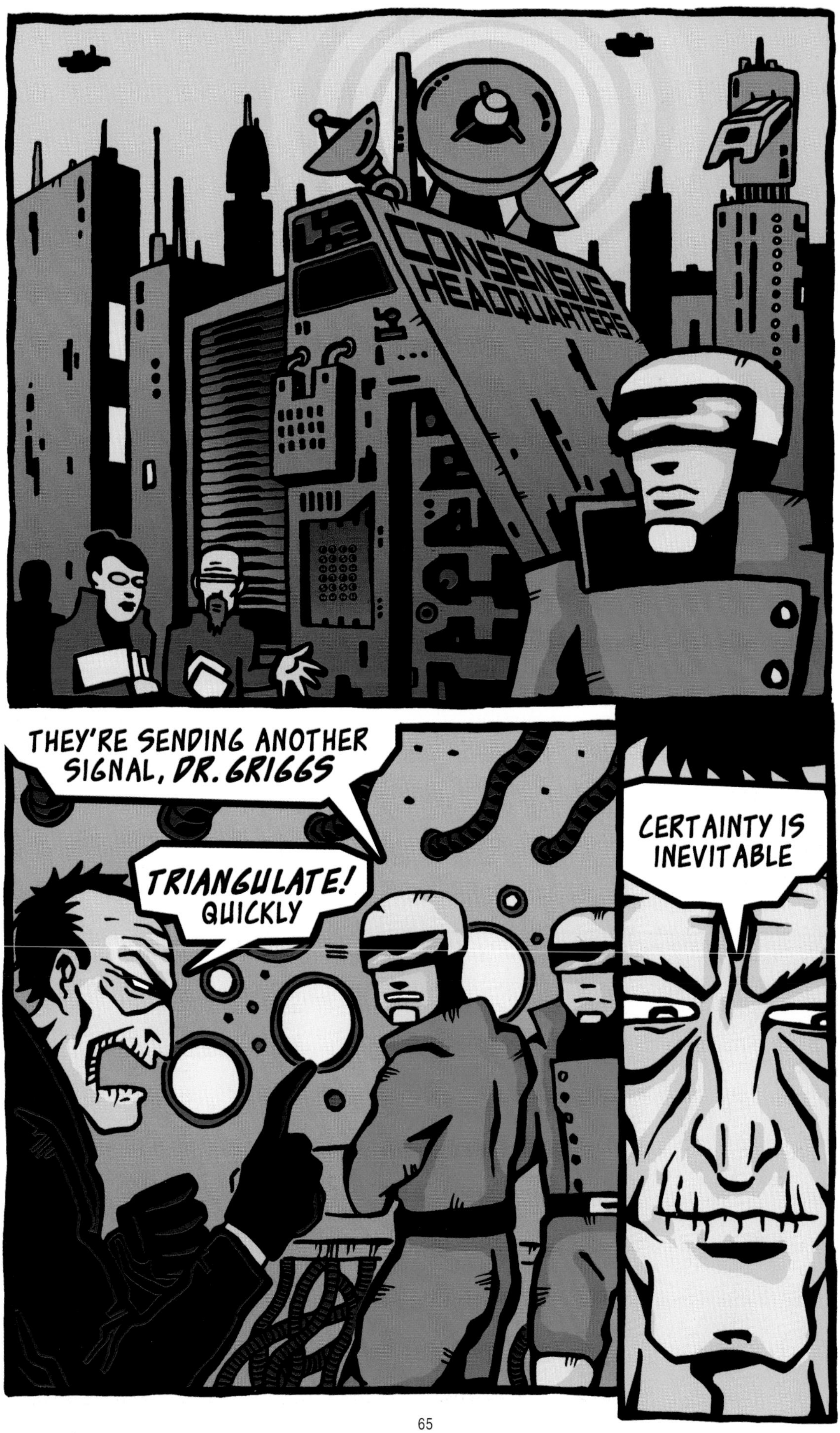
CONSENSUS HEADQUARTERS
THEY'RE SENDING ANOTHER SIGNAL, DR. GRIGGS
TRIANGULATE! QUICKLY
CERTAINTY IS INEVITABLE

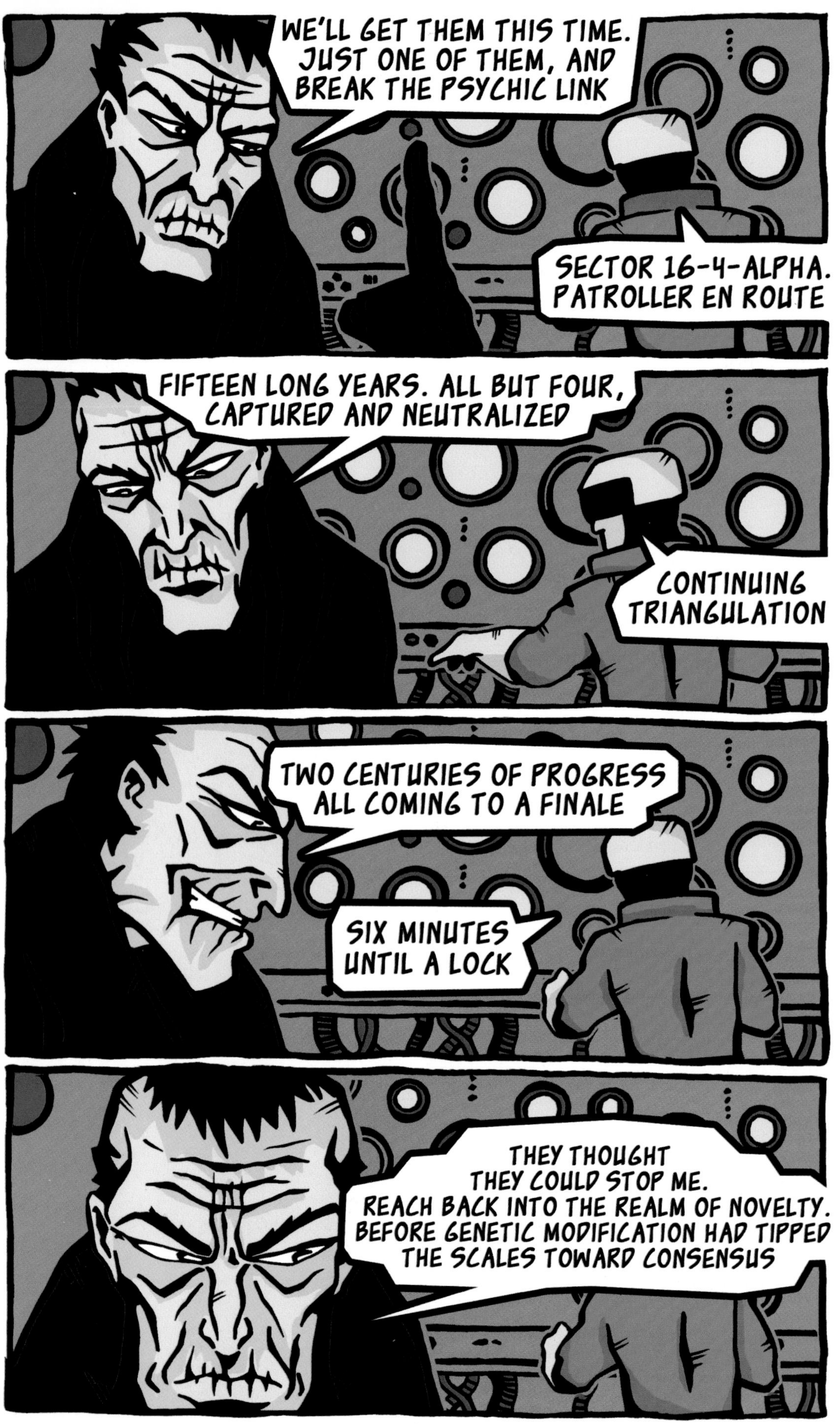
WE'LL GET THEM THIS TIME. JUST ONE OF THEM, AND BREAK THE PSYCHIC LINK
SECTOR 16-4-ALPHA. PATROLLER EN ROUTE
FIFTEEN LONG YEARS. ALL BUT FOUR, CAPTURED AND NEUTRALIZED
CONTINUING TRIANGULATION
TWO CENTURIES OF PROGRESS ALL COMING TO A FINALE
SIX MINUTES UNTIL A LOCK
THEY THOUGHT THEY COULD STOP ME. REACH BACK INTO THE REALM OF NOVELTY. BEFORE GENETIC MODIFICATION HAD TIPPED THE SCALES TOWARD CONSENSUS

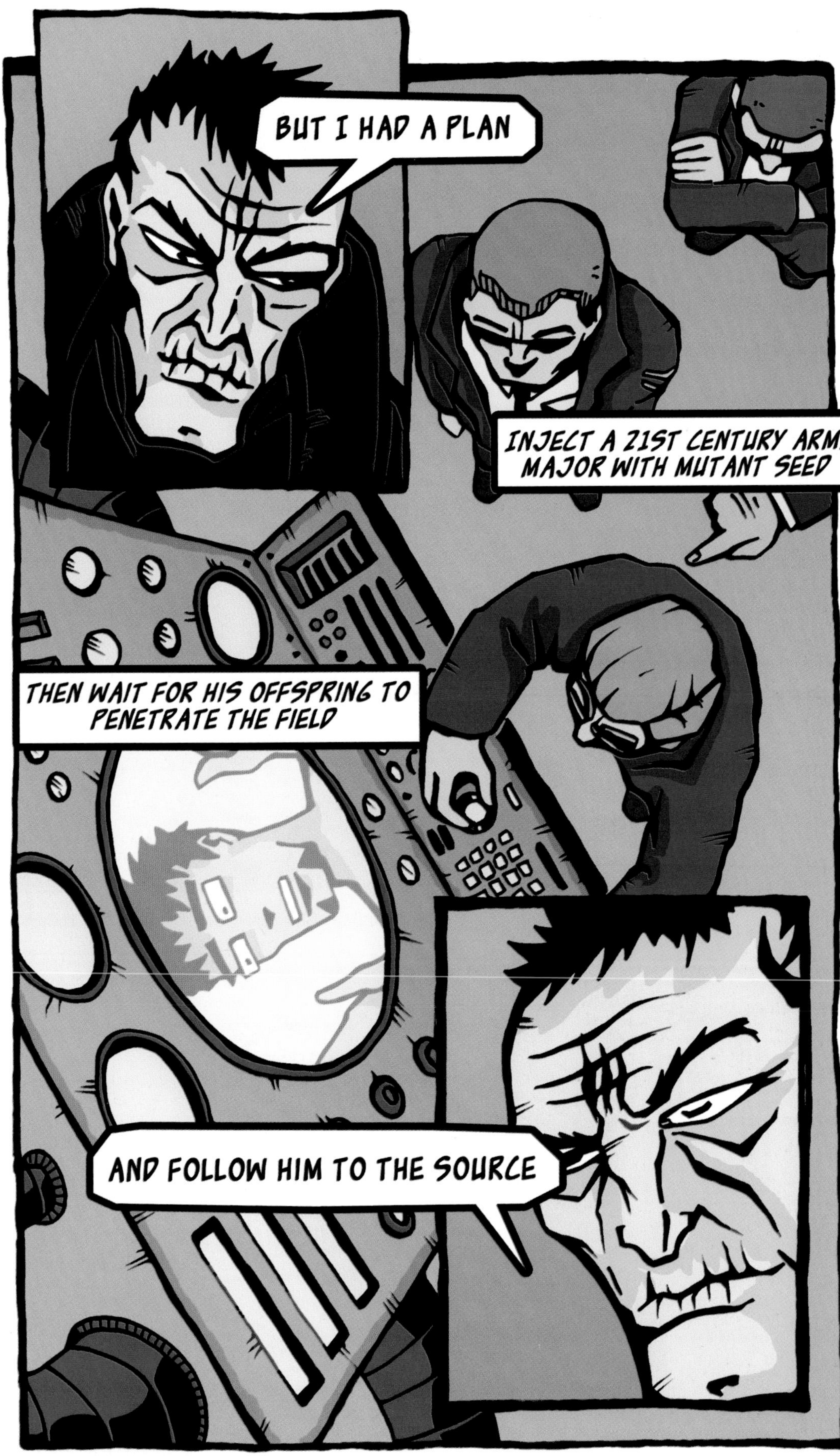
BUT I HAD A PLAN
INJECT A 21ST CENTURY ARMY MAJOR WITH MUTANT SEED
THEN WAIT FOR HIS OFFSPRING TO PENETRATE THE FIELD
AND FOLLOW HIM TO THE SOURCE

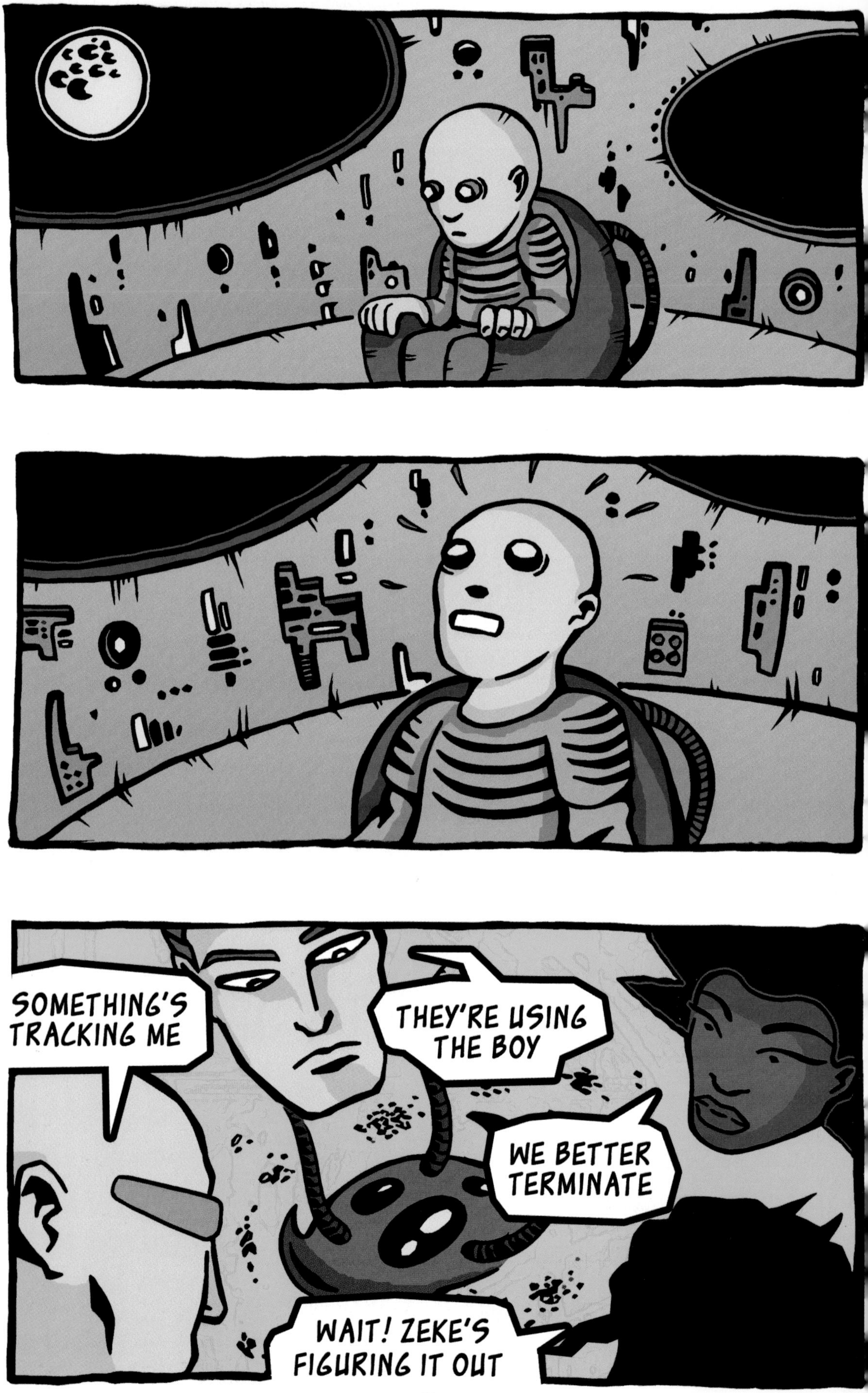
SOMETHING'S TRACKING ME
THEY'RE USING THE BOY
WE BETTER TERMINATE
WAIT! ZEKE'S FIGURING IT OUT

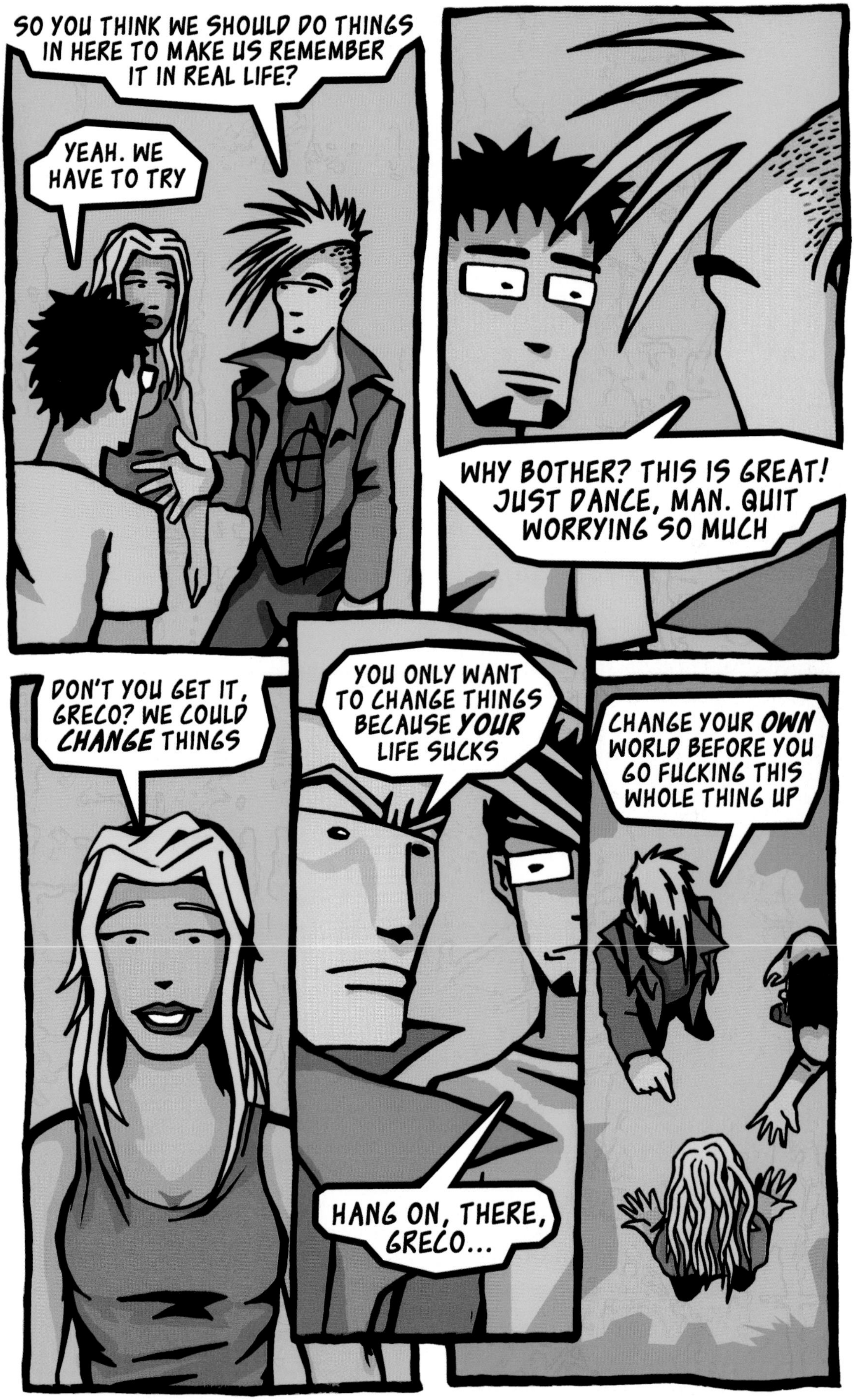
SO YOU THINK WE SHOULD DO THINGS IN HERE TO MAKE US REMEMBER IT IN REAL LIFE?
YEAH. WE HAVE TO TRY
WHY BOTHER? THIS IS GREAT! JUST DANCE, MAN. QUIT WORRYING SO MUCH
DON'T YOU GET IT, GRECO? WE COULD *CHANGE* THINGS
YOU ONLY WANT TO CHANGE THINGS BECAUSE *YOUR* LIFE SUCKS
HANG ON, THERE, GRECO...
CHANGE YOUR *OWN* WORLD BEFORE YOU GO FUCKING THIS WHOLE THING UP

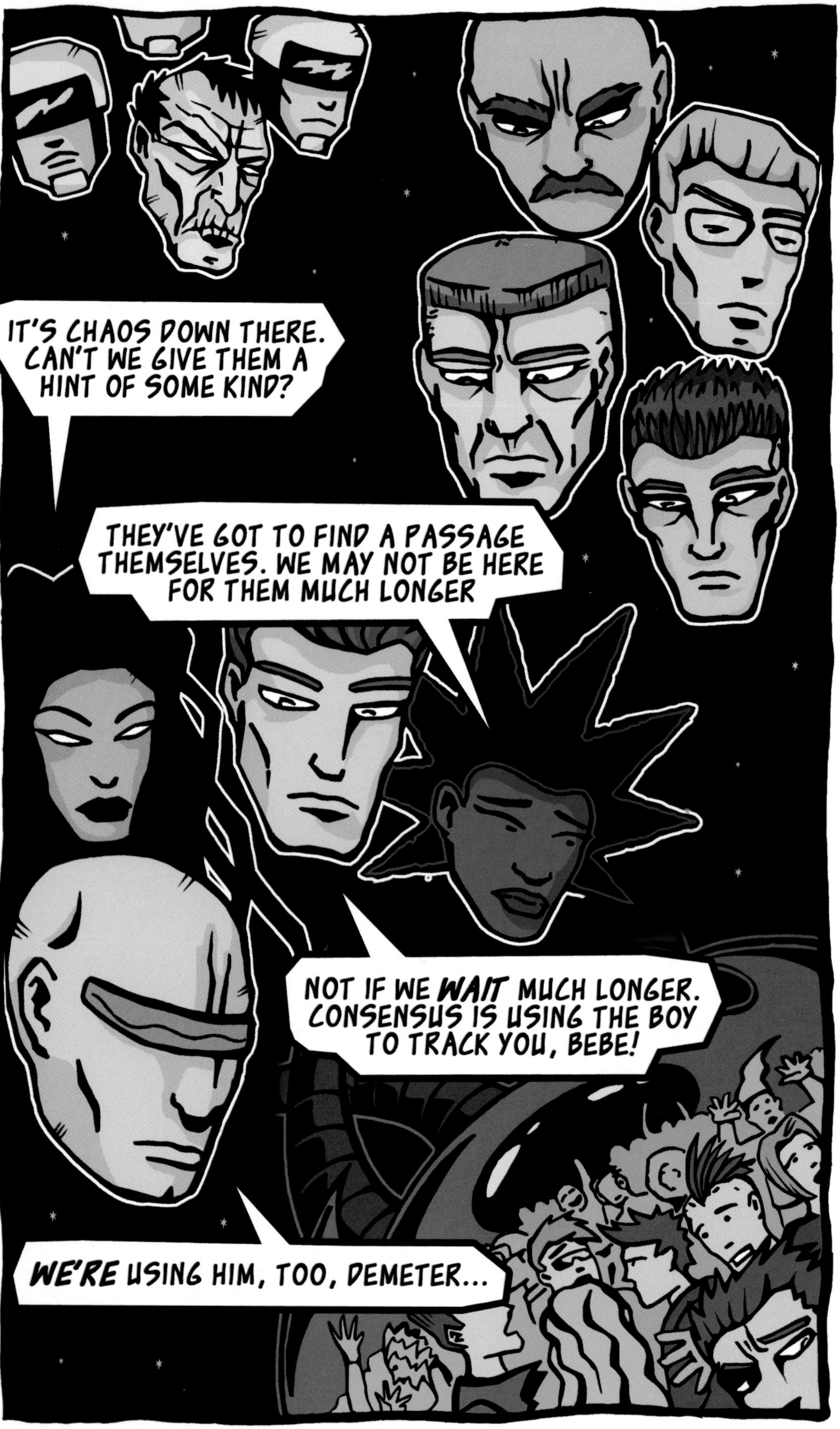
IT'S CHAOS DOWN THERE. CAN'T WE GIVE THEM A HINT OF SOME KIND?
THEY'VE GOT TO FIND A PASSAGE THEMSELVES. WE MAY NOT BE HERE FOR THEM MUCH LONGER
NOT IF WE *WAIT* MUCH LONGER. CONSENSUS IS USING THE BOY TO TRACK YOU, BEBE!
WE'RE USING HIM, TOO, DEMETER...

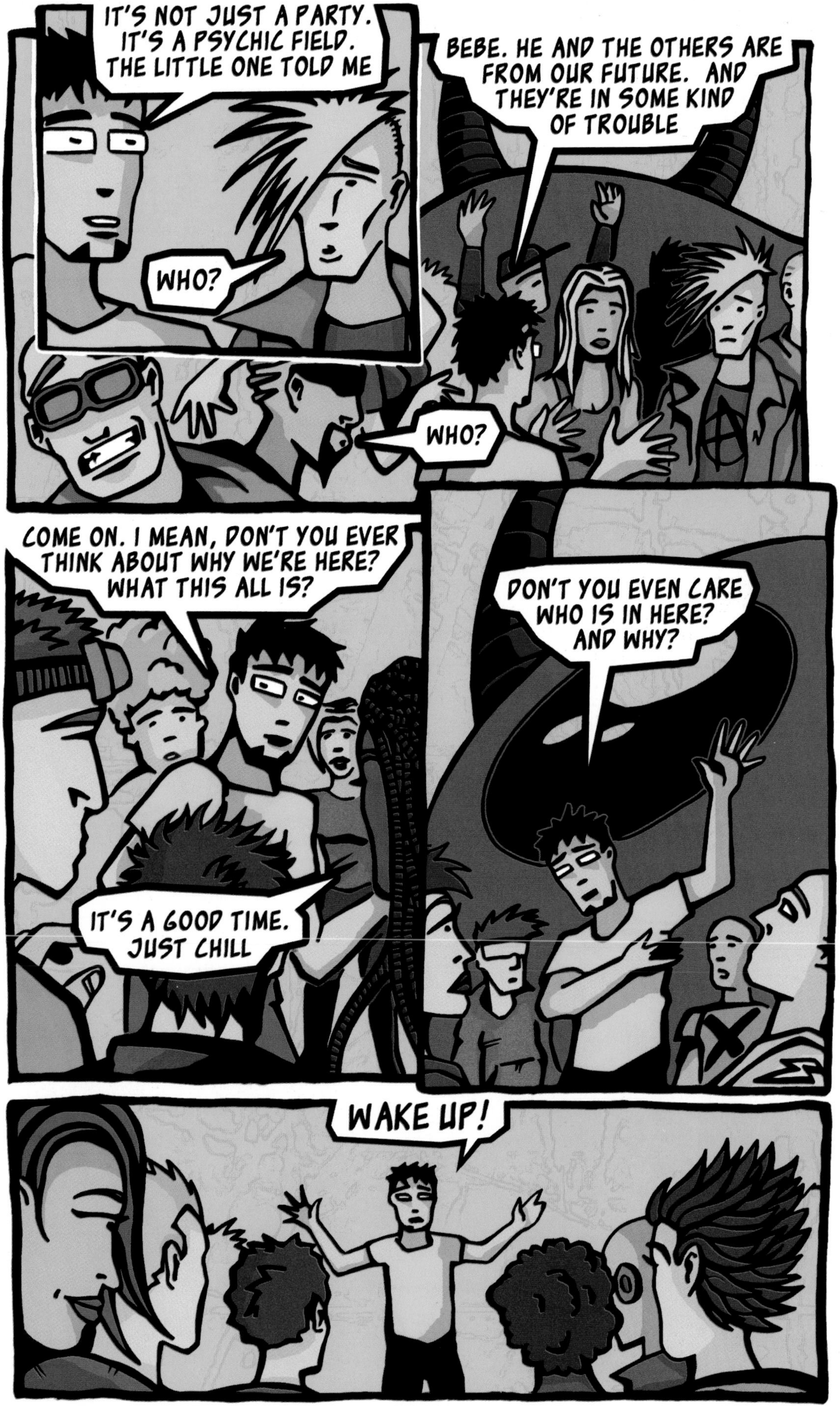
IT'S NOT JUST A PARTY. IT'S A PSYCHIC FIELD. THE LITTLE ONE TOLD ME
WHO?
BEBE. HE AND THE OTHERS ARE FROM OUR FUTURE. AND THEY'RE IN SOME KIND OF TROUBLE
WHO?
COME ON. I MEAN, DON'T YOU EVER THINK ABOUT WHY WE'RE HERE? WHAT THIS ALL IS?
IT'S A GOOD TIME. JUST CHILL
DON'T YOU EVEN CARE WHO IS IN HERE? AND WHY?
WAKE UP!

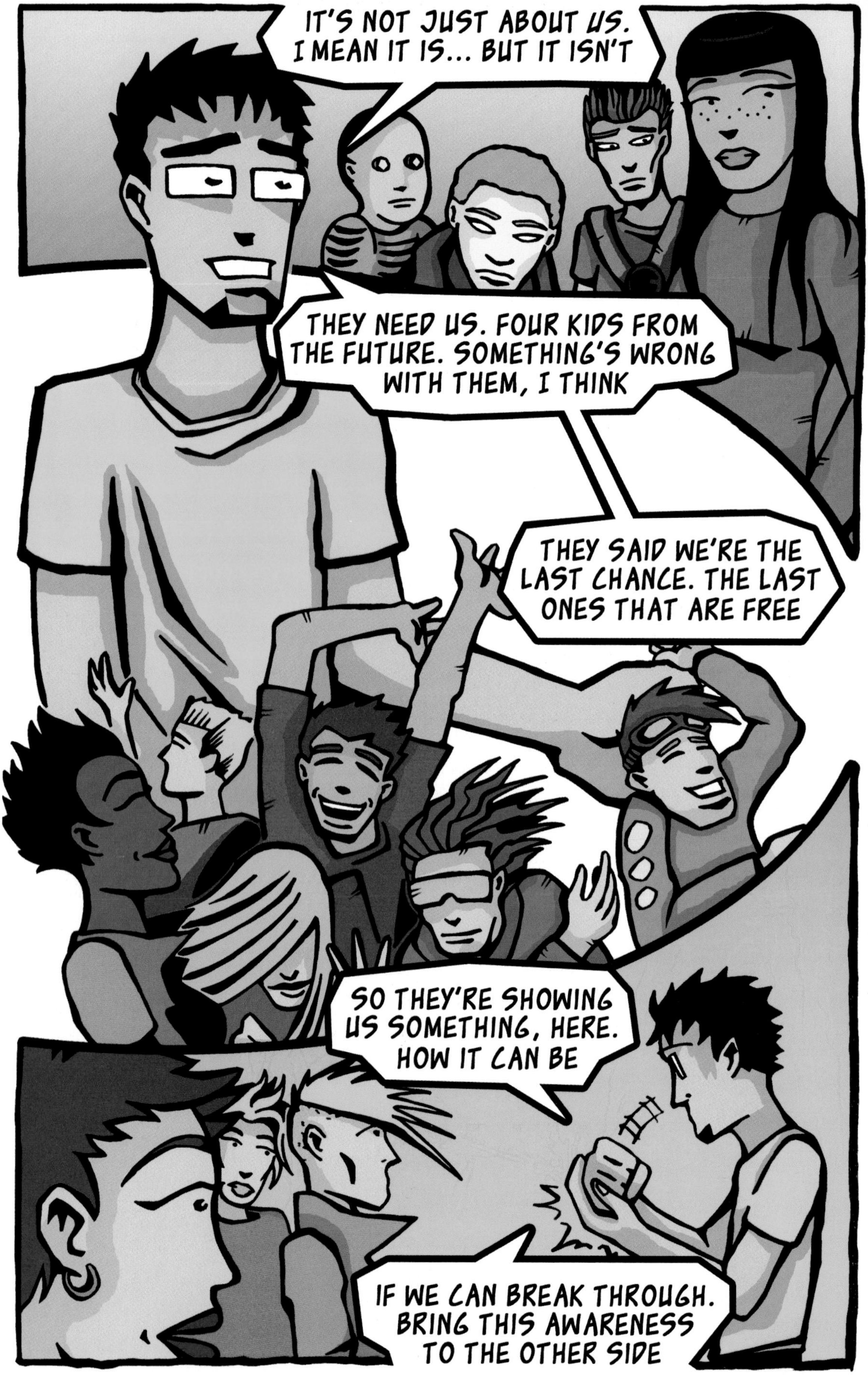
IT'S NOT JUST ABOUT US. I MEAN IT IS... BUT IT ISN'T
THEY NEED US. FOUR KIDS FROM THE FUTURE. SOMETHING'S WRONG WITH THEM, I THINK
THEY SAID WE'RE THE LAST CHANCE. THE LAST ONES THAT ARE FREE
SO THEY'RE SHOWING US SOMETHING, HERE. HOW IT CAN BE
IF WE CAN BREAK THROUGH. BRING THIS AWARENESS TO THE OTHER SIDE

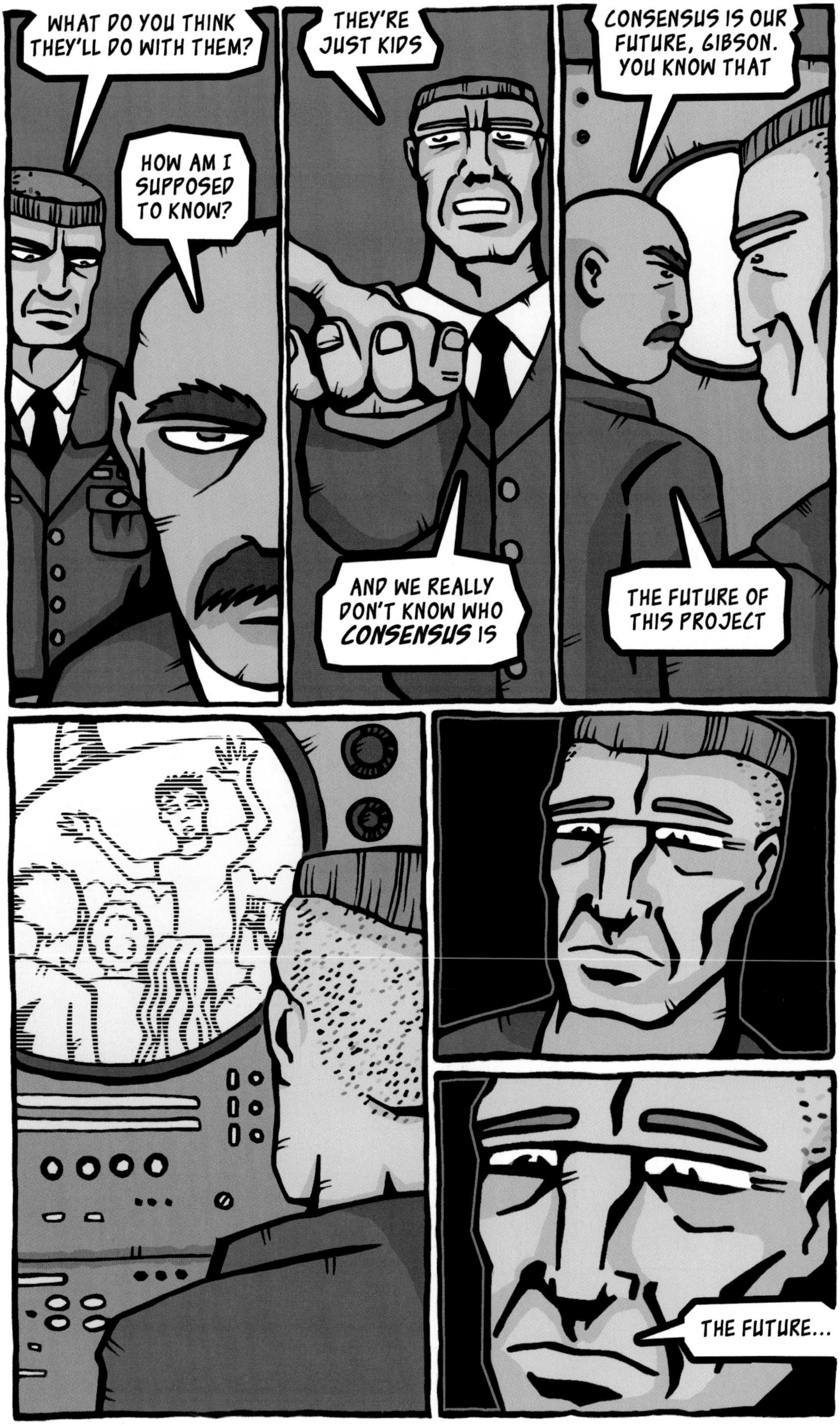
WHAT DO YOU THINK THEY'LL DO WITH THEM?
HOW AM I SUPPOSED TO KNOW?
THEY'RE JUST KIDS
AND WE REALLY DON'T KNOW WHO *CONSENSUS* IS
CONSENSUS IS OUR FUTURE, GIBSON. YOU KNOW THAT
THE FUTURE OF THIS PROJECT
THE FUTURE...

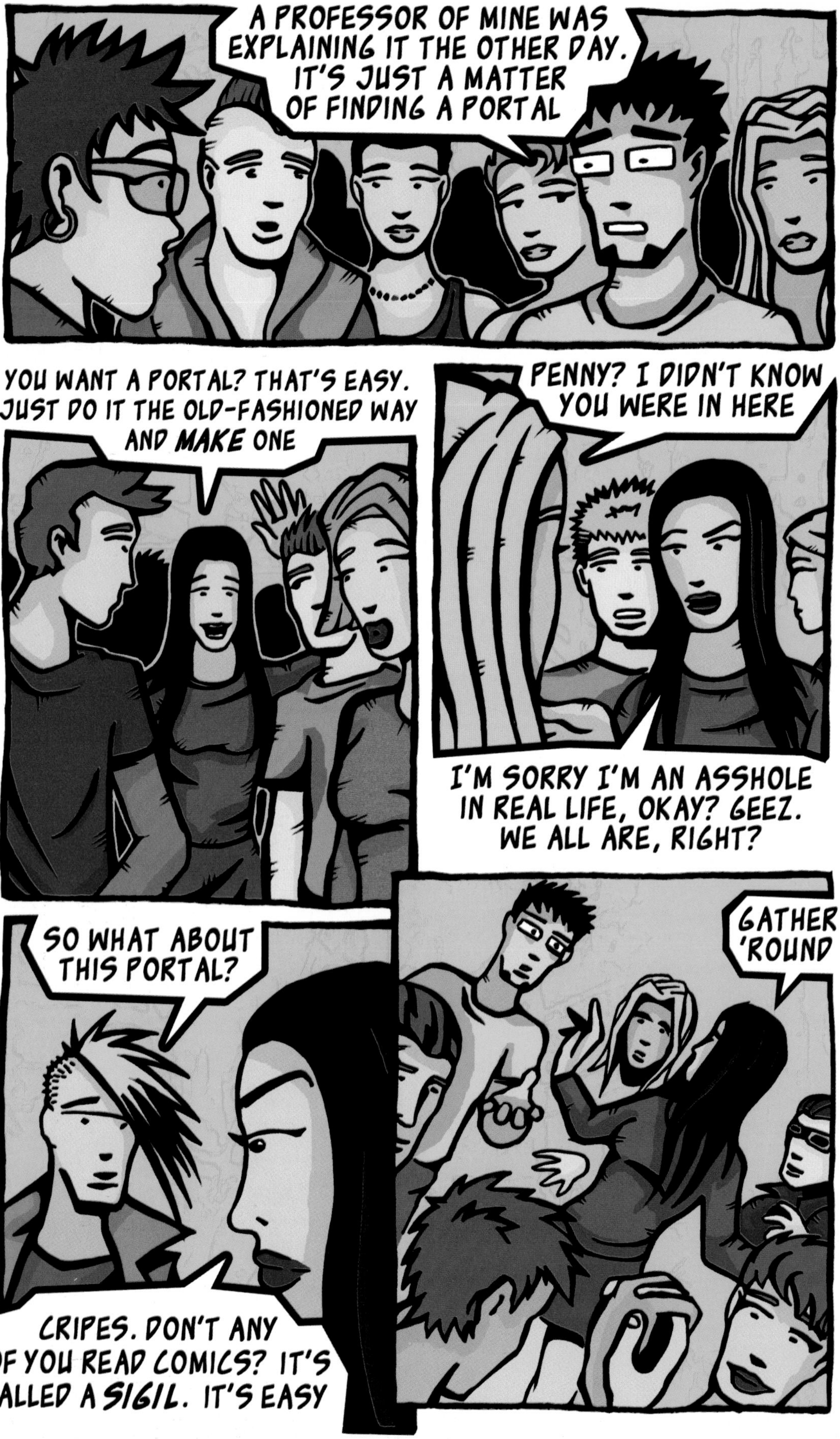
A PROFESSOR OF MINE WAS EXPLAINING IT THE OTHER DAY. IT'S JUST A MATTER OF FINDING A PORTAL
YOU WANT A PORTAL? THAT'S EASY. JUST DO IT THE OLD-FASHIONED WAY AND MAKE ONE
PENNY? I DIDN'T KNOW YOU WERE IN HERE
I'M SORRY I'M AN ASSHOLE IN REAL LIFE, OKAY? GEEZ. WE ALL ARE, RIGHT?
SO WHAT ABOUT THIS PORTAL?
CRIPES. DON'T ANY OF YOU READ COMICS? IT'S CALLED A SIGIL. IT'S EASY
GATHER 'ROUND

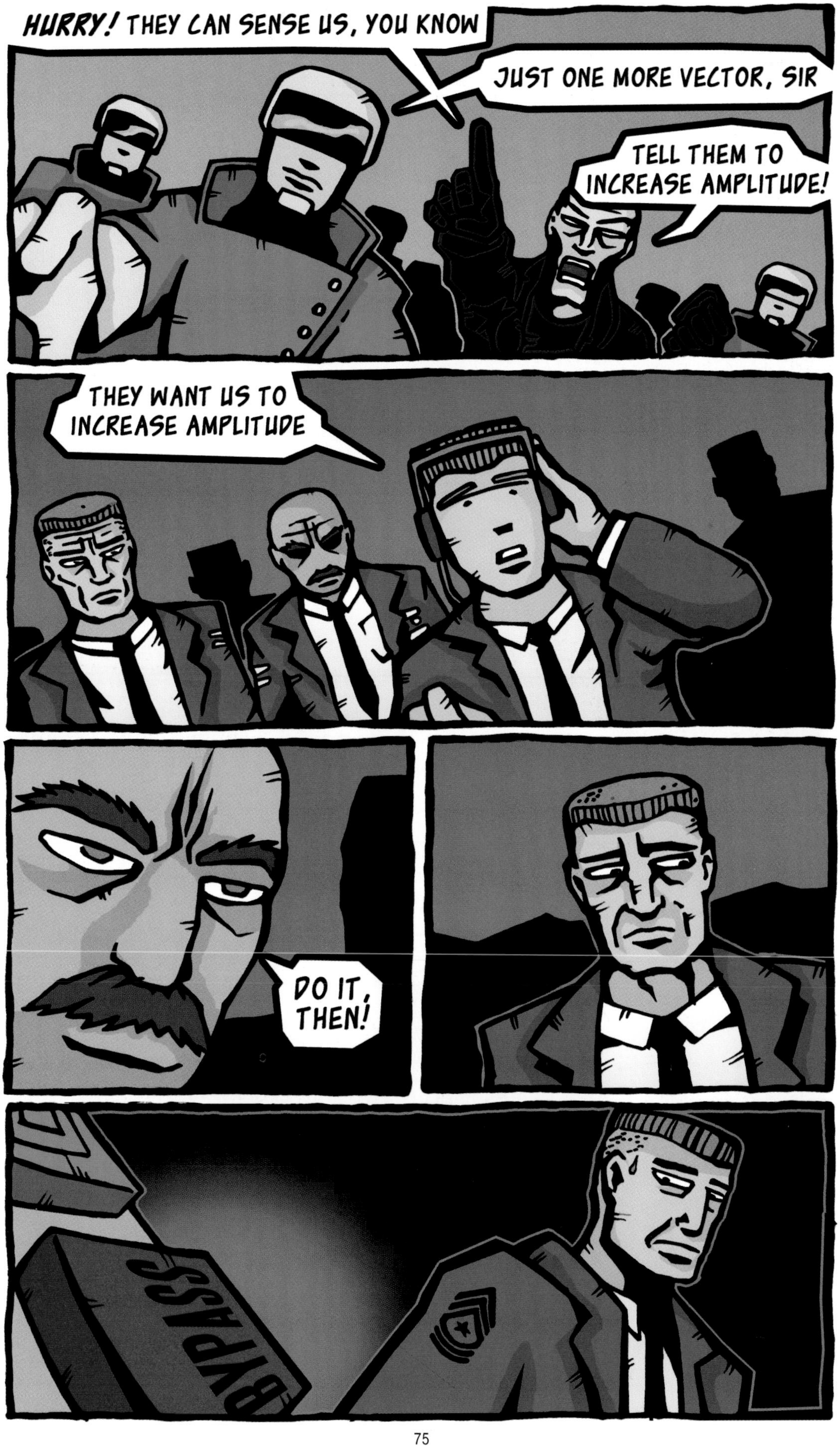
HURRY! THEY CAN SENSE US, YOU KNOW
JUST ONE MORE VECTOR, SIR
TELL THEM TO INCREASE AMPLITUDE!
THEY WANT US TO INCREASE AMPLITUDE
DO IT, THEN!
BYPASS

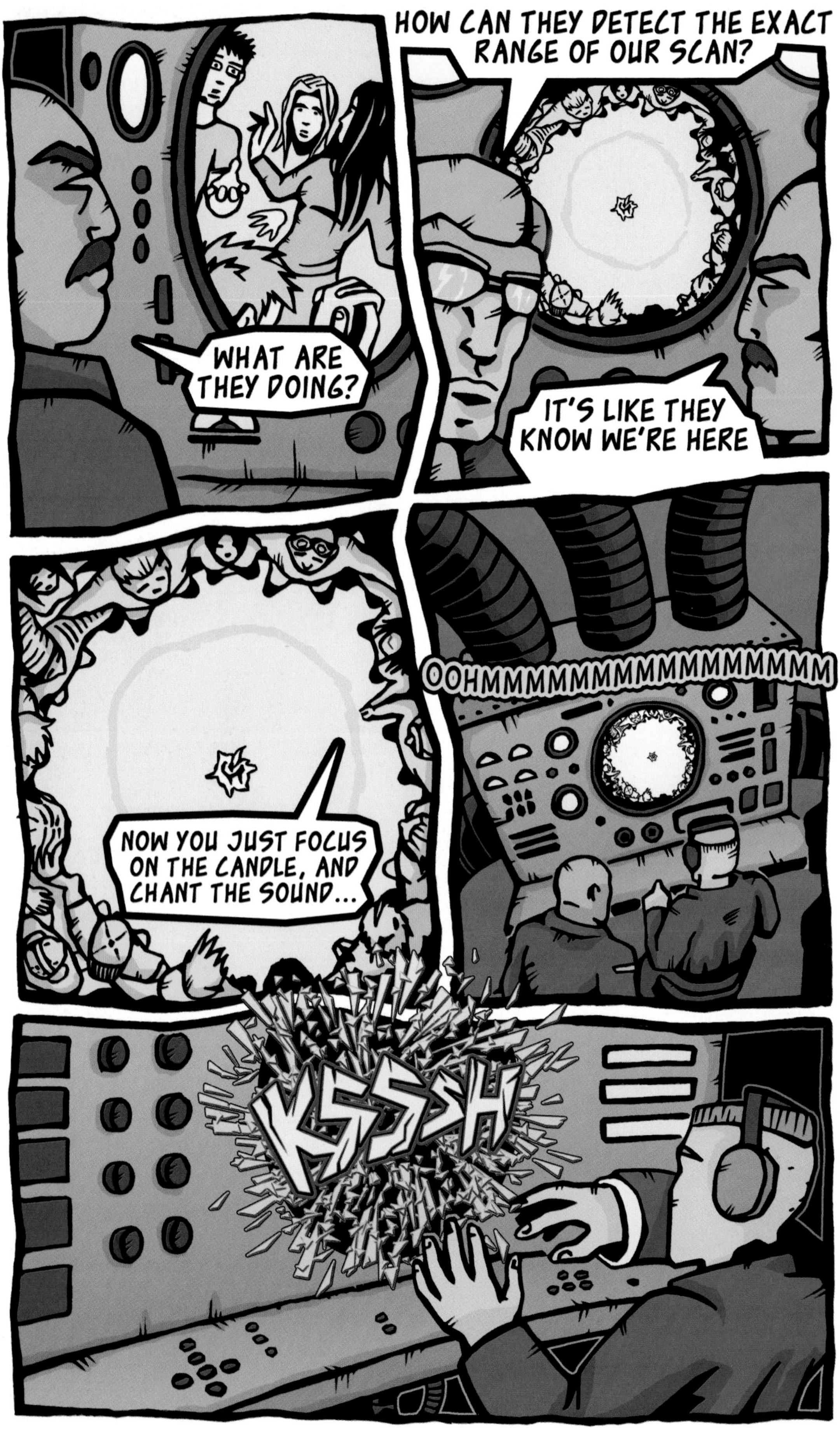
WHAT ARE THEY DOING?
HOW CAN THEY DETECT THE EXACT RANGE OF OUR SCAN?
IT'S LIKE THEY KNOW WE'RE HERE
NOW YOU JUST FOCUS ON THE CANDLE, AND CHANT THE SOUND...
OOHMMMMMMMMMMMMMMMM
KSSSH

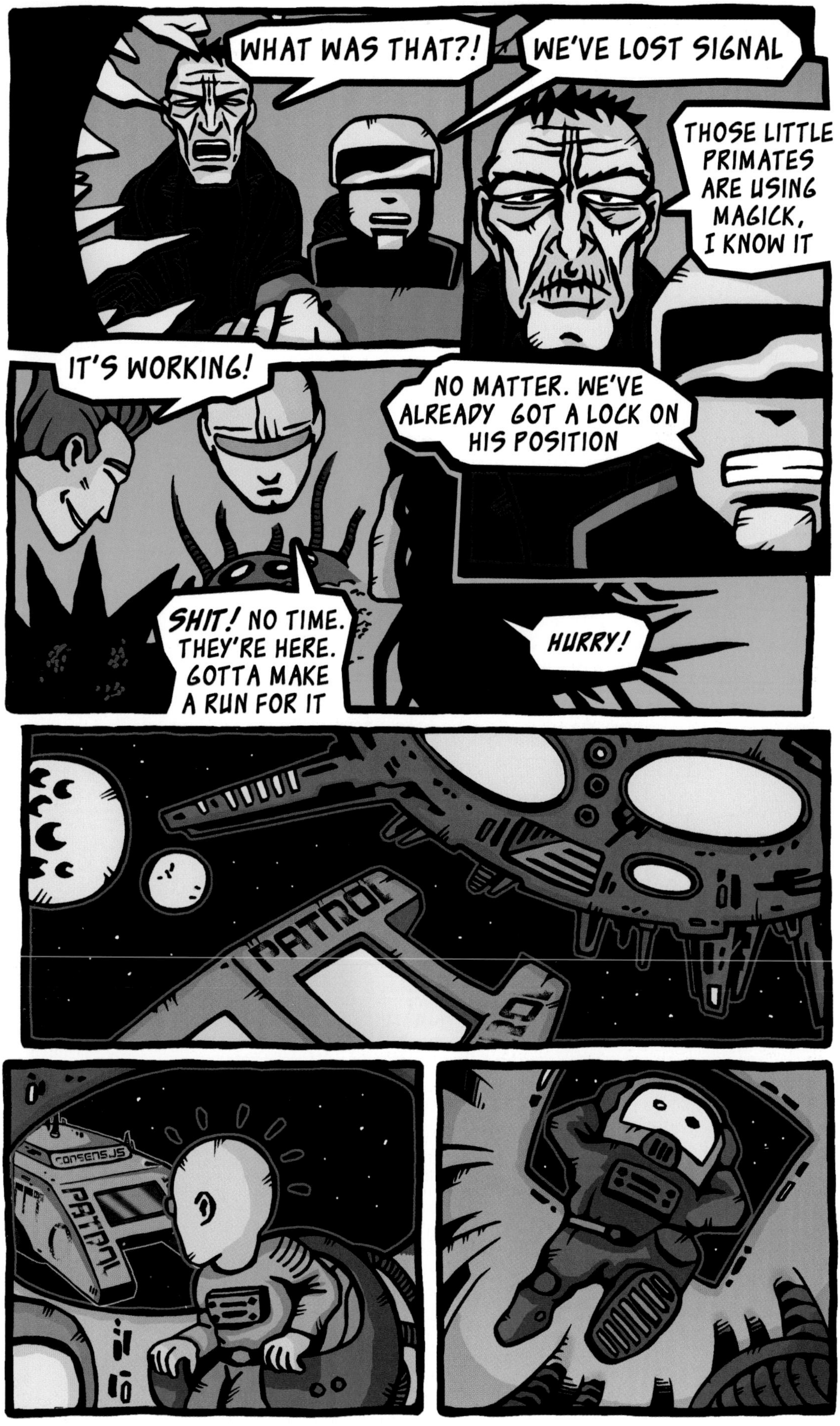
WHAT WAS THAT?!
WE'VE LOST SIGNAL
THOSE LITTLE PRIMATES ARE USING MAGICK, I KNOW IT
IT'S WORKING!
NO MATTER. WE'VE ALREADY GOT A LOCK ON HIS POSITION
SHIT! NO TIME. THEY'RE HERE. GOTTA MAKE A RUN FOR IT
HURRY!
PATROL
CONSENSUS
PATROL

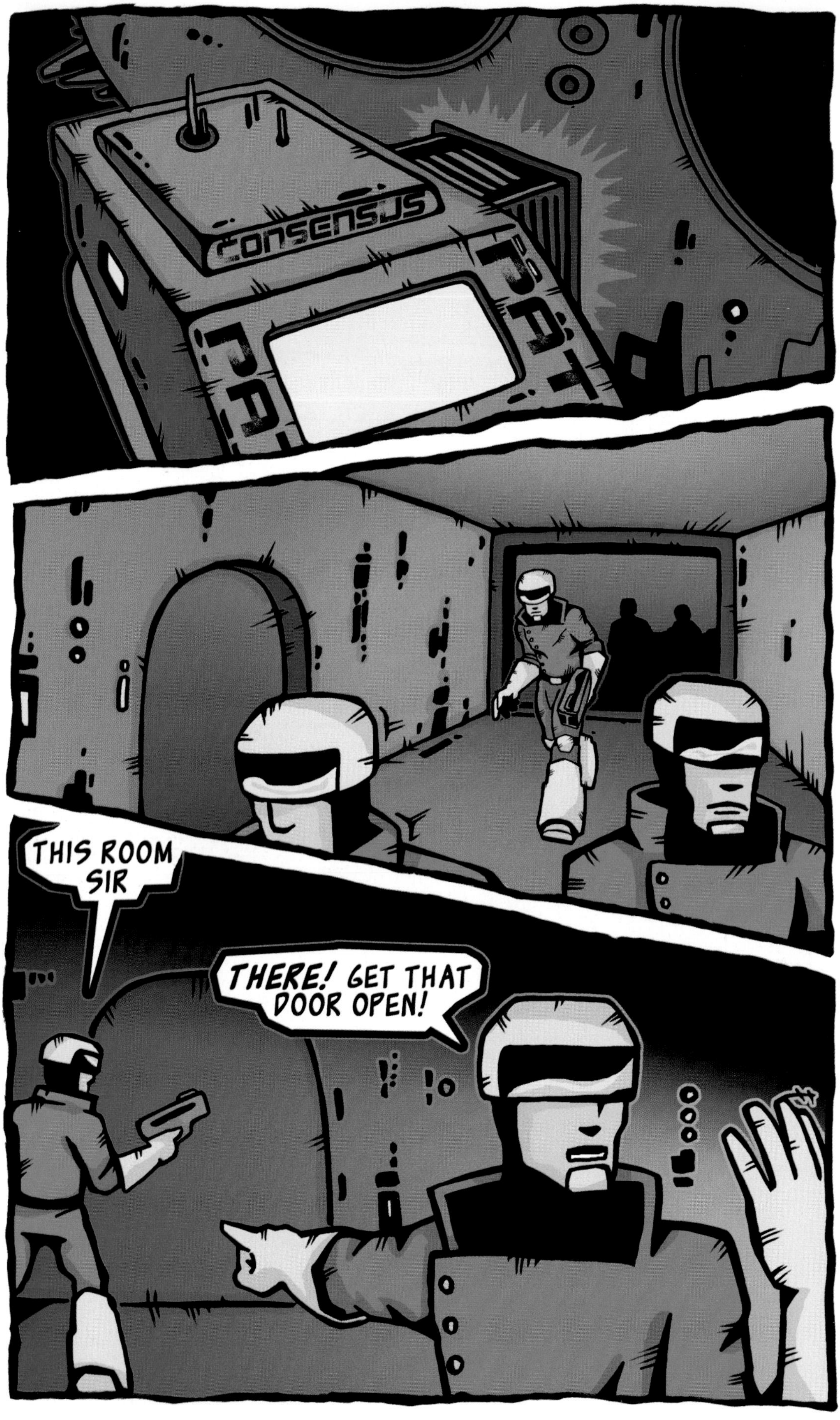
CONSENSUS
THIS ROOM SIR
THERE! GET THAT DOOR OPEN!

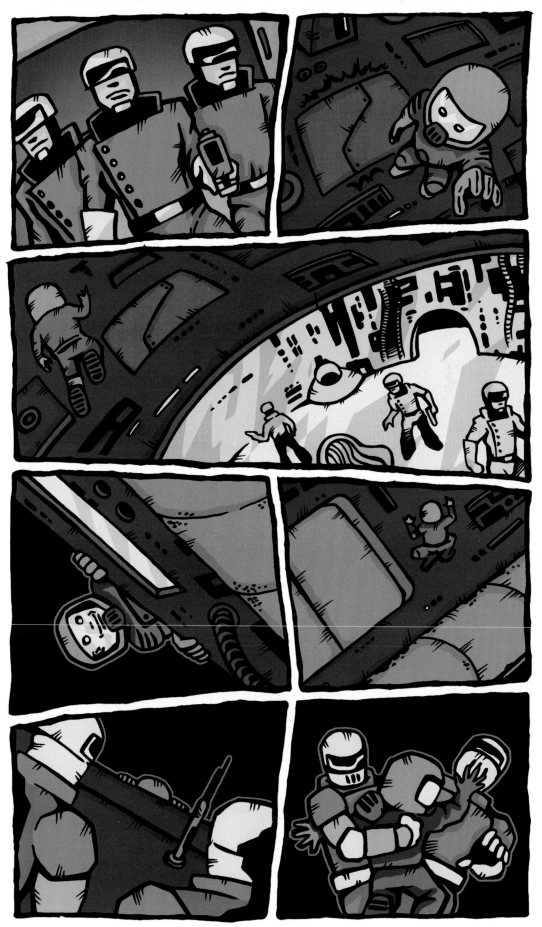

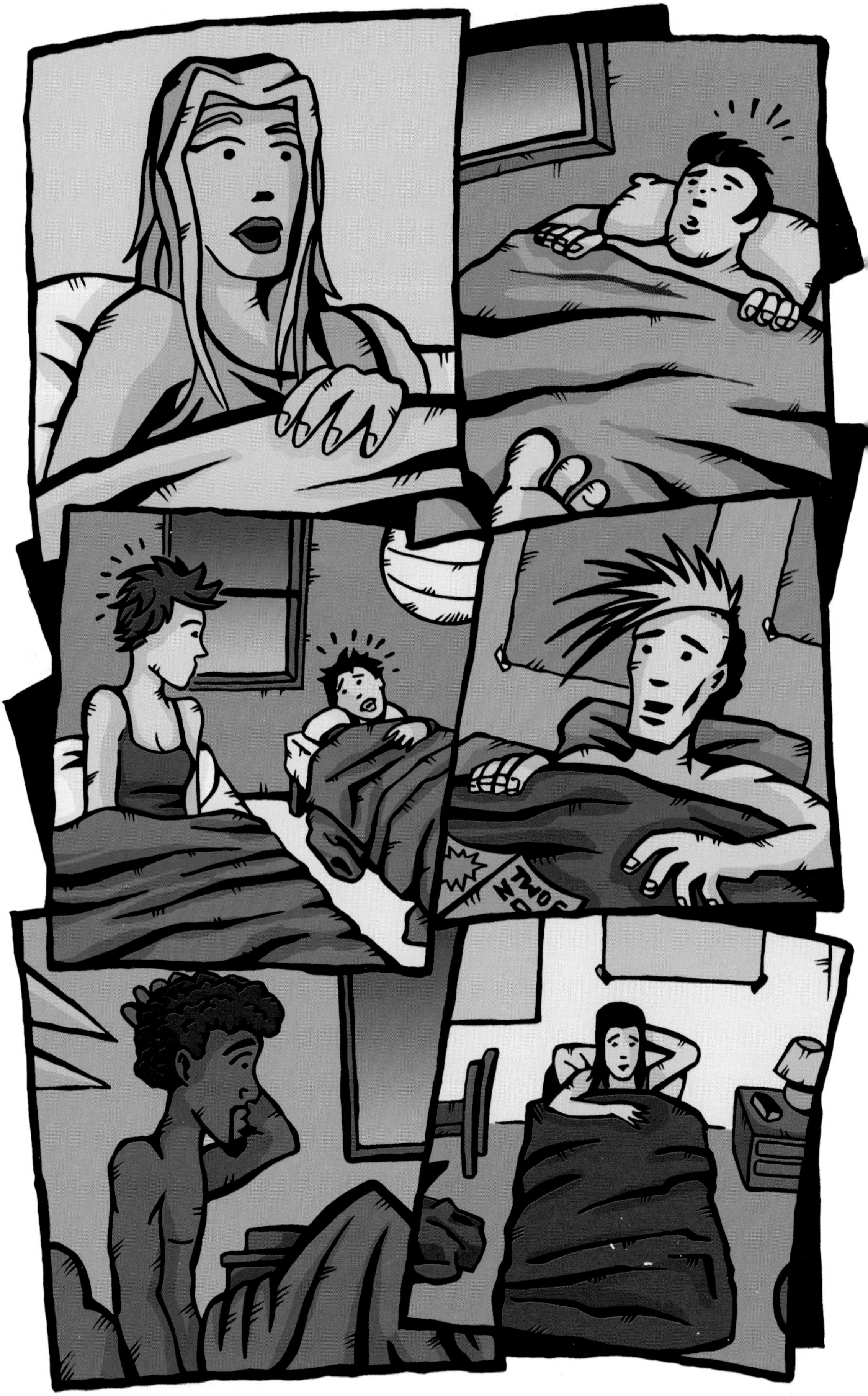

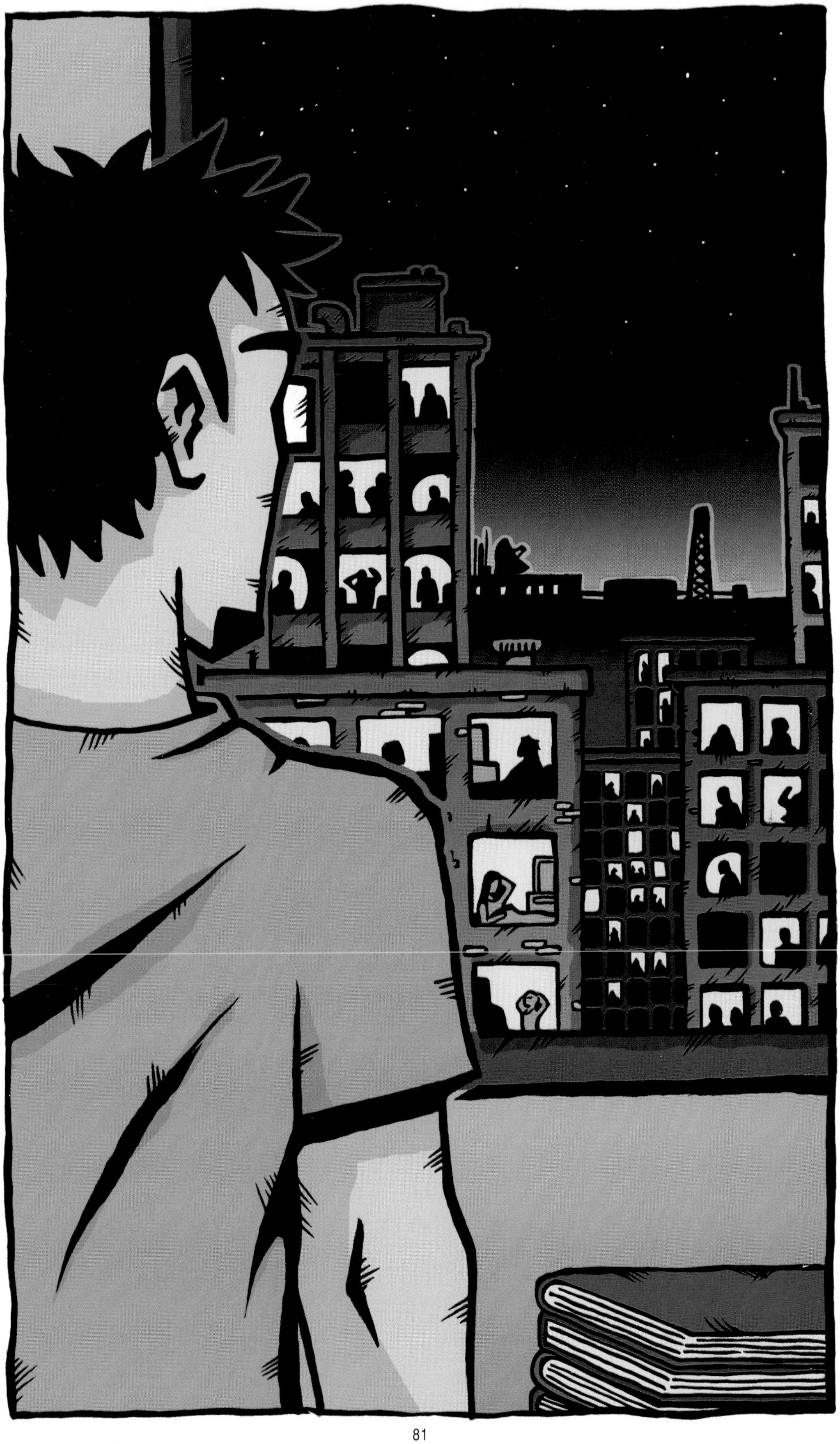

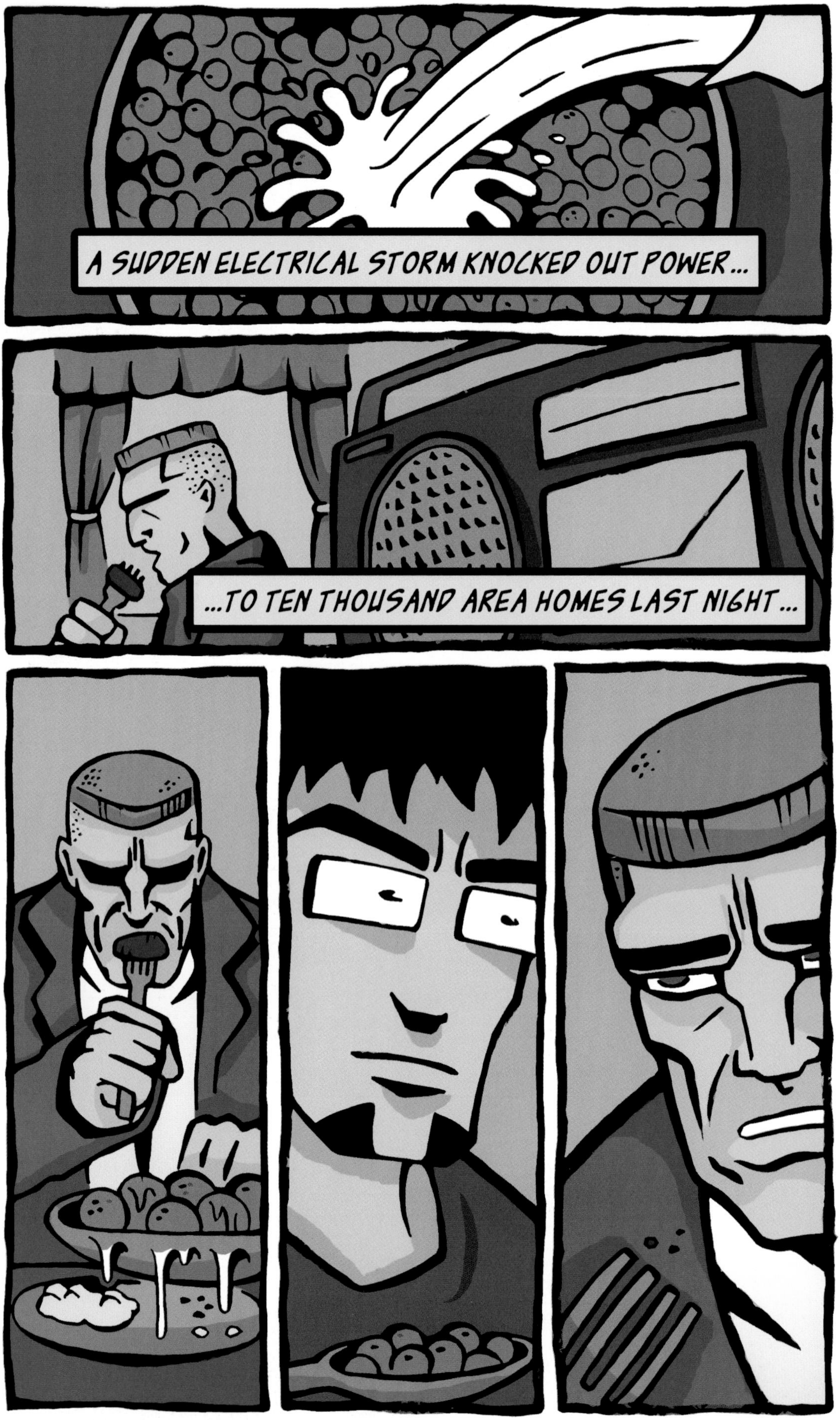
A SUDDEN ELECTRICAL STORM KNOCKED OUT POWER...
...TO TEN THOUSAND AREA HOMES LAST NIGHT...

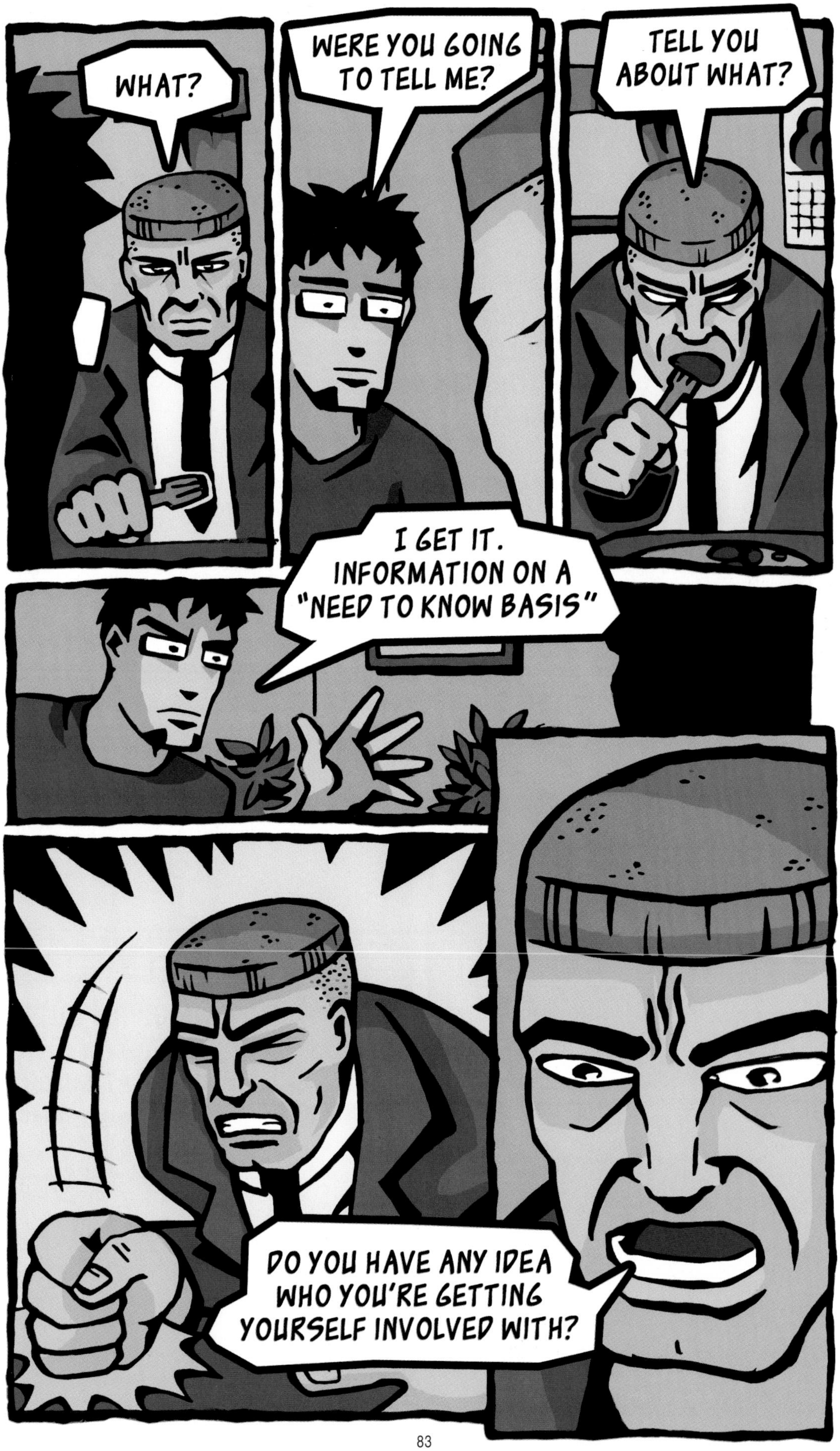
WHAT?
WERE YOU GOING TO TELL ME?
TELL YOU ABOUT WHAT?
I GET IT. INFORMATION ON A "NEED TO KNOW BASIS"
DO YOU HAVE ANY IDEA WHO YOU'RE GETTING YOURSELF INVOLVED WITH?

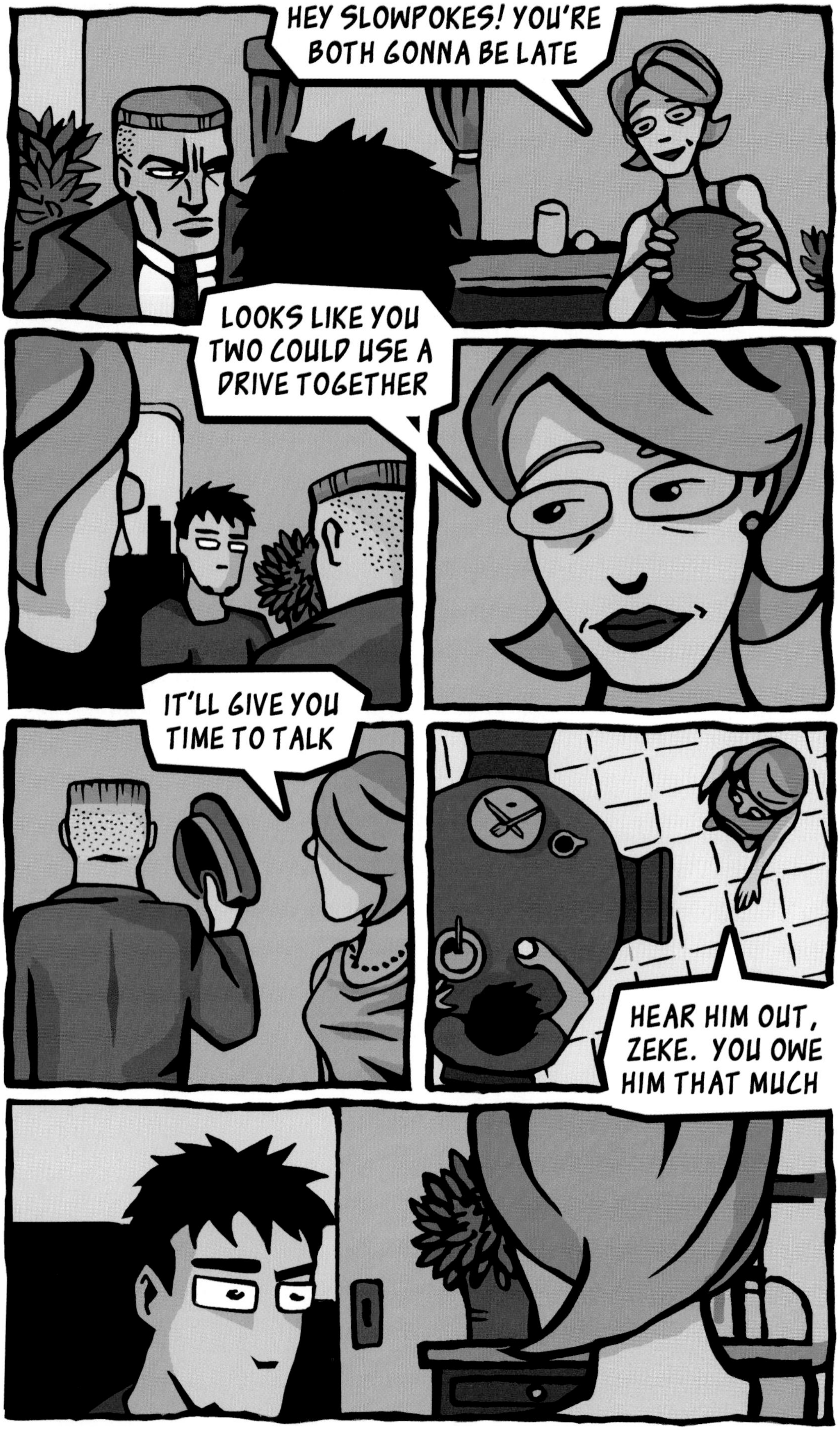
HEY SLOWPOKES! YOU'RE BOTH GONNA BE LATE
LOOKS LIKE YOU TWO COULD USE A DRIVE TOGETHER
IT'LL GIVE YOU TIME TO TALK
HEAR HIM OUT, ZEKE. YOU OWE HIM THAT MUCH

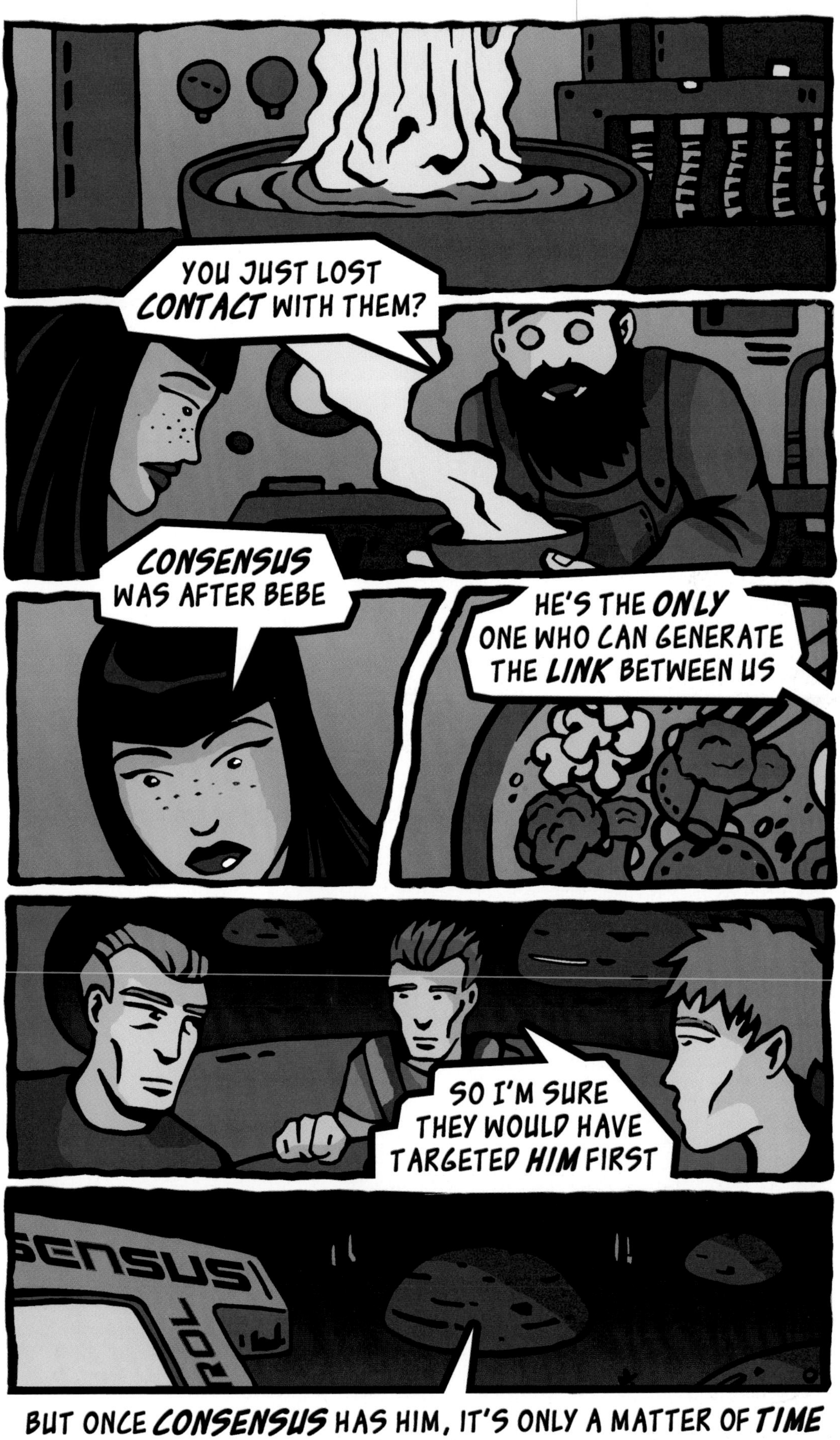
YOU JUST LOST CONTACT WITH THEM?
CONSENSUS WAS AFTER BEBE
HE'S THE ONLY ONE WHO CAN GENERATE THE LINK BETWEEN US
SO I'M SURE THEY WOULD HAVE TARGETED HIM FIRST
BUT ONCE CONSENSUS HAS HIM, IT'S ONLY A MATTER OF TIME

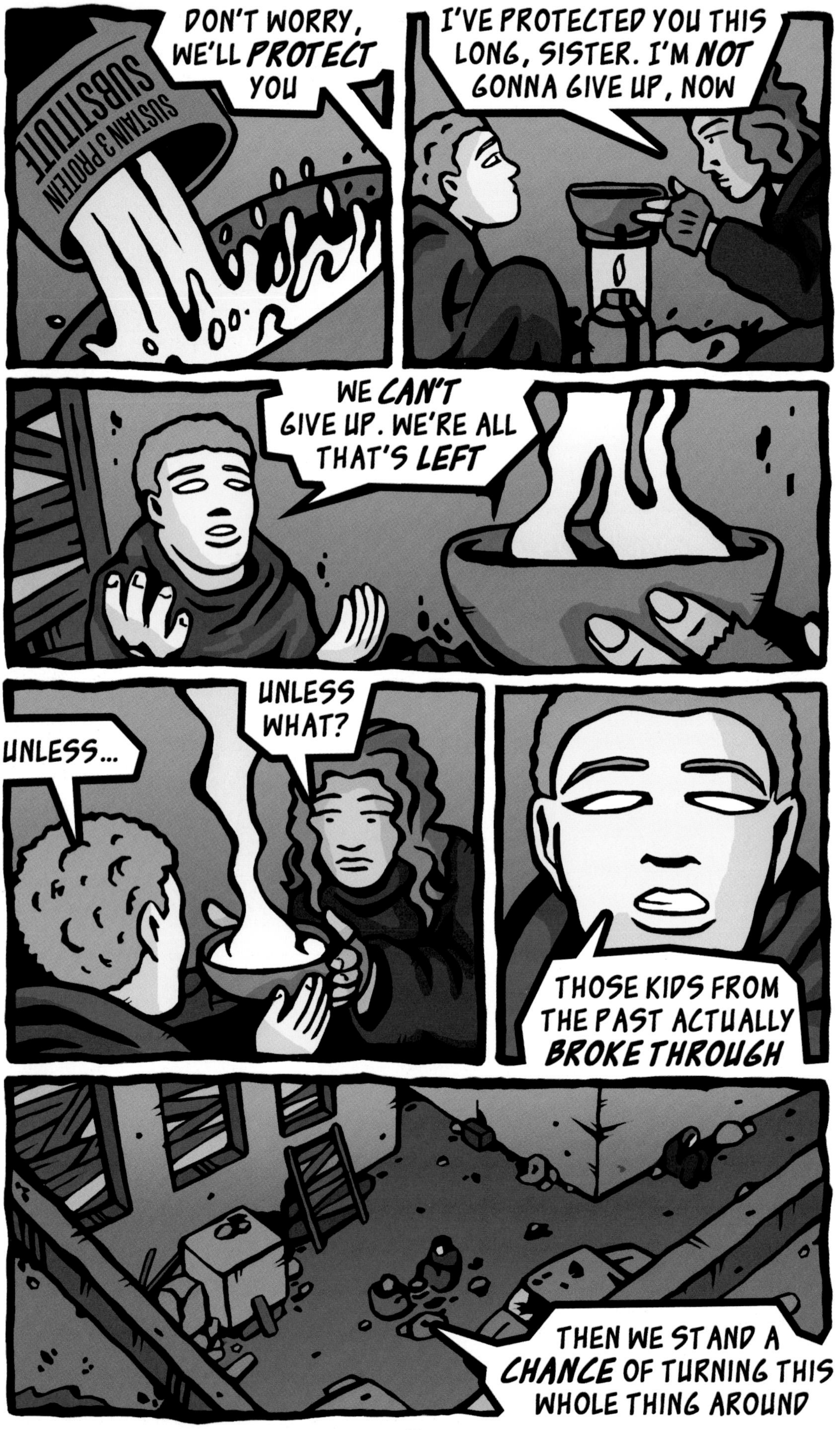
SUSTAIN 3 PROTEIN SUBSTITUT
DON'T WORRY, WE'LL PROTECT YOU
I'VE PROTECTED YOU THIS LONG, SISTER. I'M NOT GONNA GIVE UP, NOW
WE CAN'T GIVE UP. WE'RE ALL THAT'S LEFT
UNLESS...
UNLESS WHAT?
THOSE KIDS FROM THE PAST ACTUALLY BROKE THROUGH
THEN WE STAND A CHANCE OF TURNING THIS WHOLE THING AROUND

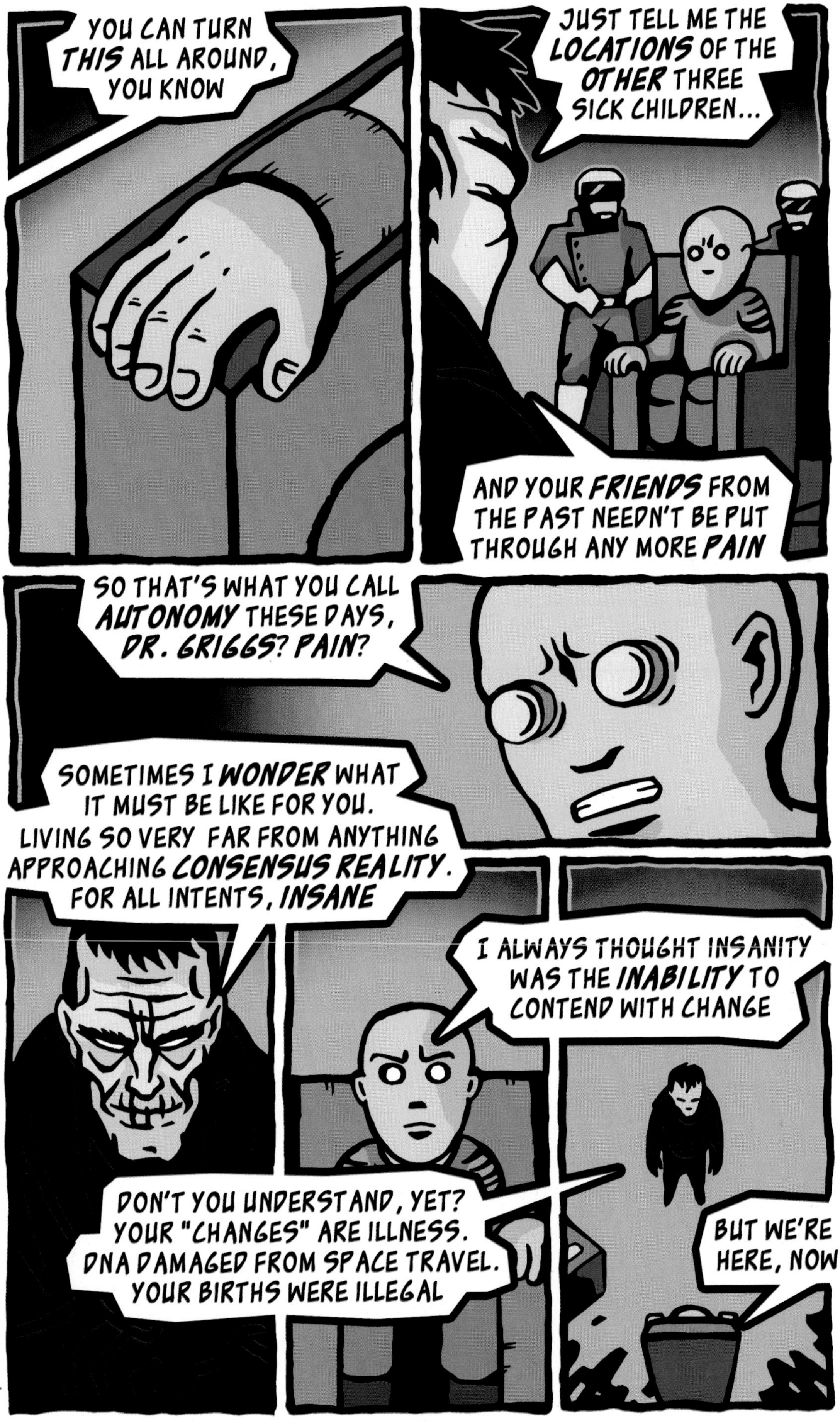
YOU CAN TURN THIS ALL AROUND, YOU KNOW
JUST TELL ME THE LOCATIONS OF THE OTHER THREE SICK CHILDREN...
AND YOUR FRIENDS FROM THE PAST NEEDN'T BE PUT THROUGH ANY MORE PAIN
SO THAT'S WHAT YOU CALL AUTONOMY THESE DAYS, DR. GRIGGS? PAIN?
SOMETIMES I WONDER WHAT IT MUST BE LIKE FOR YOU. LIVING SO VERY FAR FROM ANYTHING APPROACHING CONSENSUS REALITY. FOR ALL INTENTS, INSANE
I ALWAYS THOUGHT INSANITY WAS THE INABILITY TO CONTEND WITH CHANGE
DON'T YOU UNDERSTAND, YET? YOUR "CHANGES" ARE ILLNESS. DNA DAMAGED FROM SPACE TRAVEL. YOUR BIRTHS WERE ILLEGAL
BUT WE'RE HERE, NOW

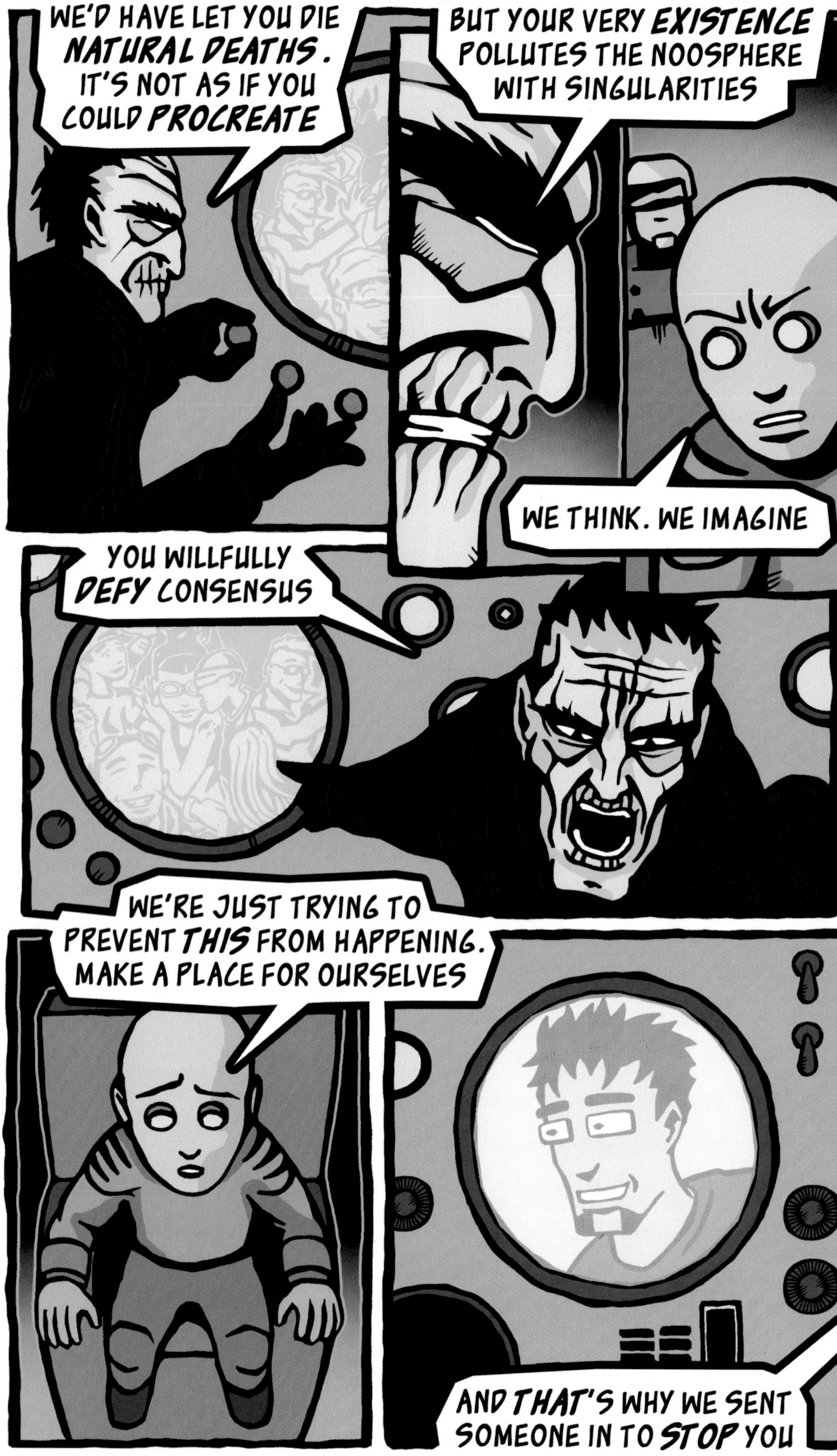
WE'D HAVE LET YOU DIE NATURAL DEATHS. IT'S NOT AS IF YOU COULD PROCREATE
BUT YOUR VERY EXISTENCE POLLUTES THE NOOSPHERE WITH SINGULARITIES
WE THINK. WE IMAGINE
YOU WILLFULLY DEFY CONSENSUS
WE'RE JUST TRYING TO PREVENT THIS FROM HAPPENING. MAKE A PLACE FOR OURSELVES
AND THAT'S WHY WE SENT SOMEONE IN TO STOP YOU

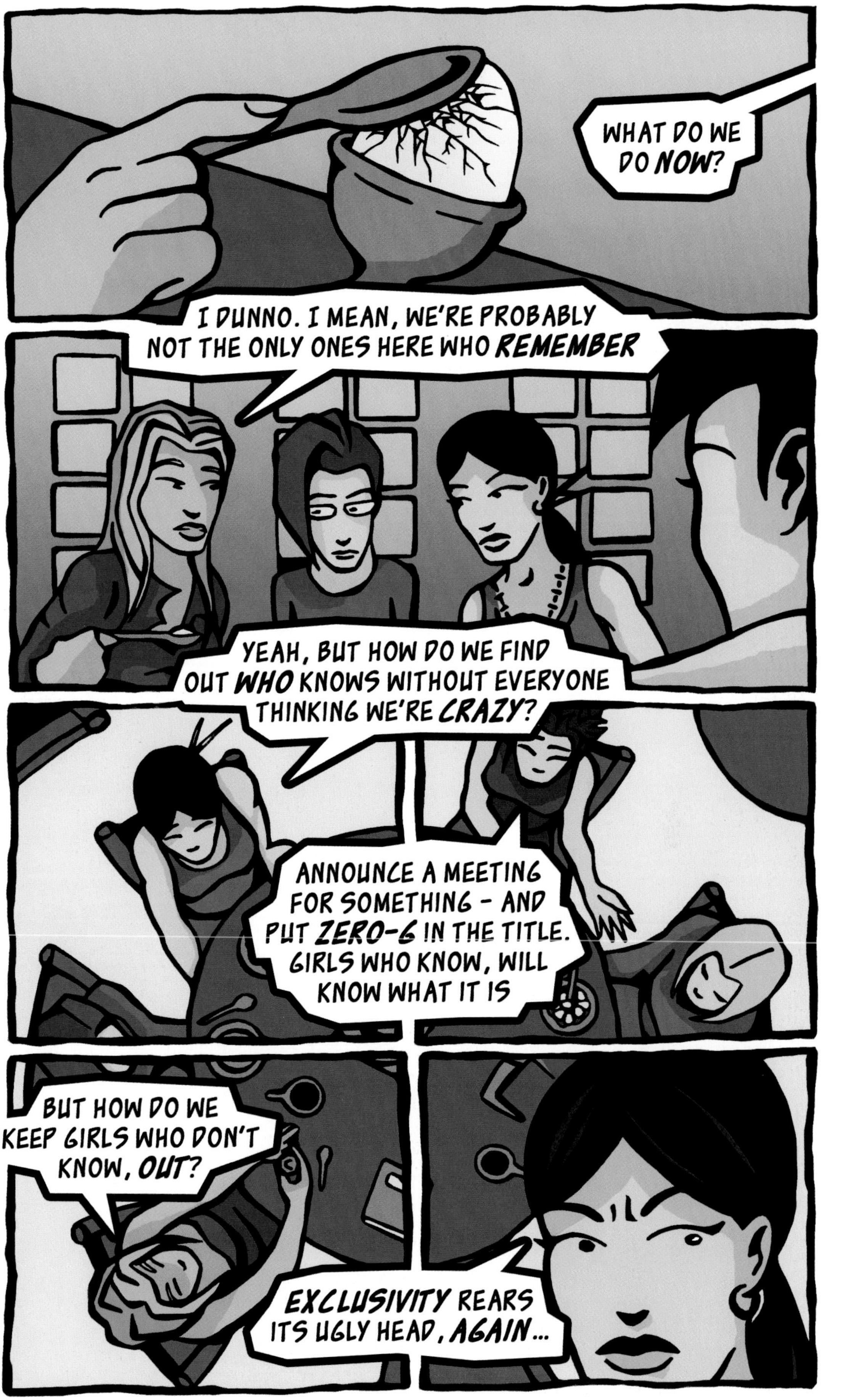
WHAT DO WE DO NOW?
I DUNNO. I MEAN, WE'RE PROBABLY NOT THE ONLY ONES HERE WHO REMEMBER
YEAH, BUT HOW DO WE FIND OUT WHO KNOWS WITHOUT EVERYONE THINKING WE'RE CRAZY?
ANNOUNCE A MEETING FOR SOMETHING - AND PUT ZERO-6 IN THE TITLE. GIRLS WHO KNOW, WILL KNOW WHAT IT IS
BUT HOW DO WE KEEP GIRLS WHO DON'T KNOW, OUT?
EXCLUSIVITY REARS ITS UGLY HEAD, AGAIN...

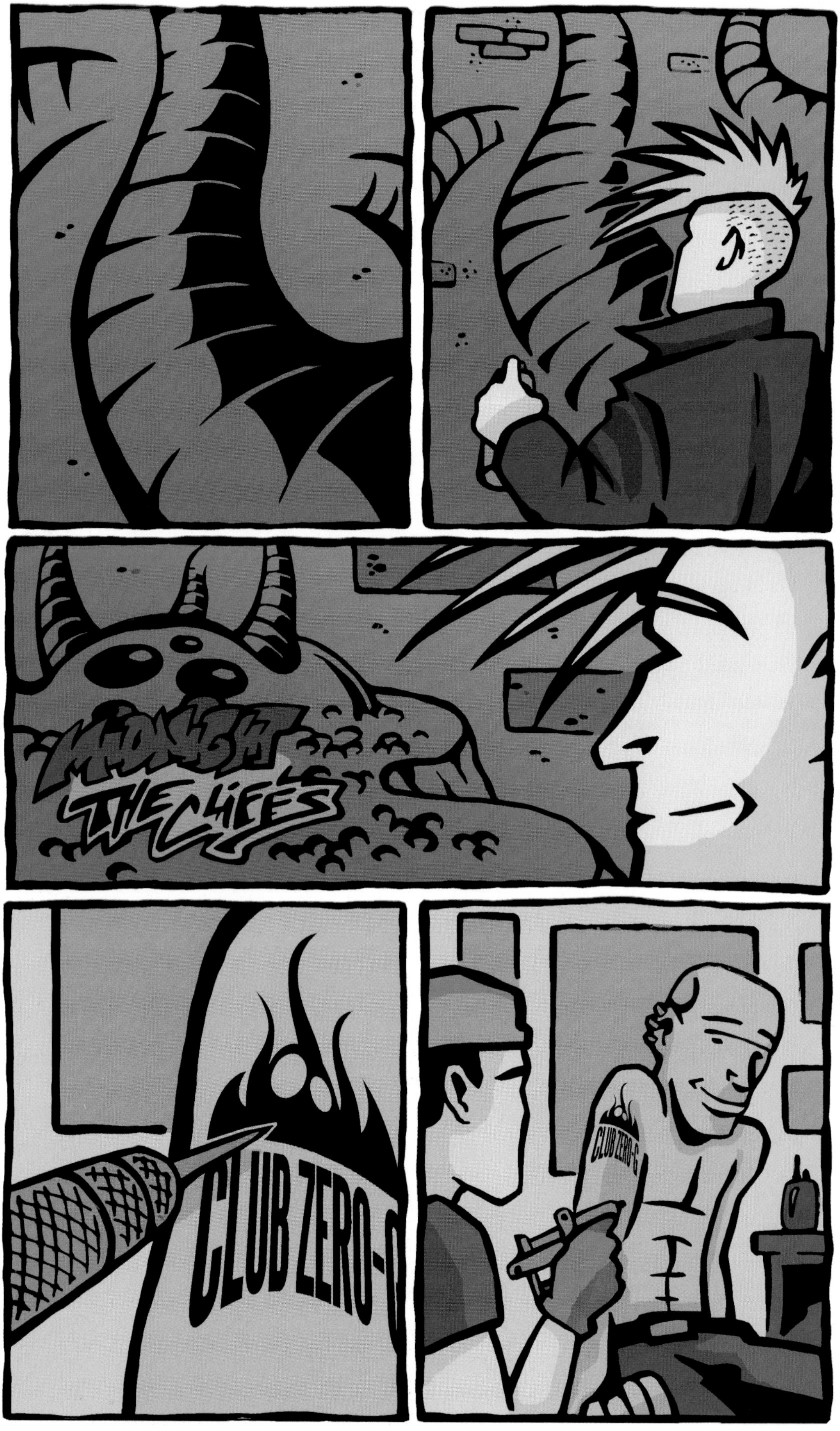
MIDNIGHT
THE CLIFFS
CLUB ZERO-G
CLUB ZERO-G

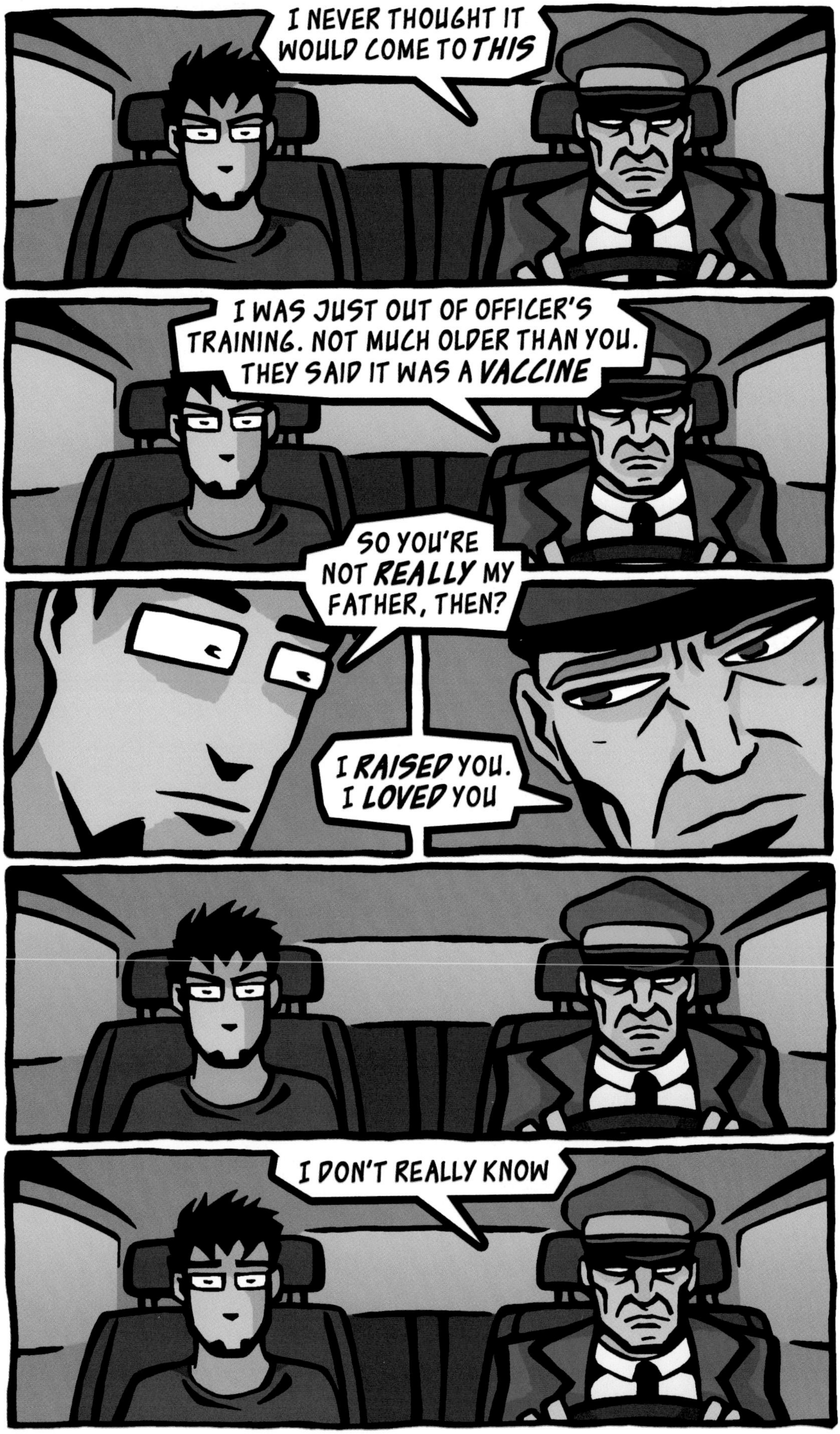
I NEVER THOUGHT IT WOULD COME TO THIS
I WAS JUST OUT OF OFFICER'S TRAINING. NOT MUCH OLDER THAN YOU. THEY SAID IT WAS A VACCINE
SO YOU'RE NOT REALLY MY FATHER, THEN?
I RAISED YOU. I LOVED YOU
I DON'T REALLY KNOW

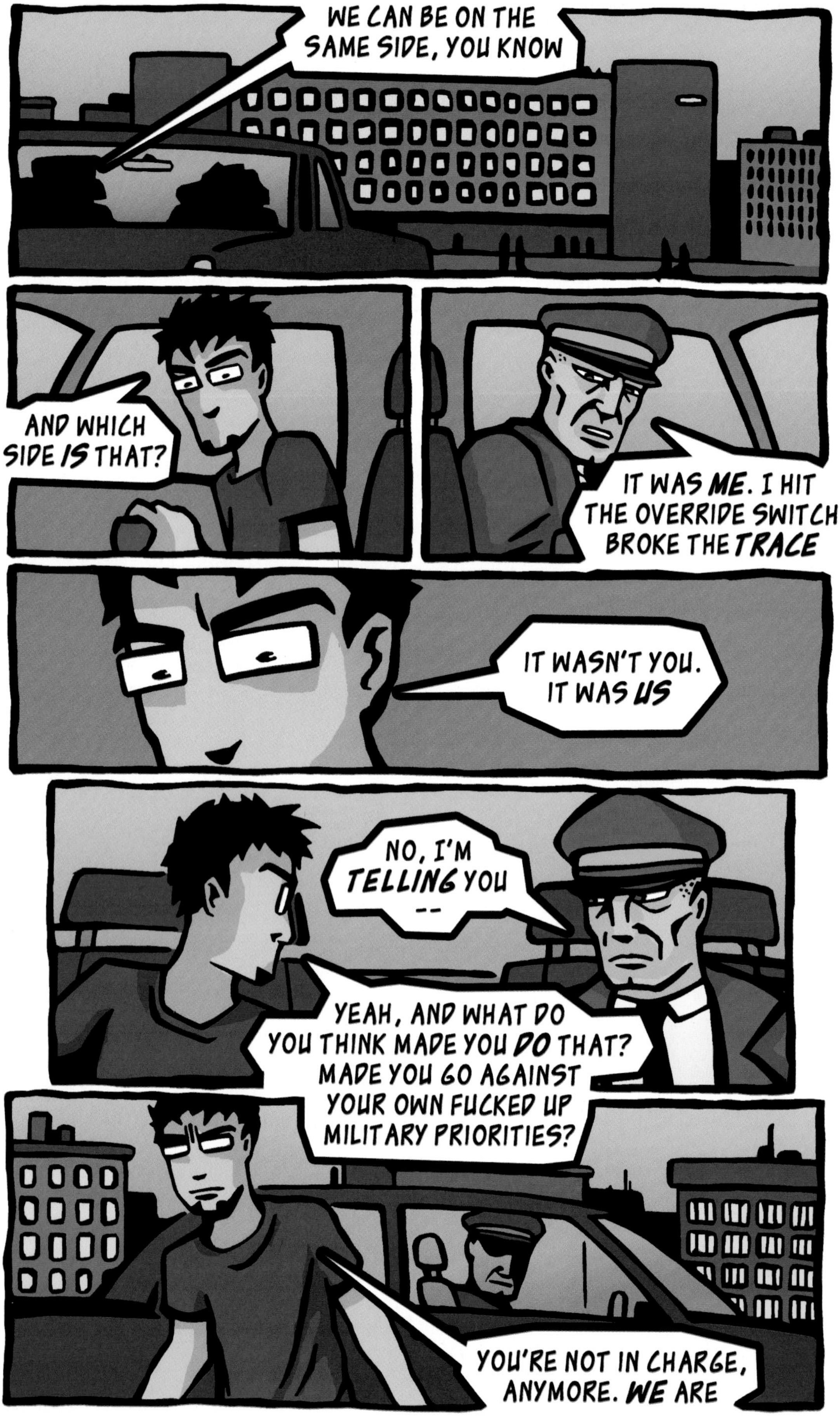
WE CAN BE ON THE SAME SIDE, YOU KNOW
AND WHICH SIDE *IS* THAT?
IT WAS *ME*. I HIT THE OVERRIDE SWITCH. BROKE THE *TRACE*
IT WASN'T YOU. IT WAS *US*
NO, I'M *TELLING* YOU --
YEAH, AND WHAT DO YOU THINK MADE YOU *DO* THAT? MADE YOU GO AGAINST YOUR OWN FUCKED UP MILITARY PRIORITIES?
YOU'RE NOT IN CHARGE, ANYMORE. *WE* ARE

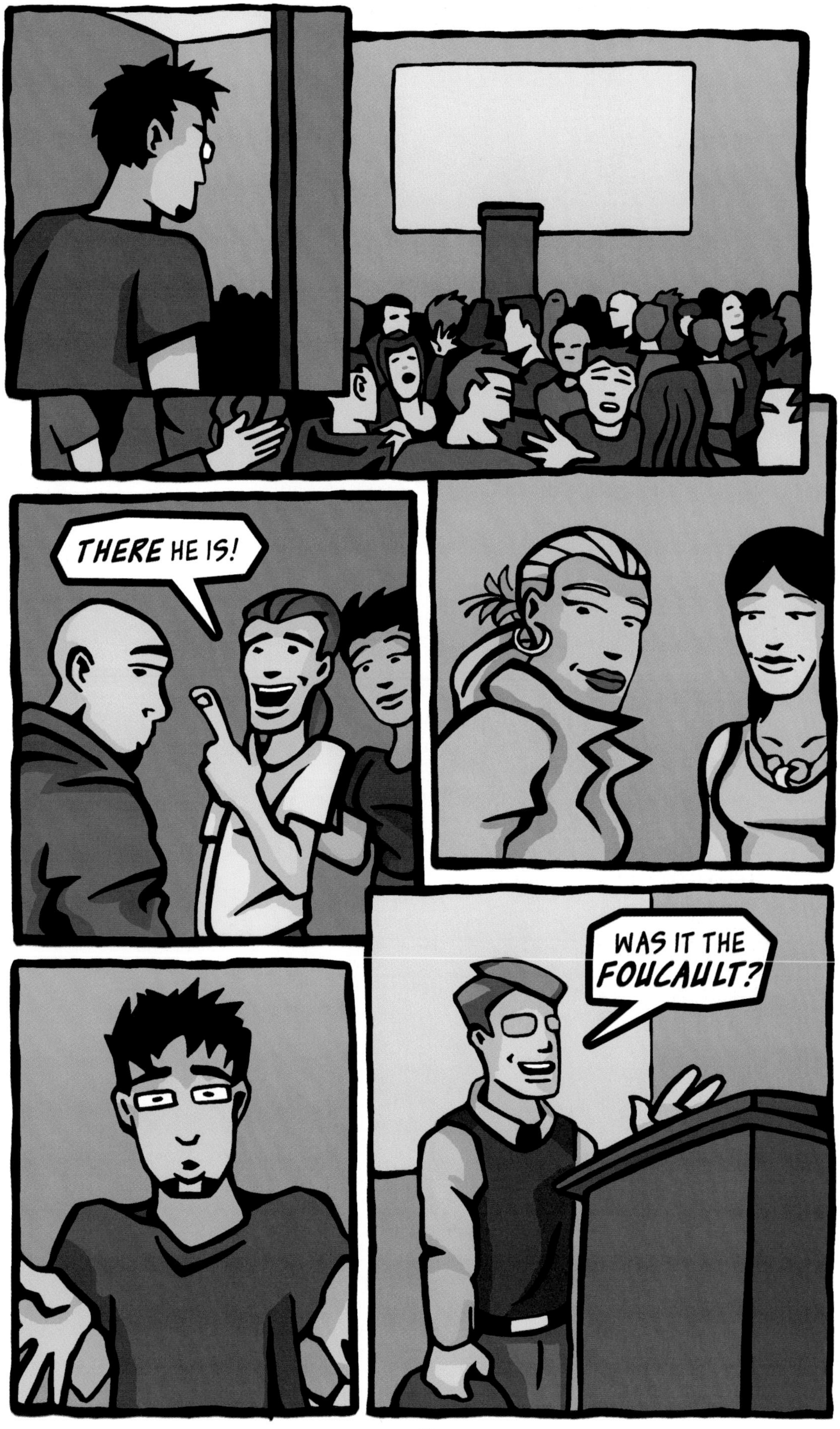
THERE HE IS!
WAS IT THE FOUCAULT?

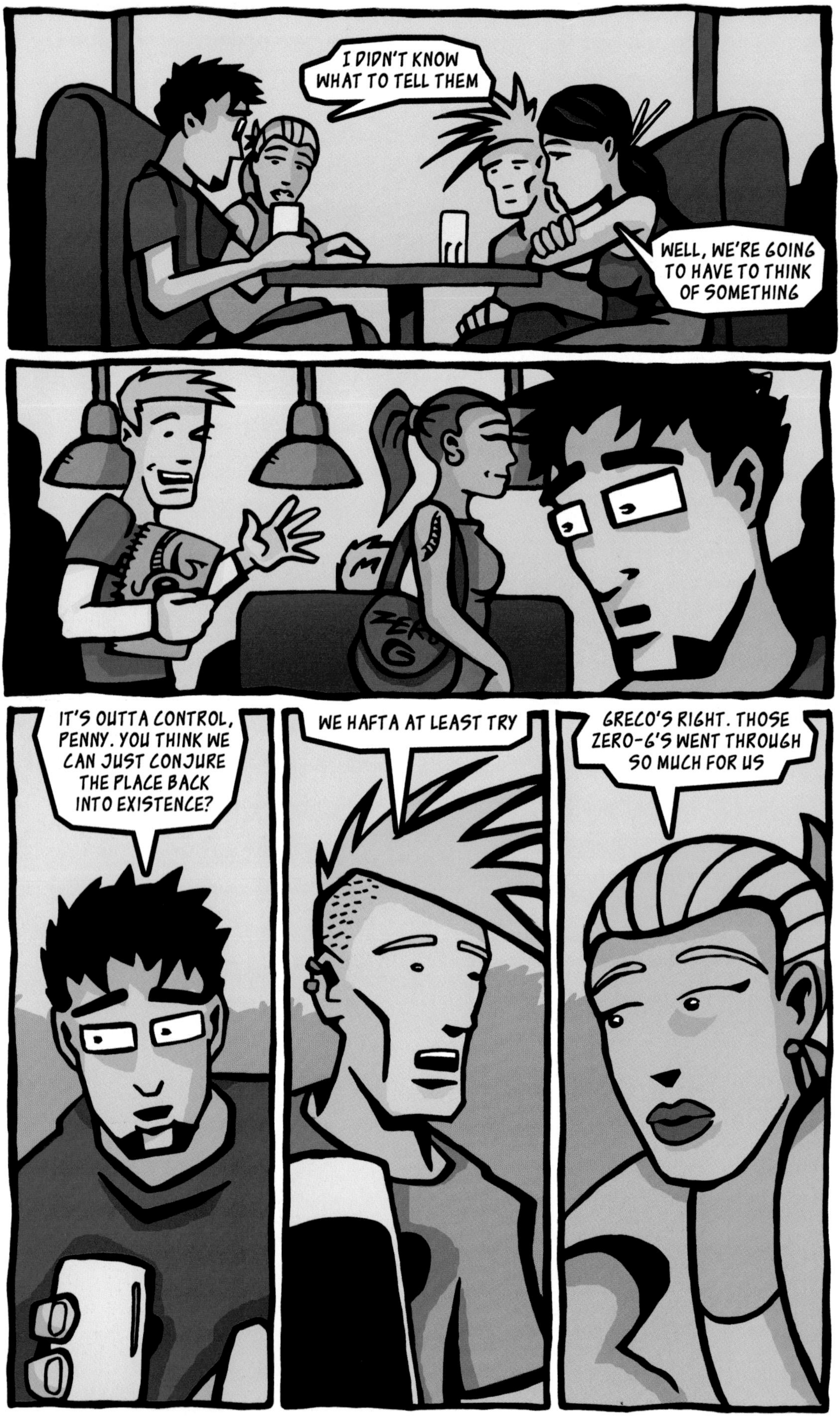
I DIDN'T KNOW WHAT TO TELL THEM
WELL, WE'RE GOING TO HAVE TO THINK OF SOMETHING
ZERO G
IT'S OUTTA CONTROL, PENNY. YOU THINK WE CAN JUST CONJURE THE PLACE BACK INTO EXISTENCE?
WE HAFTA AT LEAST TRY
GRECO'S RIGHT. THOSE ZERO-G'S WENT THROUGH SO MUCH FOR US

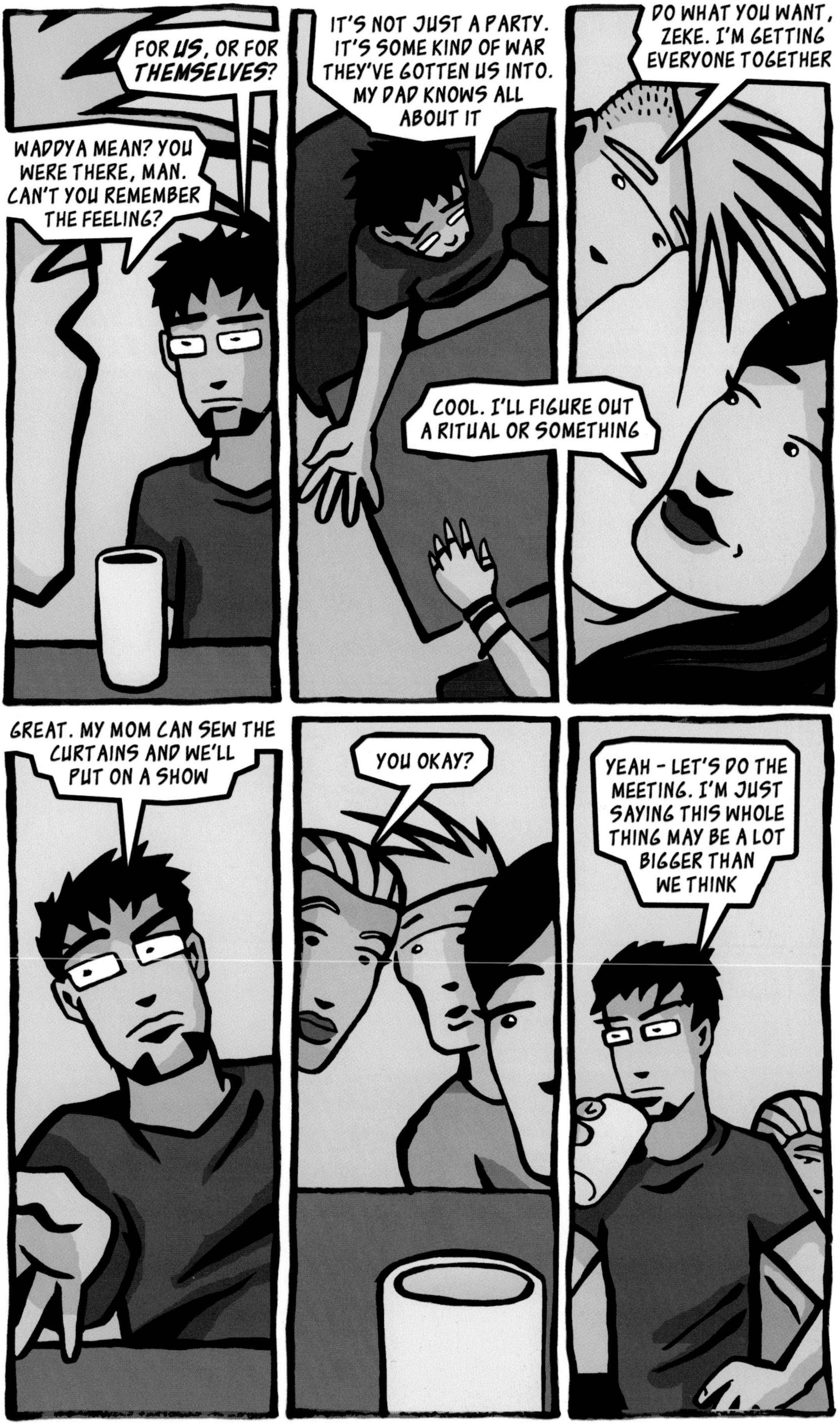
FOR *US*, OR FOR *THEMSELVES?*
WADDYA MEAN? YOU WERE THERE, MAN. CAN'T YOU REMEMBER THE FEELING?
IT'S NOT JUST A PARTY. IT'S SOME KIND OF WAR THEY'VE GOTTEN US INTO. MY DAD KNOWS ALL ABOUT IT
COOL. I'LL FIGURE OUT A RITUAL OR SOMETHING
DO WHAT YOU WANT, ZEKE. I'M GETTING EVERYONE TOGETHER
GREAT. MY MOM CAN SEW THE CURTAINS AND WE'LL PUT ON A SHOW
YOU OKAY?
YEAH - LET'S DO THE MEETING. I'M JUST SAYING THIS WHOLE THING MAY BE A LOT BIGGER THAN WE THINK

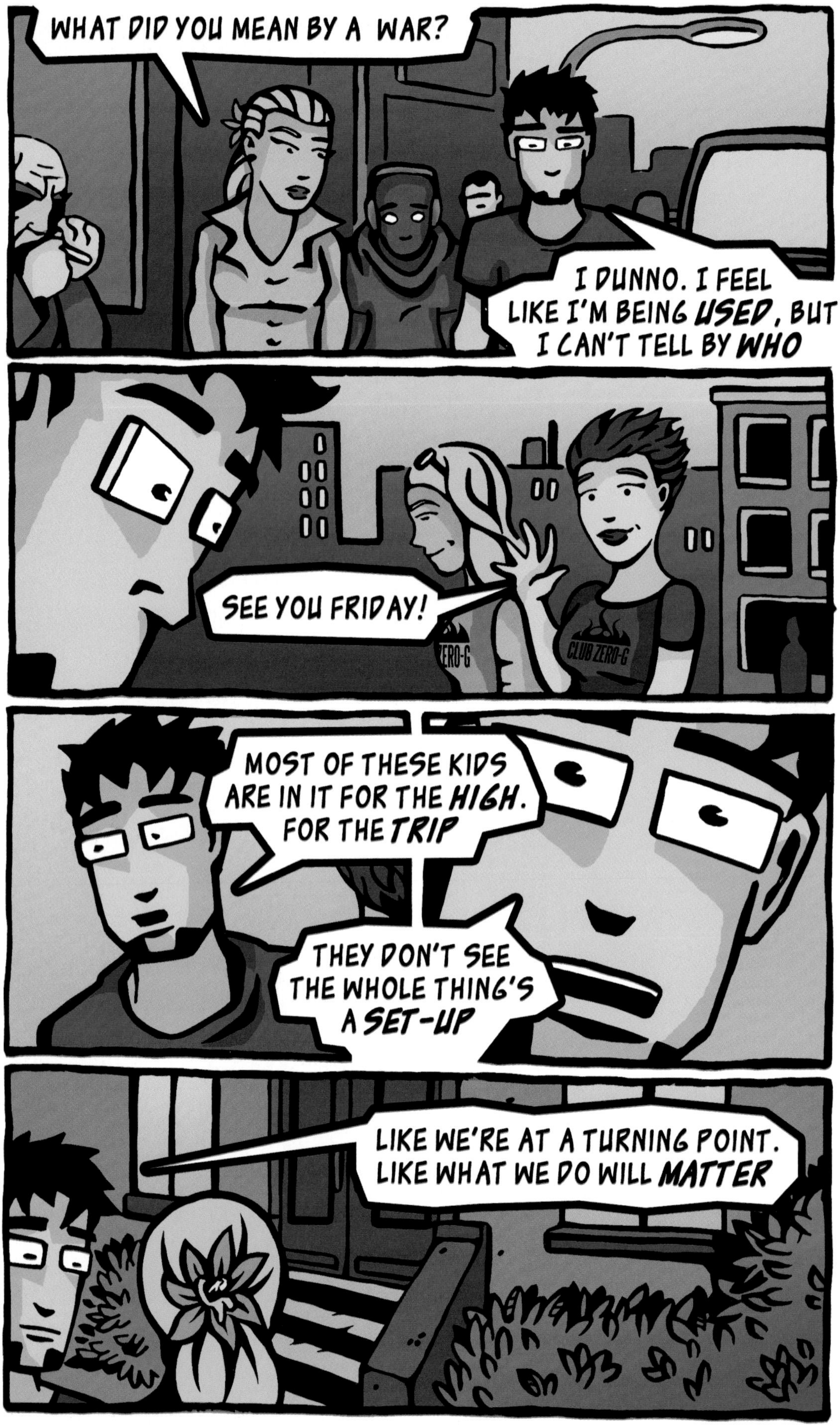
WHAT DID YOU MEAN BY A WAR?
I DUNNO. I FEEL LIKE I'M BEING USED, BUT I CAN'T TELL BY WHO
SEE YOU FRIDAY!
ZERO-G
CLUB ZERO-G
MOST OF THESE KIDS ARE IN IT FOR THE HIGH. FOR THE TRIP
THEY DON'T SEE THE WHOLE THING'S A SET-UP
LIKE WE'RE AT A TURNING POINT. LIKE WHAT WE DO WILL MATTER

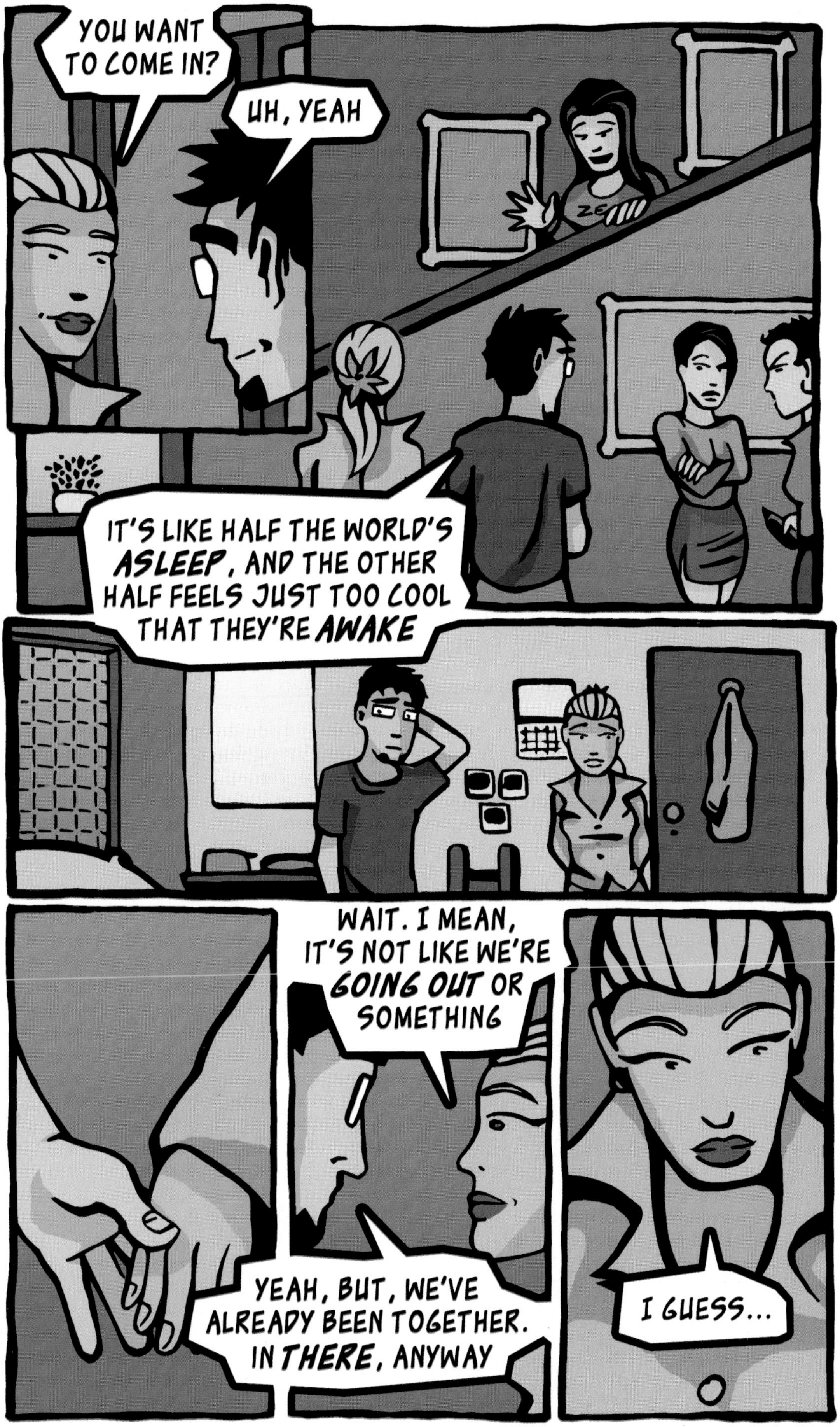
YOU WANT TO COME IN?
UH, YEAH
ZE
IT'S LIKE HALF THE WORLD'S ASLEEP, AND THE OTHER HALF FEELS JUST TOO COOL THAT THEY'RE AWAKE
WAIT. I MEAN, IT'S NOT LIKE WE'RE GOING OUT OR SOMETHING
YEAH, BUT, WE'VE ALREADY BEEN TOGETHER. IN THERE, ANYWAY
I GUESS...

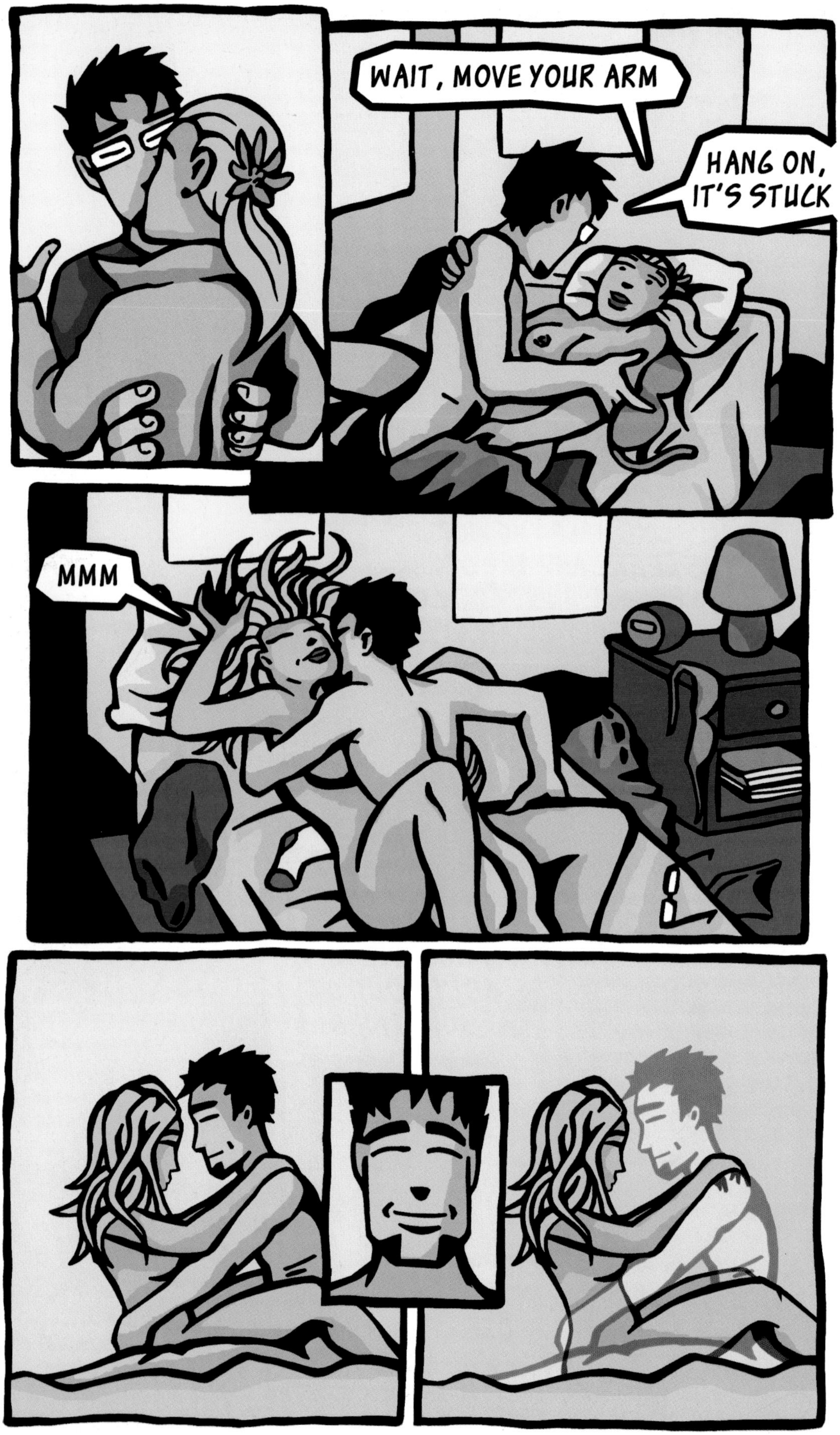
WAIT, MOVE YOUR ARM
HANG ON, IT'S STUCK
MMM

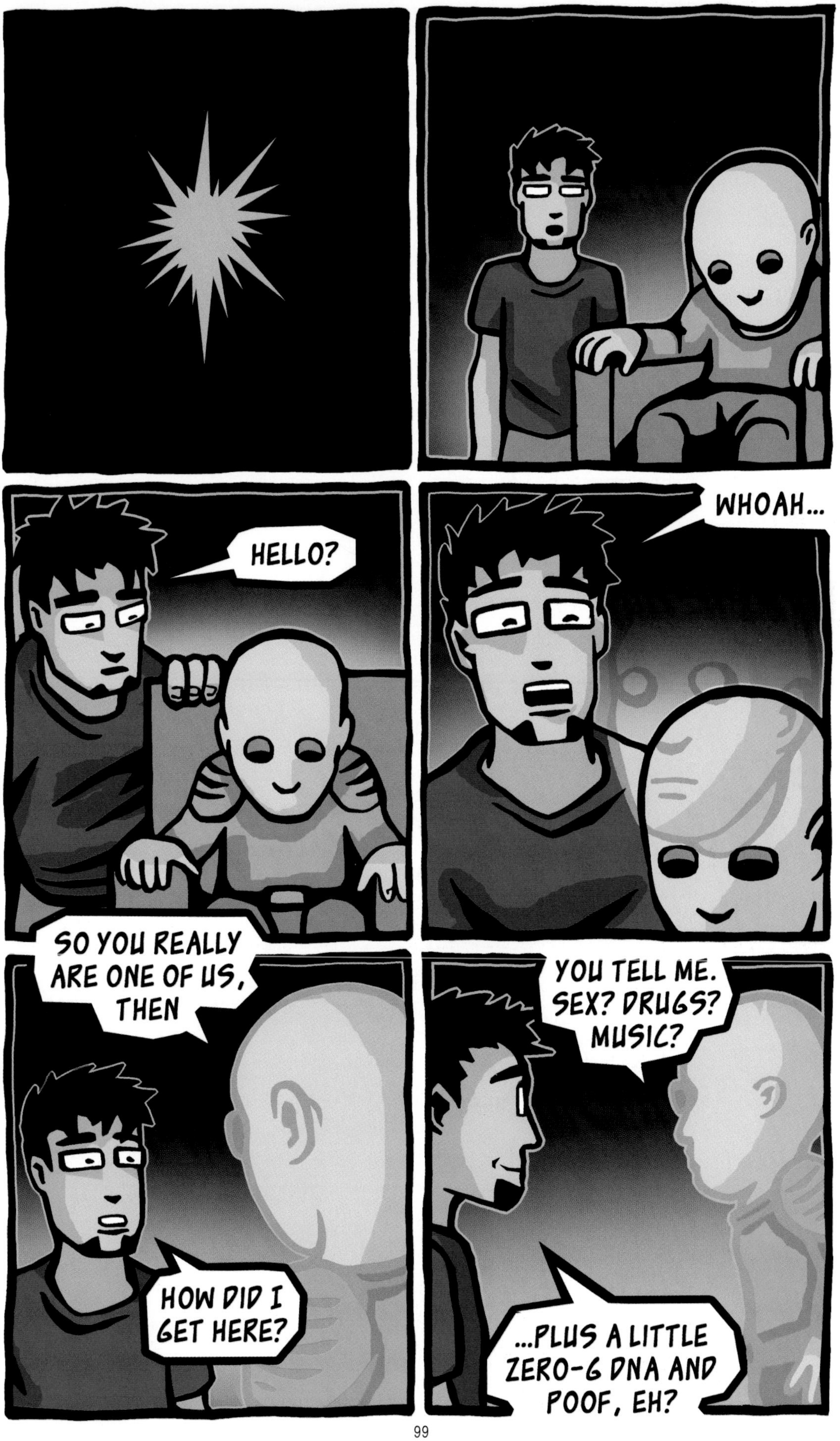
HELLO?
WHOAH...
SO YOU REALLY ARE ONE OF US, THEN
HOW DID I GET HERE?
YOU TELL ME. SEX? DRUGS? MUSIC?
...PLUS A LITTLE ZERO-G DNA AND POOF, EH?

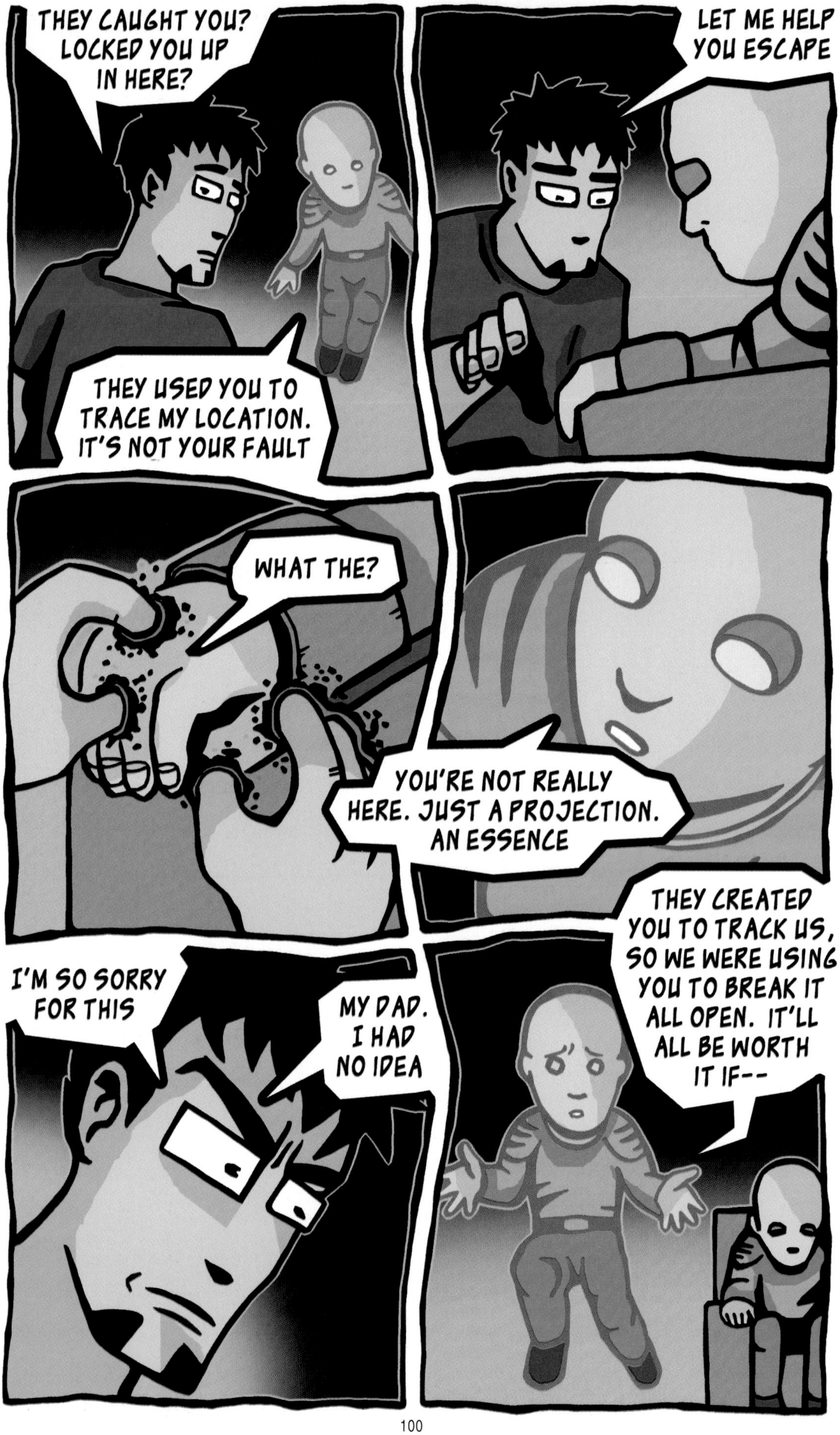
THEY CAUGHT YOU? LOCKED YOU UP IN HERE?
THEY USED YOU TO TRACE MY LOCATION. IT'S NOT YOUR FAULT
LET ME HELP YOU ESCAPE
WHAT THE?
YOU'RE NOT REALLY HERE. JUST A PROJECTION. AN ESSENCE
I'M SO SORRY FOR THIS
MY DAD. I HAD NO IDEA
THEY CREATED YOU TO TRACK US, SO WE WERE USING YOU TO BREAK IT ALL OPEN. IT'LL ALL BE WORTH IT IF--

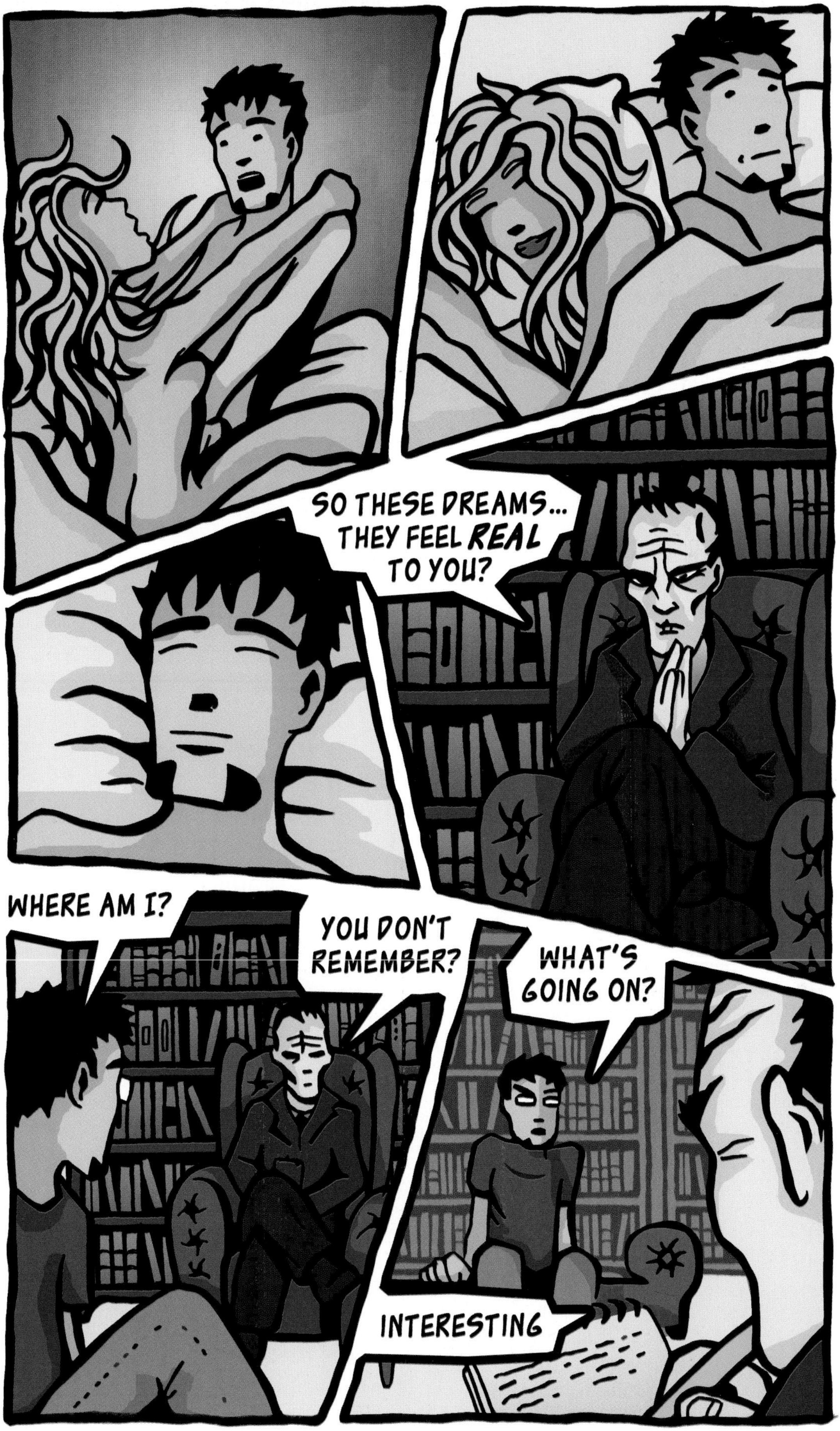
SO THESE DREAMS...
THEY FEEL REAL TO YOU?
WHERE AM I?
YOU DON'T REMEMBER?
WHAT'S GOING ON?
INTERESTING

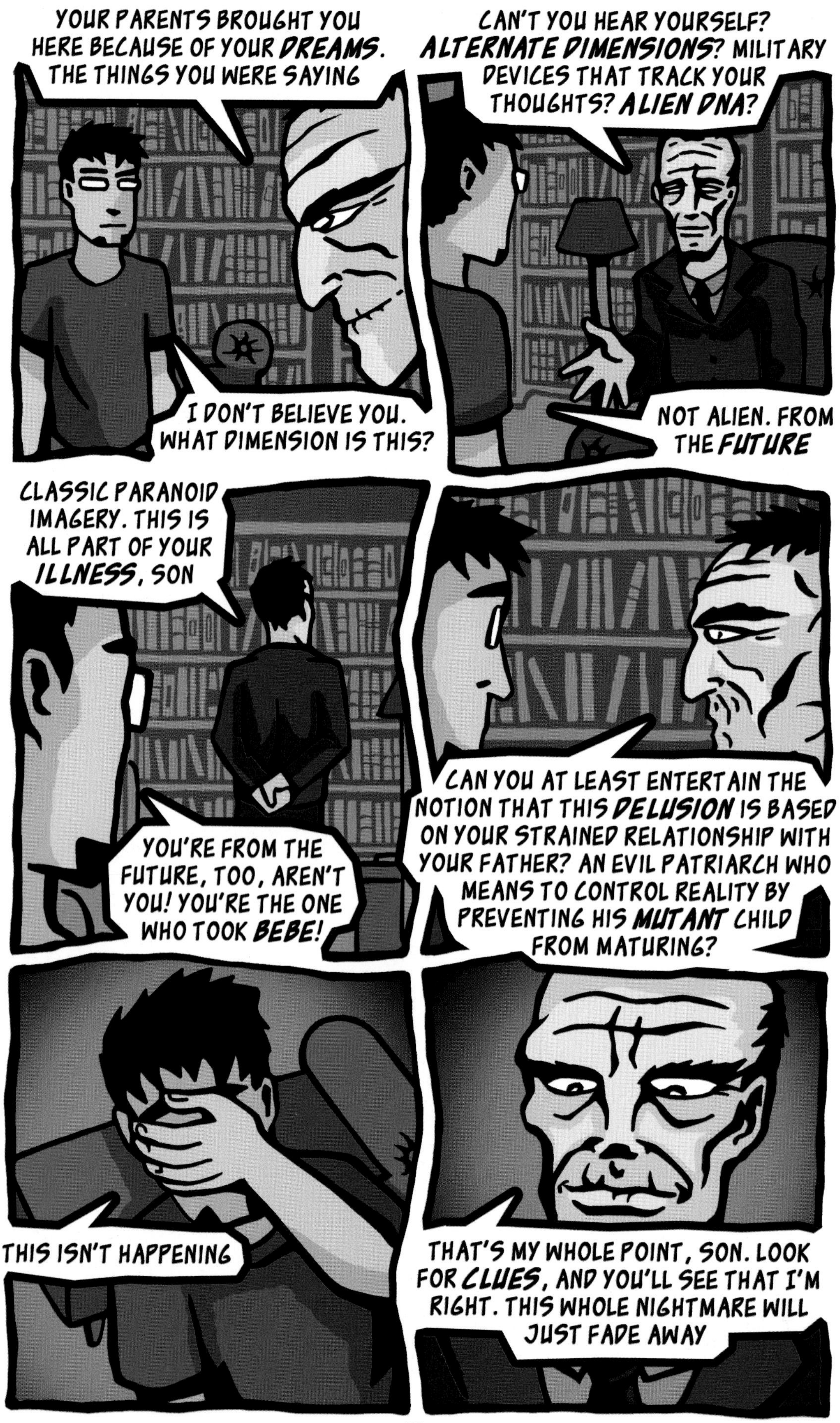
YOUR PARENTS BROUGHT YOU HERE BECAUSE OF YOUR DREAMS. THE THINGS YOU WERE SAYING
I DON'T BELIEVE YOU. WHAT DIMENSION IS THIS?
CAN'T YOU HEAR YOURSELF? ALTERNATE DIMENSIONS? MILITARY DEVICES THAT TRACK YOUR THOUGHTS? ALIEN DNA?
NOT ALIEN. FROM THE FUTURE
CLASSIC PARANOID IMAGERY. THIS IS ALL PART OF YOUR ILLNESS, SON
YOU'RE FROM THE FUTURE, TOO, AREN'T YOU! YOU'RE THE ONE WHO TOOK BEBE!
CAN YOU AT LEAST ENTERTAIN THE NOTION THAT THIS DELUSION IS BASED ON YOUR STRAINED RELATIONSHIP WITH YOUR FATHER? AN EVIL PATRIARCH WHO MEANS TO CONTROL REALITY BY PREVENTING HIS MUTANT CHILD FROM MATURING?
THIS ISN'T HAPPENING
THAT'S MY WHOLE POINT, SON. LOOK FOR CLUES, AND YOU'LL SEE THAT I'M RIGHT. THIS WHOLE NIGHTMARE WILL JUST FADE AWAY

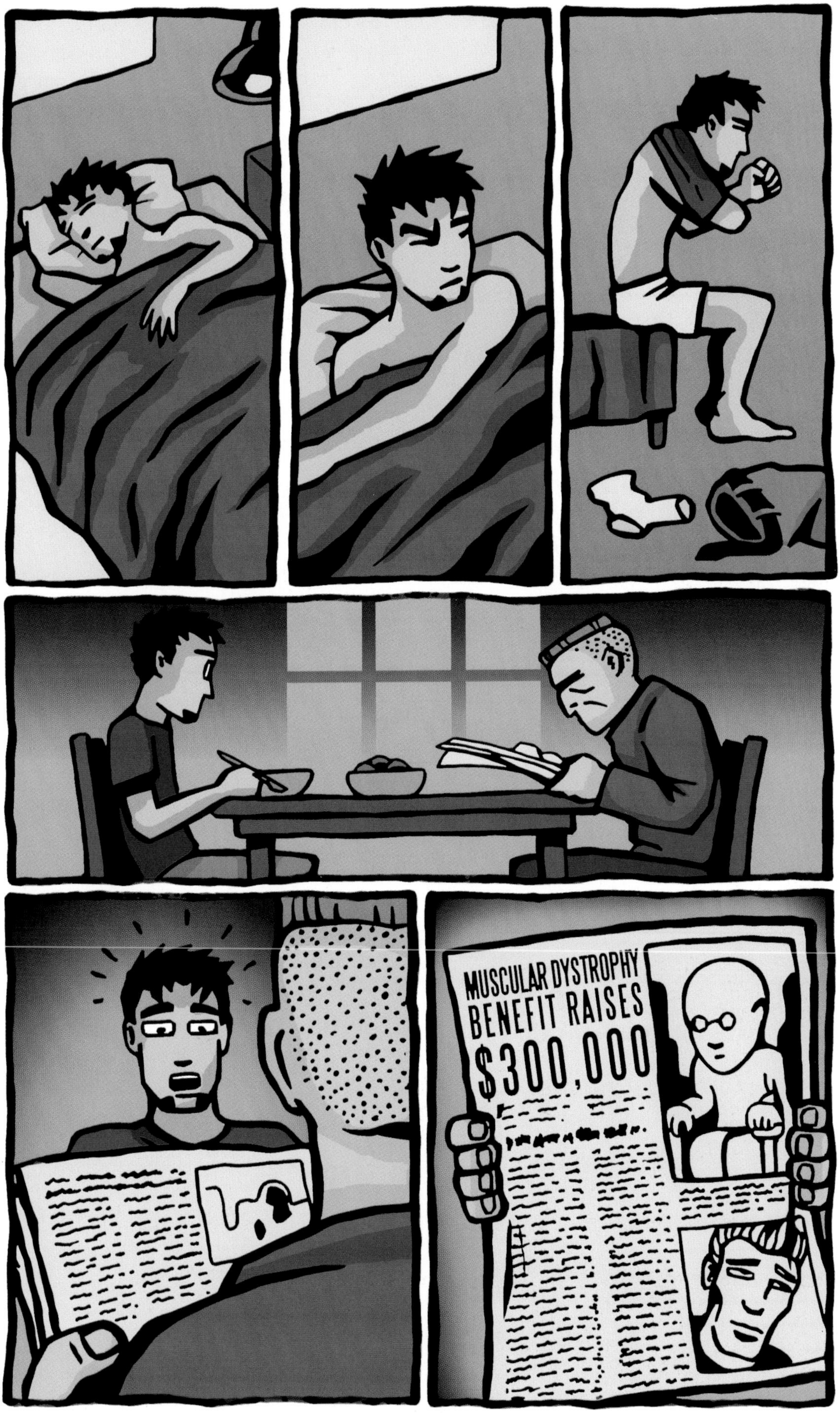
MUSCULAR DYSTROPHY
BENEFIT RAISES
$300,000

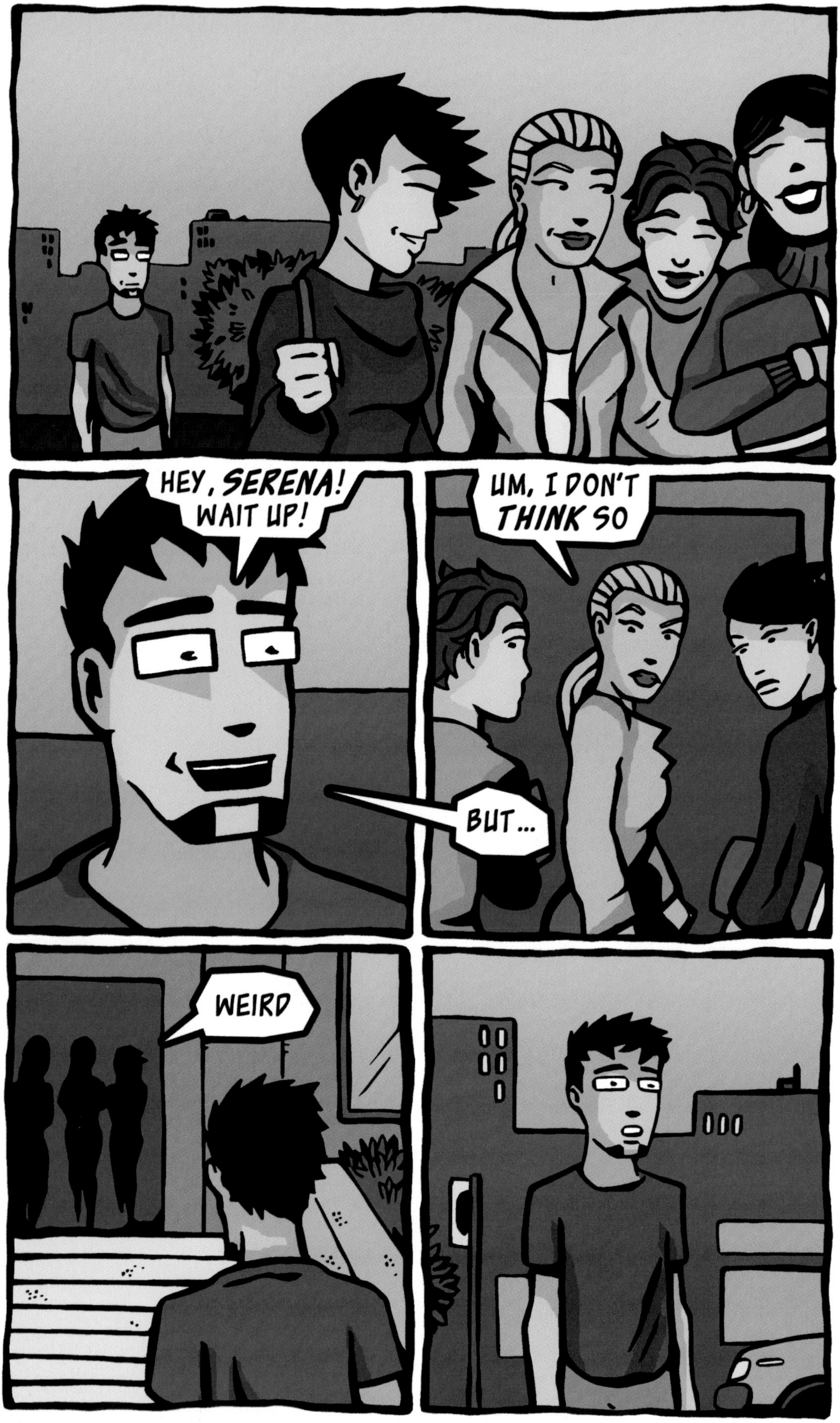
HEY, SERENA! WAIT UP!
UM, I DON'T THINK SO
BUT...
WEIRD

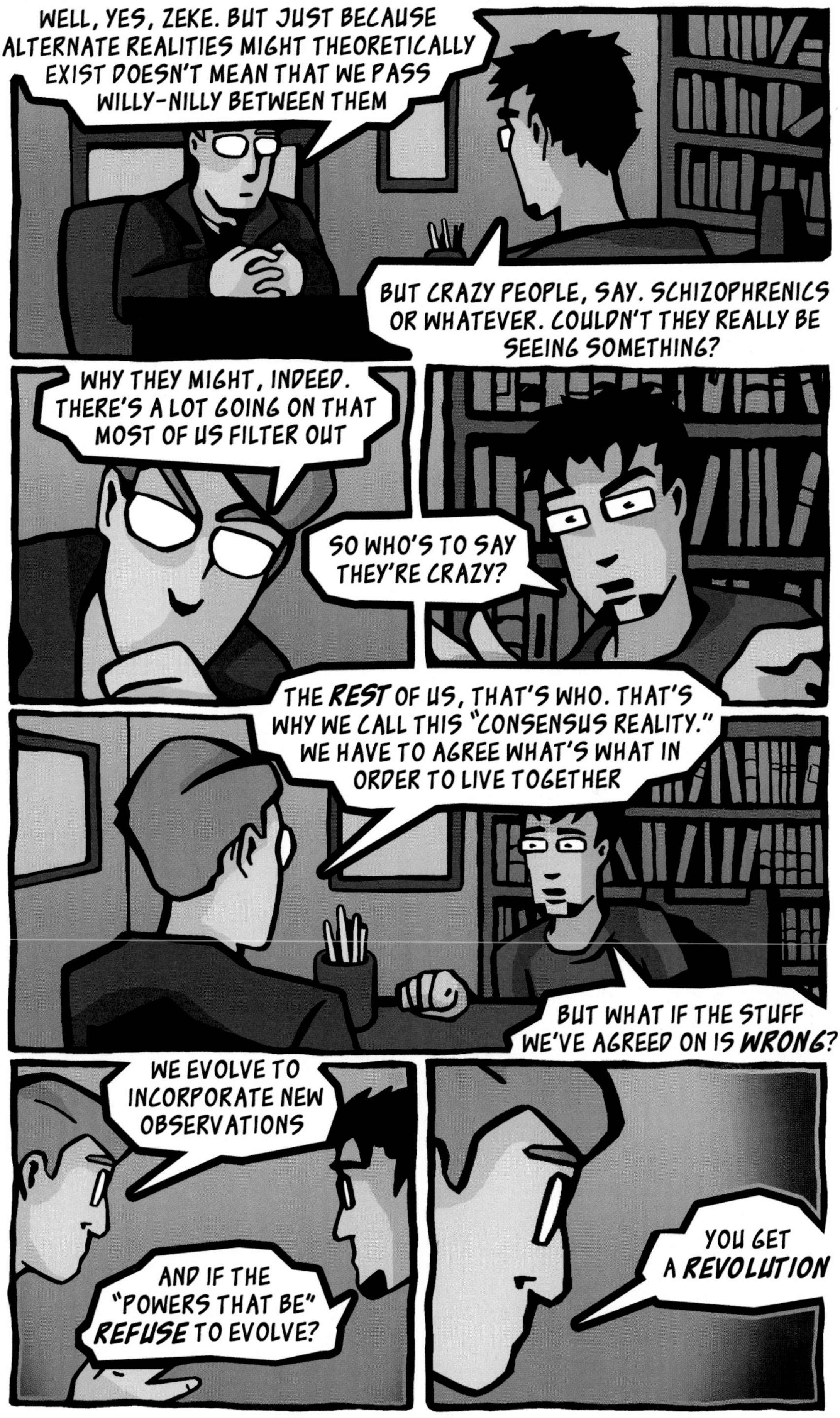
WELL, YES, ZEKE. BUT JUST BECAUSE ALTERNATE REALITIES MIGHT THEORETICALLY EXIST DOESN'T MEAN THAT WE PASS WILLY-NILLY BETWEEN THEM
BUT CRAZY PEOPLE, SAY. SCHIZOPHRENICS OR WHATEVER. COULDN'T THEY REALLY BE SEEING SOMETHING?
WHY THEY MIGHT, INDEED. THERE'S A LOT GOING ON THAT MOST OF US FILTER OUT
SO WHO'S TO SAY THEY'RE CRAZY?
THE ***REST*** OF US, THAT'S WHO. THAT'S WHY WE CALL THIS "CONSENSUS REALITY." WE HAVE TO AGREE WHAT'S WHAT IN ORDER TO LIVE TOGETHER
BUT WHAT IF THE STUFF WE'VE AGREED ON IS ***WRONG***?
WE EVOLVE TO INCORPORATE NEW OBSERVATIONS
AND IF THE "POWERS THAT BE" ***REFUSE*** TO EVOLVE?
YOU GET A ***REVOLUTION***

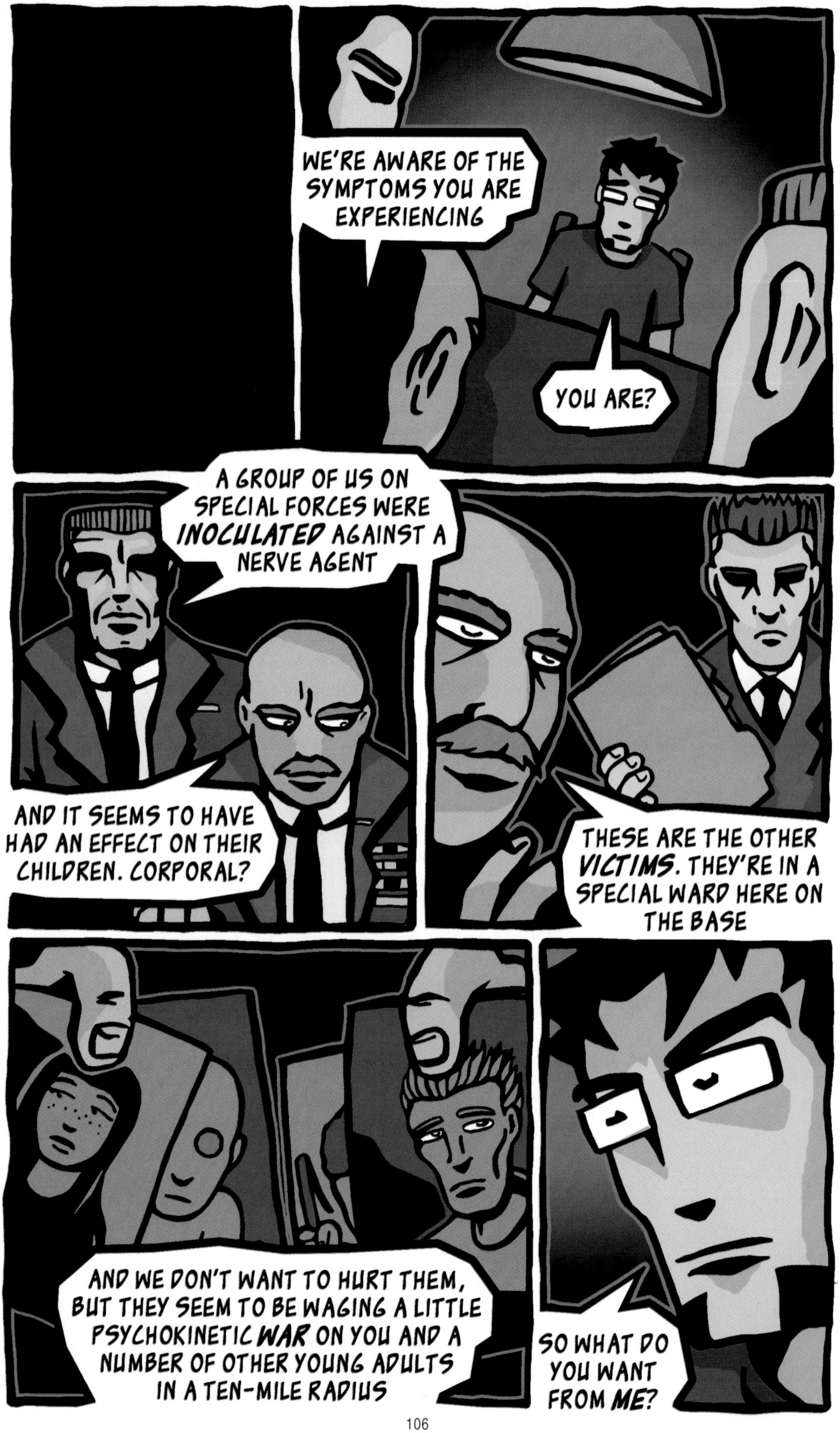
WE'RE AWARE OF THE SYMPTOMS YOU ARE EXPERIENCING
YOU ARE?
A GROUP OF US ON SPECIAL FORCES WERE INOCULATED AGAINST A NERVE AGENT
AND IT SEEMS TO HAVE HAD AN EFFECT ON THEIR CHILDREN. CORPORAL?
THESE ARE THE OTHER VICTIMS. THEY'RE IN A SPECIAL WARD HERE ON THE BASE
AND WE DON'T WANT TO HURT THEM, BUT THEY SEEM TO BE WAGING A LITTLE PSYCHOKINETIC WAR ON YOU AND A NUMBER OF OTHER YOUNG ADULTS IN A TEN-MILE RADIUS
SO WHAT DO YOU WANT FROM ME?

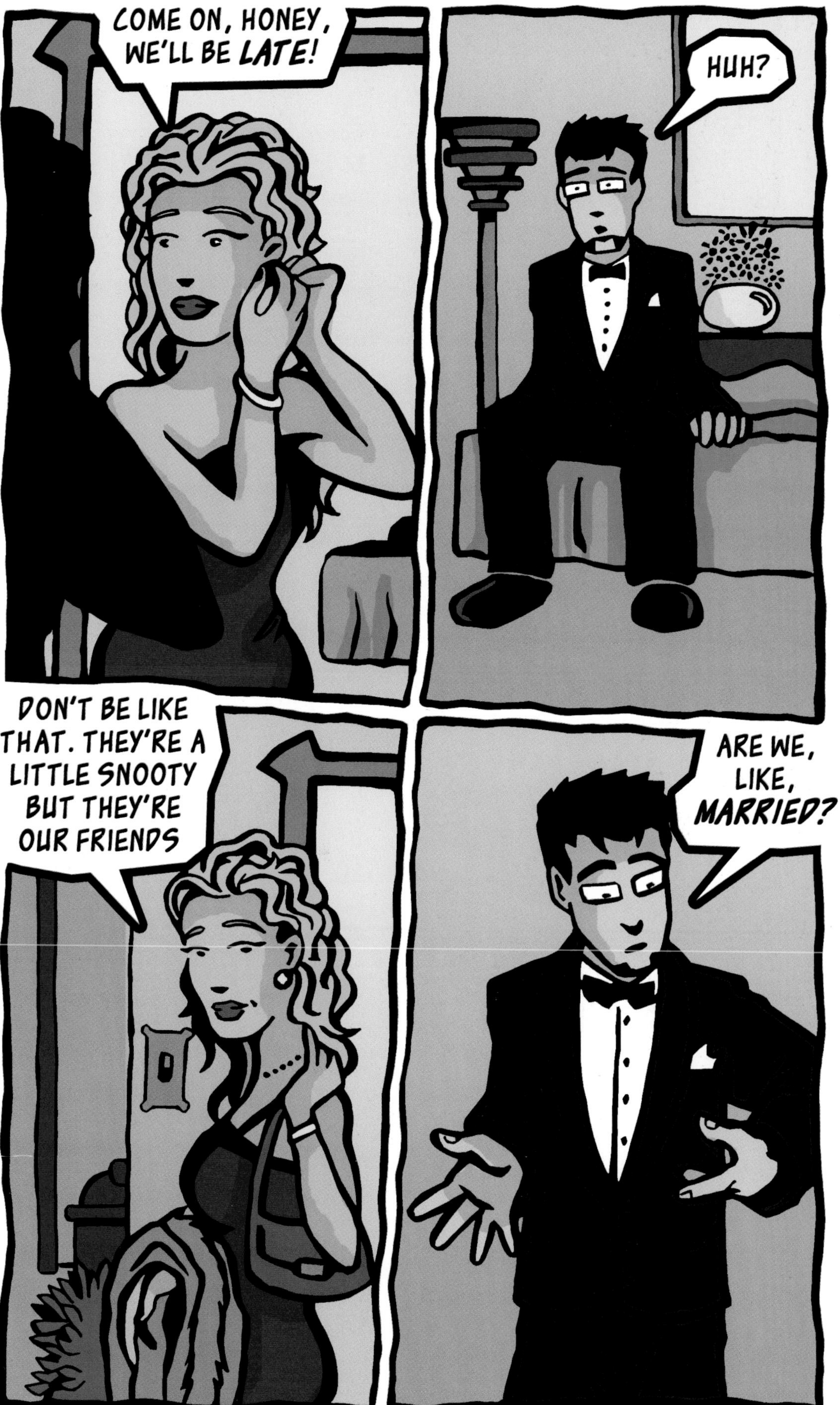
COME ON, HONEY, WE'LL BE LATE!
HUH?
DON'T BE LIKE THAT. THEY'RE A LITTLE SNOOTY BUT THEY'RE OUR FRIENDS
ARE WE, LIKE, MARRIED?

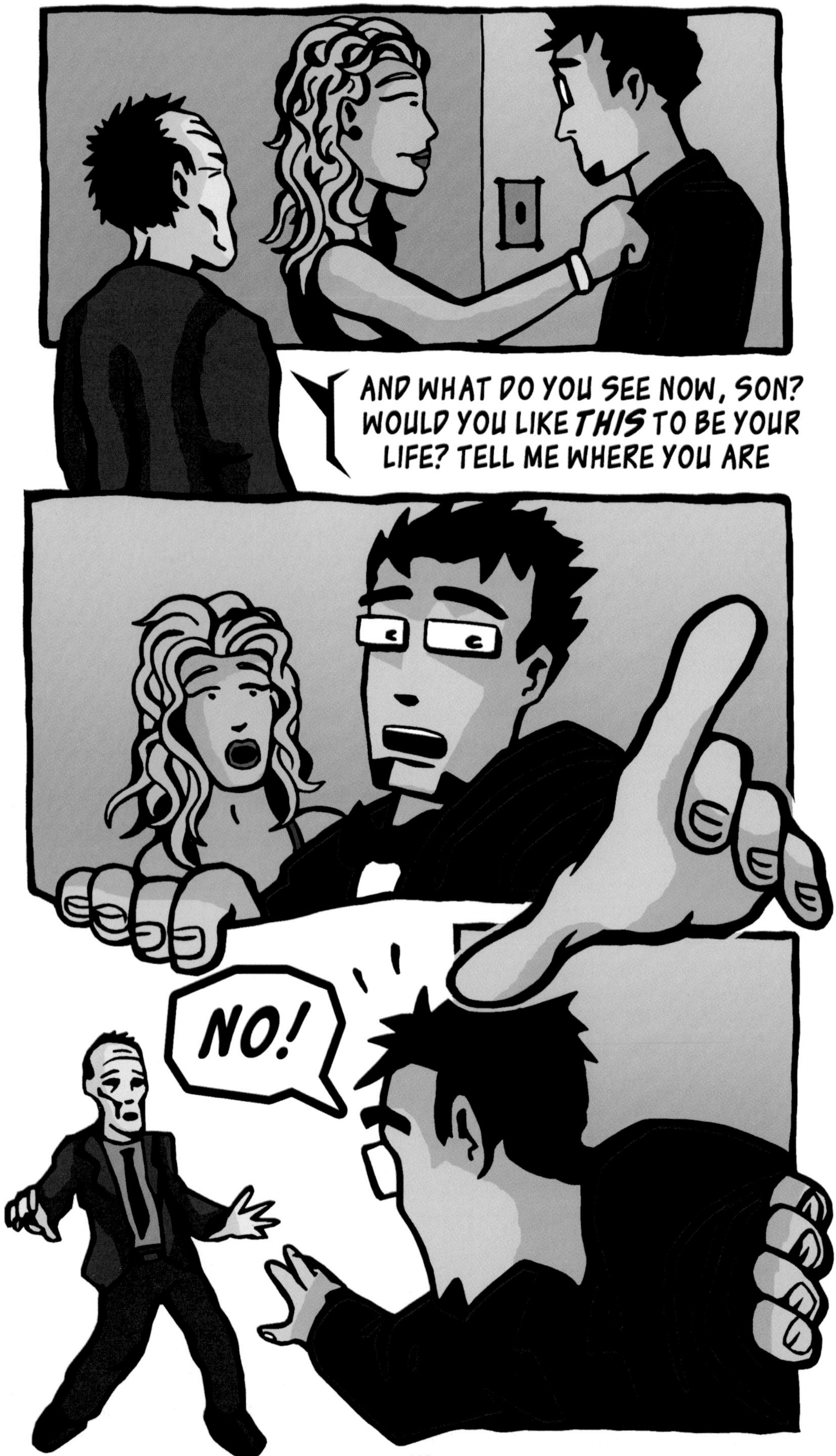
AND WHAT DO YOU SEE NOW, SON? WOULD YOU LIKE *THIS* TO BE YOUR LIFE? TELL ME WHERE YOU ARE
NO!

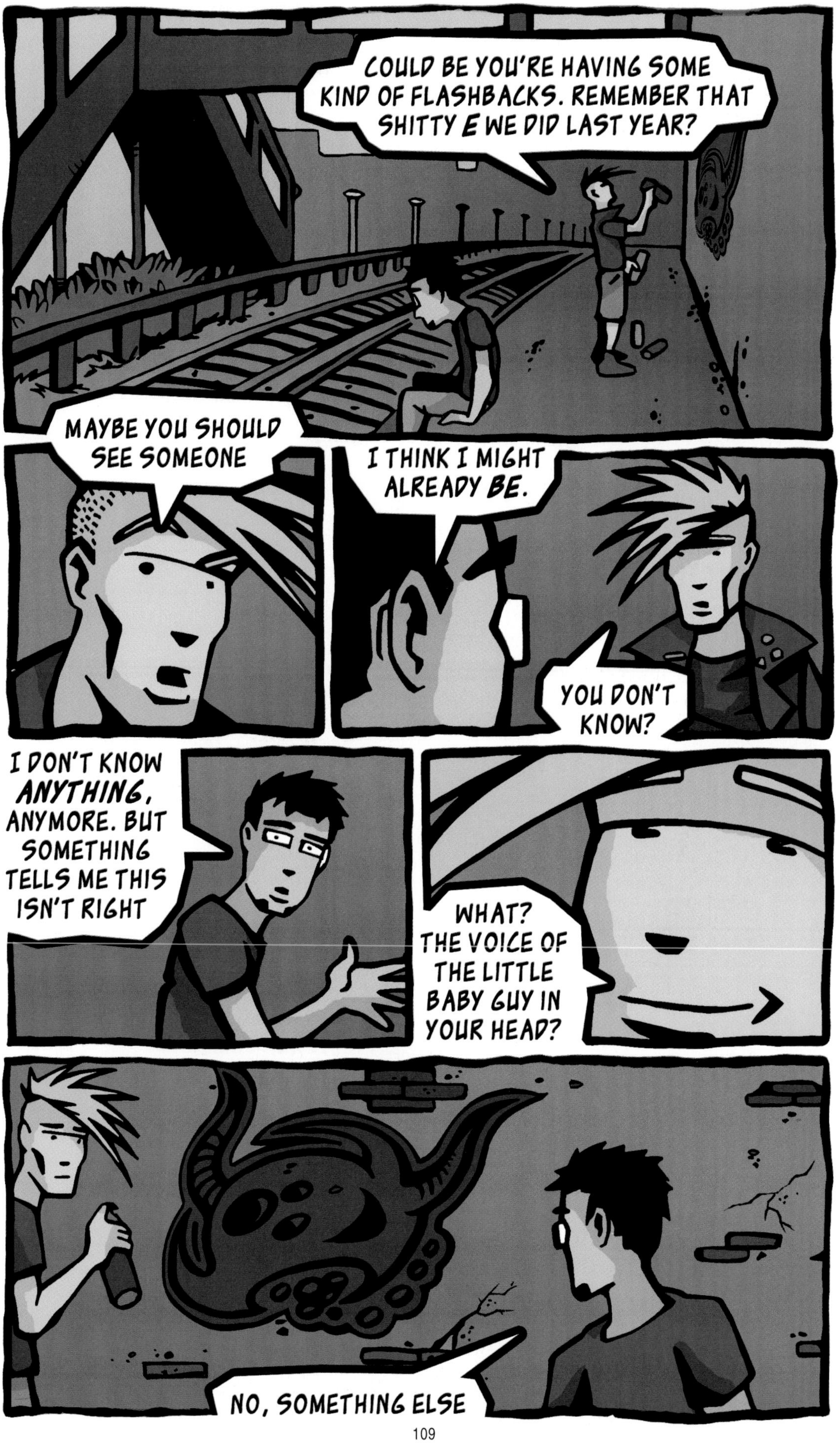
COULD BE YOU'RE HAVING SOME KIND OF FLASHBACKS. REMEMBER THAT SHITTY *E* WE DID LAST YEAR?
MAYBE YOU SHOULD SEE SOMEONE
I THINK I MIGHT ALREADY *BE*.
YOU DON'T KNOW?
I DON'T KNOW *ANYTHING*, ANYMORE. BUT SOMETHING TELLS ME THIS ISN'T RIGHT
WHAT? THE VOICE OF THE LITTLE BABY GUY IN YOUR HEAD?
NO, SOMETHING ELSE

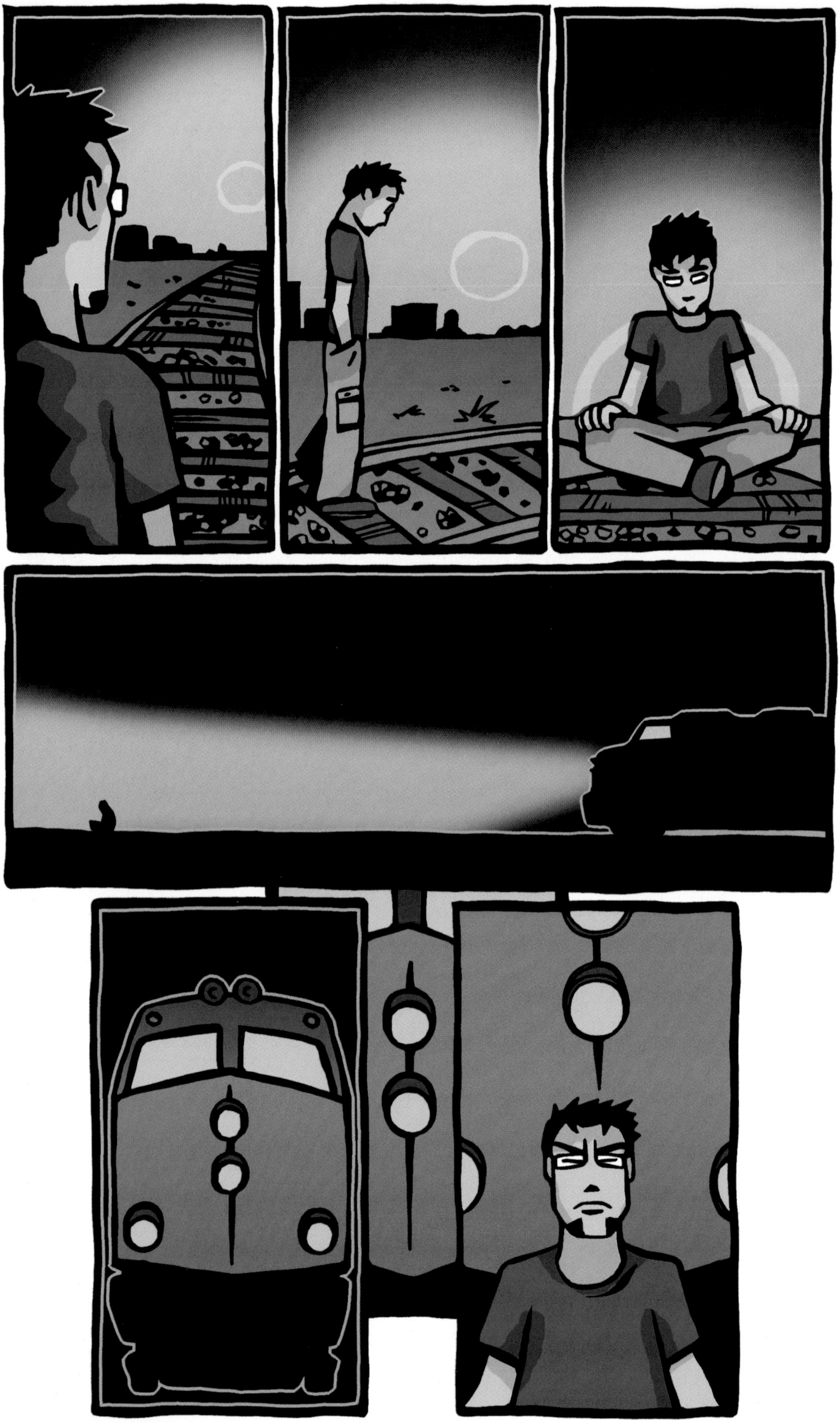

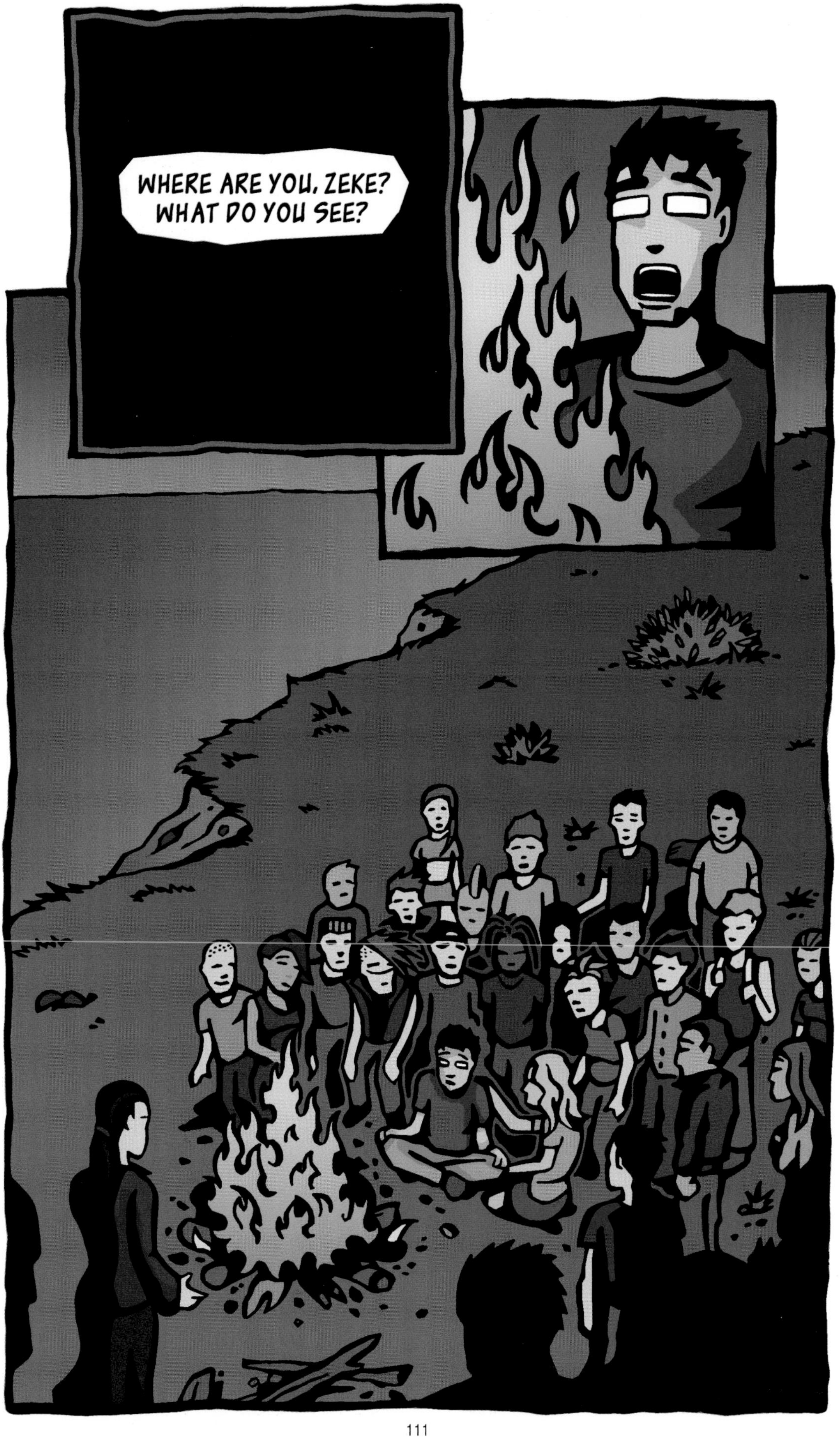
WHERE ARE YOU, ZEKE? WHAT DO YOU SEE?

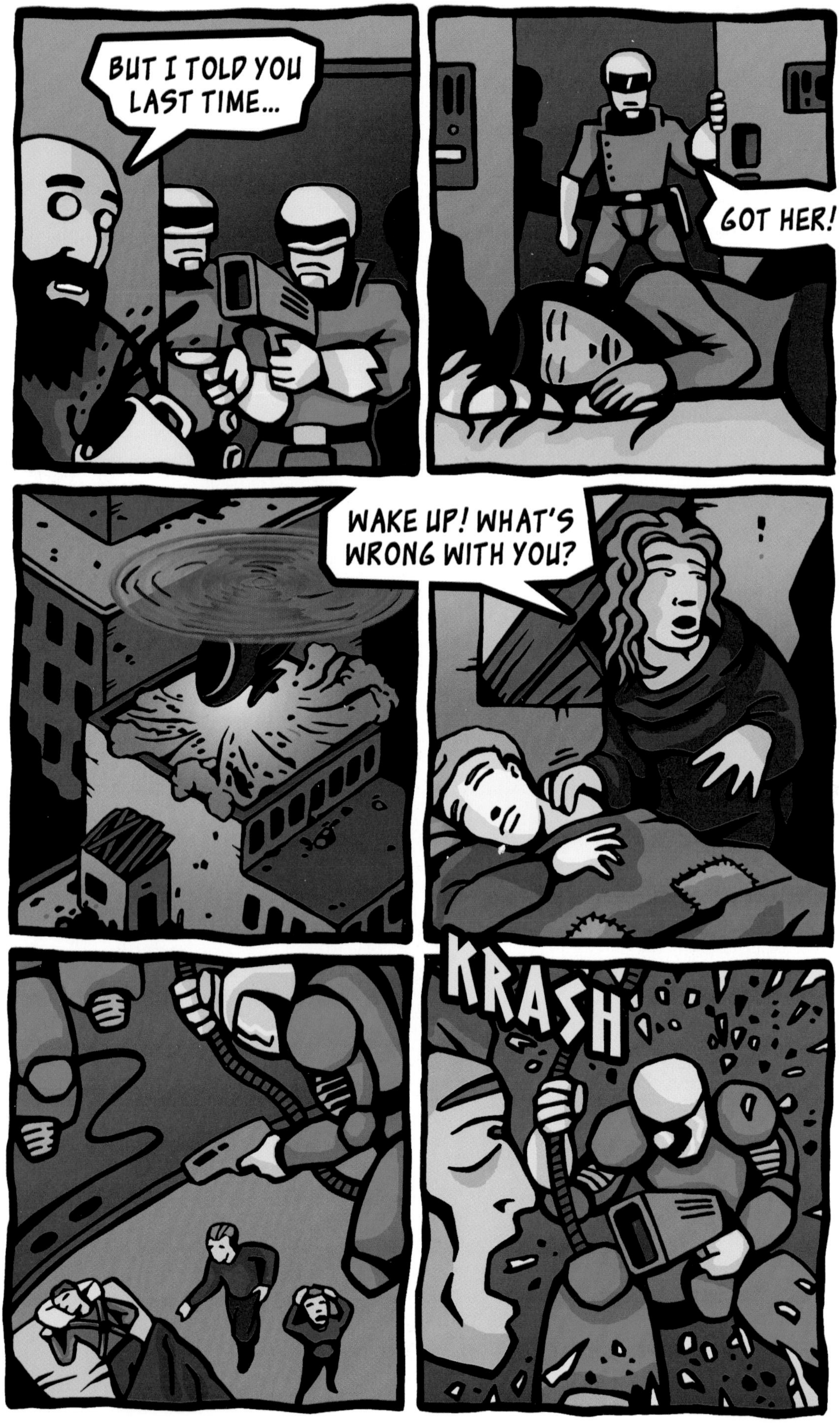
BUT I TOLD YOU LAST TIME...
GOT HER!
WAKE UP! WHAT'S WRONG WITH YOU?
KRASH

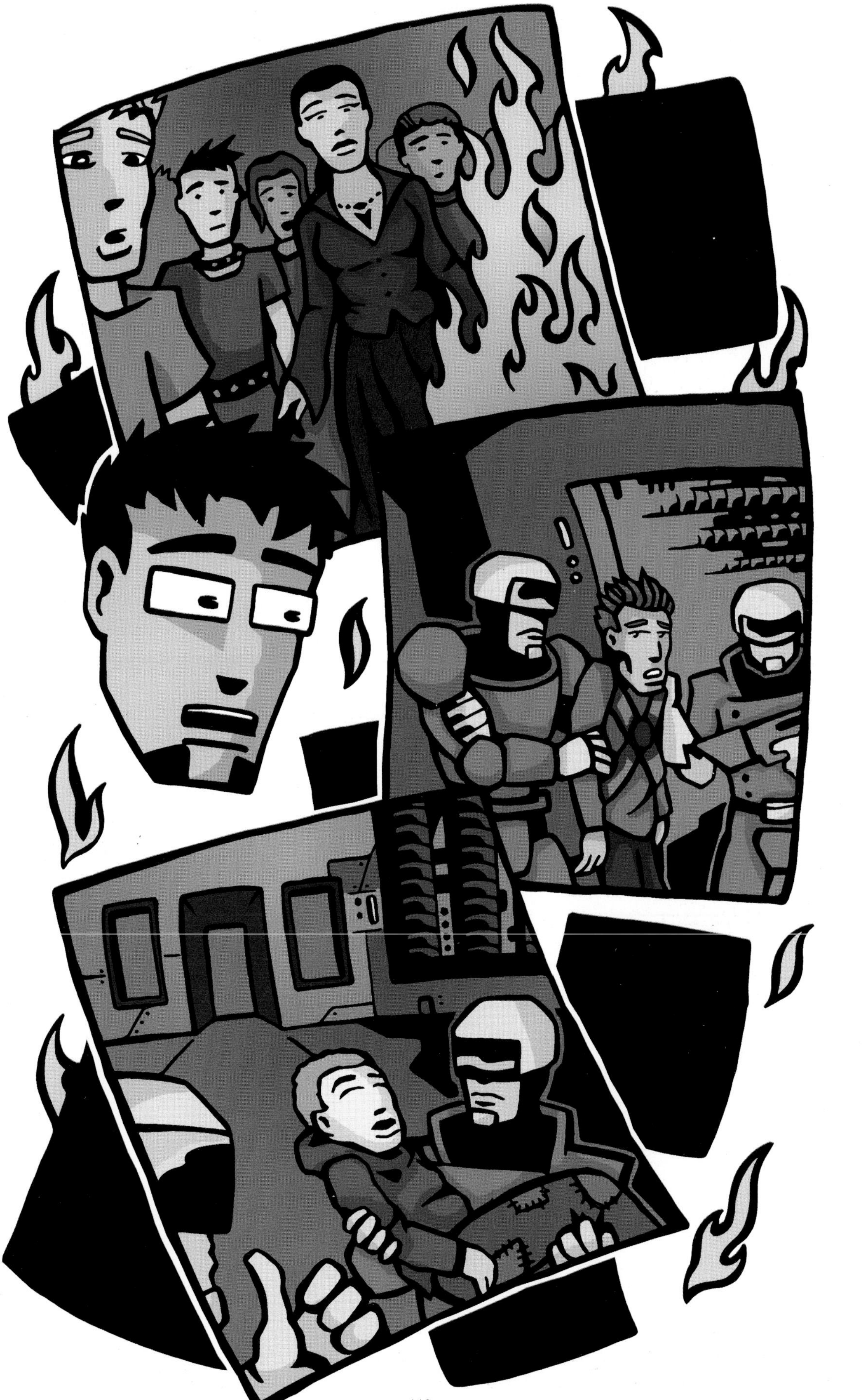

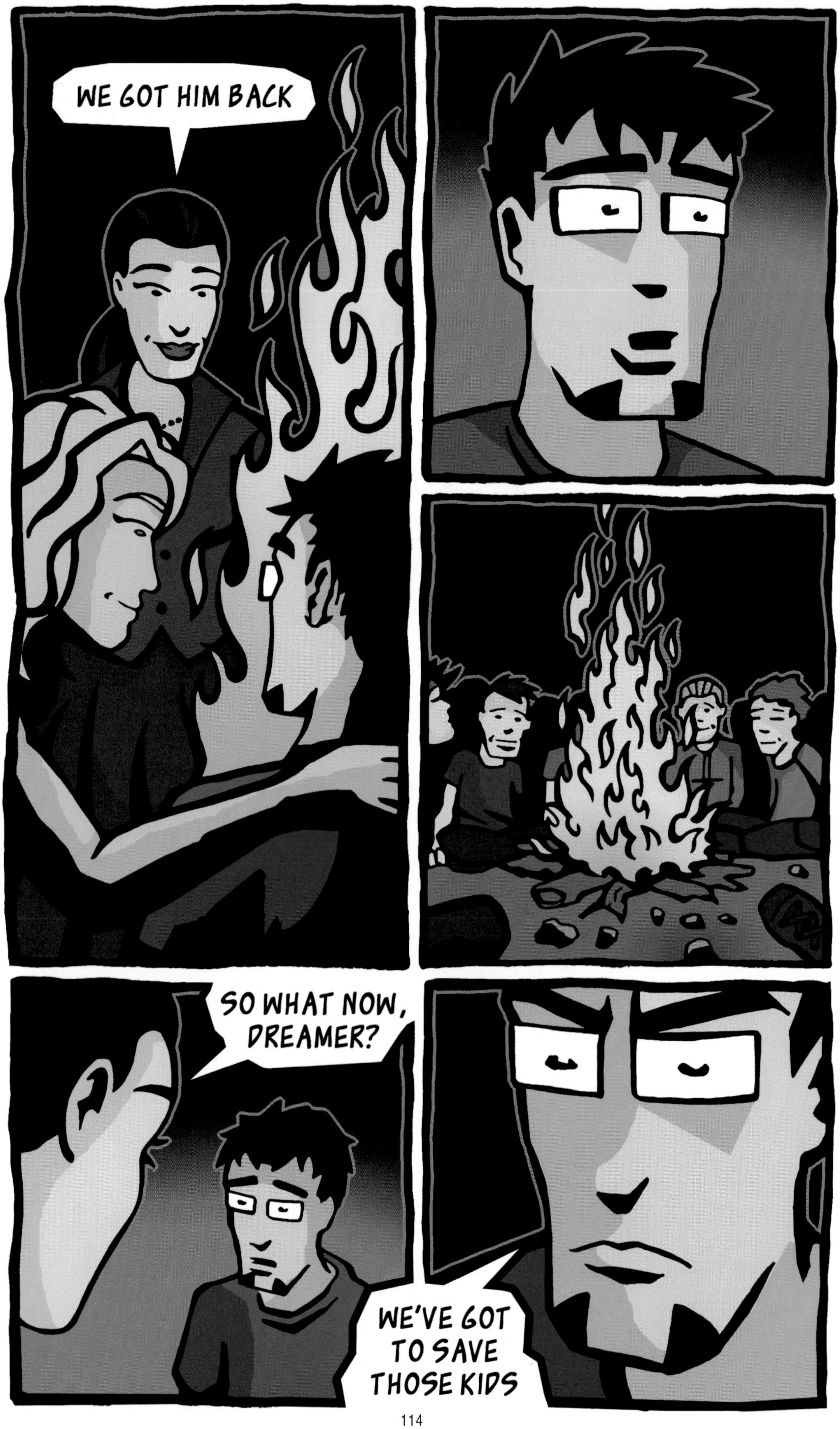
WE GOT HIM BACK
SO WHAT NOW, DREAMER?
WE'VE GOT TO SAVE THOSE KIDS

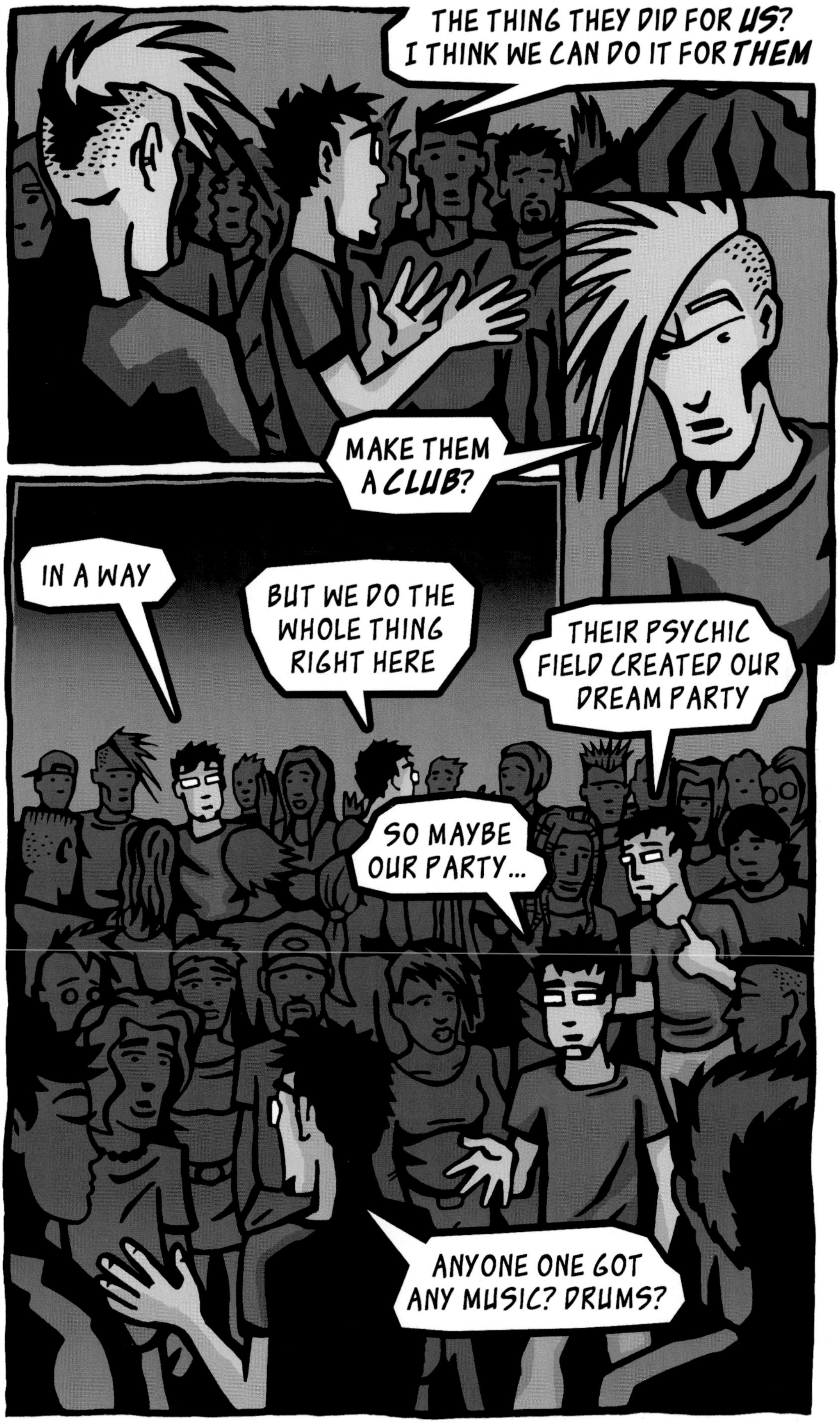

THE THING THEY DID FOR US? I THINK WE CAN DO IT FOR THEM
MAKE THEM A CLUB?
IN A WAY
BUT WE DO THE WHOLE THING RIGHT HERE
THEIR PSYCHIC FIELD CREATED OUR DREAM PARTY
SO MAYBE OUR PARTY...
ANYONE ONE GOT ANY MUSIC? DRUMS?

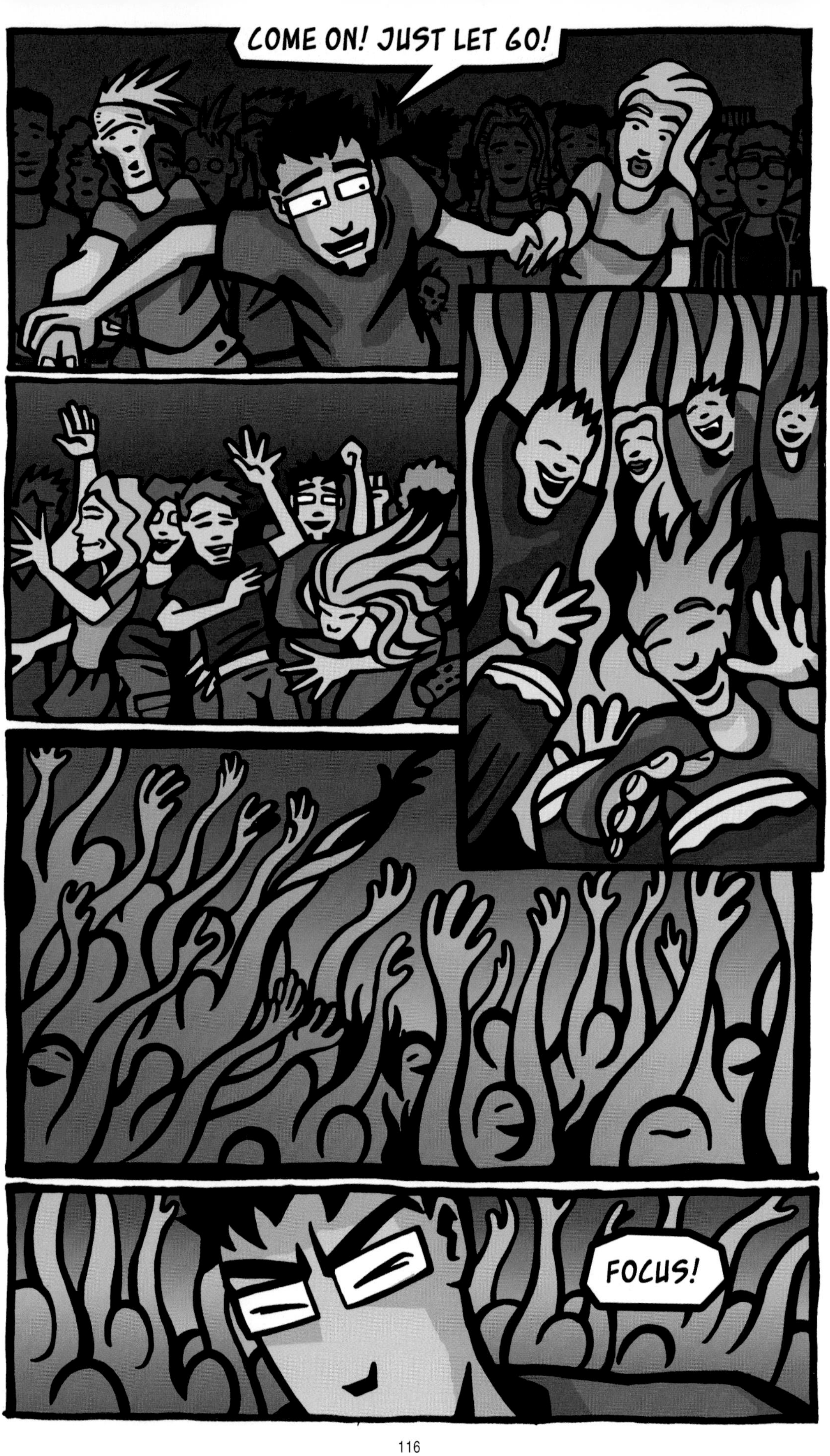
COME ON! JUST LET GO!
FOCUS!

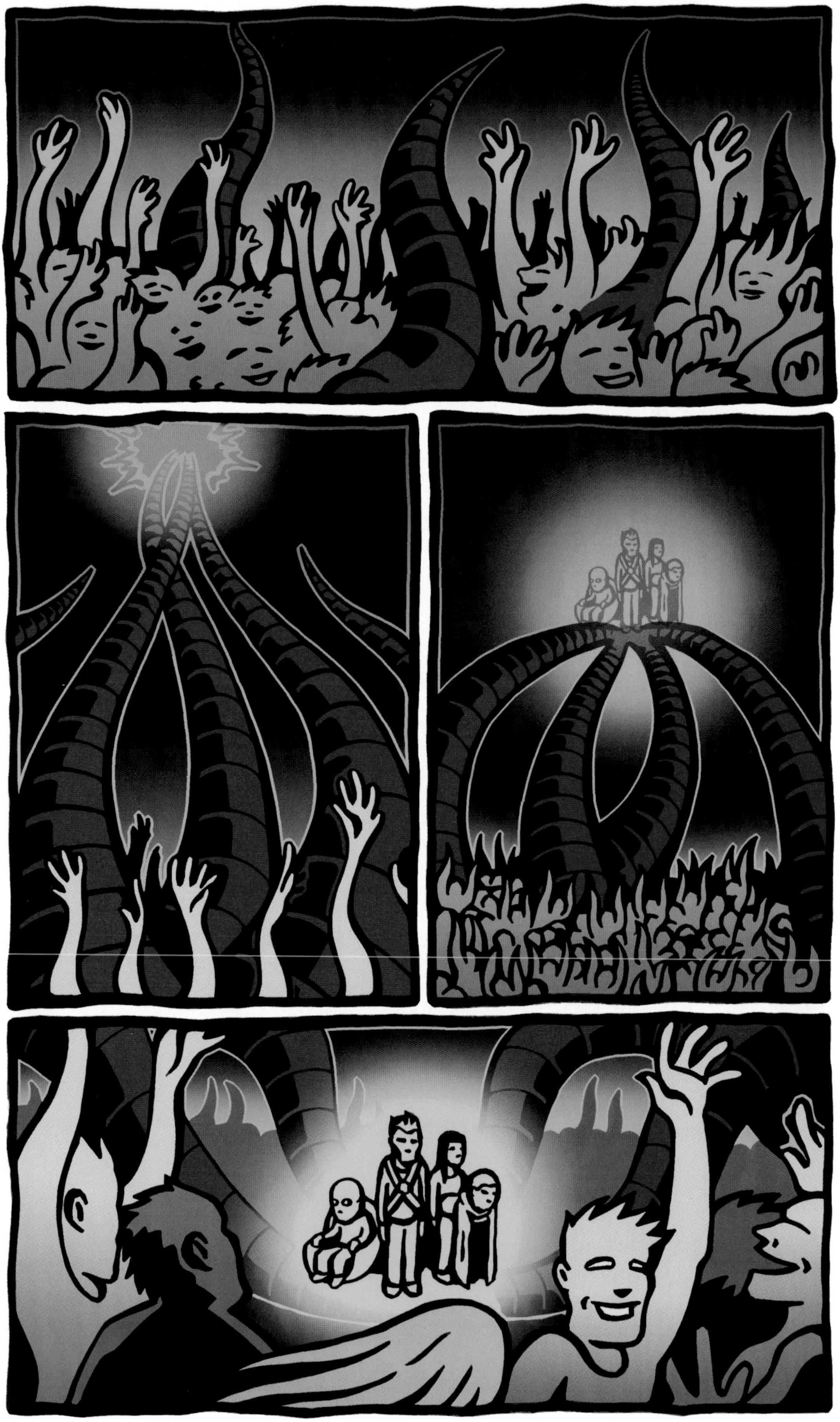

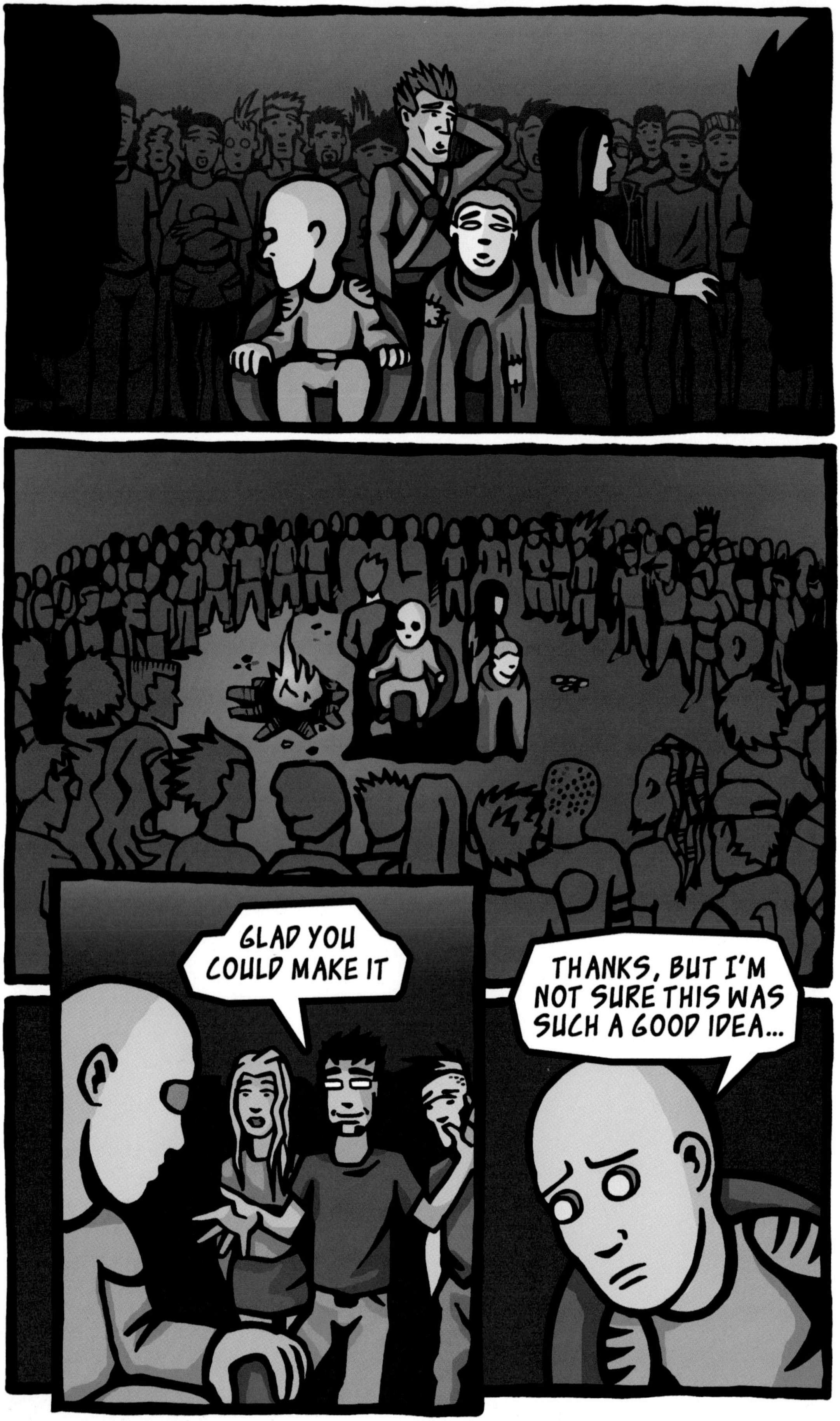

GLAD YOU COULD MAKE IT
THANKS, BUT I'M NOT SURE THIS WAS SUCH A GOOD IDEA...

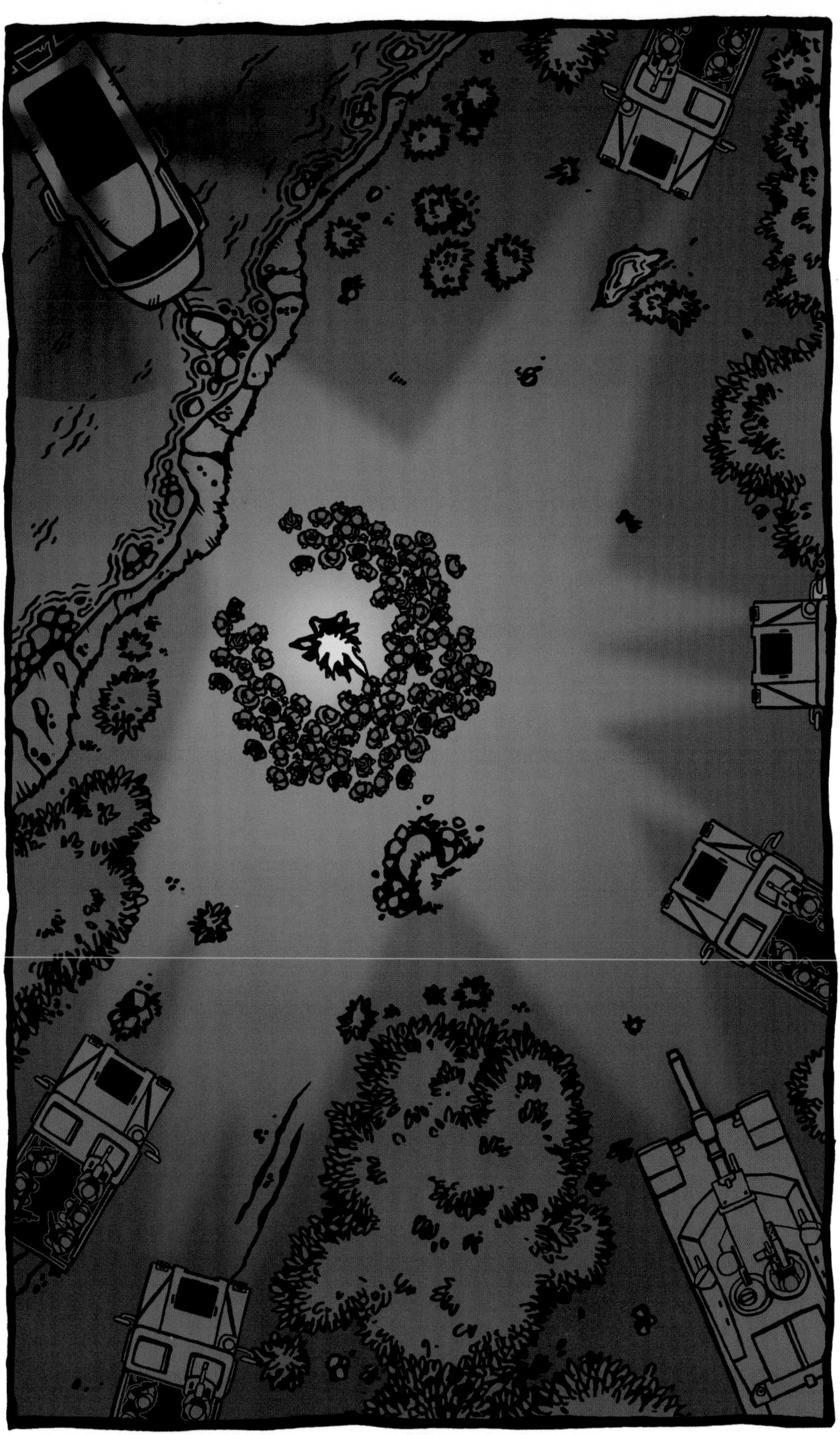

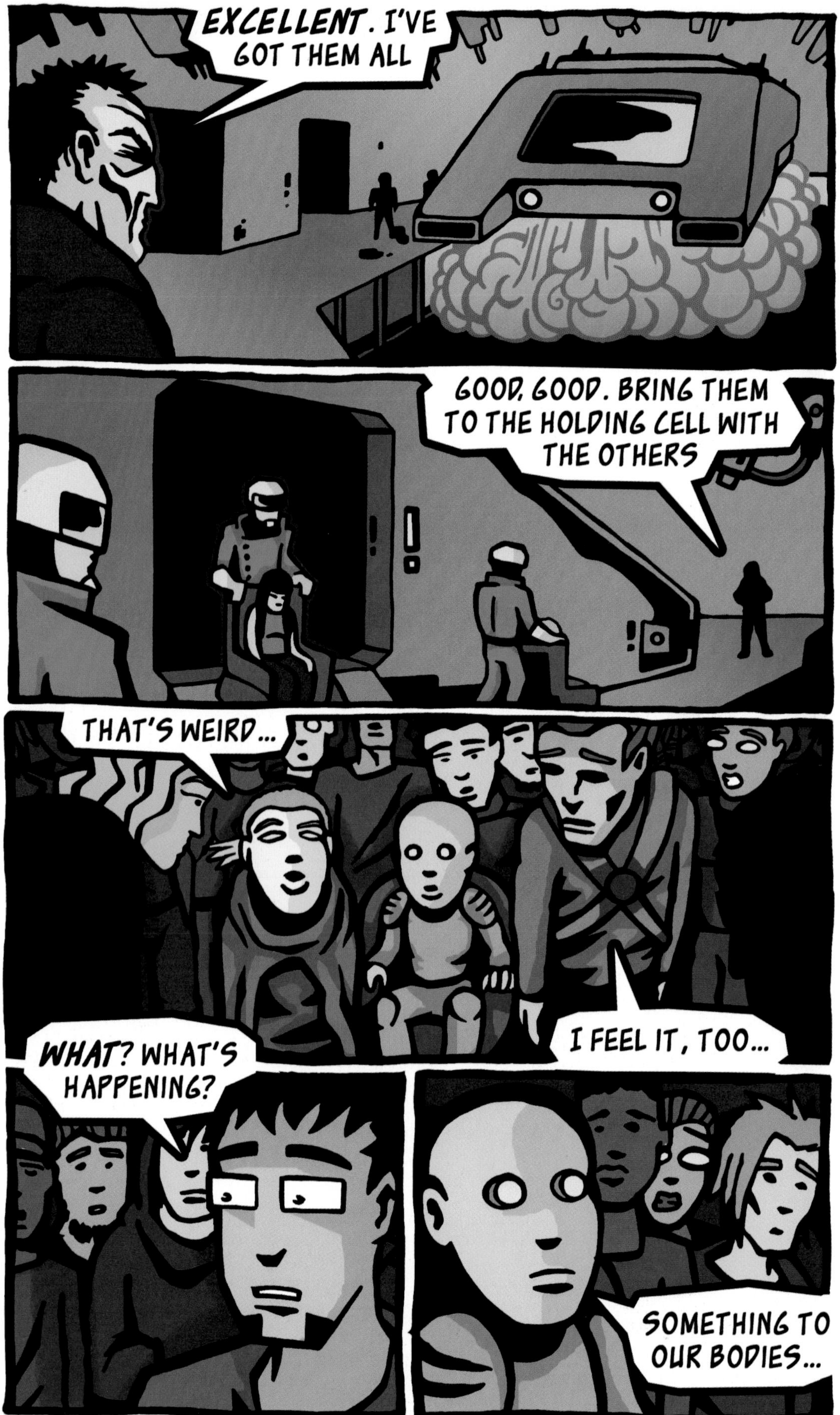
EXCELLENT. I'VE GOT THEM ALL
GOOD, GOOD. BRING THEM TO THE HOLDING CELL WITH THE OTHERS
THAT'S WEIRD...
I FEEL IT, TOO...
WHAT? WHAT'S HAPPENING?
SOMETHING TO OUR BODIES...

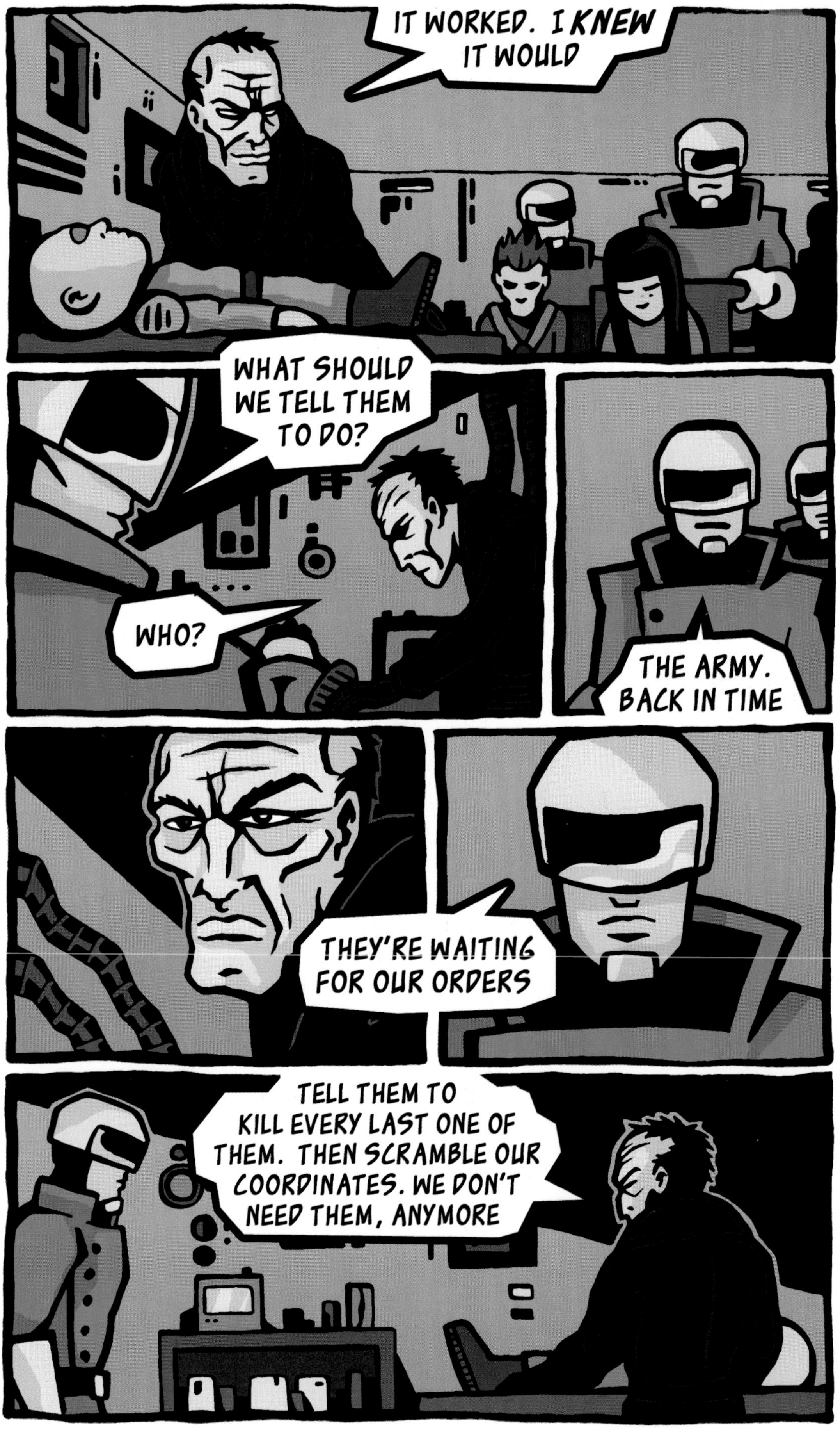
IT WORKED. I KNEW IT WOULD
WHAT SHOULD WE TELL THEM TO DO?
WHO?
THE ARMY. BACK IN TIME
THEY'RE WAITING FOR OUR ORDERS
TELL THEM TO KILL EVERY LAST ONE OF THEM. THEN SCRAMBLE OUR COORDINATES. WE DON'T NEED THEM, ANYMORE

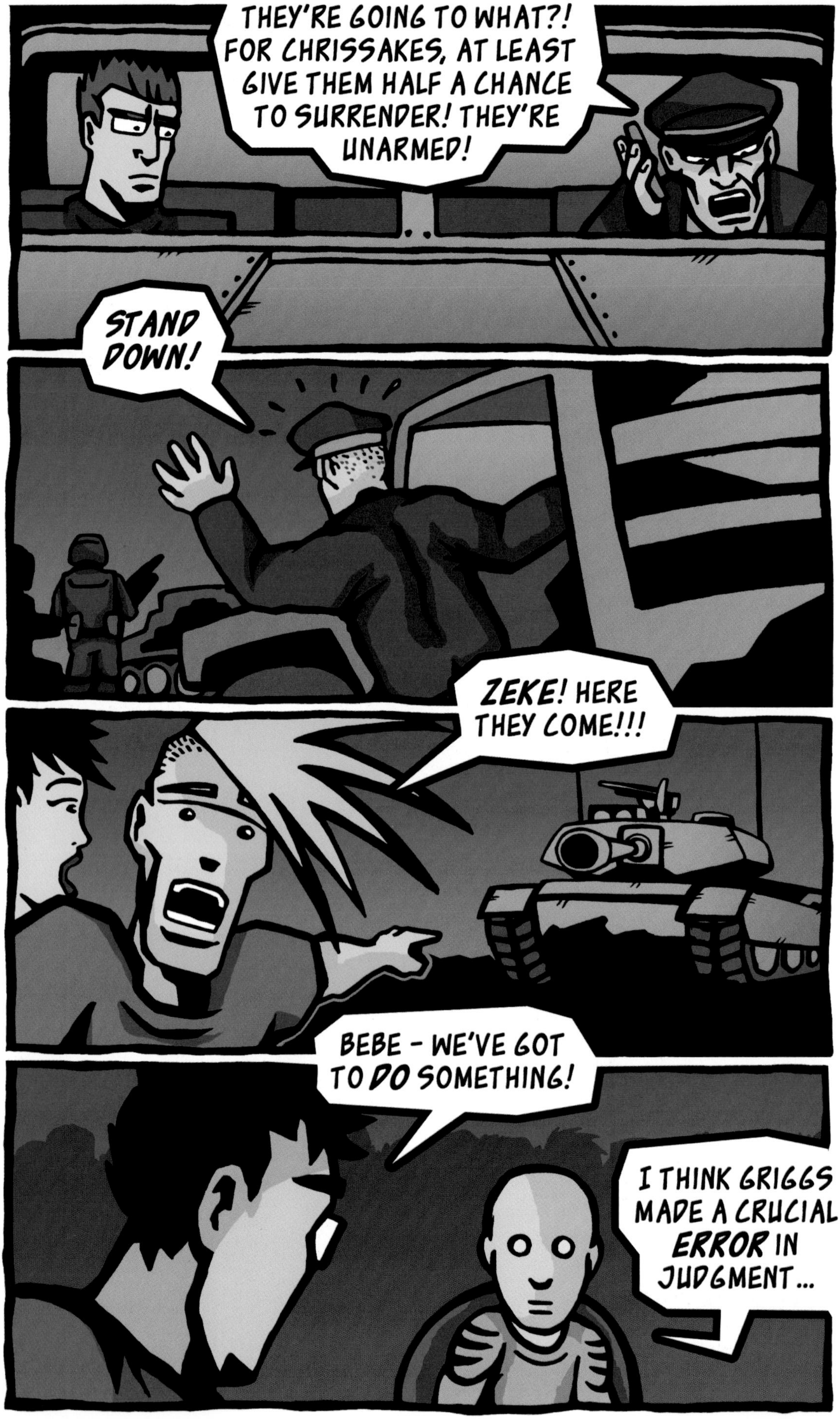
THEY'RE GOING TO WHAT?! FOR CHRISSAKES, AT LEAST GIVE THEM HALF A CHANCE TO SURRENDER! THEY'RE UNARMED!
STAND DOWN!
ZEKE! HERE THEY COME!!!
BEBE - WE'VE GOT TO *DO* SOMETHING!
I THINK GRIGGS MADE A CRUCIAL *ERROR* IN JUDGMENT...

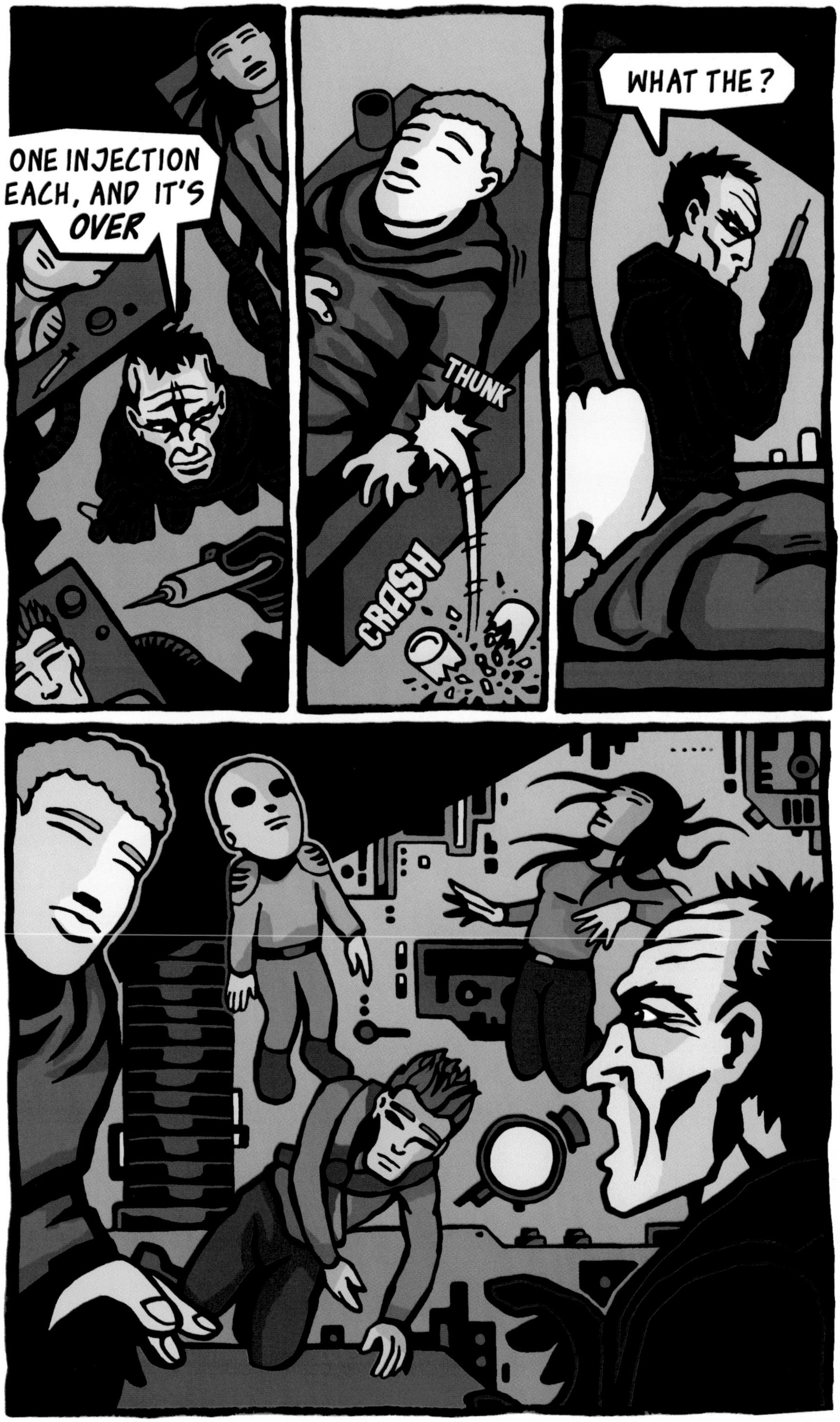
ONE INJECTION EACH, AND IT'S *OVER*
THUNK
CRASH
WHAT THE ?

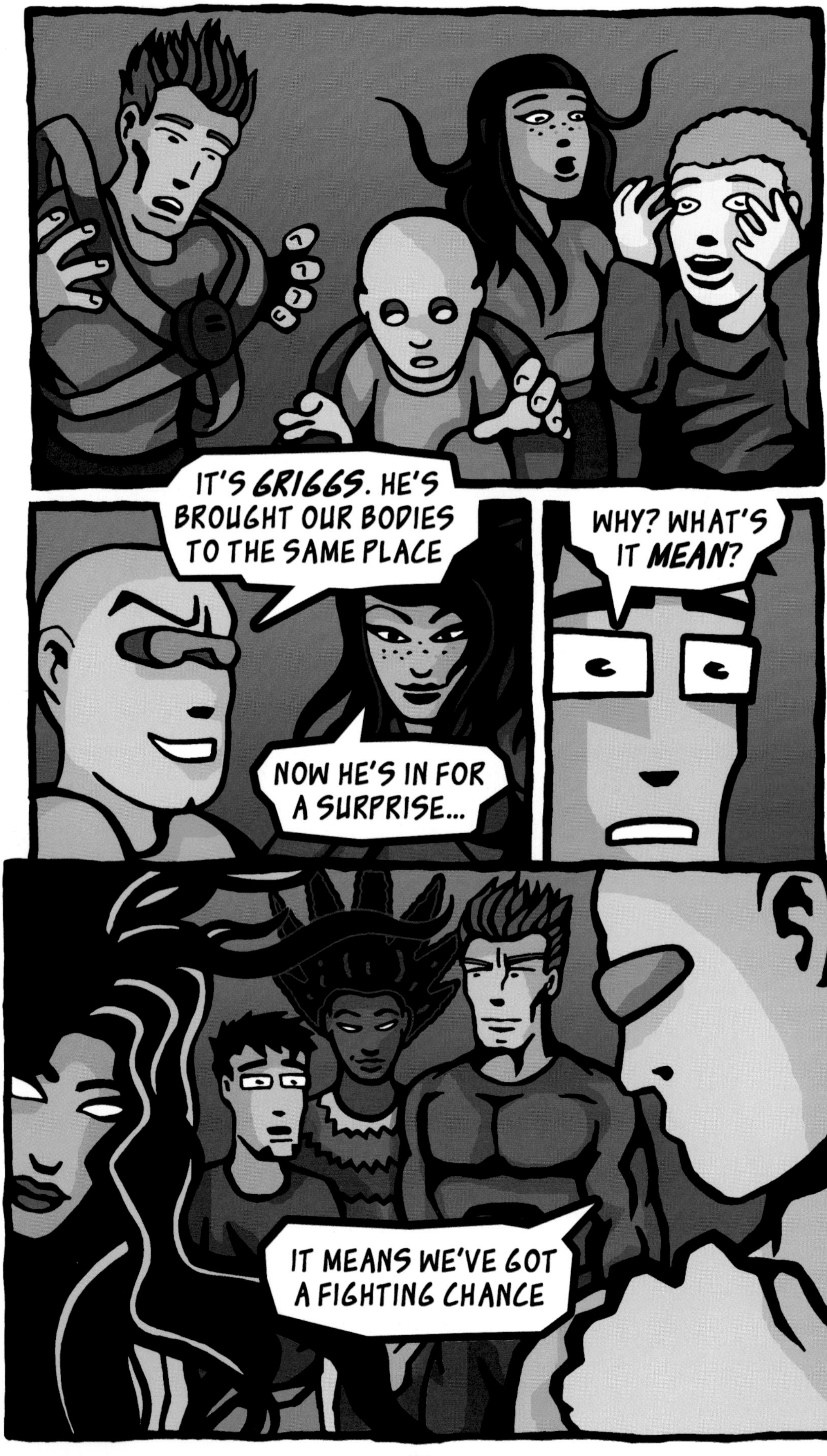
IT'S GRIGGS. HE'S BROUGHT OUR BODIES TO THE SAME PLACE
NOW HE'S IN FOR A SURPRISE...
WHY? WHAT'S IT MEAN?
IT MEANS WE'VE GOT A FIGHTING CHANCE

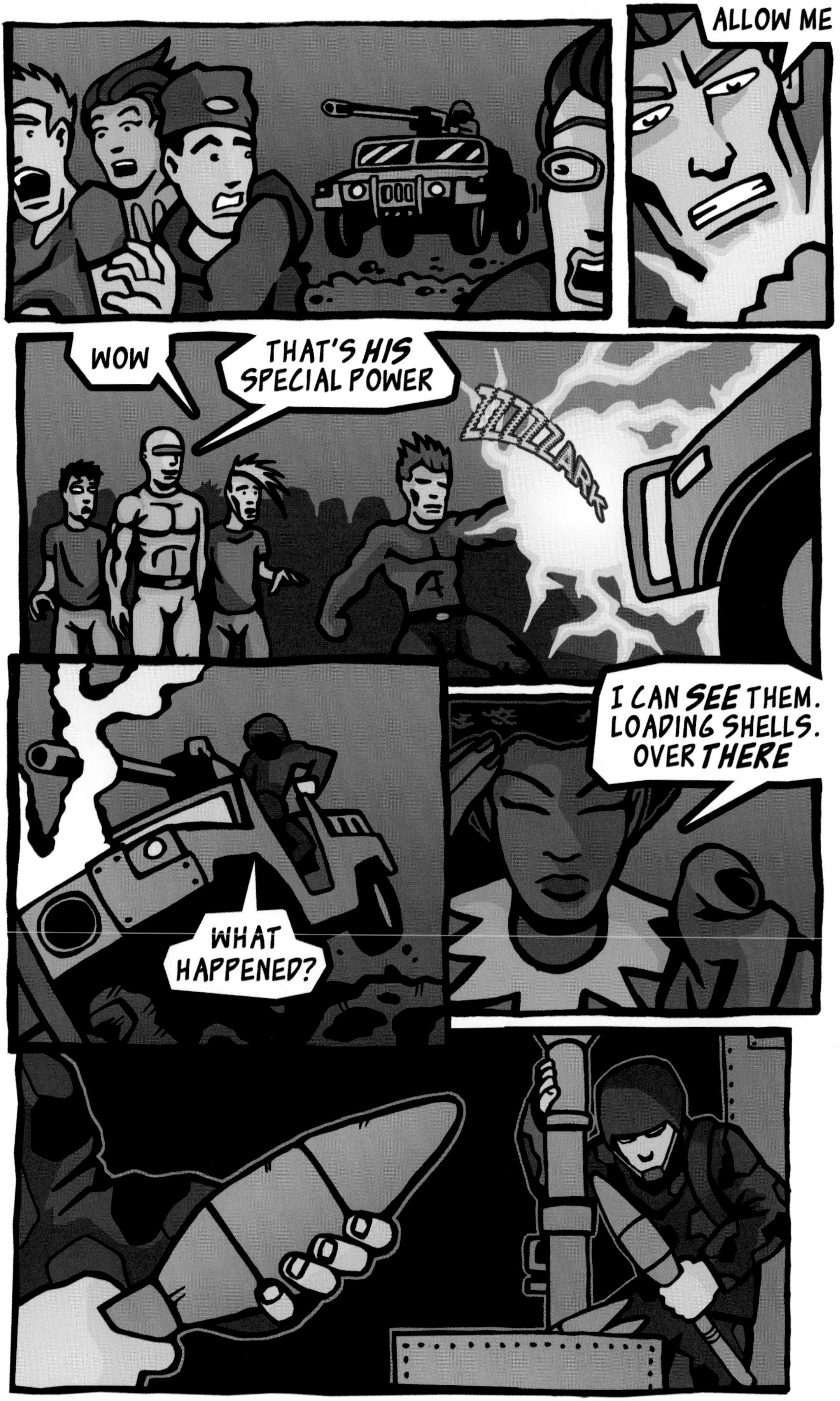
ALLOW ME
WOW
THAT'S HIS SPECIAL POWER
WHAT HAPPENED?
I CAN SEE THEM. LOADING SHELLS. OVER THERE

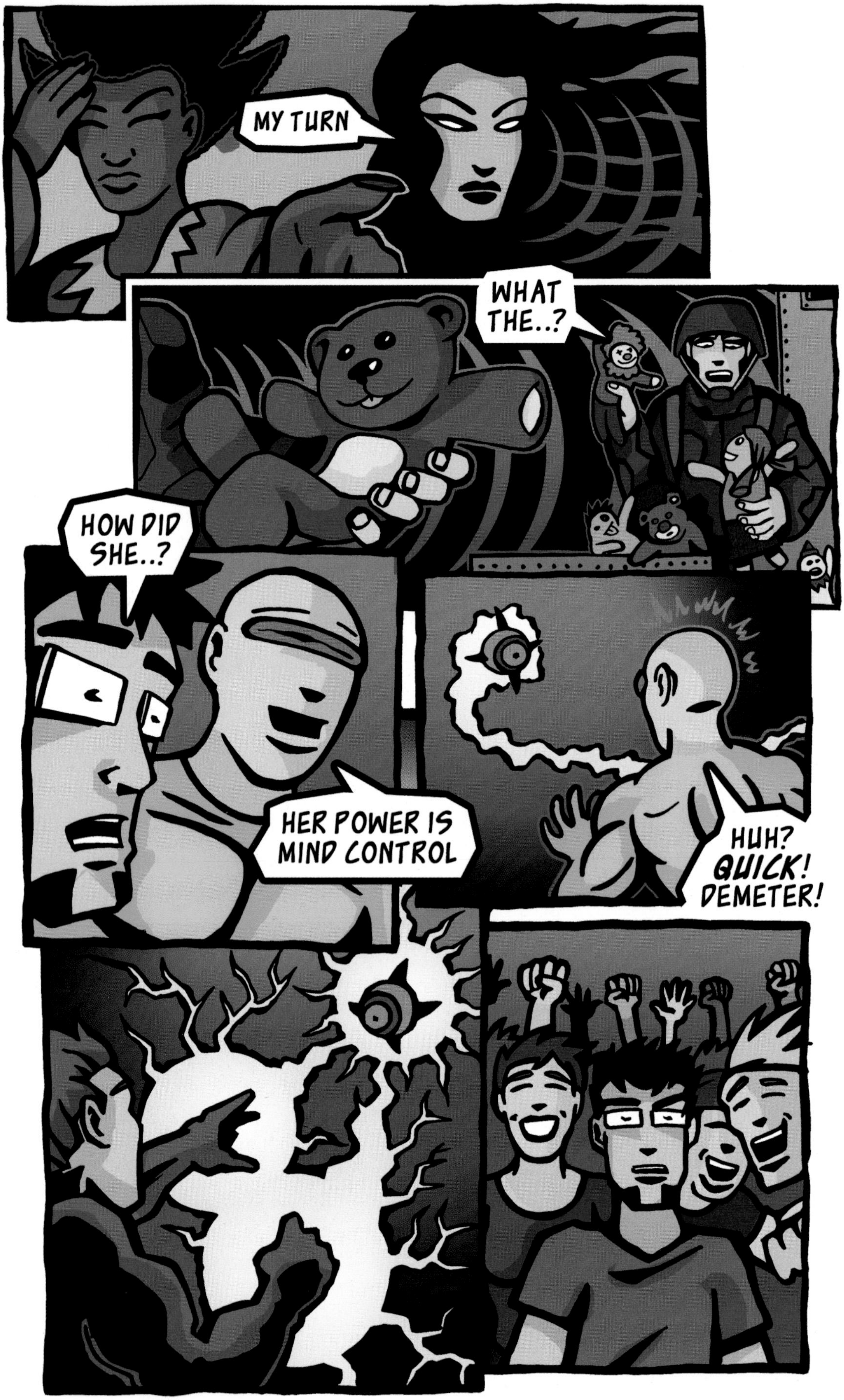
MY TURN
WHAT THE..?
HOW DID SHE..?
HER POWER IS MIND CONTROL
HUH? QUICK! DEMETER!

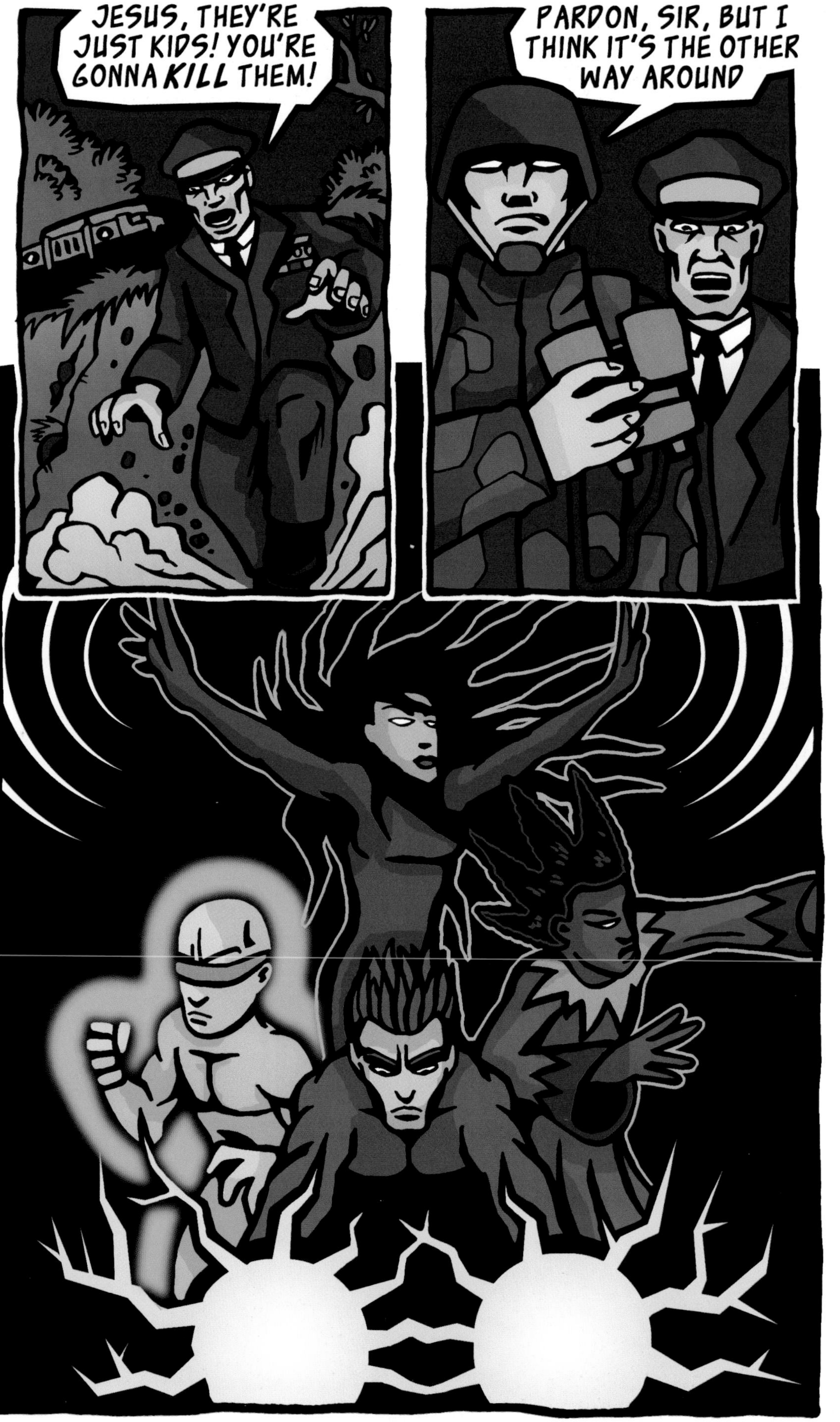
JESUS, THEY'RE JUST KIDS! YOU'RE GONNA KILL THEM!
PARDON, SIR, BUT I THINK IT'S THE OTHER WAY AROUND

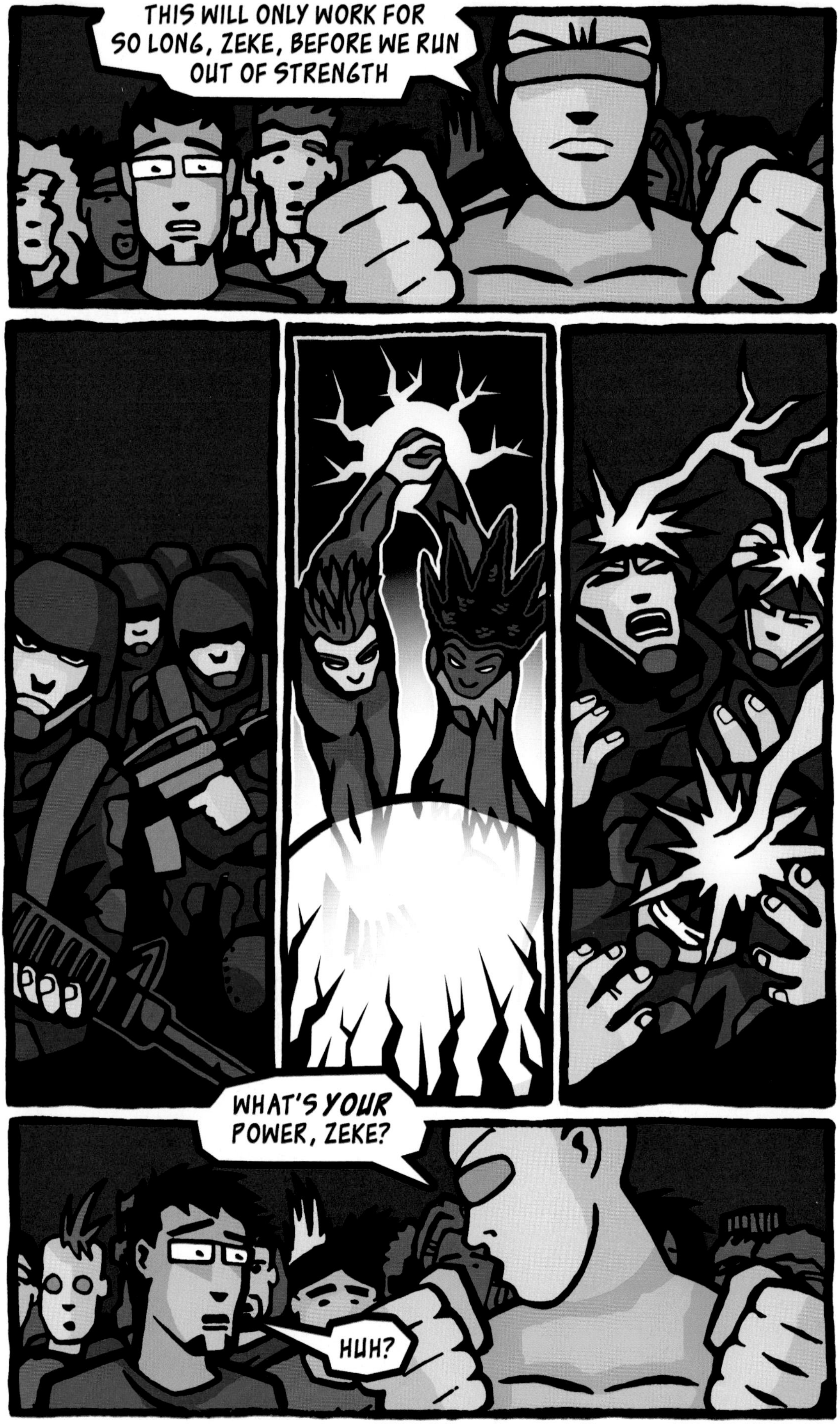
THIS WILL ONLY WORK FOR SO LONG, ZEKE, BEFORE WE RUN OUT OF STRENGTH
WHAT'S YOUR POWER, ZEKE?
HUH?

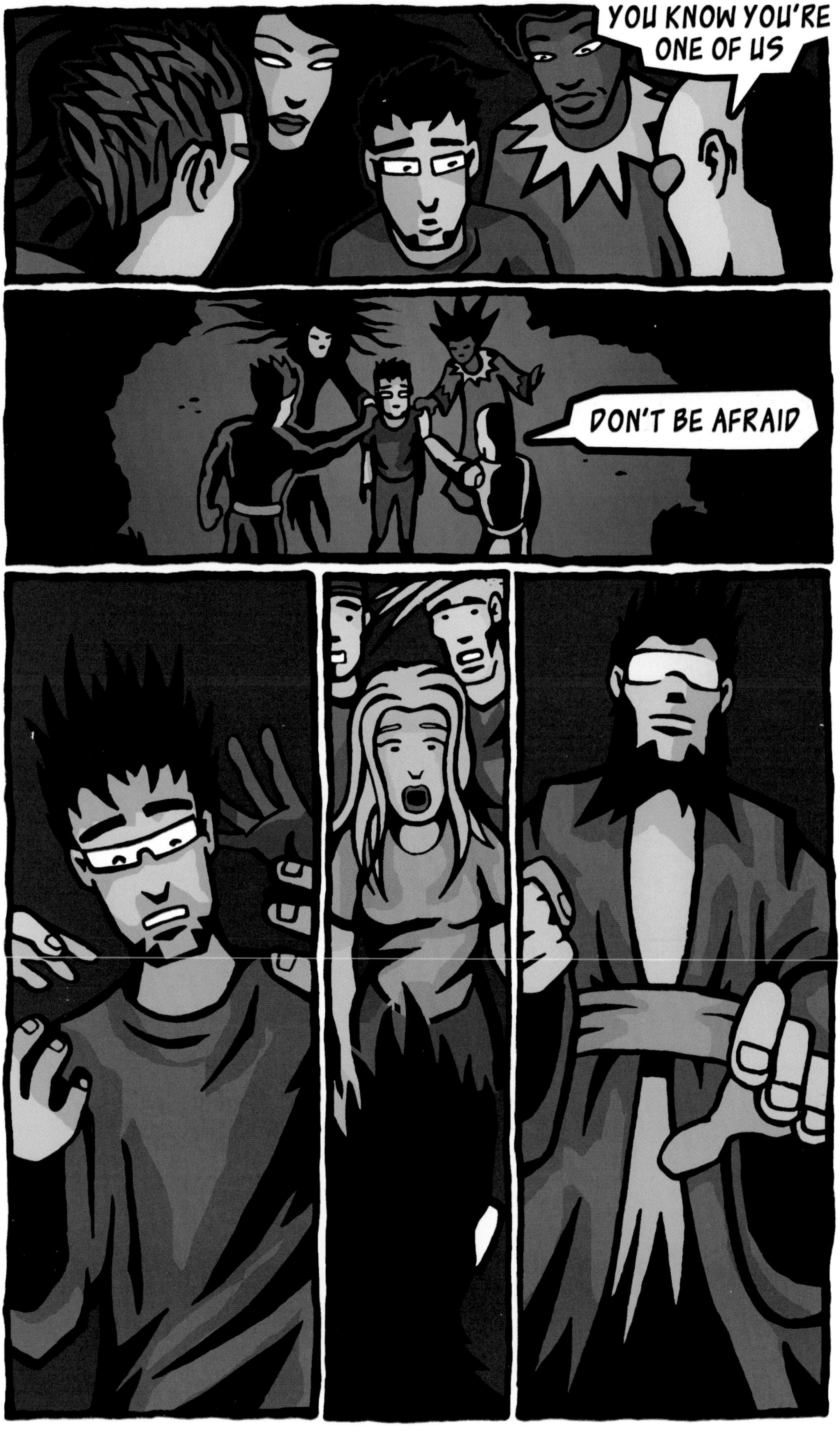
YOU KNOW YOU'RE ONE OF US
DON'T BE AFRAID

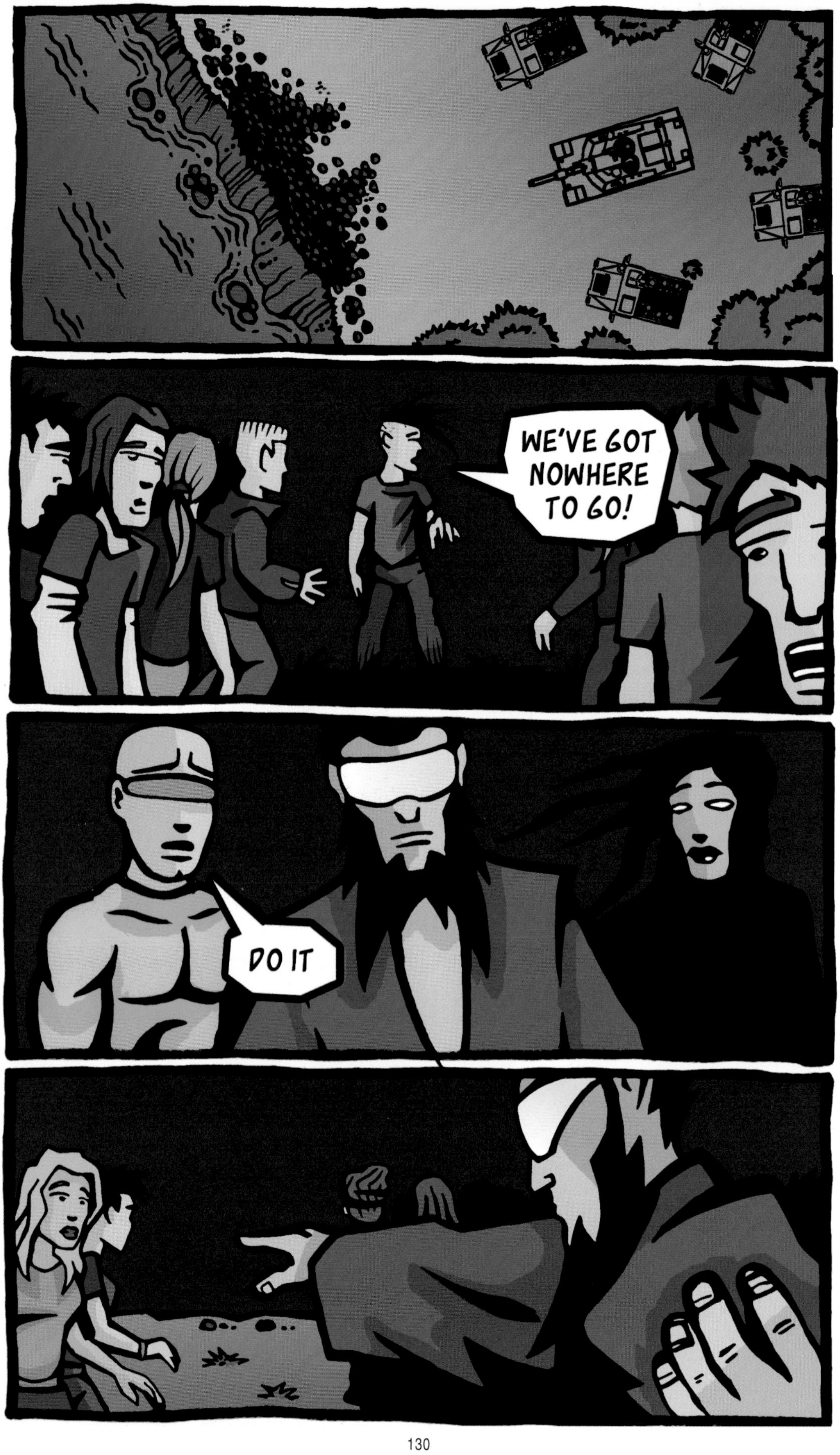
WE'VE GOT NOWHERE TO GO!
DO IT

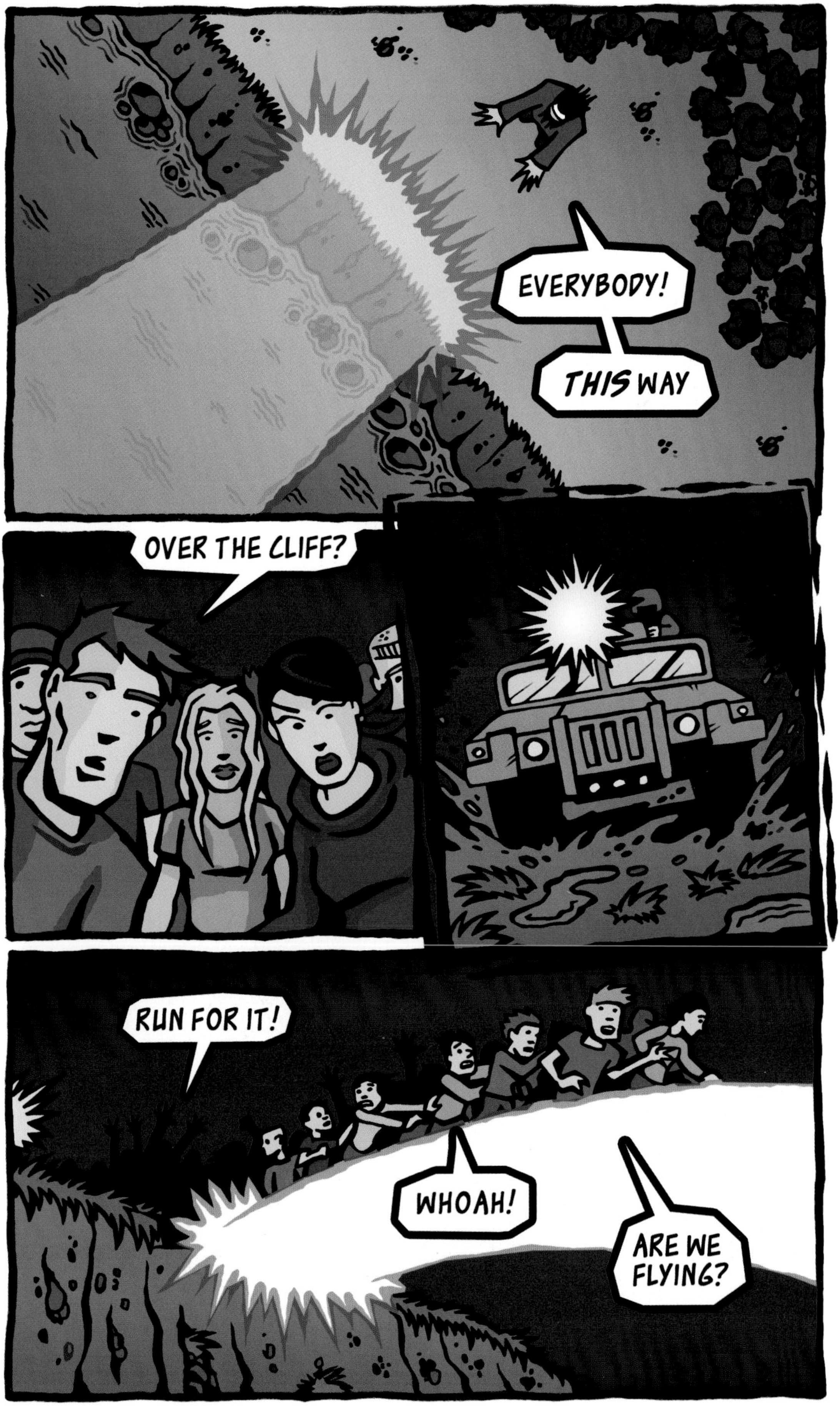
EVERYBODY!
THIS WAY
OVER THE CLIFF?
RUN FOR IT!
WHOAH!
ARE WE FLYING?

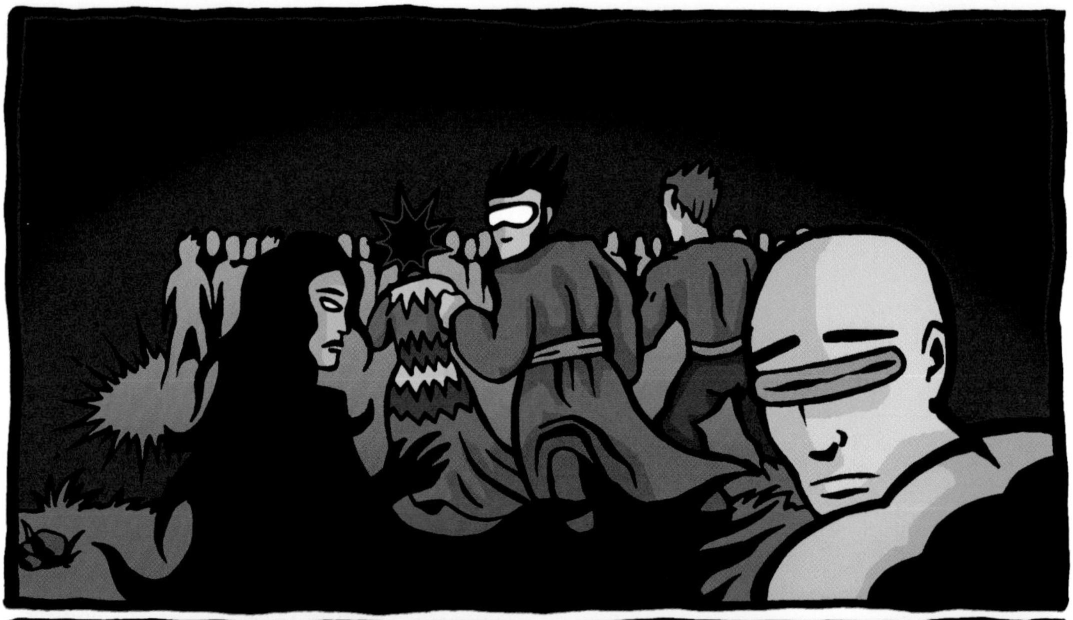

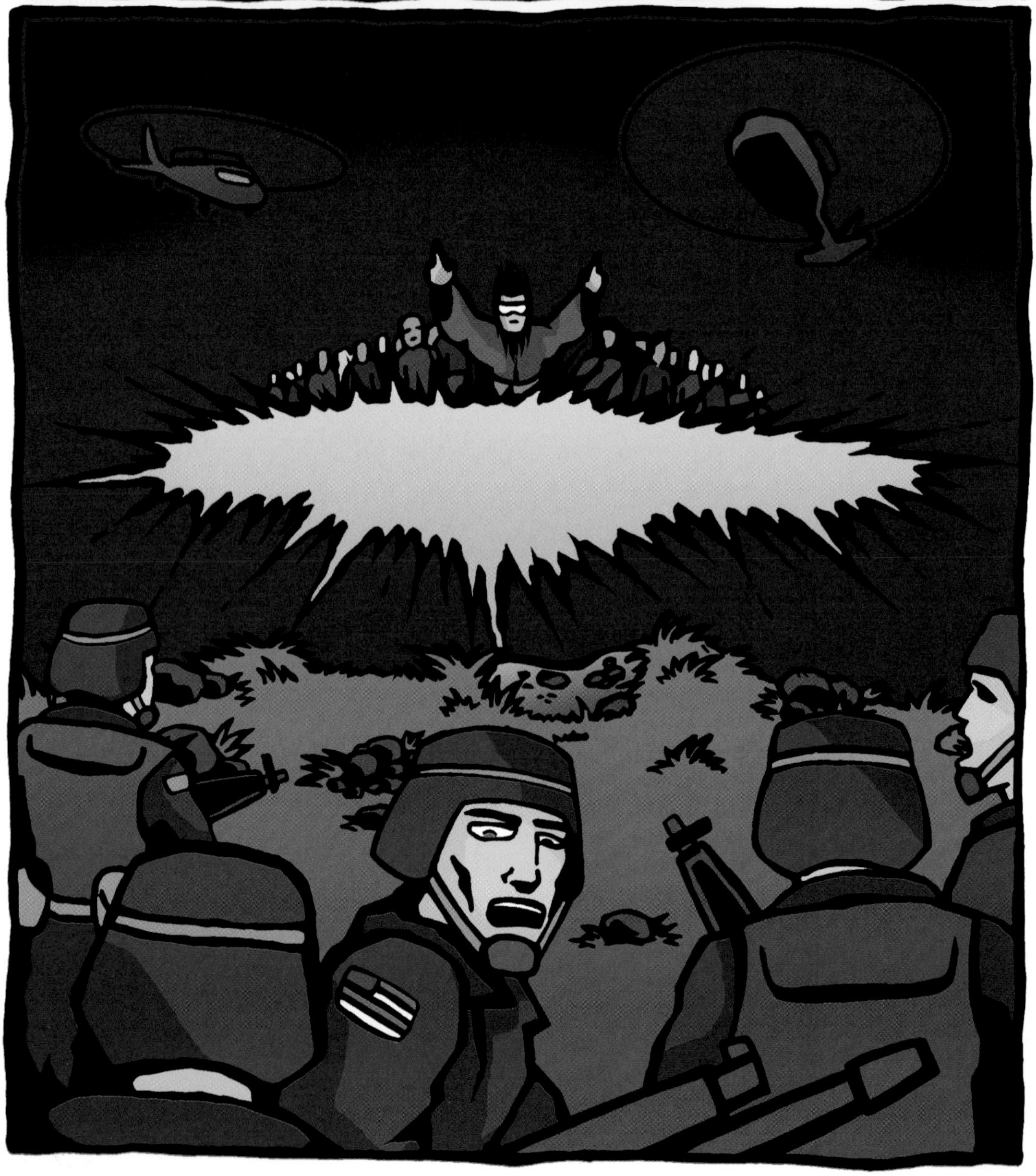

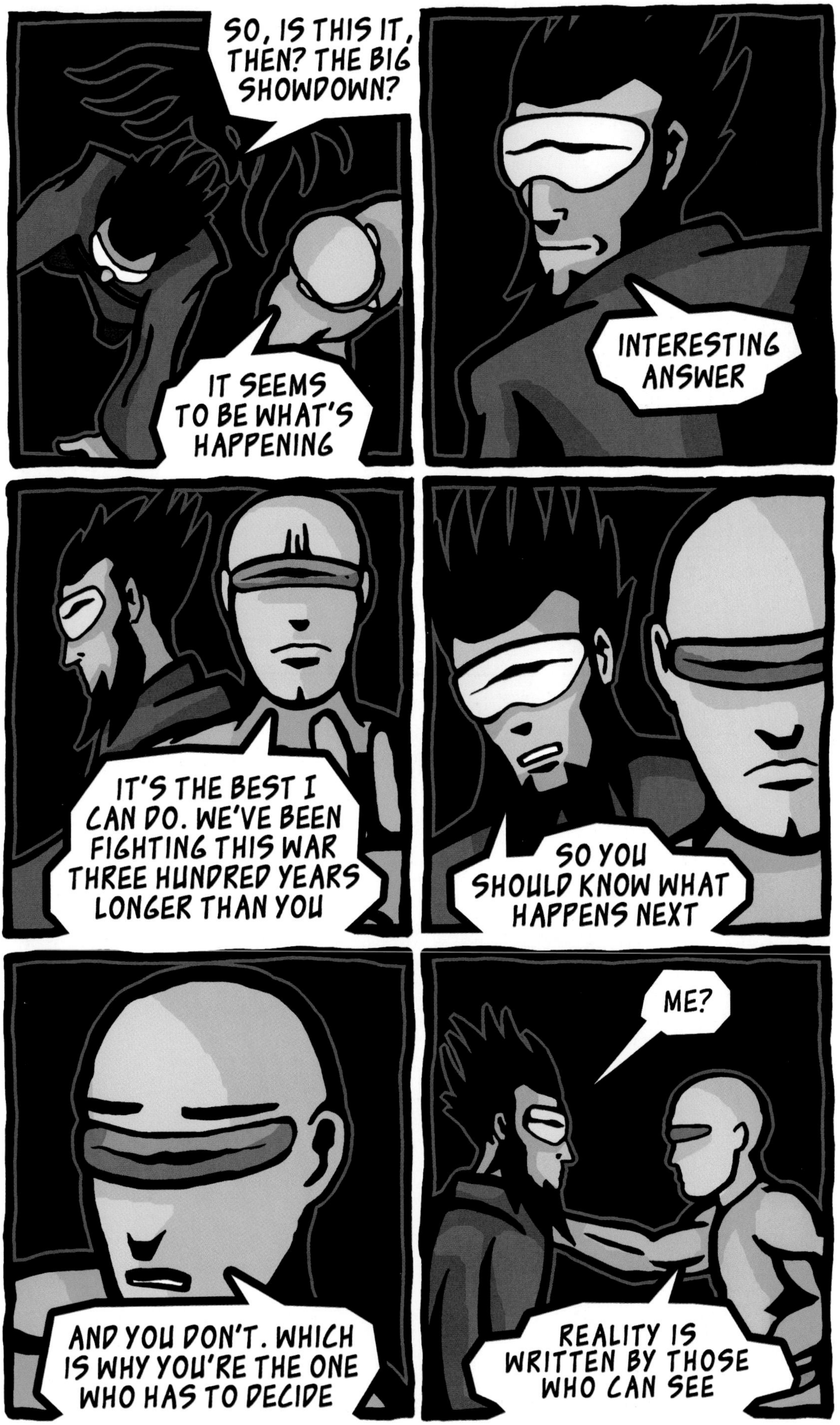
SO, IS THIS IT, THEN? THE BIG SHOWDOWN?
IT SEEMS TO BE WHAT'S HAPPENING
INTERESTING ANSWER
IT'S THE BEST I CAN DO. WE'VE BEEN FIGHTING THIS WAR THREE HUNDRED YEARS LONGER THAN YOU
SO YOU SHOULD KNOW WHAT HAPPENS NEXT
AND YOU DON'T. WHICH IS WHY YOU'RE THE ONE WHO HAS TO DECIDE
ME?
REALITY IS WRITTEN BY THOSE WHO CAN SEE

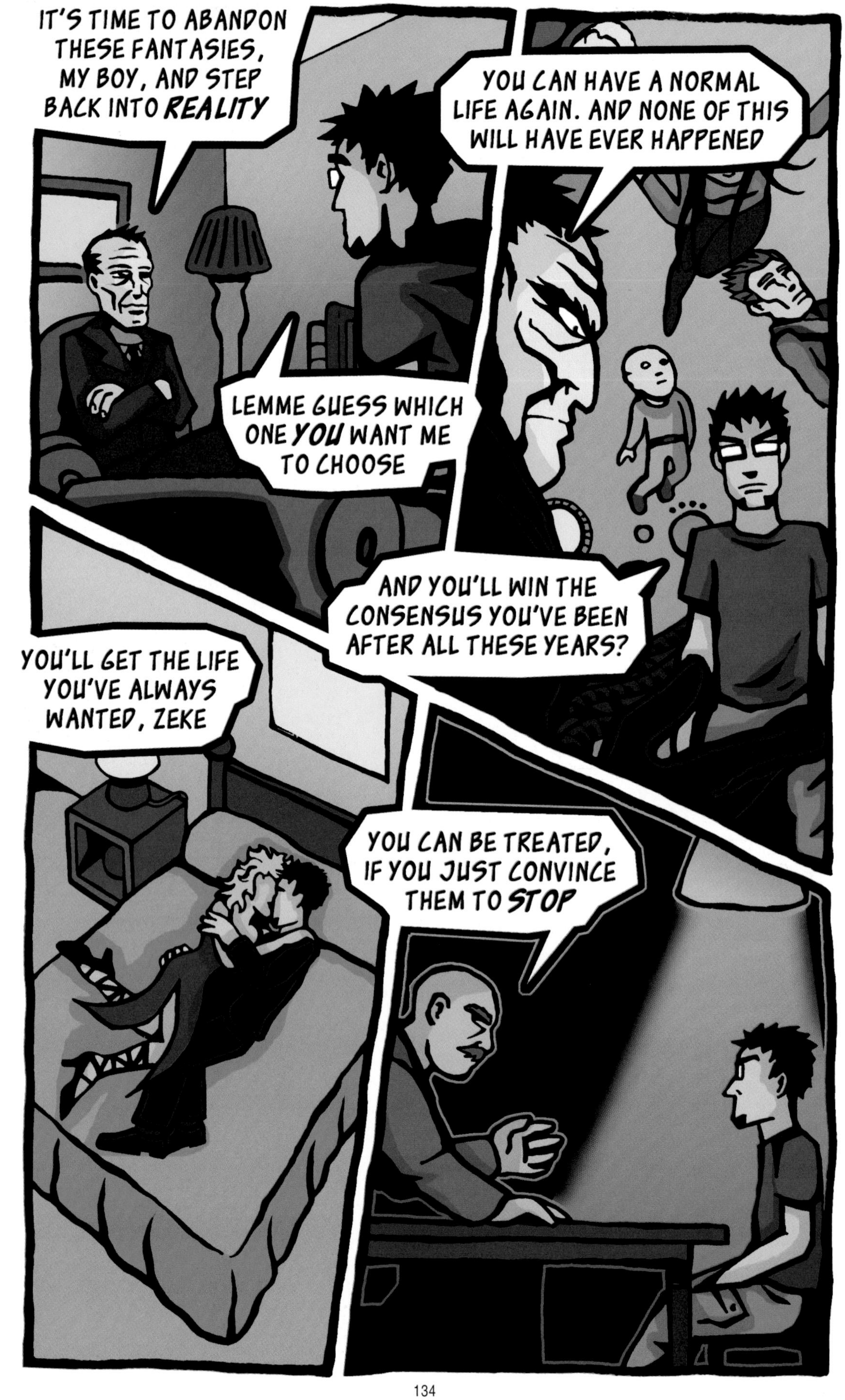
IT'S TIME TO ABANDON THESE FANTASIES, MY BOY, AND STEP BACK INTO REALITY
YOU CAN HAVE A NORMAL LIFE AGAIN. AND NONE OF THIS WILL HAVE EVER HAPPENED
LEMME GUESS WHICH ONE YOU WANT ME TO CHOOSE
AND YOU'LL WIN THE CONSENSUS YOU'VE BEEN AFTER ALL THESE YEARS?
YOU'LL GET THE LIFE YOU'VE ALWAYS WANTED, ZEKE
YOU CAN BE TREATED, IF YOU JUST CONVINCE THEM TO STOP

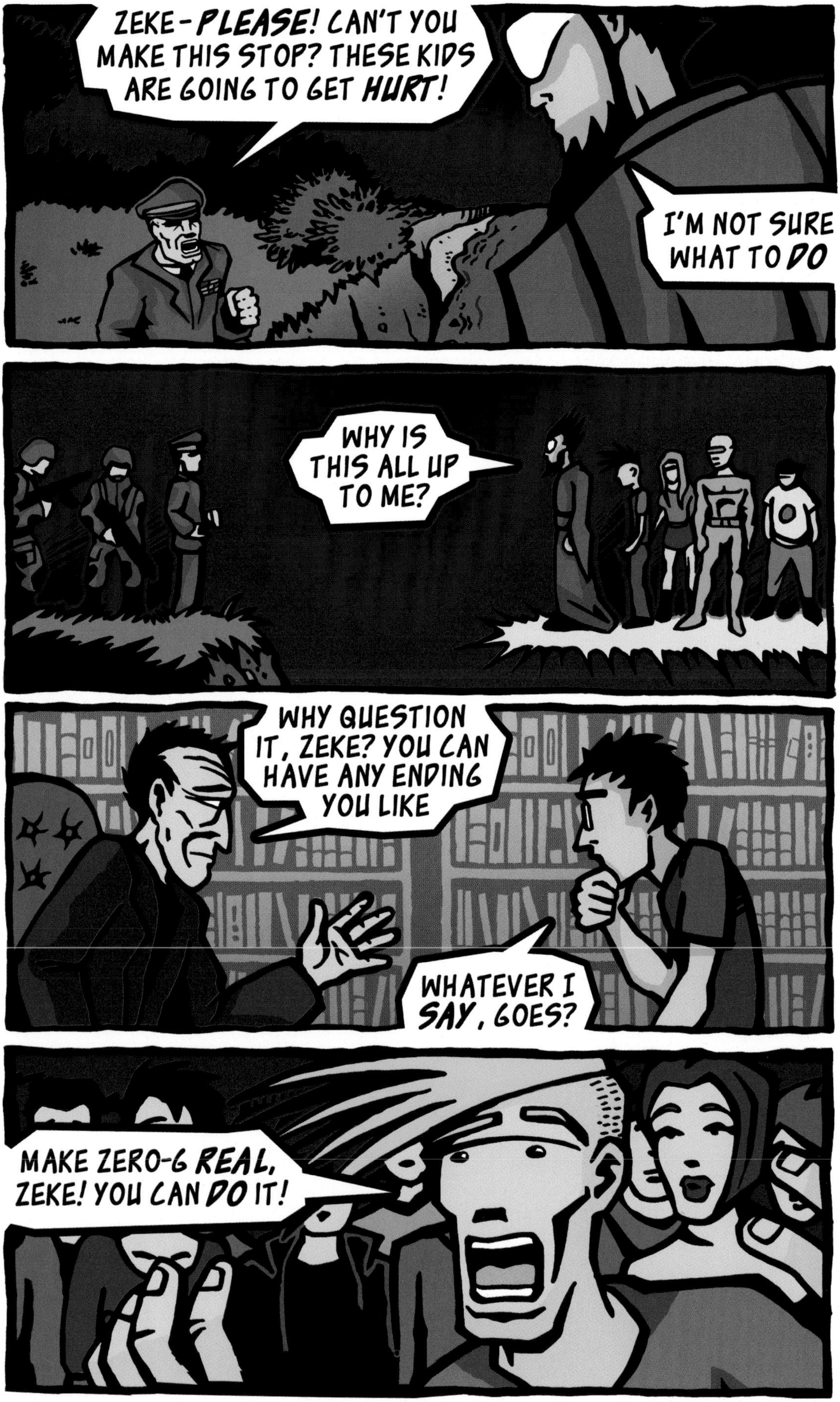
ZEKE-PLEASE! CAN'T YOU MAKE THIS STOP? THESE KIDS ARE GOING TO GET HURT!
I'M NOT SURE WHAT TO DO
WHY IS THIS ALL UP TO ME?
WHY QUESTION IT, ZEKE? YOU CAN HAVE ANY ENDING YOU LIKE
WHATEVER I SAY, GOES?
MAKE ZERO-G REAL, ZEKE! YOU CAN DO IT!

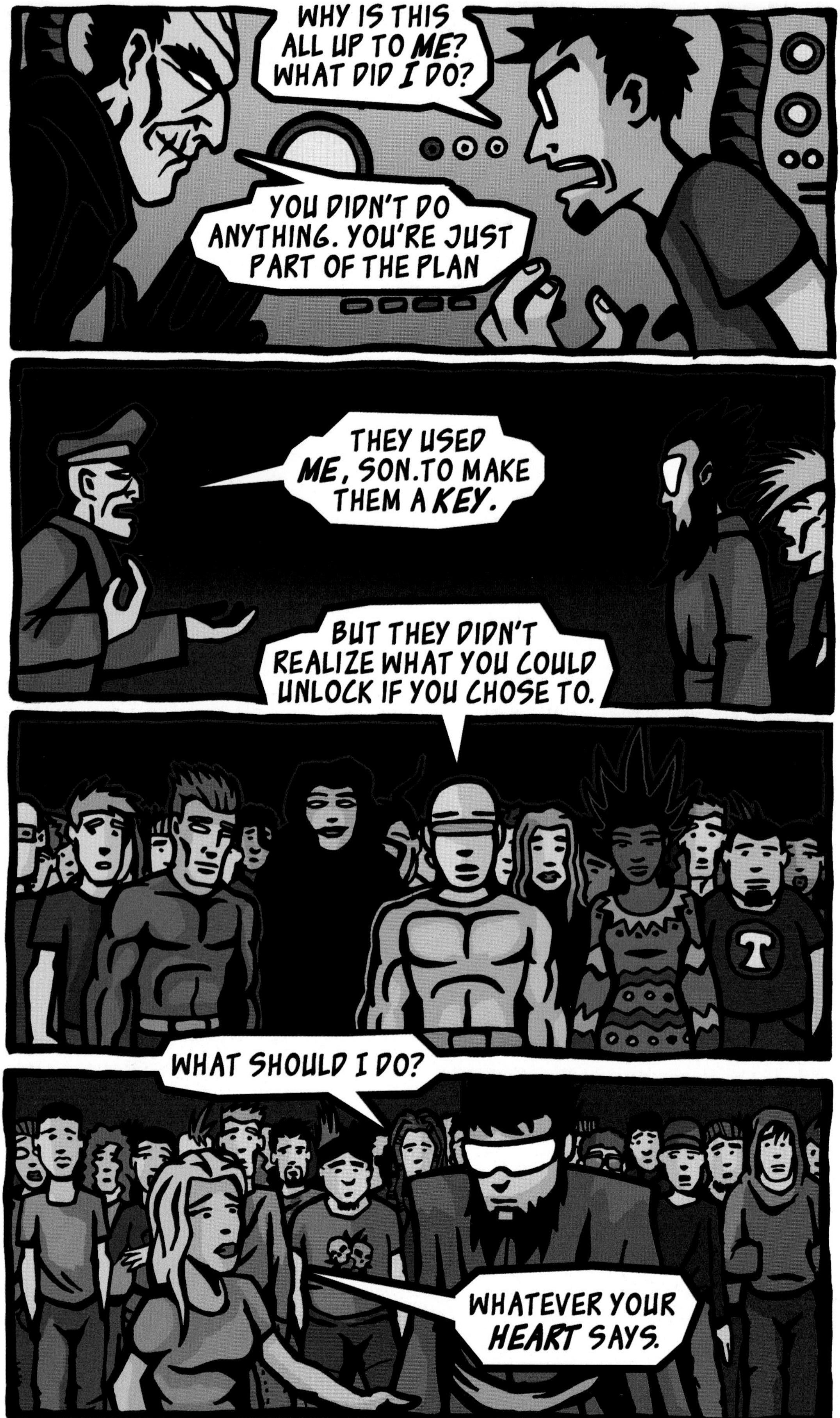
WHY IS THIS ALL UP TO ME? WHAT DID I DO?
YOU DIDN'T DO ANYTHING. YOU'RE JUST PART OF THE PLAN
THEY USED ME, SON. TO MAKE THEM A KEY.
BUT THEY DIDN'T REALIZE WHAT YOU COULD UNLOCK IF YOU CHOSE TO.
WHAT SHOULD I DO?
WHATEVER YOUR HEART SAYS.

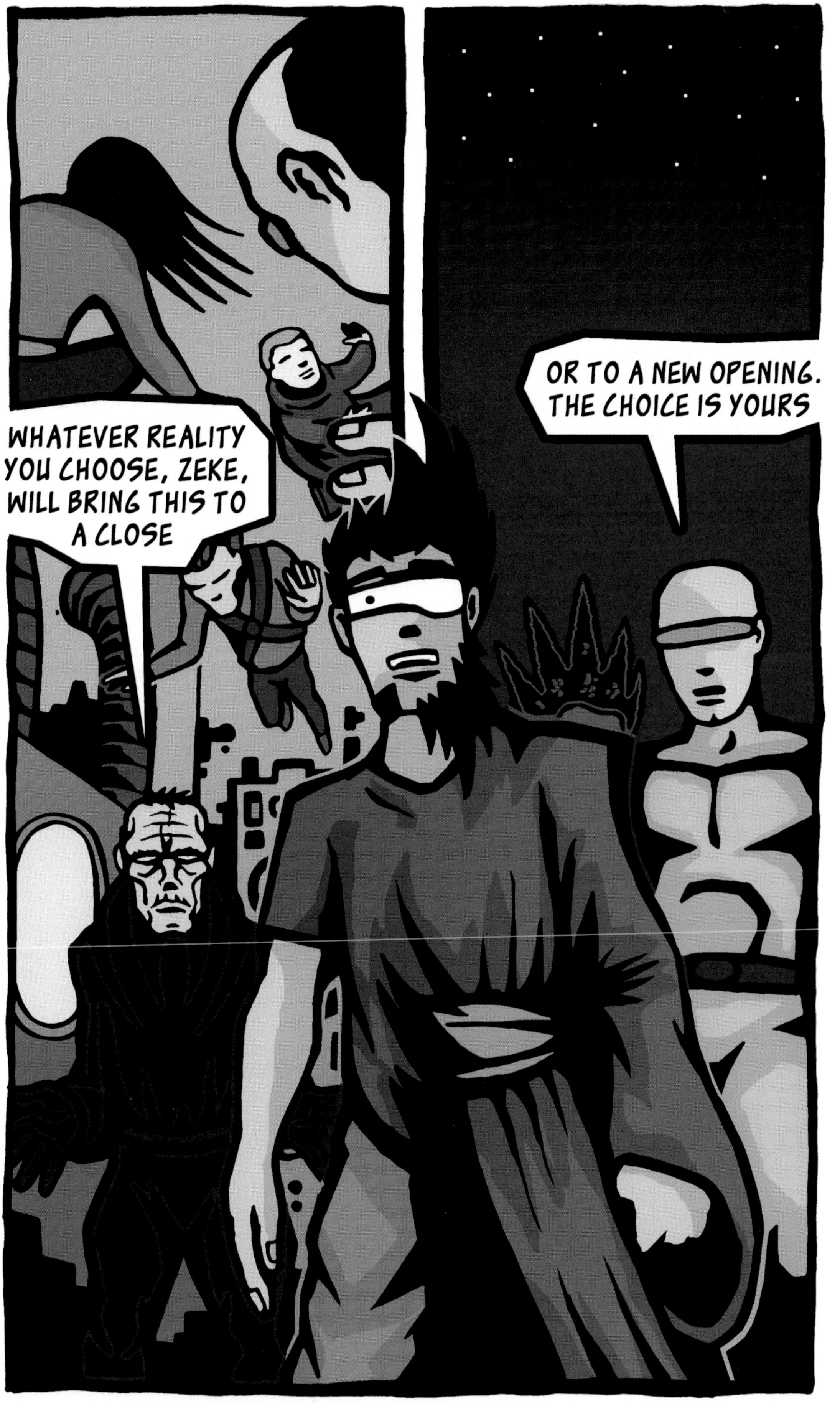
WHATEVER REALITY YOU CHOOSE, ZEKE, WILL BRING THIS TO A CLOSE
OR TO A NEW OPENING. THE CHOICE IS YOURS

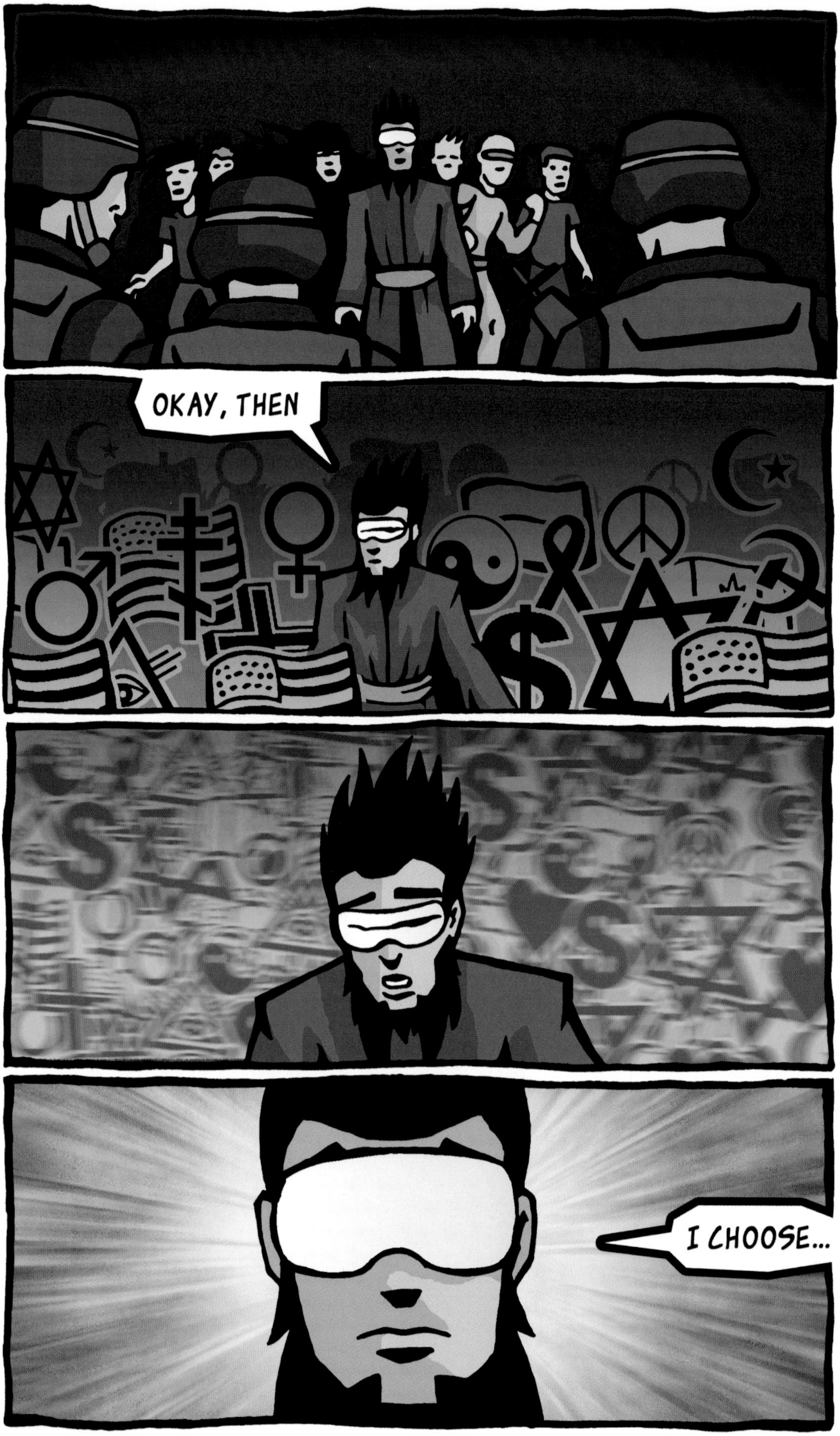
OKAY, THEN
I CHOOSE...

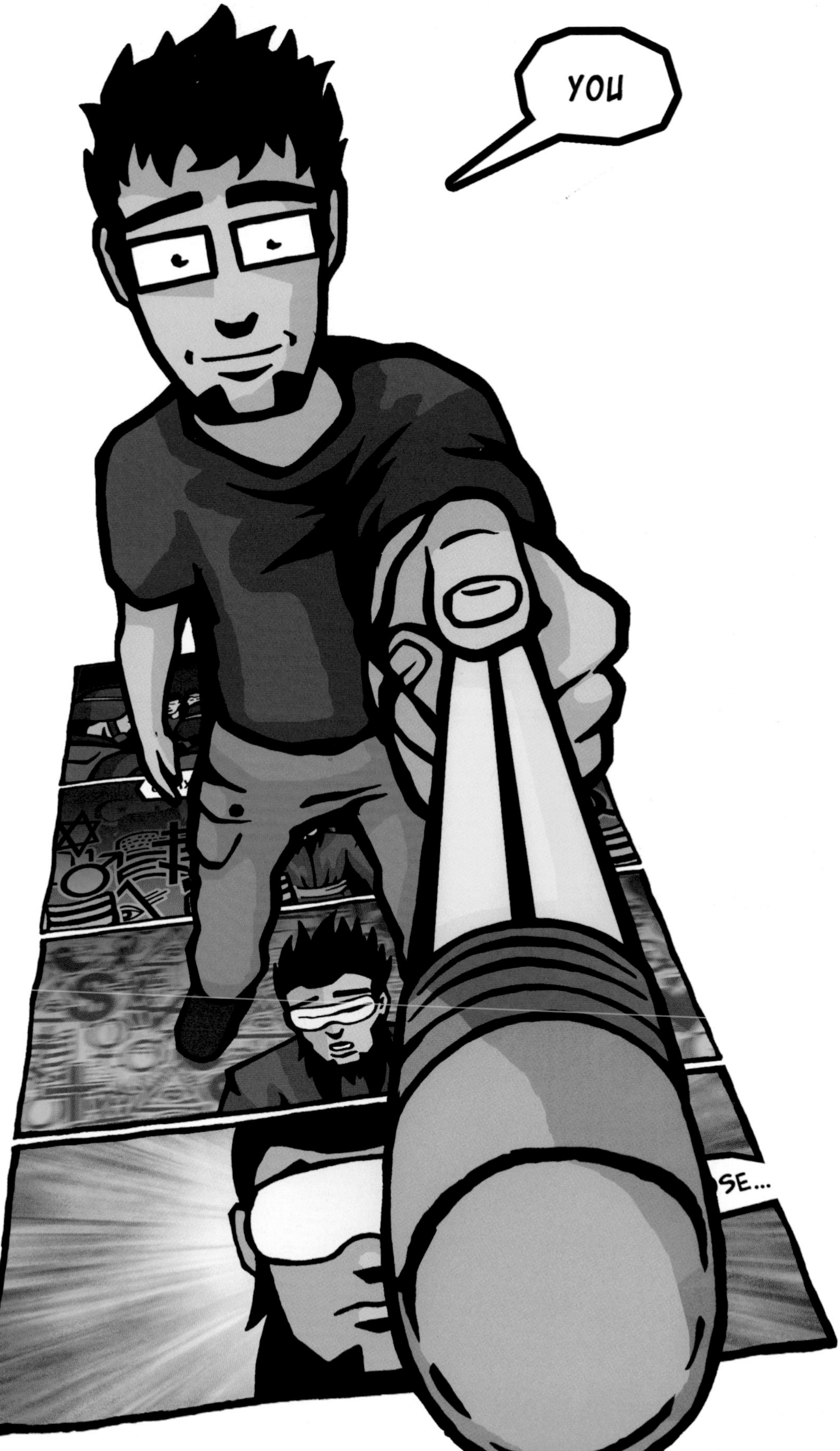
YOU

www.disinfo.com disinformation®

A FILM BY ROBERT-ADRIAN PEJO

DVD VIDEO

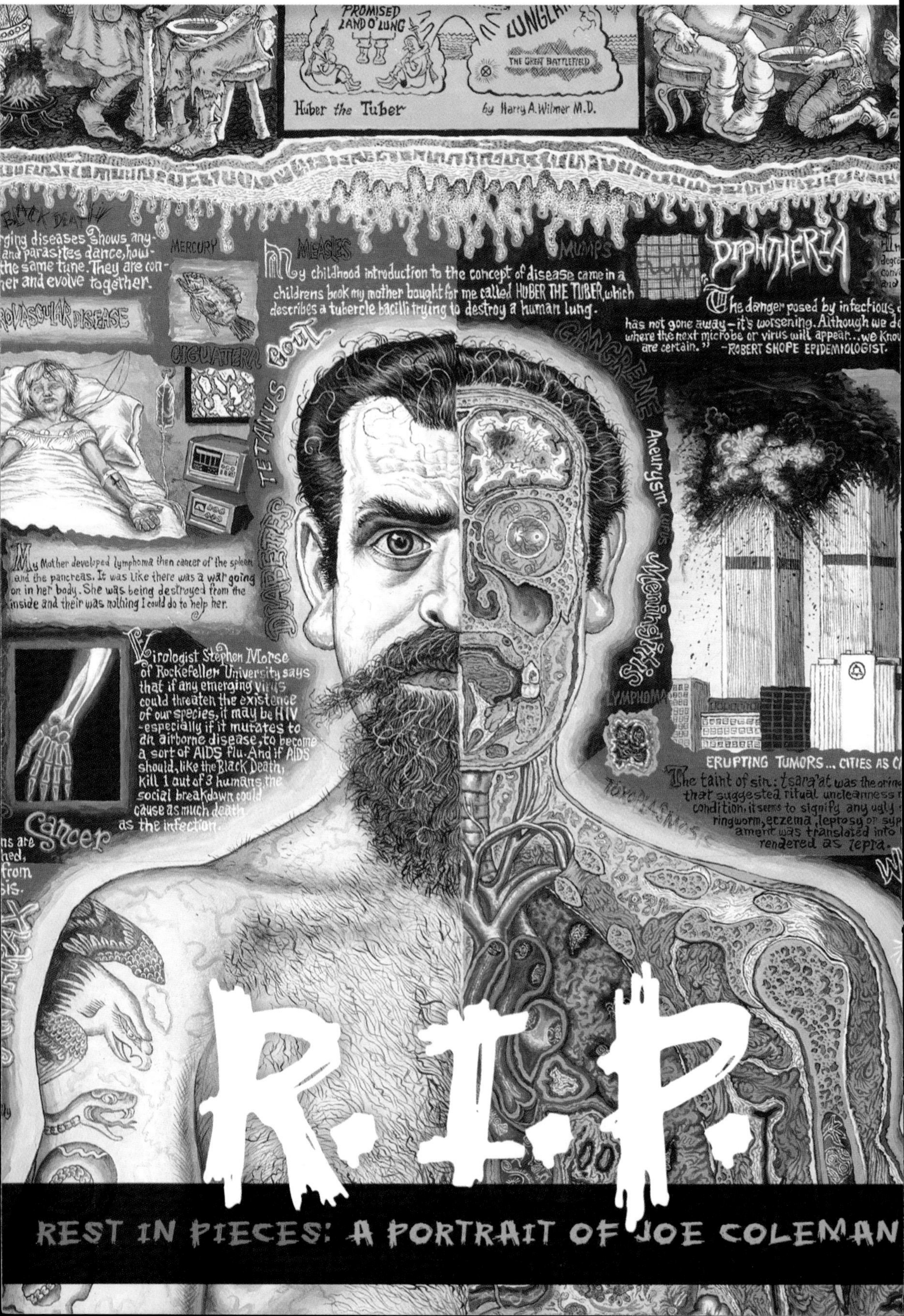
PROMISED LAND O'LUNG
LUNGLAND
THE GREAT BATTLEFIELD
Huber the Tuber
by Harry A. Wilmer M.D.
BLACK DEATH
MERCURY
MEASLES
My childhood introduction to the concept of disease came in a childrens book my mother bought for me called HUBER THE TUBER, which describes a tubercle bacilli trying to destroy a human lung.
MUMPS
DIPHTHERIA
CIGUATERA
GOUT
TETANUS
GANGRENE
DIABETES
Aneurysm
Meningitis
LYMPHOMA
My Mother developed lymphoma then cancer of the spleen and the pancreas. It was like there was a war going on in her body. She was being destroyed from the inside and their was nothing I could do to help her.
Virologist Stephen Morse of Rockefeller University says that if any emerging virus could threaten the existence of our species, it may be HIV - especially if it mutates to an airborne disease, to become a sort of AIDS flu. And if AIDS should, like the Black Death, kill 1 out of 3 humans, the social breakdown could cause as much death as the infection.
Cancer
TOXOPLASMOSIS
ERUPTING TUMORS... CITIES AS
-ROBERT SHOPE EPIDEMIOLOGIST.

R.I.P.

REST IN PIECES: A PORTRAIT OF JOE COLEMAN

ANARCHY FOR THE MASSES

THE DISINFORMATION GUIDE TO THE INVISIBLES

BY PATRICK NEIGHLY & KERETH COWE-SPIGAI

A complete guide to every issue of the cult smash comic series **THE INVISIBLES**, featuring interviews with author Grant Morrison and major behind-the-scenes players. Plus comprehensive annotatations, critical analyses, previously unpublished artwork and more!

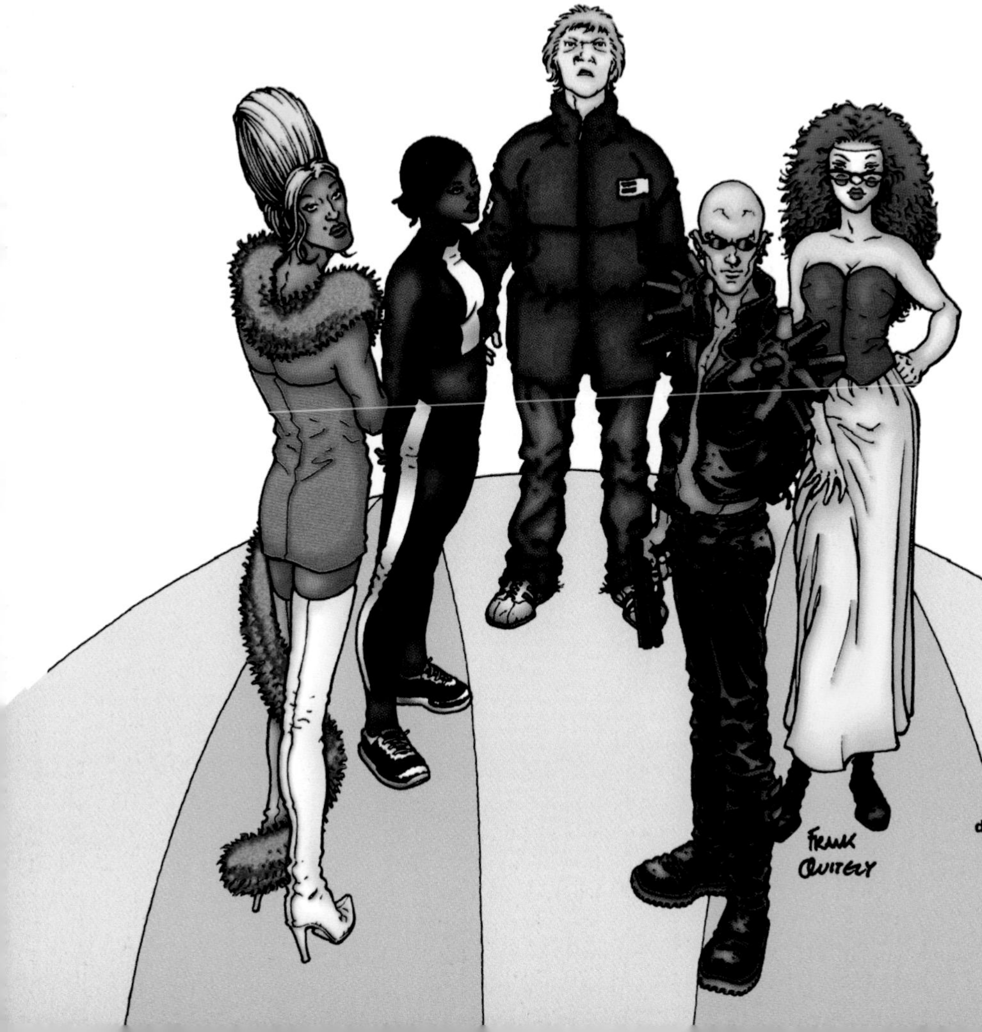
FRANK QUITELY

disinformation

MAD YAK PRESS

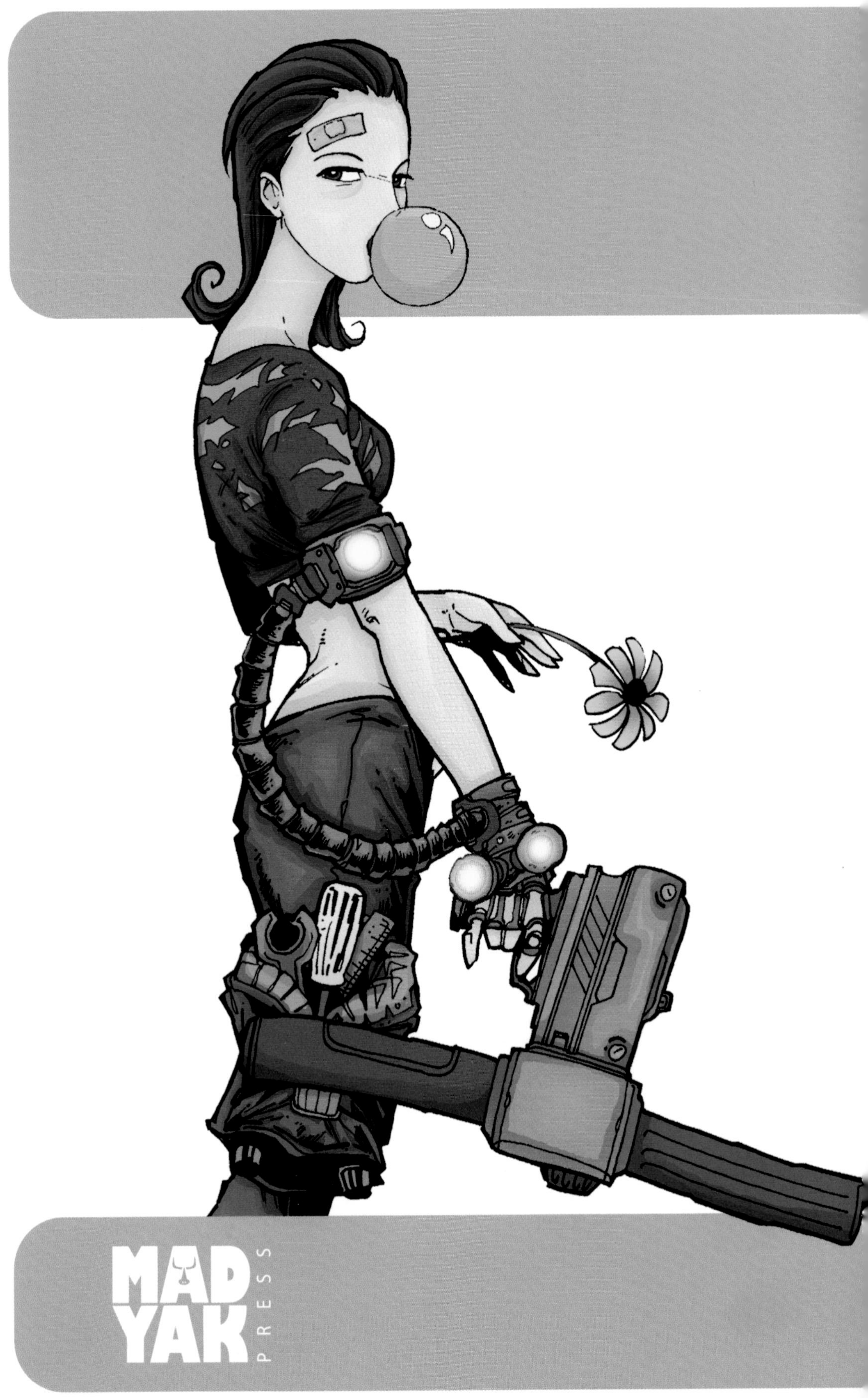

MAD YAK PRESS